Since winning the Catherine Cookson Prize for Fiction for her first novel, *The Hungry Tide*, **Val Wood** has become one of the most popular authors in the UK.

Born in the mining town of Castleford, Val came to East Yorkshire as a child and has lived in Hull and rural Holderness where many of her novels are set. She now lives in the market town of Beverley.

When she is not writing, Val is busy promoting libraries and supporting many charities. In 2017 she was awarded an honorary doctorate by the University of Hull for service and dedication to literature.

Find out more about Val Wood's novels by visiting her website: www.valwood.co.uk

Have you read all of Val Wood's novels?

The Hungry Tide

Sarah Foster's parents fight a constant battle with poverty – until wealthy John Rayner provides them with work and a home on the coast. But when he falls for their daughter, Sarah, can their love overcome the gulf of wealth and social standing dividing them?

Annie

Annie Swinburn has killed a man. The man was evil in every possible way, but she knows that her only fate if she stays in Hull is a hanging. So she runs as far away as she can – to a new life that could offer her the chance of love, in spite of the tragedy that has gone before . . .

Children of the Tide

A tired woman holding a baby knocks at the door of one of the big houses in Anlaby. She shoves the baby at young James Rayner, then she vanishes. The Rayner family is shattered – born into poverty, will a baby unite or divide the family?

The Gypsy Girl

Polly Anna's mother died when she was just three years old. Alone in the world, the workhouse was the only place for her. But with the help of a young misfit she manages to escape, running away with the fairground folk. But will Polly Anna ever find somewhere she truly belongs?

Emily

A loving and hard-working child, Emily goes into service at just twelve years old. But when an employer's son dishonours and betrays her, her fortunes seem to be at their lowest ebb. Can she journey from shame and imprisonment to a new life and fulfilment?

Going Home

For Amelia and her siblings, the grim past their mother Emily endured seems far away. But when a gentleman travels from Australia to meet Amelia's family, she discovers the past casts a long shadow and that her tangled family history is inextricably bound up with his . . .

Rosa's Island

Taken in as a child, orphaned Rosa grew up on an island off the coast of Yorkshire. Her mother, before she died, promised that one day Rosa's father would return. But when two mysterious Irishmen come back to the island after many years, they threaten everything Rosa holds dear . . .

The Doorstep Girls

Ruby and Grace have grown up in the poorest slums of Hull. Friends since childhood, they have supported each other in bad times and good. As times grow harder, and money scarcer, the girls search for something that could take them far away . . . But what price will they pay to find it?

Far From Home

When Georgiana Gregory makes the long journey from Hull for New York, she hopes to escape the confines of English life. But once there, Georgiana finds she isn't far from home when she encounters a man she knows – who presents dangers almost too much to cope with . . .

The Kitchen Maid
Jenny secures a job as kitchen maid in a grand house in Beverley – but her fortunes fail when scandal forces her to leave. Years later, she is mistress of a hall, but she never forgets the words a gypsy told her: that one day she will return to where she was happy and find her true love . . .

The Songbird
Poppy Mazzini has an ambition – to go on the stage. Her lovely voice and Italian looks lead her to great acclaim. But when her first love from her home town of Hull becomes engaged to someone else, she is devastated. Will Poppy have to choose between fame and true love?

Nobody's Child
Now a prosperous Hull businesswoman, Susannah grew up with the terrible stigma of being nobody's child. When daughter Laura returns to the Holderness village of her mother's childhood, she will discover a story of poverty, heartbreak and a love that never dies . . .

Fallen Angels
After her dastardly husband tries to sell her, Lily Fowler is alone on the streets of Hull. Forced to work in a brothel, she forges friendships with the women there, and together they try to turn their lives around. Can they dare to dream of happy endings?

The Long Walk Home
When Mikey Quinn's mother dies, he is determined to find a better life for his family – so he walks to London from Hull to seek his fortune. He meets Eleanor, and they gradually make a new life for themselves. Eventually, though, they must make the long walk home to Hull . . .

Rich Girl, Poor Girl
Polly, living in poverty, finds herself alone when her mother dies. Rosalie, brought up in comfort on the other side of Hull, loses her own mother on the same day. When Polly takes a job in Rosalie's house, the two girls form an unlikely friendship. United in tragedy, can they find happiness?

Homecoming Girls
The mysterious Jewel Newmarch turns heads wherever she goes, but she feels a longing to know her own roots. So she decides to return to her birthplace in America, where she learns about family, friendship and home. But most importantly, love . . .

The Harbour Girl
Jeannie spends her days at the water's edge waiting for Ethan to come in from fishing. But then she falls for a handsome stranger. When he breaks his word, Jeannie finds herself pregnant and alone in a strange new town. Will she find someone to truly love her – and will Ethan ever forgive her?

The Innkeeper's Daughter
Bella's dreams of teaching are dashed when she has to take on the role of mother to her baby brother. Her days are brightened by visits from Jamie Lucan – but when the family is forced to move to Hull, Bella is forced to leave everything behind. Can she ever find her dreams again?

His Brother's Wife
The last thing Harriet expects after her mother dies is to marry a man she barely knows, but her only alternative is the workhouse. And so begins an unhappy marriage to Noah Tuke. The only person who offers her friendship is Noah's brother, Fletcher – the one person she can't possibly be with . . .

Every Mother's Son
Daniel Tuke hopes to share his future with childhood friend Beatrice Hart. But his efforts to find out more about his heritage throw up some shocking truths: is there a connection between the families? Meanwhile, Daniel's mother Harriet could never imagine that discoveries about her own family are also on the horizon . . .

Little Girl Lost
Margriet grew up as a lonely child in the old town of Hull. As she grows into adulthood she forms an unlikely friendship with some of the street children who roam the town. As Margriet acts upon her inspiration to help them, will the troubles of her past break her spirit, or will she be able to overcome them?

No Place for a Woman
Brought up by a kindly uncle after the death of her parents, Lucy grows up inspired to become a doctor, just like her father. But studying in London takes Lucy far from her home in Hull, and she has to battle to be accepted in a man's world. An even greater challenge comes with the onset of the First World War; will Lucy be able to follow her dreams – and find love – in a world shattered by war?

A Mother's Choice
Delia has always had to fend for herself and her son Jack, and as a young unmarried mother, life has never been easy. In particularly desperate times, a chance encounter presents a lifeline. Delia is faced with an impossible, heart-wrenching choice. Can she bear to leave her young son behind, hoping another family will care for him? What else can a mother do to give her son the life he deserves?

A Place to Call Home
When Ellen's husband Harry loses his farm job and the cottage that comes with it, they have to leave the countryside they love in order to survive. Harry sets out to find a job in the factories and mills of nearby Hull, and Ellen must build a new life for her family on the unfamiliar city streets. But when tragedy threatens Ellen's fragile happiness, how much more can she sacrifice before they find a place to call home?

Four Sisters
With their mother dead, four sisters and their father form a close bond. But when tragedy suddenly strikes and their father disappears on his way to London, the sisters have no way of knowing what has happened to him – only that he hasn't returned home. With little money left, they're now forced to battle life's misfortunes alone . . .

The Lonely Wife
Beatrix is just eighteen when her father tells her she is to marry a stranger – a man named Charles, who shows little interest in his young wife. Soon, the only spark in Beatrix's lonely life is her beloved children. But then Charles threatens to take them away. Can Beatrix fight against her circumstances and keep what is rightfully hers?

CHILDREN OF FORTUNE

Val Wood

PENGUIN BOOKS

TRANSWORLD PUBLISHERS
Penguin Random House, One Embassy Gardens,
8 Viaduct Gardens, London SW11 7BW
www.penguin.co.uk

Transworld is part of the Penguin Random House group of companies
whose addresses can be found at global.penguinrandomhouse.com

Penguin
Random House
UK

First published in Great Britain in 2021 by Bantam Press
an imprint of Transworld Publishers
Penguin paperback edition published 2022

A CIP catalogue record for this book
is available from the British Library.

ISBN 9780552178914

Typeset in New Baskerville ITC Pro by Jouve (UK), Milton Keynes
Printed and bound in Great Britain by Clays Ltd, Elcograf S.p.A.

The authorized representative in the EEA is Penguin Random House Ireland,
Morrison Chambers, 32 Nassau Street, Dublin D02 YH68.

Penguin Random House is committed to a sustainable
future for our business, our readers and our planet. This book
is made from Forest Stewardship Council® certified paper.

1

For Daphne Glazer

Writer and novelist, for her wise and inspirational
words, who began this journey with me so long ago.
A light has gone out, but her work will remain.

CHAPTER ONE

1864

Alicia, her blonde hair blowing in the sharp breeze, took a deep breath and in a wavering voice called out at the top of her voice, 'Mama! Mama! Where are you?'

From the top step outside the front door of Old Stone Hall her voice was intended to reach a fair distance, but the ten-year-old's words didn't carry far. The heavy front door opened and Dora Hallam, her mother's right-hand companion, arms folded, looked out. 'Miss Alicia,' she warned. 'Please don't shout. It's not ladylike, and your mama will think there's something wrong; and then she'll hurry, which she shouldn't.'

'Oh, I'm so sorry!' Alicia turned tragic blue eyes towards her. 'I really am, Dora – I mean Mrs Hallam. Do I really have to call you that? I've known you for *years!*'

'Yes, you must.' Dora hid a smile and ushered her inside. 'It was different when I was Miss Murray, as you know very well,' she reminded Alicia, who did know, as she had been a flower girl at Dora's wedding to Simon Hallam.

Simon was their estate manager, and Dora her mother's long-time friend and confidante as much as her assistant. They had been married in the village church in North Fer-riby, and although Alicia's mother had had to wear a dark grey gown and a grey and black hat with raven feathers as she was

1

still in mourning for poor Papa Charles, Alicia was allowed to wear a white dress with pretty blue ribbons and a large white lacy bonnet with a brim.

Alicia's brothers Laurence and Ambrose acted as ushers and wore black knickerbockers with white shirts and black waistcoats, and Edward, who was now her new papa – she always felt a rush of pure happiness when she thought of him, for she loved him so much – had been Hallam's best man.

Alicia had been nearly seven when her father Charles had died. She hardly remembered him, as he hadn't often come home, preferring to live in London, and she had often wondered if perhaps he didn't like children. Her mama had waited for two years after Papa Charles's death before she married Edward, and she had told Alicia and her brothers that it was only right and proper to do so. It was a way of honouring his life.

Alicia had sighed when she heard this. She really wanted their mama to marry Edward at once so that she could be a bridesmaid again. Laurie remembered their father, as he was a year and a half older than Alicia, but had whispered to her that he hadn't liked him much, although she wasn't to tell Mama; Alicia had whispered back that she didn't either, though she always pretended that she did, and was pleased when he went back to London because her mother always seemed anxious whenever he came to see them. Ambrose, the youngest, said he didn't know who they were talking about, if anyone mentioned Charles's name, and that Edward was their papa.

'So what did you want to ask your mama?' Dora asked.

'I wanted to ask if I could go out on my pony by myself,' Alicia piped. 'Aaron is too busy to come with me. He says he's waiting for a message and he might have to go out.'

'You can ride in the paddock,' Dora told her, 'but not anywhere else on your own. Not today. Can you saddle up on your own?'

'Yes, but that's not fun!' Alicia pouted. 'I'll just be trotting round and round in circles and, besides, the hens get in the way and they're always squawking. I want to go up the road to see Granny Mags.'

'Well, you can't,' Dora said firmly. 'Not on your own, and not today,' she repeated. 'Your mama likes to know where you are. Otherwise she gets worried about you and we can't have that, can we?'

Alicia shook her head. 'Could I have some lemonade then? Please,' she added.

'Yes,' Dora conceded. 'Go outside again and sit at the table and I'll ask Ambrose if he'd like some too and he can join you. Your mama won't be long.'

'Where is she?' Alicia asked petulantly. 'Why didn't she ask me to go with her? I could have looked after her.'

Dora opened the door again and ushered her outside. 'I don't know where she is,' she said, although she did. Beatrix Newby always made a point of telling Dora where she was going in case of an emergency with the children. This anxiety had developed in her former marriage, but it had lessened since Charles had died.

Dora had turned back from the door when she heard the sound of wheels on the drive and spun round again to see her mistress returning in the trap. Beatrix signalled to her to come and then gave Alicia, who had started towards her, a little wave.

'Stay there, Alicia,' she called. 'We'll have lunch outside.'

Alicia continued to run to her mother. 'I'll help you first, Mama,' she said. 'I've been looking for you.'

Dora hurried down the steps and saw that Mrs Newby was hesitating before stepping down from the trap. 'Give me your hand, Dora, will you, and yes, you too, darling.' She stretched out her other hand to Alicia, who clutched it as her mother stepped on to the drive.

'Are you all right, Mama? Where have you been?'

Her mother gave a little gasp. 'Only – to see Rosie,' she said. 'She's had – a new baby.'

'Oh!' Alicia jumped up and down on the spot. 'What did she get? Can I see it?'

'Not yet.' Her mother seemed breathless. 'A boy,' she told her. 'To add to the other three.' She gave a half laugh, half gasp.

'I hope you have a girl, Mama. I've got two brothers already.'

'I'll do my best, Alicia.' Her mother sank unsteadily into one of the cane chairs on the lawn. 'They don't come to order, darling. We don't get to choose, but perhaps we won't have long to wait and then we'll know!' She looked up at Dora, who was hovering. 'I'll need someone to put the pony and trap away, Dora.'

'I know where Aaron is, Mama,' Alicia said. 'Shall I run and fetch him?'

'Please.' Her mother took a deep breath. 'But no need to run,' she called as Alicia sped away. 'There's no immediate hurry.'

Beatrix was enveloped in a lightweight summer cape which completely hid her condition, but she signalled to Dora by her raised eyebrows that her time to give birth was imminent. Dora about-turned and ran up the steps, calling to the housekeeper that her assistance was required.

'I think perhaps I won't have lunch after all,' Beatrix said when the two women came to stand at either side of her. 'If you could help me inside before Alicia comes back? I don't want to alarm her, but I don't think I can manage the steps or stairs by myself.'

'Goodness,' Mrs Gordon said. 'This is quick, ma'am. I didn't think it was your time yet.'

'It might be a false alarm,' Beatrix told the housekeeper. 'Maybe because I saw Rosie's baby!'

'I don't think so,' Dora commented. 'But there was no indication before you went out, was there?'

'None,' Beatrix said, as they entered the house and Mrs Gordon unfastened her cape and took it from her shoulders. 'Everything was quite normal, no sign at all. Dora, could you send someone to fetch Edward, please? I'm not sure where he is.'

'And the doctor?' Mrs Gordon asked.

'Not yet,' Beatrix sank down on the hall sofa. 'Sorry to be a nuisance, but could you get me a glass of water? And maybe a biscuit.'

'I'll go,' Mrs Gordon said. 'Perhaps we should wait for Mr Newby before attempting the stairs,' she murmured to Dora, who nodded.

Alicia in the meantime had run round to the back of the house towards the stables and called out for the groom, who would do anything for Mrs Newby.

'Mama needs you, Aaron,' she shouted. 'Can you come?'

He had a saddle and a cloth in his hands and swiftly returned them to the stable. He wondered whether it was the mistress's time, but wouldn't dream of asking the little girl, for she had a habit of answering questions with questions which in this case might be difficult to answer.

'She wants you to move the trap from the front of the house,' Alicia went on. 'She's just come back from Rosie's and I don't think she'll be going back out again; she seems rather tired. Rosie has had another baby and Mama went to see it. It's a boy!' She gave all the pronouncements on one single breath.

'Has Edward— your father come back?' he asked, ignoring her chatter. 'He's over at Home Farm.'

'Don't know,' she said. 'Come on. I'll race you!'

Aaron groaned; she was always doing this and always set off running as soon as she'd said it, but he always let her win.

'Edward isn't my father, you know,' she said, when he caught up with her. 'My father is dead.'

He nodded. 'I know.'

'But I like Edward being my father,' she went on. 'He's the best one I could ever have chosen. Did you know that you can't choose what kind of a baby you're going to have if you become pregnant? I mean, between a girl and a boy? They

5

don't come to order,' she finished, parroting her mother's phrase.

He sighed. 'Yes, I did know,' he muttered. 'But it isn't summat up for discussion, Miss Alicia; you shouldn't be talking to me about such matters. You must ask your mother or Dora if you want to know owt.'

'Oh, Mama's gone inside!' she exclaimed as they came round to the front of the house. 'We were going to have lunch on the terrace!'

'Never mind,' he said. 'Perhaps she needed a rest. Come on, would you like to tek 'reins and I'll show you how to negotiate 'trap round 'corner?'

'Oh, yes please,' she said exuberantly. 'Laurie knows how, so I'd like to learn too.'

She climbed into the trap and he showed her how to drive it, telling her it was like riding on her own pony, gently handling the reins to indicate what she wanted the pony to do, but also remembering that there was a cart behind them that had to be manoeuvred so that it didn't cockle into any ruts.

'I'll show you next time how to release him from 'shafts. You've done very well,' he told her. 'Now off you pop to see your ma and you can tell her what you've done. She'll be right proud of you.'

CHAPTER TWO

Edward arrived ten minutes later. He saw Beatrix's pony in the stall and went into the house by the kitchen door, taking the short flight of stairs two at a time to reach the hall. The study door was open and Beatrix was sitting in her armchair.

He bent to kiss her forehead. 'It's very odd,' he said softly, 'but I had an undeniable urge to hurry home and see my wife.'

'Thought transference.' She smiled up at him and whispered, 'It's a special energy. I was wishing you home.'

'Really?' he said. 'Do you believe in that?' He sat cross-legged on the floor at her feet.

Beatrix laughed. 'I do, but just to be sure I asked if someone would go and look for you.'

His eyebrows rose and he reached for her hand. 'Because?' he asked quietly.

'Because I wanted you home when your son or daughter makes an arrival.'

He took a deep breath to steady himself and she saw his Adam's apple move as he swallowed and how his chest rose and fell. 'It's all right,' she murmured. 'I've done it before, and besides, with my first child I was taught what to expect by an expert: a farmer,' she smiled tenderly, 'who took me to see his dog give birth to a litter of pups to prove how easy it was. You may recall?'

He shook his head and she saw that his eyes were moist. 'I lied,' he mumbled. 'It's not the same.'

'It's the most natural thing in life.' She repeated what he had told her when with an ever absent husband she was expecting her first child, and he had calmed her fears. 'It will be all right.'

Edward stood in one swift movement and gathered her up into his arms, cradling her and kissing her tenderly on her neck and cheek. 'It's not the same when it comes to our own child; that's what I didn't understand at the time. Even though I loved you when you were carrying another man's child, this is different. This,' he ran his hand gently over her belly, 'this child is my responsibility, as are you, my beloved wife.'

She closed her eyes, feeling loved and safe and knowing that he would stay with her, defying convention so that he might be there when his child was born.

They had always had the ability to know instinctively what the other was thinking. When Beatrix had been married to Charles their friendship had been platonic, and although Beatrix had been aware of Edward's feelings towards her he had always behaved faultlessly. It wasn't until after she was widowed that he confessed that he had loved her from the first. Newly married and friendless, she had arrived in Yorkshire to take possession of an empty, dilapidated, stately old house whilst Charles, her husband of a mere week, was on his way back to London for the weakest of reasons.

Edward had never forgiven Charles for leaving his young bride, a mere girl, to fend for herself with only her maid and their nearest neighbours – Edward himself and his parents Mags and Luke Newby – to advise and assist her. Knowing it was out of the question to stay with her himself, he'd brought in his cousin, Aaron, just out of school, to join the household.

Beatrix gave a sudden start. 'Ooh!' she said, making light of the signs she recognized. 'Perhaps I'll go upstairs. We don't want an arrival on the study floor.'

'Can you manage them?' he asked anxiously. 'I can carry you.'

'If I take my time,' she said, standing up. 'And I think I have plenty. Dora!' she called, as Dora crossed the hall with Alicia.

'I'm so pleased that you're here, Papa.' Alicia rushed to Edward's side and put her arms round his waist, while Dora helped Beatrix towards the stairs. 'I was beginning to feel worried. I've never seen a really new baby before.'

'Don't you remember Ambrose being born?' her mother asked her, reaching for the balustrade, and smiling tenderly when Alicia shook her head. 'Perhaps I will have the midwife after all, Dora,' she added.

'Already sent for, ma'am.'

'You know me so well,' Beatrix murmured. 'Thank you.'

Alicia trailed after them and Edward asked her where Ambrose was.

'He's upstairs finishing an essay that Mr Norman asked him to write. He's very strict, you know.' She frowned. 'I had to write twenty times that I mustn't be late for lessons. He's much stricturer than Mr Roberts used to be.' Mr Roberts had taught her and Laurence before Laurence went away to school in Pocklington.

'He's *stricter*,' her mother pointed out, and went towards her bedroom. 'Listen, darling, I'm going to lie down for ten minutes; can you entertain yourself until I've had a little nap?'

'Are you not having the baby yet?' Alicia asked. 'I'd like to see it as soon as it's born. Oh,' she clasped her hands together, 'I do wish I knew what it was. Will it know already if it's a boy or a girl?'

'Will the baby know, do you mean?' Edward ushered Alicia towards the schoolroom, whilst Dora followed Beatrix into her bedroom. 'Yes, he or she is already formed, but we'll have to wait until it makes an appearance before we find out. Perhaps you'd like to write down some suggestions for names, would you?'

'Oh, I've made several lists already.' She hopped from one foot to another. 'But I can't decide.'

Ambrose was gathering up papers on his desk as they opened the door.

'Mama's going to have her baby,' Alicia announced.

'I know.'

'I mean she's going to have it *soon*.'

'You won't be able to play with it yet,' her brother told her.

'I know that,' she said grumpily, and Edward quietly closed the door on them. The two of them occasionally had mild arguments, but Ambrose, who was more than two years younger than Alicia, was logical and practical and not in the habit of letting his imagination run away with him as Alicia was. Nor did he allow her to best him in an argument – or to act as though she were his superior, as she was inclined to try to achieve.

Edward went back to Beatrix's bedroom – their bedroom, as it usually was, but as her pregnancy advanced he had moved to a room across from hers, for she was restless and not always able to sleep, and being a farmer he was always awake at dawn.

'Will I be in the way?' he asked her, and glanced out of the window as he heard the sound of the trap on the gravel below. 'Here's your woman arriving. She must have delivered more babies than we can count. My ma says she delivered me and my sisters, but I can't believe that.'

'She told me that too.' Beatrix paused in her pacing of the floor and stood beside him to look out of the window. 'So it must be true. You can stay if you'd like to,' she said, putting her hand on his arm. 'But will you entertain the children until it's time? Alicia is so keen to be in here and I'd rather she wasn't, or at least not just yet.'

'I want to be here,' he said softly, hearing the midwife's laboured breath as she came puffing up the stairs. 'I'll take the children down and give them something to do and then come back.'

She smiled and kissed him. 'Yes, please. Mrs Beddows won't mind your being here. She knows you well enough.'

A peremptory knock on the door made him draw back as the midwife came in. 'I've asked your girl to mek a pot of tea, Mrs . . .' she paused momentarily, 'Newby. I thought you might be here to give a hand, Edward.' She huffed. 'You young farmers are all 'same. You think it's like cows and 'osses, but it's not, as you'll see; but I don't mind you staying if your missus don't.'

'I don't,' Beatrix said. 'But don't be long with the children,' she told Edward before taking a slow, deep breath, 'as I think our new arrival won't be long.'

Edward settled Alicia and Ambrose with a board game downstairs in the sitting room; they were brought lemonade and biscuits by Mrs Gordon and after about fifteen minutes he sidled out of the room, telling them he'd just find out if anything was happening upstairs.

He was anxious to be there when his son or daughter arrived in the world. He'd waited so long for the only woman he had ever loved, unable to comfort her through her unhappy first marriage and filled with jealousy when she gave birth to children by another man, who didn't seem to care for any of them. But I mustn't think of him now, he chastised himself; Charles had demons of his own to contend with and had died before his time, though in doing so had given Edward and Beatrix the chance of the happiness that had been denied them; the child about to be born would be the peak of contented fulfilment.

He tapped on the door before entering and found Beatrix flushed and perspiring, standing by the bed rail, already in labour.

'Won't be long, I reckon,' Mrs Beddows murmured. 'It's nearly here. The quickest labour I've ever known. Come, my dear, let's have you on the bed and make you comfortable.'

Edward gently stroked Beatrix's forehead, which was gleaming with perspiration, then gently moved his fingers over her belly to note the position of the child. 'You're doing fine, my brave darling,' he whispered, and she nodded, but didn't speak. He stood back, anxious not to get in the midwife's way, but he glanced at her questioningly and she briefly lifted her eyes to his.

11

'Hold my hand, Edward.' Beatrix gave a small gasp and squeezed his fingers hard when he did so.

'Come on, my lady,' Mrs Beddows said. 'There are blonde curls waiting to make an appearance. That's it, dear lady.' Mrs Beddows, it seemed, had many variations on the theme of naming her mothers and urging them on to deliver.

'That's it, my lovely,' she said now, adding, 'Here you are, Edward; if you've washed your hands you might like to take over,' and relinquishing her role so that Edward could deliver his child.

He wept, tears streaming down his cheeks so that he could barely see to take the clean soft towel to wipe the baby's face of mucus and smile at his first cry. Carefully wrapping him in a swaddling sheet, he placed their son in Beatrix's arms, whilst whispering and kissing them both on the top of their forehead.

Beatrix gave a sudden grimace and Mrs Beddows put her hand on her abdomen. 'I think we're not quite finished, dearest girl,' she murmured. 'Shall we see what else you might be hiding? It's not the afterbirth, that's for sure.'

'What?' Beatrix gasped. 'There's another?'

Edward gave a watery smile. The midwife took the new baby from Beatrix's arms, put him in the waiting cot and moved to one side so that Edward could receive his golden-haired daughter.

'My cup runneth over,' he murmured, putting the second child into his wife's arms. 'What a perfect woman you are, Beatrix.' And as he had promised, he opened the bedroom door and called downstairs for the children to come up.

CHAPTER THREE

Alicia and Ambrose raced upstairs and Edward put his finger to his lips when they reached the bedroom door.

'Quietly, now. I want you both to close your eyes and not peek, not even the tiniest bit.' He turned the doorknob and took a hand of each to lead them inside, saw a smiling Beatrix with a baby under the crook of each arm, and said, 'Open your eyes.'

Alicia was beside herself with delight when she saw the two sleeping mites and gave a little squeal. 'Oh! One each, Amby!'

Ambrose's mouth opened, and then he exclaimed, 'I won't know how to look after it!'

'A boy and a girl! We'll have to learn together, won't we?' Edward said, patting his shoulder. 'Mama will teach us.'

Ambrose, whose blond-reddish colouring was just like Edward's, so that he was often mistaken for his son, turned to his step-father. 'Laurie won't know, Pa. We'll have to write and tell him.'

'Come here, both of you,' Beatrix called, seeing how over-whelmed they were. 'Papa will send a telegram to Laurie's school and I'm sure he'll be allowed home, since it's almost term end anyway, and we'll send another to Grandmama and Grandpa and perhaps they'll come to visit us soon. Mrs Beddows, won't you pop downstairs for that pot of tea and a slice of cake?' she added, knowing that the kettle would be on the boil and the cake would be cut already.

13

'I will, m'dear,' the midwife said, 'and I'll ask them to bring one up for you. Now, don't you be overdoing things, Mrs Newby. No visitors except for family and a week in bed at least, after giving birth to two babies, even though I know you're a strong young woman.'

Not as strong as I was when I gave birth to Laurie, Beatrix thought. But I was a slip of a girl then, and now, well, my goodness! Five children, and no longer a girl. She smiled at Edward. And I'm so deliriously happy.

Later, towards evening, once Edward had received the return telegram to say that Laurence could be excused from school and needn't return until the September term began, Aaron offered to drive to Pocklington to pick him up and bring him home.

'Don't tell Laurie the outcome of the birth,' Edward told his cousin. 'We want to keep the news as a complete surprise.'

'I can't tell him, cos I don't know, do I?' Aaron grinned. 'Nobody's said yet if it's a boy or a girl.'

'Not even Alicia?' Edward asked. 'That's incredible; she's just bursting to tell somebody.'

'I'd better get off then before she lets 'cat out of 'bag.' Aaron cracked the whip over the pony's head. 'We'll be about an hour and a half, providing young master is ready and waiting.'

Edward watched him drive off. Aaron had come to work for Beatrix following Edward's own request to his aunt Hilda to allow her thirteen-year-old son to come and be Beatrix's right-hand man when she had arrived at Old Stone Hall as a young bride and knew no one in Yorkshire at all.

Aaron had stayed with her that first night, sleeping on the kitchen floor so that Beatrix wouldn't be afraid of being alone in this great old mansion, and had grown in stature and confidence as he handled the responsibility of doing whatever needed to be done. Now that she was married to his cousin Edward, he somehow kept the connection quite separate and never crossed or even straddled the social barrier.

Convention and protocol was what he had been taught by his mother and he followed these maxims seriously, considering them to be right and proper. Now he was stable manager and had a young lad, Harry, under his own charge to do what he himself had formerly done.

Edward ran back upstairs to be by his wife's side. There would be no more work today; he wouldn't be able to concentrate, not when there were two babies to watch and rejoice over. If there were a happier man in the world he'd like to meet him. His joy was absolute.

Dora had brought up a tray of tea and biscuits for Beatrix and for Edward too. 'Here you are, sir.' She beamed at Edward. 'A good strong cup will settle your nerves!'

Dora had been a constant companion to Beatrix since before Beatrix's first marriage to Charles Dawley. She had been a maid at her parents' home in London's Russell Square, and at Beatrix's request had come with her to Yorkshire, where she had stayed ever since, lending a sympathetic and confidential ear during many of Beatrix's troubles.

She peeped into the cot where the babies were sleeping, one at each end. 'Oh, ma'am, they're lovely. So sweet. I'm so pleased for you.' She looked across at Edward. 'For both of you.'

'Thank you, Dora.' Beatrix and Edward spoke simultaneously. They both knew that Dora had always had their best interests at heart. When she left to go downstairs, reminding Beatrix as everyone did to take some rest, Edward stood up.

'Come on, sweetheart,' he said to Alicia, who was sitting close up to her mother. Ambrose had gone back downstairs after taking one more peep at the babies. 'Let's leave Mama to rest for an hour. You can come up again when Laurie arrives.'

'All right.' She slid reluctantly down the bed. 'I'll watch out for him and bring him up; and I promise I won't tell him!'

'Good girl,' he said. 'And maybe later we'll have a discussion about suitable names for our babies.'

He gazed at Beatrix, who looked so serene and content,

and implicitly understood that she had already decided on names but wouldn't disclose them until the children had given their input.

Laurie was astonished and rather shy when he saw the two babies. It seemed as if he wanted to ask questions, but he hung back, as though he might say something that was out of bounds.

'I think he needs a man-to-man discussion, Edward,' Beatrix murmured, when Laurie had gone out of the room.

'He knows about birds and bees, and puppies, kittens, cows and sheep,' Edward said. 'He's just not thought about it in relation to people! It will come eventually, and I hope he'll ask me when he's ready.'

Beatrix settled into her pillow, fully content, but still unable to take in the fact that she had given birth to two babies, when she had been expecting only one.

I shall have my hands full with five children to bring up, but I'm so thrilled for Edward. He was close to tears, I could see. He's been so patient, loving me throughout my marriage to Charles, never thinking that there was the slightest hope for him, until Charles's sudden death changed everything.

Other musings flowed through her mind. Her parents would be thrilled, as would Edward's. His mother Mags had other grandchildren from her daughters, though she didn't see them as often as she would have liked; they lived in Holderness, the isolated area east of Hull, which was grain-growing land where the families were farmers, just as Edward's father had been.

Beatrix had previously told Edward that she would like the names of Luke Edward for a boy and Isolde Margaret for a girl. Luke for Edward's father, and Margaret for his mother, always known as Mags. Now they could use both. Edward would be so pleased, and so would they.

Mags was overcome with joy when she saw the two babies. No one had told her there were twins, and tears rolled down her cheeks as she gazed down at them asleep in their cot.

At last, she sat down on the side of Beatrix's bed. 'I love your other bairns to bits,' she snuffled, 'but to have these as my own kin is wonderful. I never thought I would see the day when Edward would marry and have children; he's such a loving man and he deserves to be happy, and he is. I know now that he allus loved you, Beatrix. He's so lucky to have you.' She wiped her eyes on the corner of her shawl. 'Really, really lucky.'

'I'm lucky too, Mags.' Beatrix gently squeezed her hand. 'Lucky that he didn't settle for anyone else, when I was married to Charles.'

The children brought up many names for the twins. Alicia's were the most fanciful, such as Princess and Prince; Laurie said Henry as he had a best friend with that name, and Ambrose shrugged and said he didn't know.

Edward said, 'Mm, those are all very interesting, but I like the idea that Mama mentioned to me earlier. She suggested that we give them two names each: have Granny Mags's proper name Margaret as a middle name for your new sister, and so that Grandpa Newby doesn't feel left out choose Luke as a first name for the boy.'

Alicia opened her mouth to speak and drew in a breath, but before she uttered a word Edward went on, 'I think you'll like this, Alicia. What about Isolde Margaret and Luke Edward?'

He gave a beaming smile, and Alicia jumped up and down. 'Oh yes, Papa, and then you're in too! Iz-old-er!' She wrinkled her brow. 'How do you spell it?'

'I S O L D E,' he said, 'and say it as you did. What do you think?'

'I love them both,' she said, and turned to look into the cot. 'Hello, Isolde Margaret. Hello, Luke Edward.'

'I've heard of Isolde before,' Laurie commented. 'There's a book called *Tristan and Isolde* in the school library, but the younger students aren't allowed to handle it as it's so old. Perhaps we should call the baby boy Tristan. Oh but . . .' He hesitated. 'Maybe not. Three names would be too many.'

17

Beatrix smiled. She was proud of her eldest boy and his clear thinking, and thought that he wouldn't know that the ancient story was of a doomed illicit romance. 'I think you're right, Laurie.' She looked at them all, her precious family. 'So are we all in agreement? Luke Edward and Isolde Margaret.'

'Yes!' They all cheered and clapped and Ambrose added, 'Welcome, little babies.' Edward blinked and smiled. He was sure that Ambrose relished the fact that he was no longer the youngest child in the family.

CHAPTER FOUR

When Laurie had reached the age of eight, Charles had insisted that he went to the boarding school in Hampstead where he and Laurie's grandfather had been educated. This decision almost broke Beatrix's heart. She missed Laurie terribly, and considered that he was far too young to be such a long way from his Yorkshire home. But Charles was adamant and warned Beatrix that she was becoming neurotic.

In the end, Laurie ran away from school and caught a train home, explaining afterwards that it wasn't so much that he disliked school as that he didn't like being so far away from his mother and siblings. After Charles's death, Beatrix took him away from the Hampstead school, and when he was ten he began as a weekly boarder at a school in nearby Pocklington on the York road, which he enjoyed so much that Ambrose asked his mother if he might be allowed to go to school soon as well, because Laurie seemed to have made lots of friends and had lots of fun too.

'I don't really mind waiting until I'm ten,' he'd said placidly, 'because I think that Alicia might miss me if I go now. The twins won't miss me, because they're only babies and don't know me yet.'

'But what about us?' his mother asked. 'Pa and me? We'd miss you dreadfully and you're such a help on the estate.'

'Yes, it's true that I am,' he said solemnly. 'I'm doing very well with my pigs and the lambs, and I suppose if I went away to school I'd have to ask Pa or maybe Mr Hallam to look after them for me; and of course I wouldn't want to miss the harvest.'

'You'd be on summer holidays during harvest,' his mother told him, 'but perhaps we'll wait, do you think, perhaps give yourself a little more time to think about it? There's really no hurry, is there, when you have such a good tutor?'

Ambrose had nodded and agreed, torn between wanting to join Laurie and not wanting to leave Alicia behind, because he could barely remember a time when they weren't all together, except when the other man, the one who used to live with them sometimes, had taken Laurie away and they had all cried, including his mother. But that man had gone now, and Edward was his papa.

When his tenth birthday came along, he'd waited anxiously for Laurie to come home for the summer holidays, so that he might discuss the prospect of school with him at more length than was possible at weekends; Laurie was fourteen now, and if he agreed that he was ready, he would ask his mother if he might start next term.

He'd spoken to his father earlier to ask what he thought about it, and Edward had rubbed his fingers through his beard and said they really should discuss it with his mother.

'We'd miss you not being here, you know,' Edward had commented. 'Although you'd be home every weekend, so I suppose we could manage. Yes, by September, I think your mama and I could probably cope without worrying too much about you.'

And so they had had a family conversation during which Alicia's mouth trembled and she came and put her arms round Ambrose and he felt like crying too, but he mustn't because then they would think that he was far too young to go to boarding school and he really, really wasn't.

But it turned out that his mother had already written to the headmaster suggesting that Ambrose might start in September, and if he was still sure that that was what he wanted, then all they had to do was confirm that he was coming, and order his uniform.

He stood as tall as he possibly could whilst he was being measured, and although he was a good deal shorter than Laurie when they stood side by side he was almost up to Alicia's shoulder, and, he thought, she's going to be thirteen by Christmas.

'Oh, goodie,' he said, when they had finished the measuring. 'Now there'll be two Newby boys at school. Maybe Luke will come too when he's old enough. But that will be ages,' he said, with all the wisdom of a ten-year-old. 'Laurie, do they have a board with names on, like the one you said they had at the London school?'

Beatrix and Edward exchanged startled glances, and Laurie looked towards them.

'Erm, I'm not sure,' he muttered. 'I expect so.'

'The thing is, Ambrose,' Edward said slowly 'the three of you – you and Laurie and Alicia – all have the Dawley name, while Luke and Isolde are called Newby.'

Ambrose frowned and Laurie bit on his lip, whilst Alicia gazed at them all in turn and then said forthrightly, 'But we're all still brothers and sisters, aren't we?'

Ambrose interrupted. 'Why? Why don't we all have the same name?'

'Cos we had a different father,' Laurie murmured.

'But I didn't know him!' Ambrose objected. 'And besides, he's dead now.'

His mother broke in. 'But a child keeps the father's name, or at least the boys do, and if a girl gets married then she takes her husband's name.'

Ambrose crossed his arms. 'Well, that's not fair! I want to be a Newby like Pa and Mama and Luke and Isolde.'

'But then you'll be different from Laurie and me,' Alicia said crossly and almost crying.

'Wait! Wait,' Edward interrupted. 'We'll look into it, your

mama and I. We'll look into the legalities. What would you like to do, Laurie? And you, Alicia?'

Alicia shook her head. 'I don't know! I'd like us all to be the same. Did you have to change your name when you and Papa got married, Mama?'

Her mother paused. 'I'm not sure whether I *had* to or whether it's just a tradition that women are expected to follow.'

'Laurie?' Edward turned to him. 'Any thoughts?'

'I don't know either.' He seemed rather nonplussed. 'What, erm, what would we do about the Dawley estate if we all changed our names?'

And this was a question that neither his mother nor his stepfather could answer directly; the estate was designated as the inheritance of the eldest son in the Dawley family, and that was Laurence.

There's something wrong here, Beatrix considered as the children drifted off elsewhere, and Luke and Isolde were carried off to the nursery. Surely Charles would not have intended his second son and his daughter to be left with nothing at all. He had been a complex man with many issues, but he must have had some plan for them, mustn't he?

Yet he hadn't set up the original entail; someone, way back in time, had decreed how the estate should be passed on. It was nothing to do with Charles, or Charles's father either, for that matter, even though Alfred Dawley had insisted that the terms should be followed to the exact letter, even to choosing a suitable wife, and that was me.

Charles had left only a letter of intent, not a will, and he had died so suddenly and unexpectedly that he obviously hadn't given any consideration to explaining his wishes.

Oh dear, Beatrix thought. This must be discussed, and before the children grow up, for Ambrose and Alicia will surely wonder why they have been left with nothing. I can't think why, as an adult, I haven't considered this before. I suppose I thought that I had; after Charles's death it was up to me to look after the estate on Laurie's behalf until he was old enough to do so for himself. But now I have remarried and the family has grown. This, she thought, is a different life for all of us.

She felt a sudden lightening of spirits. Can we shed the Dawley shackles? We surely don't need to be hampered by what happened in the past. After Charles died the details of the inheritance were swiftly and legally wrapped up by their solicitor Stephen Robinson-Gough so that Charles's devious father, Alfred Dawley, couldn't alter or exploit it, which he assuredly would have done on the pretext that he was doing so on Laurence's behalf.

'You need to speak to Stephen.' Edward was sitting in a fire-side chair, leaving her to her contemplations whilst he too pondered the issue.

'Yes, we do,' she murmured, her head filled with questions and possibilities.

He looked up. 'No, darling Bea. *You* do. This isn't some-thing I can help you with.'

'We always discuss—'

'Yes, farming issues and the like. But this is something that only you can decide, and possibly Laurie – though he's still a tad too young, and I don't know if he's ready for decision-making yet – but *not* me. I can't advise on something from which I might profit.'

'Oh! Of course.' She sat and gazed at him. 'Someone – Alfred Dawley springs to mind – might say that you married me so that you could take control of the estate.'

He gave her a wry smile and nodded. 'Exactly. Isn't that why you brought Stephen in in the first place?'

'Not for protection from you!' Her forehead creased. 'From Alfred Dawley! I'd trust you with my life – *and* our children's!'

'Ah hah! But your money?'

She came across to him and sat on his knee. 'You forget.' She tapped him on the nose. 'I haven't got any!'

He gave a false groan. 'Oh, I forgot that! What a good thing I married you for love, not for money!'

CHAPTER FIVE

'It seems like a complex issue,' Stephen Gough said, when he came across from his York office to discuss the affairs of the estate. 'But it doesn't need to be.'

He and Beatrix were in her office alone, although Edward had said he would give his opinion if they should ask for it. A tray of coffee and biscuits had been brought in and Stephen listened carefully to what Beatrix had to say as he sat comfortably in an armchair sipping his coffee.

He leaned forward to put his cup back on the tray and brushed the shortbread crumbs from his fingers, murmuring, 'Your cook makes the best shortbread I have ever tasted. Now,' he began. 'There is no difficulty whatsoever about changing your surname to anything you like; for instance, I decided to drop the Robinson in my name and only use Gough. There is no law that says you must keep the one you were born with, or indeed that a woman must take her husband's name on marriage. There are a few exceptions, such as changing your name with intent to defraud, or pass yourself off as someone else, or commit a crime, that kind of thing, but nothing that need concern us here.

'An estate is slightly different, though there are similarities,' he went on. 'Anyone expecting an inheritance does not necessarily have to accept it. It can be given away to another member of the same family, or turned into a limited company, or whatever the inheritor desires. After all, the person who made the bequest will no longer be around to object, as in the case of Neville Dawley – Charles's great-uncle, if I'm not mistaken – who bequeathed it to Charles. Who' – he raised his eyebrows significantly – 'perhaps didn't want it either but was pressured into it, as you said, by his father, who might have had ulterior reasons of his own. If Charles had given any thought to it he could have simply sold the estate or passed it on immediately to his son.'

He sat back and took another sip of coffee, watching Beatrix's face. 'You're relieved!' he declared. 'So what would you like to do? For a change of name you simply discuss it between yourselves. Strictly speaking, the inheritance isn't for you to decide, as it is willed to Laurence as the eldest son, and in effect you are just the caretaker of it until he comes of age, but it is your right to talk to him about it.'

Beatrix thought carefully. How could she possibly make a decision on Laurie's behalf? In six or seven years' time he might want to become a farmer and run the estate; or he might choose to travel the world, or share the inheritance with his brothers and sisters. It is worth a lot of money; far more now under my stewardship than it was originally. I think we should wait; Laurie shouldn't have this burden thrust upon him now. He's still a child, although he wouldn't like to hear me say so.

'I'm willing to talk to Laurence if you wish,' Stephen offered when he saw her hesitation. 'There might be things that he doesn't understand.'

'Yes,' she said, with some relief. 'I'd like that, Stephen. You could explain it all without the risk of his misinterpreting any confusion on my part, or of fearing to be thought mean for having more than his siblings have.'

'My thoughts exactly,' he said. 'I'll try to persuade him to wait until he's older before even thinking of making any decision. How old is he now?' Stephen took a notebook and pencil out of his briefcase.

'He's just turned fourteen,' she said tenderly. 'Too young to be making choices about his life, although I expect he will be thinking of what he would like to do. That is for sure; didn't we all do that when we were young? So many dreams.'

'I have to say, it took me a long time before I decided on law,' Stephen replied, 'although I remember longing for a briefcase when I was young. When I eventually received one as a present I used to collect caterpillars and store them in the inside pockets!'

He pondered for a while and then said quietly, 'I met Charles at school, as you know; I would have been about Laurie's age when Charles invited me and some other friends to come to Yorkshire and see the estate that rumour had it Charles was due to inherit. It was most impressive, this lovely old house and the grounds; I never thought then that I would ever visit at the request of his widow.'

She nodded. 'I needed someone I could trust to advise me,' she murmured. So much had happened since then, so much that no one would believe. Poor Charles, she thought, so many demands made on him. At another time or in different circumstances he might have been considered a reasonable kind of man, for he could be charming, but his family's expectations and the avaricious thread that ran through them were too strong to break.

Too strong for me, at least, she thought, having been brought up to think of others as much as myself, and far too young to have married a man like Charles, who was only looking for a suitable wife. For that was one of the conditions of the inheritance: that he married someone who would keep him on a steady path and bear him a son to be the next heir to the estate. She gave a small sigh. At least I have fulfilled all my obligations, but without receiving the consideration or love I expected in return.

A soft tap on the door brought Edward back to them. He knew Stephen well, having met him here when he was a boy, on the occasion of Stephen's visit with Charles.

'You'll stay for lunch, Stephen, won't you?' Beatrix asked. 'It will give Laurie the opportunity to meet you under friendly circumstances and not formal ones before you speak to him alone.'

'Yes, a good idea,' Edward agreed. 'Perhaps we could bring up the change of name over lunch and the children could give their opinion too?'

Stephen smiled. 'I'd love to,' he said. 'I've given myself the day off. It was such a lovely drive from York, I felt very relaxed.'

'Perhaps you'd take Stephen for a look around the garden, Edward,' Beatrix said. 'Lunch will be twenty minutes, so if you'll excuse me until then, I'll pop up to see the twins.'

'There's a great family atmosphere, Edward,' Stephen commented as they went outside. 'It was apparent as soon as I came through the front door.'

'That's Beatrix's doing,' Edward said. 'She's created it. When I first met her she had been married less than a week. Charles had taken her to the Lake District, which she loved, but they left after three days and came here, to a house full of old furniture, a massive empty kitchen and no staff at all.'

He pressed his lips together; it was as if he was still angry after all these years. 'Charles upped and left for London after a couple of days and I happened to come by and found her quite alone, wandering about the barns and stables wearing a battered top hat that she'd found in one of the tack rooms.'

He smiled fondly as he remembered. 'She looked so young, which she was, and vulnerable, which really she wasn't, except that she could have been. She found her niche here, fell in love with the house and gardens and made them her own, whilst Charles showed up every now and again.'

'So in a word, it really is *her* home?' Stephen questioned.

Edward nodded. 'Oh, yes, and I'm of the opinion that Laurie is very much like her; all her children have her hallmark, thank heavens, and I haven't seen a single one of Charles's. I don't think for a moment that Laurie would want to take any

27

of it away from his mother when he comes of age, which is coming up so fast it's hard to contemplate.'

'You have an estate of your own?'

Edward laughed. 'I wouldn't call it an estate exactly, although it is a farm of reasonable size and doing well. Officially it belongs to my father; he bought it from Neville Dawley, the one who left Old Stone Hall to Charles.'

Stephen was probing, Edward knew that. The lawyer was getting a feel of how the family worked together, how their lives conjoined. He wanted to tell him that there was no division between them, that although Beatrix already had three children when he married her he loved those children as his own, and as for Beatrix herself, he had loved her from the moment he met her; that young woman wearing the old top hat had eased her way into his heart even though she was wed to another. Now he must try to make it possible for her to keep the home that she loved, at least until her children were grown up themselves.

Lunch was a jolly affair. As she always did, Beatrix brought the twins downstairs to sit in separate high chairs to join the family meal. Stephen roared with laughter as he watched Luke and Isolde each try to escape their confinement and join the other so that they might sit together in one chair. Both were teething, and chewing on hard biscuits that Cook made for them specially, but most of them had been hurled across the room to land on the floor. When chuckles threatened to turn to tears, Beatrix rang the bell to summon the nursery maid, who tucked one under each arm, and Edward opened the door to let them out so they could finish their lunch in peace.

'Eventually, they will realize that if they're good they'll be able to stay,' Beatrix laughed. 'But it's quite a long process.'

'I wasn't like that, was I, Mama?' Alicia said, and added in a very grown-up manner, 'How mortifying,' when her mother nodded that she was.

'I wasn't,' Ambrose said.

'No, you weren't, but you always dipped your fingers into the food to scoop it up rather than use a spoon,' Beatrix said. 'As for you, Laurie, you were always hungry and so eager to eat you used to bang the tray with your spoon until food was put in front of you.'

Laurie groaned. 'I don't really wish to hear that,' he said, putting his hands over his ears.

'No, and I'm sure that Mr Gough doesn't either. He has children of his own,' Beatrix said. 'If we're finished, shall we have our coffee in the sitting room? I thought we could ask Mr Gough's opinion on the question of names, which we discussed previously. What do you think?'

She looked between them all: Laurie, Alicia, Ambrose and Edward. 'We're taking up more of your time, Stephen. Is that all right?'

'By all means,' he said heartily. 'I have enjoyed myself very much, thank you all.' He included everyone in his gaze. 'It has been so nice to meet you in your delightful home.'

They trooped into the sitting room and the three children waited until the grown-ups were seated before they took their own seats, Alicia choosing the padded window seat where she tucked her feet beneath her skirts and put her arms round her knees. Beatrix smiled at her. She remembered doing the same in her parents' house when she was Alicia's age.

Stephen stood up in front of the fireplace, where a vase of flowers stood in the hearth. 'So, ladies and gentlemen, this is the case of the naming of the family of . . .' He tucked his thumbs beneath the roll collar of his elegant, pale blue spotted waistcoat as if he were in court, and they all laughed as he continued in a pompous voice, 'Dawley versus Newby.'

'*Yes*,' all but Beatrix chorused. She remained silent, and Laurie's reply was more muted than the others.

'I would say there is no case to be answered,' he continued in his normal voice, 'if in accordance with my views you might consider, without fear or favour – meaning,' he added, 'in a fair and equal way – combining the names of the person who made this house a home and gave birth to the children of this family, namely Beatrix Newby, formerly Dawley, née Fawcett . . . and using the name Fawcett-Newby.'

CHAPTER SIX

The suggestion was accepted unanimously. Beatrix gave a long sigh of relief; she could shed her unfortunate memories and concentrate on making happier new ones. No longer need she think of Charles as a dark presence in her life, but remember only that he had given her three much-loved children; he had been a troubled soul and had needed someone to blame for his own complicated life.

Edward could barely hide his delight in knowing that the long shadow hanging over his beloved wife could be dispelled; she could now be her own person, no longer tied by an invisible thread to Charles, as she had been even after his death. The question of the inheritance could be resolved at some other time, when the children, especially Laurie, were old enough to speak their opinions on the matter.

Ambrose was pleased and gave a jig of approval. It had been his idea after all. He hadn't any clear recollection of Charles and considered that someone he had never really known shouldn't have any influence over him. For a ten-year-old child, the adults had thought him very clear-thinking.

Alicia was thrilled to be using her mother's name. She had always considered herself to be equal to her brothers, but had gradually become aware that women had to do better than men in order to prove themselves to be on the same level. She worshipped her mother's friend Rosie, who was very controversial and always gave her opinion whether asked for it or not.

As for Laurie, his feelings were about to be shared with Stephen Gough, who, to his surprise, asked if he might have a private word.

Essentially, Laurie was modest and reserved; at school he had made special friends, who, bright and intelligent as he was, had discovered as they got to know one another that they had similar views and a sense of humour which was subtle and sometimes absurd.

'I asked your mother if I could have a word with you,' Stephen told him in the privacy of the study, 'only to reassure you, as heir to the estate, that the details of an arrangement that was made before you were born are *not* set in stone.'

Laurie's face lightened. 'Really, sir? That's good news.' He sat down opposite Stephen. 'I've never told my mother, but I've been worried about the inheritance for ages. I've often been on the verge of discussing it with Pa,' he added, 'but I never have. I thought that I was being a weakling. I've had sleepless nights for years – since I was very young – wondering if I was up to the responsibility of it.'

It was Stephen's turn to be surprised on hearing this. 'Really?' He repeated Laurie's expression. 'For years?'

Laurie nodded. 'Yes, since before I went to the school in Hampstead. My father – Charles, that is – bought me a pony and all the equipment, boots, hat, everything, and told me that as heir to the Dawley estate I must always look the part and behave as a potential owner of a successful estate should. I was only about eight and a bit and didn't properly know what he meant, and I was scared of doing something wrong. He hardly ever came to visit us, and for a long time before I'd thought it was my mother's house and he was a guest.'

He clasped his hands together. 'It was about then that I realized that whenever he came to stay my mother was always tremendously nervous and careful about what she said to him. He had a fearful temper and that frightened me.'

Stephen nodded. He didn't say anything immediately, but thought of how Charles had tried to influence the boy. His words had probably affected Laurie's behaviour, but fortunately Beatrix's guidance was much stronger.

'So to know that I don't have to claim it is wonderful,' Laurie went on. 'I love living here. This is my home and the best place in the world and . . .' He hesitated. 'Well, it feels safe now. I've talked to Alicia and she said she'd always felt safe, especially since Mama and Pa married, because she knew Edward would always look after us, but I've always had the inheritance hanging over me and what Charles said I must do with it. He told me I had to follow it to the letter.'

'You can do whatever you wish.' Stephen gave a smile. 'Providing it's legal! You might want to travel; there will be money enough to do that, apart from the actual land and property. You can go to university if you work hard enough, or go to farming college if you decide you want to run the estate. It's a considerable asset, of course; your mother has worked very hard to make it so.'

'But I don't have to decide now, do I?' Laurie's voice cracked as boys' voices often do when on the verge of manhood. 'I can enjoy myself at school without worrying about taking on all that responsibility when I reach twenty-one. I'll be the same as Ambrose and Alicia, who never seem to worry about anything!'

That's because they've not had the millstone of an inheritance hanging round their necks, Stephen mused as he pondered on the boy's words. They've had a normal childhood, sheltered from all responsibility and without Charles's undue influence bearing down on them in the way it did on Laurie. It's a wonder the boy isn't a nervous wreck. Fortunately he was saved by Charles's early death, though it seems unduly harsh to think so. But he has a sensible mother. He'll be all right.

He stood up, and Laurie did too, putting out his hand. 'Thank you, sir. I'm very grateful to have had the chance to talk to you. I sort of guessed that Mama worried about me, but now I can tell her that she needn't any longer. I'm free to make my own choices.'

'Thanks for coming.' Edward shook Stephen's hand as he prepared to leave. 'It's a weight off our minds to know that's a problem over and done with. I know that Beatrix can relax, now that the shadow of the Dawley name has been removed. It's a pity in a way, for old Neville Dawley was a good friend to us Newbys.'

'Time to move on,' Stephen said mildly. 'Keep in touch; let me know if you have any problems. Beatrix could, if she should wish, change the estate name for business matters; most folk will know it as the Dawley estate, I imagine.' He paused for a second. 'Perhaps sometime in the future you might consider amalgamating your own property into the Dawley holding. You've your twins to consider eventually; but send a note over if you'd like to discuss it.' He grinned. 'I'll always be happy to come to such a splendid residence.'

Edward nodded. 'Not my doing!' he said, lifting his hand in farewell. 'It's my estimable wife; she could have been a born and bred country woman for all anyone knew. But you are welcome at any time, Stephen, and your wife and family too.'

Beatrix had excused herself to go up to the nursery but Laurie, Ambrose and Alicia came to wave goodbye.

'He's a very nice man,' Alicia said.

'A good sort,' Laurie agreed. 'I'd like to meet his sons.' He put his hand affectionately on Edward's shoulder and Edward smiled, but Ambrose broke in to say, 'I must go and look at the pigs. They'll be *really* hungry.'

CHAPTER SEVEN

1866

'You don't mind not coming with me, Mama?'

Ambrose stood in the hall in his new school uniform, waiting for Laurie to come downstairs and Edward to bring the carriage round to the front of the house.

'I mean, you can if you'd like to.' He was rather choked, now that the day had come, yet he had insisted that he'd be perfectly all right without the whole family going with him, and that he'd travel with just Laurie and his father.

'We are rather a crowd, aren't we?' Beatrix gave him a tender smile, knowing that she would shed a tear once her sweet and sensible boy had gone.

Alicia ran down the stairs and gave Ambrose a hug. 'I'll miss you, Amby,' she said. 'There'll just be me and the twins left at home now. Mama, could you and I drive to fetch the boys home next weekend, and we'll get all the news first?'

'Not me.' Laurie came down carrying his luggage. 'I've arranged to stay on with a couple of friends who can't go home as their parents are away.'

'They could come here,' his mother said. 'Your friends are always welcome.'

Laurie kissed her cheek. 'I know, but they've been planning

a trip into York and sent me a postcard to ask if I'd like to join them. I meant to tell you earlier but I forgot. Sorry.' His forehead creased. 'It won't upset any of your arrangements, will it?'

'No, of course not. That will be lovely for you. What are you planning on doing?'

The sound of the carriage wheels trundling over the gravel reached them. 'Jonathon is a history buff,' he said. 'He wants to look at some ancient Viking sites; he says there's more history still to be discovered in York. He's longing to find something of significance.' He turned to smile at Ambrose. 'Come on then, young Fawcett-Newby,' he said in a big-brotherly kind of way.

Beatrix felt her eyes well up; suddenly she had a memory of Laurie going away to school in London when he was only eight. 'I'll look after Amby, Mama, don't worry,' Laurie murmured into her ear as he gave her a hug. 'He'll love it there.'

She nodded, not trusting herself to speak as Ambrose came to give her a kiss.

'I'm very excited,' he said, 'but I'll miss you. Will you make sure that Papa doesn't forget my pigs?'

She gave a choky laugh. 'I won't forget, and Papa won't either. Be good. We'll see you on Friday afternoon. I'll be longing to hear all about everything.'

Edward came inside to collect their luggage, which wasn't a great deal as they were weekly boarders, but new boys were encouraged to take a few personal things to remind them of home. Some of the staff were coming up from the kitchen to say goodbye, and Cook brought each boy a cake that she had made specially.

'Goodbye,' Dora said, giving both boys a kiss on the cheek, for she had known them all their lives. 'See you soon.' Mrs Gordon, the housekeeper, also gave them a hug; both she and Dora had been here so long that they felt like part of the family.

After Edward had driven them off, Dora turned to Beatrix,

who was coming back inside wiping away a tear. 'Pot of tea, ma'am? Though I don't know why I ask!'

'Yes, please, Dora,' Beatrix snuffled. 'I need something to cheer me up now that another of my babies has flown the nest.' She reached out a hand to Alicia. 'Will you join me, darling?'

'Yes.' Alicia gave a pensive smile, and Beatrix, knowing her so well, knew she had something to say. 'But it will soon be Friday, Mama. I don't know about Laurie, but Amby has plans for the future and I'm sure he'll tell us about them soon.'

When the maid brought in a tray of tea, she followed the usual procedure and left it on a side table for Beatrix to pour. This was something that Beatrix's mother had taught her to do: to pour without spilling or making slops on the tray cloth, and handing out biscuits. Now it was her daughter's turn to learn.

'Would you like to pour, Alicia?' she asked, sitting back in her chair.

Alicia nodded. 'Are you very upset about the boys going?'

'Not upset. A little emotional, perhaps; these last few weeks have been unsettling, deciding on the name change for all of us and Ambrose going off to school for the first time. But he's wanted to go for some time so I know he'll be content, and I think Laurie is too, don't you?'

'Yes.' Alicia concentrated hard on pouring without dripping tea on to the tray cloth and triumphantly passed a cup and saucer to her mother, before handing her a small plate containing thin slices of lemon and then offering another holding shortbread biscuits. 'I do. He's happier than I've seen him in a long time.'

Beatrix nodded approvingly. 'Well done,' she murmured. 'Thank you.'

They both sipped their tea for a minute or two and Alicia crunched on a buttery biscuit, and then Beatrix asked, 'And what about you, Alicia? What's next for you?'

'Well, I was going to ask you, Mama. Now that Amby has

gone to school, would you mind if I had a governess, rather than Mr Norman? I don't think he understands girls; I don't mean that he's not a good teacher, but he's . . . well, he doesn't expect the same from me as he did from the boys. He never asks if I understand what he's saying, but he was always asking Ambrose.'

'Perhaps he assumes that you do. Understand him, I mean.'

'He once told me that I was . . .' she took a breath and spoke carefully, '*exceptionally numerate* for a young girl and if I'd been born a boy I could have been a mathematician or an accountant or able to work in a bank; but as I wasn't it seemed a waste, because I would marry and wouldn't need a career.'

Beatrix gave an exasperated huff; she had once been told the self-same thing. Does nothing ever change, she wondered?

'I'll write to him. I don't suppose he expects to come back in any case, now that Ambrose has gone away to school.'

'No,' Alicia said glumly. 'He won't want to teach just a *girl*!'

Beatrix sat pondering. Alicia wasn't thirteen until December, but she was old enough to go to school if they could find a decent one that would see her potential. 'How would you feel about going to school? I don't mean just yet, but maybe next year. Do you think you'll be bored without Amby?'

'Yes, I will be, though I could look after Luke and Isolde so you wouldn't need a nursery maid. Or,' she asked eagerly, 'could I help you with the estate accounts and things? I love doing figures and working out dimensions and quantities and so on.'

'Do you? My goodness! What a help that would be.' Beatrix gazed at her daughter. 'But I want you to enjoy what's left of your childhood; it's so fleeting.'

Beatrix had become engaged to be married when she was eighteen, was married at nineteen, and felt that she hadn't experienced much of life in those early years. She wanted more for Alicia; for both of their daughters, though Isolde was still only a toddler.

'Supposing I teach you what I know about farming facts? Acreage, the price of corn; the cost of rearing and selling live-stock, for instance? Or would that be too mundane? And then, if you'd like to, you could go to school next year.'

'Oh, yes, I would,' Alicia said eagerly. 'When we last visited Rosie, she told me that one of her cousin's daughters had got a place at Cheltenham Ladies' College and loved it there.'

'It has an excellent reputation,' her mother agreed. 'But it's rather a long way from here; and besides, it's a day school. You'd have to live in lodgings and I wouldn't want that.' She smiled. 'You know that I need my children close by me until they're older.'

Alicia nodded and gave a little sigh. 'I'll wait, then. Perhaps I could go to York? That wouldn't be too far, would it?'

'I'll look into it, but in the meantime we'll find you a gov-erness, and she can give you a good grounding until we reach the next of phase of your education, which will come soon enough.'

It was ridiculous, she knew, but the altercations that she had had with Charles had left an indelible mark upon her, making her anxious to ensure that her children were safe and within her reach for as long as possible. She had talked to Edward about it; she could talk about anything with him and knew that he would understand her fears.

'You know that they are in safe hands,' he had told her, drawing her close. 'No one is going to run off with the little monsters; they're growing up so fast, and apart from our twins no one has any power over them except you. But you must let them grow up to be strong independent adults.'

'I do, I do,' she said hastily. 'And of course I didn't mean *you* in any case; of course I didn't. It's only because Ambrose has gone off now, and—'

'He'll be back on Friday,' he insisted. 'Now come on, Beat-rix! Where's that spirited young woman I fell in love with all those years ago?'

She laughed. 'Still here,' she said. 'She's still here. I'll be all right once I see him again and know that he isn't unhappy.'

'He won't be,' he said softly, 'and I can tell you something: Ambrose will definitely want to come home on Friday because he'll want to know if I've looked after his blessed pigs! As if I had nothing else to do!'

CHAPTER EIGHT

Dora had been fourteen when she entered employment as a housemaid at Beatrix's parents' home in London. She hadn't been there long before Beatrix became engaged to Charles Dawley and asked her if she would go with her to Yorkshire when she married, not as a housemaid but as her personal lady's maid.

Dora had said yes, immediately. She was a practical and sensible girl, with an old head on young shoulders, as her own mother said, and although remaining in service to Beatrix she had soon become a friend and confidante as well.

Since Dora had married Simon Hallam, and although she was still Beatrix's personal maid, she no longer lived in. The couple had moved into a rented cottage in the village of North Ferriby, barely ten minutes away from the estate, and Dora walked up to Old Stone Hall every morning. Beatrix no longer needed someone to button her into her everyday gowns, for she had a husband who was willing to do that, but she still liked to have Dora near at hand, to accompany her on visits, or simply to sit and sew with her.

Dora had been married from Old Stone Hall, and her parents had travelled from London for the wedding. Not only was it the first time they had ever travelled on a train, even though they lived within a mile of King's Cross; they were also totally overwhelmed when they saw for the first time the lovely old house where their daughter had been living and working for so many years.

'I'd be lost without you, you know that, Dora,' Beatrix had told her on her wedding day as their roles were reversed and she helped Dora to dress, 'and so would the children. Will you come part-time for as long as you can? Simon won't mind, will he?' 'For as long as you can' was a well-mannered expression for *until you begin to carry a child.*

But that hadn't happened, and Dora in her practical manner had said to Beatrix that if she were meant to have a child, then it would come when it was good and ready, and in the meantime she would come up the hill on four days a week, or more if Beatrix needed her, as a companion for visiting, to dress Beatrix's hair, mend tears, lengthen or shorten shirts or skirts, sew on buttons for the children's clothes, or indeed anything else, for she liked to be useful.

Lily Gordon, on the other hand, had been a housekeeper in London for most of her working life, but when her last employers retired to live abroad and asked her to go with them she had felt a sudden desire to come home to her native county. Offered a position as housekeeper in East Yorkshire, and in particular near her birth town of Hull, where her mother still lived, she grasped the opportunity and arrived just when her young employer had discovered that she was pregnant with her first child, Laurence.

Now that Laurence and Ambrose were at school, with the nursery maid looking after the youngest children and Alicia at almost thirteen perfectly able to look after herself, Mrs Gordon, after first conferring with Dora, asked Beatrix if she might take a few days off to stay with her mother.

'Of course you may. Heavens above, I miss my parents too,' Beatrix replied. 'Though perhaps I might ask them to come here. It would be less complicated than if I travelled to them.'

'Well, I wouldn't go off at the same time, ma'am,' Mrs Gordon said. 'If you were intending going to London, do say if it isn't convenient.'

'Oh, I didn't mean I wanted to go yet! Nearer Christmas, maybe, and do some shopping at the same time. No, go whenever you want. Just let me know when.'

Lily decided to take three days midweek, for the weekends were often busy at the Fawcett-Newby home and she thought that the short break would be just right for her and her mother to catch up with news.

She sent her mother a postcard to say she was coming and caught a morning train, arriving in Hull's Paragon station just over half an hour later. She'd told her mother not to meet her but that she would walk or catch a horse-cab and later they'd go out for lunch, and with that in mind she called in at the Station Hotel and booked a table.

A row of vehicles was waiting outside the station, and looking out for a familiar face amongst the drivers she saw the very one she was hoping would be there. He wasn't sitting aloft his vehicle, though; a younger driver was. Joseph Snowden was standing talking to another cabbie, but Lily Gordon's observant eye noticed that on the door of the cabriolet the name *Joseph Snowden* was etched in gold and black letters; beneath his name were the engraved words *Carriages for Hire.*

'Hmm.' She gave a satisfied mumble, and thought that young Joseph was doing well. Then she smiled to herself: Joseph Snowden in fact wasn't so young any more; he must be in his early thirties now, she mused, probably ten years younger than her.

As if he sensed someone was behind him he had put up his hand to lift his top hat, about to greet the newcomer, when his face lit up with surprised delight.

'Well, by all that's wonderful. Lily Gordon! How good to see you. You don't change. Have you come over to see your ma? I heard you were back in 'district but I've never once caught even a fleeting glance of you.'

'Which is strange, isn't it, in a place like Hull?' Lily said. 'Where everybody knows everybody. But I've been back many a year now, Joseph, fourteen or more. I'm housekeeper out

North Ferriby way and come regularly to see my mother, but your path and mine have never crossed. I hear about you, though, how well you're doing, and now I see for myself.' She indicated the cabriolet.

'That'll be through my ma and yours, I imagine. They often have a natter; known each other a long time.'

'They have indeed,' she said. 'And home is where I'm heading now. Do you have a driver who can take me?'

He looked up at the young man sitting atop the cab, waiting for a customer. 'Rogers!' he called. 'A very special customer so drive wi' care.' Then he added, 'Second thoughts, I'll come along. Drop me off at 'yard.'

He helped Lily into the cab and picked up her bag, lifting it into the interior. 'Not stopping long,' he asked, sitting by her side, 'if this is all your luggage?'

'Only a couple of days, just to check up on Ma, make sure she's all right. Spoil her a bit, you know.' She smiled. Joseph Snowden was the kind of man who made you smile.

'We'd keep an eye on her if she wasn't,' he said, 'but mebbe you might leave us 'name of your place o' work just in case she ever isn't.'

'That's kind of you, Joseph. My mother has it, but I'll write it out for your mother. Ma told me some years ago that you were married and have a daughter,' she chatted on. 'How old will she be now? A schoolgirl, I should think? Time passes so quickly.'

He cleared his throat. 'I, erm, never . . . I didn't get married. I was almost tempted, and yes, I have a daughter. Olivia. She lives with Ma and me, and you're right, she's at school now, and beautiful and bright as a button.'

'Oh!' She was embarrassed at her indiscretion. 'I'm sorry. I assumed . . .'

'Not many folk do know; there are countless suppositions. My ma confided in yours.'

Lily felt a glow of pride in her mother's ability to keep a secret that wasn't hers to share.

44

'I don't mind her knowing,' he murmured. 'But nobody's bothered now; it was onny at 'beginning when Olivia came along and folk were curious.'

'Everyone has a story to tell, Joseph, rich or poor,' Lily said. 'It's up to them whether or not they want to share it.'

'Olivia knows now, and that's what's important. I didn't want folk calling her names and her not knowing why.' He gave a deep sigh. 'We had a good reason for keeping her and I'm glad that we did. She's brought a light into our lives that we didn't expect.'

The carriage drew to a stop as it reached his livery yard in Charlotte Street mews and he put his hand on the door handle to get out. Lily was impressed by the painted board above the brick wall publicizing *Snowden's Livery Stables. Carriages For Hire or Sale.*

This was a tightly packed area of tall three-storey houses, some with basements, such as the houses of Lily's mother, and the one where Joseph lived with his mother and daughter; there was also a public house and a shop. Only a street away was Kingston Square, or Jarrett's Square as some called it, after the man who had thought of landscaping the central area into a fenced garden of trees, flowering shrubs and rose beds, to which only those living near had a key to the gate. A very desirable area in which to live.

'I'll see you around, Lily,' Joseph told her. 'If not this time, I'll mebbe see you on your next visit.' He lifted a thumb up to the driver. 'Drop Mrs Gordon off where she tells you. Don't charge her.'

CHAPTER NINE

Lily kissed her mother's cheek. 'It's good to see you, Ma. I'm sorry it's been a while. There's always something to do at the Fawcett-Newbys'. They're a busy household.'

'Good.' Her mother turned to put the kettle on the fire. 'That's what you need. Don't you worry about me; it's best that you're kept busy, then they'll want you to stay on.'

'Oh, I think I'll always be needed. I'm almost part of the furniture. There was a time before Mr Dawley died when I gave thought to leaving. There was such a lot of tension, but I knew I'd feel guilty, because Mrs Dawley, as she was then, relied on her staff to keep her sane, bless her.'

'And two more babies to her new husband.' Her mother made the tea and took cups and saucers out of a cupboard. 'And she's happy now, is she?'

'You can see it in her face, and in his as well; Mr Newby adores his wife. They've changed their name, too. They're now all Fawcett-Newby.' She took a sip of tea, but refused a biscuit. 'Don't forget we're going out for lunch.'

'I can soon make us a spot of dinner,' her mother objected, calling the midday meal *dinner* in the way they always used to.

'No, it's a treat for you,' Lily insisted. 'I'm going to spoil you for a couple of days. Hey, guess who drove me home!'

'Drove you home! Lost 'use of your legs, have you?'

'I wanted to spend more time with you, so I picked up a cab at the station.'

'You must be made o' brass; you've got used to 'good life,' her mother muttered, but Lily was quick to tell her that she'd used Joseph Snowden's cabriolet and he hadn't charged her.

'That's all right then. He'd have been offended if you'd insisted,' her mother nodded.

'Ah, well, I gave the driver a tip.' Lily smiled. 'It's what the London cabbies expect. He's doing well, isn't he, our Joseph?'

'Deserves to, doesn't he? He's a hard worker, allus was. Tom Henderson took him on as a stable hand just after he left school, and then found out he was Samuel Snowden's lad; do you remember Joseph's father? Died sudden like. By, he was a clever chap: well educated and mainly self-taught, and young Joseph took after him. Samuel had taught the lad bookkeeping, thinking he'd get a good job and a pension at Hull Corporation just like he did. White collar work, you know, but young Joseph was fixed on working outdoors.'

Lily nodded. She knew all this; it was well known that Tom Henderson, who kept horses and had a couple of old carriages, couldn't read or write and that he'd asked Joseph if he could do bookkeeping like his father had done for him. He could, Joseph had told him, but he wanted to work with the horses, and to get the job he wanted he agreed to do both. Before long, he wasn't only working for Tom Henderson, for word got around the district that Samuel Snowden's lad was a good and reliable bookkeeper and might fit in a few extra hours after work, looking after the accounts of local shopkeepers.

Whilst Joseph ate his midday meal he told his mother that he'd met Lily Gordon. 'She's come to stay with her ma for a few days; you might like to call on her?'

'Aye, I would. I've not seen Lily for a long time; her visits are allus short,' Irma Snowden said, then added, 'I've never said owt, you know. About 'bairn, I mean. Onny to her ma, and then not much.'

'Aye, well, she'd be discreet, I don't doubt, but we don't need to talk about it, Ma, it's done with now. It's past history. Olivia is under my protection. My ward. Signed. Sealed. Official!'

His mother opened her mouth to say more, but then, seeing Joseph's set expression, decided not to. She nodded. 'Aye,' she said. 'Course it is. It's for 'best.'

Joseph had had a follow-on plan when he started work for Tom Henderson; it hadn't been properly formulated in his head, for he was only just out of school and had to earn his living, but he knew that one day he would like to own his own horse and cabriolet, and Tom Henderson had unwittingly provided the opportunity to learn the business.

As Joseph grew out of his youth and into adulthood, Tom realized that, being smart and quick-thinking, and with a ready smile and willingness to please, Joseph would one day want to leave him and set up on his own. Tom knew that when that happened his own business would fail, just as it almost did when Samuel Snowden had died so suddenly and he had no one to look after his account books; no one to tell him if he was doing well, or if he was paying over the odds for feed, or indeed if anybody was cheating him.

'Now then, lad,' he had said one morning, having contemplated the matter for most of the previous few days. 'I've had an idea.'

Joseph looked up as he rolled up his sleeves in preparation for mucking out. 'Yeh?'

'How would you like to come into 'business wi' me?'

Joseph licked his lips. 'I've got no money to buy in, Tom. I've onny got my wages from you and 'bit that I earn from bookkeeping.'

'But would you, if I said there'd be no ingoing? I've nobody else to ask, no son, no family.'

'Heck!' He couldn't believe what he was hearing. 'Do you mean it?'

'Aye. I wouldn't have asked, would I?'

'Oh, aye, I would! I'd be proud to, Tom. Honoured! I never thought . . .'

And as they shook hands on the deal, Joseph suggested that they ask a solicitor to draw up a company plan to ensure that all was fair and equal. He couldn't quite believe that his dream of running his own business was coming true and he was still only eighteen.

He had already made an incredible difference to Tom's business, even better than the one his own father had, for although Samuel had been an honest, clever man, he was very cautious and didn't take any chances with other people's money. Joseph had come up with suggestions and ideas to improve the business; one that he proposed was that Tom bought another second-hand carriage, for he had enough money, took on a young man as a driver, and taught him to handle a horse and memorize the shortcuts in the Hull streets, so that the customers would know their time and money wasn't being wasted.

Tom and Joseph were now in a position to improve the stables and the carriage shelter; with Joseph overseeing their expenditure they took on an experienced driver who would drive the second carriage on the busier days, picking up passengers from the railway station and from the ships that plied the German Ocean and arrived at the Hull docks.

It turned out to be a sound idea, and it changed Joseph's life completely.

Two days later, Joseph's mother called on her neighbour and friend and knocked vigorously on the door. Lily Gordon opened it. 'Mrs Snowden! Please come in. It's nice to see you again. Ma's taking a tray of scones out of the oven so you've timed it right.'

'Oh, I don't want to deprive you,' Mrs Snowden protested.

'You won't,' Lily answered, ushering her into the parlour, a cosy room that overlooked the street. 'Ma always makes plenty, and besides, I'm leaving to catch a train back later this afternoon. She's been telling me that you've a French pastry cook living with you.'

'Oh, aye, for a long time now. I'm surprised you hadn't heard. She's not a lodger, though she used to be. Lucille's part of 'family, even though she's French. Like a sister to our Joseph and an aunt to Olivia, she is.'

'Intriguing,' Lily said curiously, and she was curious, for her mother had told her snippets of information over the years since she had come back to work in North Ferriby. She had generally dismissed them as her mother's habit of getting hold of the wrong end of the stick, but she now thought, after meeting Joseph, that perhaps she had been wrong and her mother was right.

She poured the tea and offered Mrs Snowden a plate of scones; there was a small dish of jam on the table and another of thick cream.

'My word.' Irma Snowden wiped her lips with a napkin after taking a bite from the warm scone and depositing a smear of jam round her mouth. 'Your ma doesn't lose her touch. She was always a good baker.'

Mrs Gordon senior looked suitably modest and her daughter Lily, who, on becoming a housekeeper many years before, had followed convention and taken the traditional title for this role of Mrs Gordon, agreed that she was, adding, 'I'd like to hear about your pastry cook, Mrs Snowden. What brought her to Hull? Is there a place for a French pastry cook here?'

Mrs Snowden took a sip of tea. 'There is now. I don't think she intended to stay for so long, but let's just say that circumstances changed their plans.'

'Their plans?' Lily's sharp ears picked up the inference. 'She was not alone, then?'

Mrs Snowden drew in a breath. 'N-no, she wasn't. She had a friend, Margot, with her. They were both very young. Lucille was the younger; she'd come as a companion to Margot and was much more sensible. Margot was flighty,' she said with a sniff. 'She went to stay with an aunt in London eventually, and never came back.'

Lily saw the way the older woman's nostrils flared and her lips pinched when she said the name. Here is a story worth hearing, she thought, but she wasn't the prying kind, so wouldn't press her. It seemed as if it might be a sensitive issue. One day she might hear the full story, but for now she changed the subject back to Lucille by asking if she was baking commercially.

'She began working in a bakery; she needed to earn money. The owner of the bakery saw her potential, I suppose, and taught her the business, and then after ... well, it's a long story ... she opened a shop with a small café attached, where she bakes these pastries that she calls *croissants*' – Mrs Snowden rolled the name around her tongue as if she had carefully rehearsed it – 'and serves them in the café with coffee from eight o'clock until two,' she said proudly. 'She's very successful, catches all 'dock and office workers. She bakes from five every morning and she's back home at four in the afternoon.'

Home, Lily thought? There's definitely a story here. Why would a French woman come to Hull and set up a pastry shop to make French pastries?

That, she thought, is for another day; and Olivia is an old English name, but not common to this part of the country. A child with a father, but no mother? She gave a small secret smile. I love a mystery.

CHAPTER TEN

When Ambrose came home after his first week at school he was brimming with news, and in Laurie's absence had centre stage as he regaled his mother, father and siblings with all the things he had done and learned.

'It's a very important time for me,' he announced at supper on the Friday evening. 'It's a time when I'll have to make some serious decisions about my future.'

Beatrix and Edward looked at each other, and Edward said with a straight face, 'You don't think it's rather too soon to make decisions, Amby? Would you not prefer to take some time to think carefully about your options?'

Ambrose drew himself up to look taller as he sat at the table. 'My options? Hmm! Well, yes, perhaps,' he said thoughtfully, and then turned to his older sister. 'Have you thought about yours, Alicia?'

'I'm not sure if I have any,' she said, cutting into a slice of cold ham. 'What do you think, Mama?'

'I think it's a little early to be considering options, to be honest, Alicia,' her mother said. 'I'd like to think you'll enjoy your girlhood before thinking about the next part of your life. You'll be happy at home with a governess, won't you? Unfortunately there don't seem to be any schools in the district that would suit your requirements.'

'What are my requirements?' Alicia questioned.

'I meant, that would improve on the education you've already had.' She smiled at her daughter. 'You're very clever. Mr Norman must have seen that, but he was concentrating on Ambrose.

'But what about me?' Ambrose butted in. 'My form teacher said it was a very important time for us to learn everything so that we would find out what we were best at.'

'Well, that's very true, and of course it's important,' Edward told him. 'But it's also a time to have fun with your friends; you don't have to decide now what you might like to do when you're a grown man.'

'Don't I?' Ambrose turned a relieved expression towards Edward. 'Well, that's good, because I was wondering how I'd fit everything in, looking after my pigs as well as doing homework *and* deciding what to do in another' – he thought for a second as he mentally counted – 'ten years, which is a long time off.'

Beatrix and Edward both nodded, and his mother said, 'I think that after you've been at school for a little longer you'll find out which are your best subjects; you've only been there for a week and everything is still new to you. You've always been busy at home, haven't you, organizing the pig feed, growing vegetables, looking after your pony and so on?'

'I have, haven't I, and I've missed going out riding and feeding the pigs. I think they've missed me.' His mouth wobbled. 'Maybe I went to school too early after all, cos I've missed everybody.'

Alicia leaned over and patted his arm. 'Well, you're home now, and if I come out with you after supper to put the pigs to bed you could tell me what you've been doing and then maybe in the morning we could ride out together?' She looked at her mother for permission. 'I'm allowed out on my own now, so maybe we could go and visit Gampa Luke and Granny Mags. I'm sure they'd love to hear all about school.'

'Oh, yes, I'd like to do that. Granny Mags will say how much

I've grown since I've been away.' Ambrose perked up, and Beatrix wondered whether, as the youngest child in the family before Luke and Isolde were born, he had been indulged more than Laurie or Alicia, and was missing out on that pampering, being now in the middle of the family.

The following morning, the two children went off on their ponies up the quiet road to visit their grandparents. Beatrix watched from the back gate to see them off, holding hands with Luke and Isolde.

Alicia was a very sensible girl, and Beatrix knew she could trust her to look after Ambrose. She looked down at the twins and thought how quickly time was passing. Luke was jumping up and down with excitement at seeing the horses and Isolde was looking up at the birds that were twittering above them in the elm and ash trees that were already shedding their golden leaves.

It will be lovely to have the twins still at home when Laurie and then Ambrose, and possibly Alicia too, fly the nest; Laurie to university, and Ambrose too if that's the future he desires. As for Alicia, so bright and intelligent: what will she choose to do with her life? Pondering, watching the two children until they turned the bend on the hill, she thought: Alicia must seriously consider her own future. I won't let her be under any pressure from anyone; she must choose her own future life.

Prompted by her father, Beatrix had followed the rigid rules of society in accepting what seemed to be a good marriage. Mr Fawcett had been persuaded by Charles's father, Alfred Dawley, that it would be an excellent match, and as he wanted the best for his only daughter, he had arranged the marriage. It had not been a happy one, but, as she told herself time and time again, in spite of her unhappiness she had gained her beautiful children.

Sometimes, life works out a pattern, she considered, and perhaps I wouldn't have changed anything: I'm safe and happy now, which I never was with Charles. With him I was always fearful and anxious, but by his death he freed me to know what happiness is. But poor Charles, he didn't deserve to die so soon.

Alicia helped her brother down from his pony. His legs were not quite long enough to dismount alone. He'd grow into his pony, his pa had told him; in another few months he'd fit him perfectly.

The kitchen door of the cottage was wide open and Alicia stepped inside. 'Hello,' she called. 'Anybody here? I've brought someone to see you!'

Mags appeared at the top of the narrow staircase and put her fingers to her lips. 'Ssh, Gampa is asleep,' she whispered.

'Is he?' Ambrose asked. 'But it isn't bedtime. It's morning!'

'I know, dear,' Mags said, coming into the kitchen. 'But he didn't sleep well, so he stayed in bed.'

She gazed at Ambrose. 'So who are you? Do I know you? I have a grandson who looks just like you, but he's not as tall.'

'It's me, Granny Mags.' Ambrose grabbed her apron and gave it a little tug. 'Amby. Don't you know me? I've only been away a week!'

Mags reached for her spectacles on the table and carefully put them on, hooking the sides over her ears and pushing the round metal frame up her nose. 'Well, bless me; so it is. I swear you've grown since I last saw you.'

Ambrose gave an exaggerated sigh and raised his eyebrows. 'You always say that, Granny Mags. You know very well who I am.'

She held out her arms and he snuggled into her warm and plump embrace. One thing he knew for certain, one thing that was steadfast and comforting, was that the welcome he looked forward to from Granny Mags would always be there.

He loved his other grandparents too, his mother's parents: his grandfather Ambrose Fawcett after whom he was named, and who knew about so many things, and his grandmother who took him on tours of London, which was where they lived. But Granny Mags and Gampa Luke were very special.

Alicia, in the meantime, had quietly crept upstairs. Seeing her grandparents' bedroom door was open, she peeped inside. Luke was lying on his back with his eyes closed. His face was creased and his lips puckered, and Alicia wasn't sure whether he was asleep or not. Perhaps he's too tired to speak to us, she thought, but risked whispering, 'Gampa, it's Alicia. I hope you'll soon feel better.'

Her grandfather opened his eyes and gave a faint smile. 'I'm sure I will,' he said hoarsely. 'Come here; I want to ask you something.'

She tiptoed to the bed and bent towards him.

'Listen,' he said, slowly and, she thought, painfully, as if speaking was difficult. 'Will you ask your da if he'll call in when he has a minute? There's no hurry and I know he's busy, but there's . . .' he took a laboured breath, 'there's summat I want to tell him.' He put a shaky finger to his lips. 'Don't tell Granny Mags.'

'I won't,' she whispered. 'It will be our secret.'

He nodded. 'Good girl.' She blew him a kiss and backed away and went downstairs.

'You haven't disturbed Gampa, have you, honey?' Mags asked as she came into the kitchen again.

Alicia shook her head. 'No,' she improvised. 'He's asleep, I think. I just wanted to see him. Mama or Papa will be sure to ask how he is. Did Amby tell you that we rode over on our ponies to see you?'

'Yes, he did. You're getting to be very skilful, aren't you?' She meant Alicia, but Amby stood up tall.

'Yes, we are,' he said. 'I wish I could take Jasper to school with me, but then everyone would want to ride him and I don't want him spoiling.'

'Of course you don't,' Mags agreed. 'Animals need looking after, don't they, especially when they're working for us.'

'Like my pigs, you mean?' Ambrose asked. 'At least I get to keep Jasper; I'll feel very sad when I have to sell my pigs.'

Mags's mouth formed an O. 'You've thought about that, have you?' she asked.

'Yes, I have,' he said. 'But I'll maybe keep some for breeding,' he added seriously. 'They have to be useful, that's what Pa says anyway.'

Mags smiled. 'I'll have to tell Gampa that. He'll be pleased to hear it. Mebbe you'll become a farmer when you're older?'

'Oh, I will,' he said earnestly. 'But I need to have an education as well. I have to know about a lot of things.'

'Like doing accounts, as Mama does,' Alicia tripped in. 'Come on, then, we'd better move on. We've a lot to do; we've only got today and half of tomorrow. You'll need to be back at school just after tea.'

They said their goodbyes and Ambrose asked Mags to say goodbye to his grandfather and that he'd hope to see him next time.

Alicia led the way down the hill, and then halted by a track. 'Let's just see where Papa is. I think he might be working on Newby land, so we can take a short cut. It's a bit rough down here, so mind the potholes and keep Jasper on a firm rein.'

She was a good rider, always in charge of her mount, and Ambrose followed her closely. 'There he is.' He caught sight of Edward close by the farmhouse which had been his home before marrying their mother. 'Pa!' he shouted. 'Pa!'

'Keep Jasper steady,' Alicia called over her shoulder. 'Don't make him jumpy. Hello, Papa,' she waved, and Edward stood back from the fence he was repairing and waved back.

'Where are you both off to?' he called.

'Come to see you,' she said, and Ambrose added, 'We've been to see Granny Mags and Gampa, but he was asleep so we didn't see him.'

'Oh.' Edward frowned and looked up at the sun. 'At this time of day?'

He came up closer and looked at Alicia, who held his eye and nodded. 'Perhaps you might go up,' she murmured, and, lowering her voice further, said, 'He would like you to, but you're not to tell Granny Mags.'

CHAPTER ELEVEN

'Now then, Da,' Edward greeted his father. 'I heard you were still abed at dinner time. What's up? Not feeling good?'

'No, I'm not,' Luke mumbled. 'Don't tell your ma, but I don't think I'll be getting up again.'

'Oh, don't say that, Da.' Edward was dismayed. 'I'll ask the doc to call. Give you a tonic or—'

'No! I don't want no tonic. I'm sick o' 'pain. I've put up wi' it for long enough. I'm going to stop in bed; at least 'pain isn't so bad when I'm lying down.'

He tried to sit up but couldn't. Edward came to his side and gently hoisted him up, then put another pillow behind his back before sitting down on the bedside chair. 'If you don't come downstairs, you do realize that Ma will have more to do, up and down the stairs like a yo-yo?'

His father was silenced, but not for long. 'She can bring a jug o' water up in a morning and a slice o' toast, and I'll not ask for owt else.'

'Would you consider coming to stay with us? Beatrix and me? We've plenty of folks who could look after you, and you'd see the children more often.'

He saw his father's expression waver; then the older man made an effort and pulled himself together. 'You don't seem to realize what I'm saying, Edward,' he grumbled. 'I don't want looking after. There's no pleasure in life any more, and I hate that your ma has to run around after me cos I can't walk.'

'What about a wheelchair? We could get you one of those.'

Luke stared at his son. 'An invalid chair! I don't want one of those blasted things; and who would push it? Not your ma, that's for sure. It'd break her back and then where would we be?'

'Then come and stay with us, you and Ma; we've plenty of room, or you could stay in the annexe – Little Stone House, I mean – have a few days' holiday, both of you, whilst we consider what would be for 'best.'

Edward saw that his father was warming to the idea. He'd become desperate at his inadequacies, which had grown worse over the years. Edward had been ten when his father had been trampled by a disturbed herd of cattle, and Mr Newby had suffered since then with barely a murmur. Now it seemed he had had enough.

'Let me talk to Ma and to Beatrix, see what they can come up with. You can stay a few days, or a week, or as long as you like until you're in a better frame of mind.'

Luke bent his head. 'Aye, all right,' he muttered, and Edward heard the croak in his voice as he added, 'I just don't want to be a bother, and I don't want your ma wearing herself out looking after me.'

Edward knew what it had cost his father to say what he had; by telling him what he intended to do he was actually asking him for help. Luke had been a proud man who had been Neville Dawley's foreman when he'd been young, and was brought low through a boy's stupidity. Charles Dawley, Beatrix's first husband, had been showing off to his friends with no thought for the consequences of his actions.

Damn Charles, Edward thought. Will I never get him out of my life? Then, taking a deep breath, he reconsidered. No use dwelling on what had gone before, and Charles was dead, unable to make amends. We need to give Da some purpose in life, help to make him feel useful again.

'I'll talk to Ma and to Beatrix,' he said again. 'Shall we have a family meeting and discuss the options that would suit you?'

'Aye,' Luke agreed, reluctantly. 'But I'll not put anybody about. I'll not be a trouble to anybody!'

'You won't be,' Edward said. 'Now then, what about coming downstairs? There's something simmering in the oven. I'm surprised you can't smell it.'

'I can.' Luke threw the bedclothes back. 'It's your ma's shepherd's pie. My mouth won't stop watering.'

'This is what we're going to do.' Edward stood up and turned his back to him. 'Now give me your hands.' He took hold of his father's hands, and bending his own knees said, 'I want you to lean forward and I'll pull you up.'

Edward heard his father give a gasp but then he had him, leaning on his back. 'Now, clasp your hands round my neck and I'm going to pull you forward. If you can propel yourself with your feet, then do so, otherwise I'll pull you along to the top of the stairs and then take one step at a time.'

When he reached the top step, his mother appeared at the bottom.

'What in heaven's name—'

'Move back, Ma. We don't want to land on top of you. Get a chair ready – and cushions.'

Mags withdrew with no more questions, plumped up the cushions on Luke's armchair and put a blanket on top of them. She wiped her eyes. She was exhausted, but would never have said so.

'Right, Da? Off we go, nice and steady. No rush.' Edward took hold of both stair rails to steady himself, then descended the stairs slowly, one step at a time, whilst his father trailed his bedsocked feet after him. Edward felt a rush of gratitude that the staircase was so narrow that the sides kept them straight; he just had to move down carefully so that they didn't tip forward and fall heads first to the bottom.

'Huh! We've made it,' he huffed as his father eased his weight off his back.

'I'm sorry, lad.' Luke's voice was choked. 'I won't go up again. I'll sleep downstairs from now on.'

Edward didn't answer as he carefully manoeuvred him across the kitchen and turned round so that he could drop him into his waiting chair. Mags fretted over Luke, adjusting his cushions and wrapping him in a blanket.

'Don't fuss, woman,' Luke grumbled at her. 'I'm all right. It's our Edward; he's the one who'll have an aching back. Better put 'kettle on,' and he lifted his face to hers to give her a kiss.

Edward and Beatrix drove Ambrose back to school and he told them he'd really enjoyed his weekend at home and that his pigs and pony had been well looked after, and that the dogs were just the same as they'd been when he'd left for school last Sunday.

'Because it was my first time away from home, I was rather nervous that they might have felt neglected, you see; animals do have feelings, you know,' he said earnestly.

Beatrix smiled as she considered that Amby was more concerned about the animals than he was about the family. 'We'd always take care of them on your behalf,' she assured him. 'That's what farming is about. Everyone has to pull together in order to safeguard our livelihood.'

Edward tried to hide a grin, not because of Ambrose, who was passionate about his pigs, but because his wonderful wife, London born and bred, now sounded like, and indeed was, a typical country woman.

'What?' she asked, obviously picking up some not so well hidden message in that grin. 'It's true!'

'Of course it's true.' He turned to her. 'And you put it so well.' He lowered his voice. 'I want to talk to you later about Da and Ma, too.'

'Gampa didn't want to get out of bed,' Ambrose interrupted from the back of the trap. 'And I think that Granny Mags is very tired.'

Beatrix glanced at Edward, who gave a discreet nod, whereon she began to consider what they could do to help, as the last time she had seen Luke he had seemed very low and Mags was exhausted.

Laurence came out of school to see his parents and gave them both a hug, then tousled Ambrose's hair, which made him frown. 'We had a splendid time in York,' he said, 'and wished we could have stayed longer, but we had to get back in good time for supper. When we get to be sixteen we'll be able to stay out later.'

Beatrix was pleased that Laurence had behaved sensibly. She considered that being at school had been good for him; he'd spent most of his early years close to her and his siblings in the country district of his home, apart from the short time at the London boarding school. Now, she couldn't be prouder of him, knowing that he was growing up responsibly.

The two boys waved their parents goodbye and stepped inside the school doors. 'Anything you need, Amby?' Laurie asked his brother. 'Don't forget to change before supper and wash your hands and face.'

'I won't,' Ambrose said, and shouldered his satchel to take upstairs to the dormitory. Then he turned back to Laurence. 'There is something I need to ask you, though. If you don't mind, I'd rather you didn't call me Amby any more. I'd like my full name, please. Amby sounds very babyish now.'

'Oh! All right. I quite understand. Do you still want to call me Laurie? I don't mind either way. Laurie is quite a friendly name, I think.'

'Yes, it is,' Ambrose agreed. 'Perhaps I'll call you Laurie at home and Laurence at school.' He paused to consider. 'As a matter of fact there's something else I'd like to discuss with you. I haven't thought it through yet but when I have I'll let you know.'

Laurence smiled as his young brother strode confidently away and thought how easily Ambrose had fitted into his new environment; he wasn't afraid of speaking to anyone, or asking questions. Quite unlike how Laurence had been when he had started at the London school. He'd been only eight; aware that his father, Charles, wanted him to make a good impression, and anxious to succeed.

Charles had died not long afterwards and for some time he had thought it had been his fault for worrying him; his mother had said that it wasn't, that his father had tripped and cracked his head and died instantly. When he was told of the accident, he hadn't been sure if he was sad or happy that he had gone.

CHAPTER TWELVE

As they drove home, Edward told Beatrix of his father's wish to stay in bed and not get up again because the pain in his legs was unbearable.

'I carried him downstairs on my back,' he said, 'and he's no light weight. I dread to think what might happen if he should fall or if Ma tried to help him up.'

'Which she would,' Beatrix murmured. She had known Edward's mother long enough to know that she would think that she was strong enough. 'She's looking tired,' she said. 'But she never says that she's finding it hard to look after your father.'

'They need some help,' Edward said, and Beatrix added quickly, 'But we're here. Do you think that they'd come and stay with us for a while, give your mother a break from cooking and helping your da? We could maybe ask the doctor to call to see him,' she went on. 'Maybe give him something to help with the pain?'

Edward gave a grimace. 'I suggested that. Nearly bit my head off. He was having a bad time. I think he was ready to call it a day.'

'What do you mean?'

He shrugged. 'He'd had enough of life, I think, though there's enough spark left in him to give me the sharp end of his tongue.'

Beatrix smiled. 'So he's not ready to give in yet, although I suspect he was asking for help. In his own independent way.'

Edward slowed the horse and stopped at the top of a rise. From here they could glimpse the estuary. They could smell wood smoke and saw hazy grey curls drift up as bonfires burned the stubble and smoke issued from cottage chimneys below. The estuary was dark silver in the fading light as the river slid endlessly on its route towards the sea, whilst above them the sky was suffused with gold and purple smudges, creating contours of mountains and castles in the air.

'I love this view of the estuary,' he murmured. 'It's so eternal, perpetual.'

'I agree. The river just rolls along on a ceaseless journey.'

'It was Alicia who alerted me to Da's predicament.' Edward changed the subject and Beatrix guessed that was why they'd stopped, not simply to admire the view.

'She went upstairs to see him and found him still in bed,' he said. 'Alicia said he'd asked her to tell me he needed a word, but not to tell Ma.'

'So he *was* asking for help,' Beatrix said. 'We should have noticed, Edward. He shouldn't have had to ask us, but they both hide their difficulties. They can come and stay with us, or,' she said thoughtfully, 'they could stay in Little Stone House. Would they prefer that, do you think? The twins can be rather exuberant but maybe they'd like the distraction? We'll ask them,' she said positively. 'They can choose.'

He nodded and caught up the reins again. 'I think we need to discuss a couple of things,' he suggested. 'Ma and Da for one, the other . . .' he hesitated. 'He won't be able to participate in the running of Home Farm for much longer. He says he likes to do odd jobs and look after the accounts and so on, but I don't think his heart is in it. He should retire and let me take over; put it into my name, I mean. I feel as if I've been running it all my life.'

'And the Dawley estate?'

He shook his head. 'No. It's Hallam who does the most

there; I think he only comes to me for confirmation that he's doing the right thing for you and the future.'

She was silent for a moment, and then said, 'But we're family, and Hallam isn't. We're all Fawcett-Newbys now.'

It was Edward's turn to be silent. Then he said, 'It's a question of trust, isn't it? We have to think of our children. You know that I think of yours as mine. I've known them since they were born and love them as much as the twins.' He gave a little chuckle. 'I suppose no one would believe that. And of course young Luke and Isolde are special to me, blood of my blood; any man would say that having sired them and delivered them at birth. But I still care very much for Laurie and Alicia and Ambrose.'

He paused. 'The estate was intended for Laurie, which I feel was unfair, when no provision was made by those early Dawleys for any other member of the family, or even their wives. Not that Neville Dawley had a wife, but even if he had, he would have followed the same guidelines, though I don't think for a moment that it was truly necessary in law. I'm sure Nev could have left it to anyone he wanted.'

Beatrix licked her lips. She too had always thought it unfair that only the eldest son should inherit, and what if Laurie didn't want it? Charles hadn't wanted it, not to work at. He had only wanted it for the prestige of being a landowner. None of their children had avaricious longings as he had had. She had brought them up to enjoy the simple things of life; true, they had dogs and ponies, but they were expected to look after them themselves, and not to think of animals as mere playthings.

And, she pondered, if anyone should run the estate, the natural successor should surely be Ambrose. He had his pigs and intended to breed them; he had chickens and his own vegetable patch, and he had asked if he might have a cold house for his next birthday so that he could grow vegetables over winter: carrots, he'd said, and greens like cabbage and spinach.

Never once have I heard Laurie say what he would like to do with the estate when he's older; and then there's Alicia. She is bright and intelligent and why shouldn't she benefit from being a member of an industrious and successful family? In my opinion she has as much to offer as her brothers.

'We need another family discussion,' Edward murmured, busy with his own thoughts. 'But not yet. Let the children enjoy life; let us enjoy *them* whilst they're young. Childhood is so fleeting. Let's make the most of it whilst we can.'

Luke and Isolde were just the tonic for Gampa Luke and Granny Mags, who were always available to entertain them with a story or mend a toy when their mother brought them over to Little Stone House. A downstairs room had been converted into a bedroom for Luke senior, whilst Mags now had her own bedroom upstairs and both were able to rest whilst a young maid attended to their every need. Their meals were brought over from the main kitchen, and if Mags felt like making a pot of tea of her own, or even baking, she could, using the smaller, though adequate, kitchen in the little house.

They had plenty of company, for apart from the twins Alicia came over each day after her lessons and always had something to discuss; Edward also came each evening to tell them what he'd been doing on the farm, and Cook, Mags's sister and Aaron's mother, often popped over with a little savoury or sweet to try.

When there was a fine day, Aaron would come and ask if they would like a ride out in the trap or carriage as he had a few errands to do for Miz Beatrix, and would drive them down to the estuary and on to Hessle or Brough, often calling in at a local hostelry for their benefit.

They were into their third week before they both began to feel restless, Luke mumbling that he needed to turn over the vegetable plot before the first frost, and Mags ruminating that she must get on with preparing the fruit for the Christmas cakes. She always made Christmas puddings and cakes, even some for her daughters out in Holderness, though they were perfectly capable of making their own, and she decided that she would ask if they could borrow Aaron to drive them there.

'Holderness is too far for me to drive there and back in a day,' she told Luke. 'Mebbe we could use the old clarence that Charles bought Beatrix all that time ago. Hardly anybody uses it since they got the newer one, and I expect that'll be used to transport 'boys backwards and for'ards to school in winter.'

There was no comment from Luke, who was dozing with his slippered feet stretched out towards the fire, when she'd expected him to suggest that she should ask their Holderness offspring to come and collect the baking, rather than have them trail all that way, especially as the weather was becoming unpredictable.

We ought to stay the night, she was thinking, rather than come back the same day, but Luke is never happy sleeping in anyone else's bed, although he hadn't made any objection to sleeping here at Little Stone House.

She glanced at him for a comment, but he was lying with his head against the back of the chair and his eyes closed. She gave a little smile; his lashes were still long and dark against his skin, and she thought of when she'd first met him and his long lashes were the first thing she had noticed about him, those and his kind grey eyes.

'P'raps I'll mek a cup o' tea,' she whispered. 'It's about that time o' day and it'll save 'young maid from bothering.'

She eased herself out of the chair and tiptoed out of the room into the kitchen, where a small fire was burning in the range and the kettle humming on it. She made the tea and rattled the teacups, putting an extra teaspoon of sugar in Luke's before carrying the tray through into the parlour and placing it on the small table.

'Cup o' tea, honey?' she said, pouring the rich golden liquid into each cup before she added milk and stirred.

'Luke, are you awake? Come on. Have it whilst it's hot. It's freshly brewed.'

Mags glanced at her husband. He was lying exactly as he had been when she'd gone into the kitchen and she felt a sudden sinking of her heart. She picked up Luke's cup; her hands trembled and shook as she put it to her mouth. She'd need the extra sugar that she'd spooned into it.

'It's not a good time, Luke,' she murmured, her voice suddenly husky. 'I thought we'd have a bit longer than this. I'd thought that if you'd agree to our Edward tekking over completely – well, he does everything already, just about, doesn't he – I thought mebbe if 'weather was settled we could have a few days and go to Bridlington or Scarborough, for a change of air, you know. But now I don't know what I'll tell our girls; they've not seen much of us over 'last few years, and they'll be upset.'

She heard the front door open and close and the fresh young voice of the maid who'd been at their beck and call since they'd come to stay call out, 'It's onny me, Mrs Newby. Kitty. Just going to mek you a pot o' tea.'

'Just a minute, honey,' Mags called back. 'Afore you do that, is our— erm, Mr Newby at home?'

'He is.' The girl put her head round the door. 'He's just come in. Did you want him?'

'Aye, I do, lovey. Will you pop back and tell him I need to talk to him when he's got a minute? Don't bother about 'tea. We've just had one. Tell our Edward there's no rush. No rush at all.'

She heard the front door open and close again and she reached out and took hold of Luke's hand. 'We'll just sit and wait here quietly, shall we, Luke?' she murmured. 'Like I just said. There's no rush.'

CHAPTER THIRTEEN

Edward came immediately. He'd seen the uncertainty on young Kitty's face when she'd given him the message from his mother.

'She said there was no rush,' she'd said throatily, but to him that communication and the way that Kitty pressed her lips together and looked at him with anxious eyes told him that it was urgent.

He got up from his chair and went to the front door to put his boots back on. 'Beatrix,' he said, as she appeared at the top of the staircase as if she were on her way out, which she was, to visit the tenant farmers, something she often did, even though Hallam gave her regular reports, 'I'm going next door.'

'Yes? Shall I come?'

'Give me five minutes, will you?' He swallowed. 'I think something's happened.'

She nodded. 'All right.' She took a faltering breath. 'I'll follow you.'

She ran down the kitchen stairs in search of Mrs Gordon, but she wasn't there, only Cook and the maid, Kitty, who, rather strangely, was sitting at the kitchen table drinking tea.

'Will you let me know if our Mags needs me, ma'am?' Cook said. 'We've allus been close.'

'Of course.' Beatrix said. Sometimes she forgot that Mags and Hilda Parkin were sisters and that Aaron too was part of the family; it seemed sometimes that practically everyone working at the Old Stone House was related.

'I'm just going next door,' she told them. 'Could you tell Mrs Gordon – and Alicia too – that that is where I am? I won't be long.'

As she finished speaking, the back door opened and Aaron came in. He gave a grin and touched his forehead to Beatrix, but when he saw their solemn expressions his smile faded and he stood stock still.

'Don't worry about anything, ma'am,' Hilda said. 'We all know what to do.'

Of course they did, Beatrix reflected as she ran back up the stairs into the hall. Everything runs like clockwork. They are all so faithful. How lucky we are.

She wouldn't go to see the tenants after all; it seemed that there might be some urgency and as the maid, Kitty, seemed upset, it could only mean that it was something to do with the Newbys. Luke? I hope not. Mags? No, please, not Mags. She cared for Mags almost as much as for her own mother.

She lifted her skirts and ran up the front steps of the annexe just as Edward was opening the door. Mags was holding on to his arm, looking shaken but regarding her with brave eyes.

'Oh, Mags! What's happened? Is it Luke?'

Mags nodded and swallowed. 'Aye, m'dear, it is. He slipped away whilst I was mekkin' 'tea. Never waited to tell me he was going. Typical of him. He allus wants to do things his way.' Her throat dried up and tears began to fall. 'He should've waited.' She began to weep, heavy sobs that came from deep within her.

Beatrix took her other arm and together she and Edward helped her down the steps to walk the few yards to the main house. Over his mother's head, he mouthed to Beatrix, 'Do you know where Aaron is?'

She nodded and mouthed back, 'Kitchen.'

Everything happened quickly after that. Mags wanted to go into the kitchen to tell her sister the news: as Hilda had said, they were very close. Aaron was despatched to the doctor to ask him to call and make what arrangements were necessary. Beatrix told Alicia, who was heartbroken, but they didn't tell the twins as they were too young to understand.

'Your mother must stay with us tonight,' Beatrix said to Edward when he came back to the sitting room; Mags was still in the kitchen with Cook.

'Mebbe,' he said. 'She might want to go home. Isn't that what we all want when we're in a state of distress?'

'Then one of us should stay with her,' Beatrix insisted. 'And – she might want to be with your father.'

'I'll stay with her.' Alicia looked up, red-eyed with weeping, and they both smiled and said how kind of her.

But it was Edward who stayed with his mother, who said she would stay the night and keep watch over Luke in the room that had become his bedroom, and then go back home the next day to 'sort things out'.

He didn't ask her what kinds of things needed sorting out; she would have her own ideas and he knew that she would want to write to his sisters and their families.

'Would you like me to drive over to Holderness and tell them?' he suggested.

But she said not. If she posted the letters first thing tomorrow, she said, the chances were that they would arrive by the afternoon post, or at latest the following morning.

Edward nodded. 'Write them now, Ma,' he advised, 'and I'll ask Aaron to drive to Hessle. It's an earlier collection there, I think.'

'There's no rush, son,' his mother said gently. 'Your da isn't going anywhere in a hurry.'

Edward sat down, clasping his fists to his mouth. 'I know, Ma.' His voice was choked, and it was as if his father's death had just become a reality. 'I know.'

It was the first time that the older children had seen death so close at hand. They had been too young to attend Charles's funeral and it would not have been expected, but all three wanted to be present for their much-loved grandfather, although with a black armband on his sleeve Laurie found that old forgotten memories of his late father resurfaced and caused him some disquiet.

The boys had been allowed time off school, and the day after the funeral, after breakfast was over, Ambrose changed into what he called his working clothes and told everyone that if anyone wanted him he would be either down on his vegetable patch or with his pigs.

'I'll come with you, Amby,' Edward called after him. 'You've got a couple starting to graze; they might be ready for weaning.'

'Oh?' Ambrose questioned. 'I thought it was too soon.'

'It is for some of them,' Edward said. 'But at twelve weeks the bigger ones are probably ready.' He grinned at Beatrix. 'Farmer Ambrose!' he said, and to Ambrose, 'Gampa would be proud of you; he always loved his pigs.'

'He did, didn't he?' Ambrose said delightedly as father and son headed for the piggery. 'I like pigs best of all.'

Laurie gazed after them, his head on one side, contemplating. He too liked the animals – especially the horses, the Shires as much as the riding or carriage ones – more than the business of growing crops when weather-watching was paramount, but he wasn't as keen to rear cows or pigs as he was to make sure that they were healthy, which led him to scour various farming journals for articles on the best treatment for sick or injured stock. As for running the financial side of the estate, he had as little interest in that as he had in growing crops, although of course he knew that it had to be run at a profit in order for it to thrive as a business. He had overheard his mother once say to Edward that Laurie had no self-centred ambitions, and Edward had muttered that he didn't take after his father then, thank the Lord. He'd puzzled over this until it had dawned on him that it was Charles that his pa was talking about, and not himself.

Following Luke's death, Beatrix and Edward discussed many

things about the Newby farm. It had nothing to do with the Fawcett-Newby estate, but Edward had run it on his father's behalf since he was a very young man and it would now become his. They thought too that perhaps Mags would no longer want to live in the cottage attached to Home Farm, now that Luke was gone.

Laurie, who was present during one of these discussions, voiced his thoughts. 'Could the Newby farm not become part of the Fawcett-Newby estate, Pa? It would make sense, wouldn't it?'

Edward looked up; he had forgotten that Laurie was in the room. 'I need to think about my sisters too,' he explained. 'But we can't make any decisions until Granny Mags finds the will.'

It was eventually found in the bottom of a cupboard, and as expected the farm was left to Edward. A reasonable sum of money – for Luke could never have been called a spendthrift – left to his wife to see her comfortable for the rest of her days, and a smaller sum to each of their daughters, who were all quite comfortably established with their farmer husbands.

There was not enough left over for his grandchildren, for, as Mags explained, there were so many of them. Their daughters had several each; Edward had the twins, and although Luke had said many times that he cared for his step-grandchildren too, he knew they were well provided for. Nevertheless, he had left each of them a small keepsake, Ambrose's being a sack of pig feed and an ancient hoe.

Stephen Gough was invited to visit again to discuss the implications of the Newby Home Farm, which Beatrix and Edward had talked over at length. They were anxious to do the right thing, particularly in relation to the twins Luke and Isolde.

'They have to be included in the estate,' Edward said, and Beatrix looked guardedly at him.

'But of course,' she said, her voice rather tense.

'I'm sorry, my darling – I didn't mean – I'm sorry!' He leaned from his chair to hers, holding out his hand. 'You don't think – surely not – that I'm anything like Charles?'

He could have kicked himself. Charles had been so manipulative in his dealings with Beatrix and the three older children, threatening to divorce her and take them away from her for no other reason than that he could; the law was on his side and not on wives' or mothers'. She had been determined that he would not take them from her, but had not felt safe until fate had taken a hand and Charles's accidental early death had released her from the menace of that threat.

She stretched out her hand to his. 'It's all right,' she murmured. 'It was a slip of the tongue, I know, and I'm still so sensitive. Of course our little ones must be the same as the others.' Luke and Isolde were still infants, being not yet three, but both had their own determined personalities, and must be considered.

CHAPTER FOURTEEN

1869

'Mama, are you busy?'

Alicia had been attending school in York for the last year. She was very sociable and had already made friends amongst young people from local families when accompanying her mother on visits, but they were mostly scattered around the villages, often quite a few miles apart, and rarely was she allowed to ride her pony any distance on her own.

Laurie would be seventeen in May, Alicia sixteen in December, both burgeoning into adulthood, although to their parents Alicia seemed to be more grown up and have more confidence than Laurie did. Once she had settled in at school, she had made her own decision that she would prefer to board for the full term, rather than weekly as Laurie and Ambrose did. Ambrose still came home every weekend to tend his animals and check on his vegetable plot, although Laurie sometimes stayed on to visit York with his friends, who were considered to be sensible and level-headed young adults.

The children were home for Easter and Alicia had found her mother in her study off the hall. 'I wanted to ask you if I might bring a school friend to stay during the summer?' she said. 'Not for the whole summer, but maybe for a week or two?'

'Of course you can,' Beatrix agreed, leaning back from her desk, where she was looking over the farm accounts. 'Your friends are always welcome.' She knew that Alicia was extremely particular about friendship. She had never been a giggly, immature child; she was happy, intelligent and advanced for her years, easy to talk to and always respectful, and her friends tended to be the same. 'Is she a special friend?' she asked. 'Someone new?'

'She began school at the same time as I did,' Alicia explained. 'But because she's slightly younger than me she was put with a different age group and I didn't meet her until – because she's so *incredibly* clever,' she raised her hands and eyebrows dramatically, 'she was moved up a year. She lives in Hull and used to go to a local school, but she also had private lessons, and her governess suggested that she should try for the York school and gave her a recommendation.'

'Ah! And is she nice? I suppose that she must be if you want her as a friend,' Beatrix said.

'She's lovely,' Alicia said, 'You'll like her, Mama. She's rather shy; no, not shy, *reserved* maybe is a better word, and quiet on first meeting, but she has a great sense of fun and irony. I looked that up,' she added. 'I couldn't think how to describe her humour, but I think that's what it is: ironic. Maybe she gets it from her father; she hasn't got a mother. She died at Olivia's birth. Isn't that so sad? I can't think how I would have coped without you, dearest Mama.'

She came up to the desk and put her arms round her mother and squeezed her tight. Beatrix kissed her tenderly on her cheek and indicated that she should sit down on the other old leather chair. 'It is very sad,' she agreed 'But if she never knew her mother she'll miss the gap in her life rather than a remembered vision of her, and that will be how she copes.'

'Of course,' Alicia said thoughtfully. 'I hadn't thought of that. She has an aunt, though, who she says is like a mother to her, so she doesn't miss her own so much.'

'Oh, I see. And does her aunt describe what her mother was like? I'm assuming she was her mother's sister?'

Alicia considered. 'I don't know. Olivia hasn't said that she was. She's French. Olivia speaks perfect French, too.'

'Who is French?' Beatrix asked. 'Her aunt? So Olivia must be half French too?'

'I don't think so.' Alicia shrugged. 'Olivia calls herself a typical Yorkshire girl. She looks French, though, or slightly foreign anyway. She has thick, shiny black hair with a long fringe down to her eyebrows and a plait that reaches her waist. She said her aunt wants her to have it cut into a French bob and says it would be *très chic*, but her father won't let her.

'Olivia doesn't look in the least like him,' she went on. 'I haven't met him but I saw him once when he came to collect her. He's huge, much taller and broader than Papa, and has brown curly hair. I saw it when he took off his top hat; Olivia is very *petite*,' she said, assuming a French accent again.

'Well, I'll look forward to meeting her,' Beatrix smiled. 'I'm sure you'll have lots of fun.'

Next to have a cosy chat with his mother and father after supper was Laurie. He said that he had been wondering if he might ask a friend to come and stay for a few days during the summer holidays.

'Andrew's older than me by a few months,' he said. 'He's seventeen already, and I might not be able to ask him again for quite some time. He'll be busy studying as he's taking exams early; his tutors have suggested that he should. He wants to study medicine, but not to be a doctor or a surgeon. He's interested in testing and finding cures for various diseases.'

'The sciences?' Edward asked.

'Yes, I think so. He's interested in tropical disease.'

Beatrix took a breath. 'Really? My goodness, and he's only seventeen?'

'The exams are just a kind of test,' Laurie explained. 'A general assessment to see how he copes with the set questions. If he does well he'll move up a year to prepare him for university.'

Edward leaned forward with his elbows on his knees. 'Is he prepared for that? It's quite a challenge!'

Laurie nodded. 'He's keen to do it. He likes a challenge. I, erm . . . well, because Andrew has begun thinking about his future, Jonathon and I have been discussing our options too. Jonathon is the history buff, so he thinks he'll go into teaching.'

'And you?' Edward said lightly. 'Have you any thoughts yet? Though there's plenty of time. Your mother and I are agreed that you don't have to rush over your choices.'

'Would you expect me to take over the estate?' Laurie asked in a low voice. 'I know that Mr Gough said that it wasn't set in stone that I had to, even though I'm due to inherit, but would you be disappointed?'

Beatrix smiled. 'I wouldn't be disappointed, Laurie. I want you to be happy and to choose your own path in life; I wouldn't want you to feel constrained to decide on something you didn't want to do because you thought you should, or because someone else had decreed it was expected of you.'

'I have a few ideas,' Laurie confessed. 'Not for running the estate; to be honest, I think Alicia would be better than me, and Ambrose is more interested in crops than I am, but . . .' He hesitated, and his mother broke in.

'You don't have to discuss your plans if you haven't thought them through; you have plenty of time, and no one's putting any pressure on you, Laurie. You're only sixteen. You have years ahead of you.'

He nodded, and laughed. 'Ambrose has decided,' he said. 'He's going to invest in his pigs!'

Edward laughed too. 'That's probably my fault.' He looked across at Beatrix. 'I came across to the house for some reason or other when Ambrose was three or thereabouts and he was grizzling; Ma and Aunt Hilda were trying to entertain him in the kitchen, but I could tell they were getting flustered. We'd had a litter of pigs at Home Farm, so I put him on my back and took him off to see them.'

'You stole him!' Beatrix said in mock horror.

'Aye, I did.' Edward grinned. 'He tried to reach down from my back to play with them. Haven't I ever told you?'

She shook her head. She only knew that back then Edward had always been somewhere near as soon as Charles had left for London, checking to be sure that she was all right after her husband's visit.

'I forget sometimes – mostly, in fact,' Laurie broke in, 'that you haven't always been our father. I mean . . .' He tailed off self-consciously.

Edward gave him a friendly cuff with his fist and Beatrix knew that he was moved by the declaration. 'I know,' Edward said. 'And yet I've been in your life from even before you were born, although you'd never have known it. I always had to keep a distance' – he swallowed – 'because of Charles.'

Laurie nodded. It had taken him a long time to be free of the disturbing remembrance of his late father and it was Edward, his stepfather, whom he knew he could trust with his life, who had helped him over that.

'Poor Charles,' his mother murmured. 'He wasn't a bad man; he just hadn't received love and kindness from his own parents and didn't know how to give it himself.'

And that's just it, Laurie thought. I'm safe and loved here within my family circle and I have special friends at school, but how will I be if I look for a career away from home, outside my own circle? How will I get on if I attend university?

He was aware that he conveyed confidence to those who didn't know him well, whereas in reality he had very little self-assurance. He sighed. And I don't know how to get over that.

CHAPTER FIFTEEN

At the end of the summer term Edward went to York to collect Alicia from school and met Olivia and her father, who had driven from Hull to collect his daughter.

The two men drew into the entrance, one behind the other. Alicia had said that her friend was Olivia Snowden; Edward saw that the carriage in front of him had *Joseph Snowden* etched on the door, and went across to introduce himself.

Olivia had told her father that Edward was a country man, which was obvious as he was carrying a wide, battered felt hat and wore a tweed sack coat and cord trousers. Joseph could tell that he was a man of the soil by his hands, which were scrubbed clean but bore a few nicks and scratches as Joseph's did too, but he had none of the fancy airs and graces that Joseph had expected. Olivia had told him that the family were estate owners, and he'd met one of that kind many years ago from the same area and hadn't liked him.

He prided himself on never forgetting a face, and he knew this wasn't the man he'd met before. He remembered that one perfectly, for it was seldom he had customers going to or coming back from that region, and generally, after one particular occasion, he had tried to avoid it.

A toff, he would have called the other fellow, and from London probably, certainly not from these parts. He'd met him again subsequently, when he had not been alone.

They waited in the large hall with other parents and Joseph mused that maybe the estate – surely it must be the same estate? – had been sold; the other chap wasn't a country type. So this is Alice's father? No, not Alice, *Alicia*! That's the name of the friend that Olivia is always talking about. He watched as Alicia flung her arms around Edward and he in turn gave her a huge bear hug, lifting her off her feet.

'Oh, Papa,' Alicia cried excitedly. 'It's so good to see you. Olivia, come and meet my darling papa, and Mr Snowden, how de do? I'm Alicia Fawcett-Newby; I'm very pleased to meet you.'

Joseph lifted his top hat and declared that he was very pleased to meet her too. Alicia held out her hand and dipped her knee to him and he was instantly charmed, returning the grin that was plastered over Edward's face. 'My daughter Olivia,' he said proudly. Edward gave a small neat bow, his hand to his chest.

'Hello, Olivia. I'm pleased to meet you.' He smiled at her. 'We've heard much about you. You're coming to stay with us soon, I understand? We're looking forward to that. Papa doesn't mind?' He raised his eyebrows. 'He'll miss you, no doubt?'

Olivia slipped her arm into Joseph's. 'It will be the first time I've been anywhere without him,' she said shyly. 'I've explained it will only be for two weeks, so he says he'll be able to manage. Grand-mère will be at home and Tante Lucille too. They'll look after him.'

The two men glanced at one another, Edward sympathetic at Snowden's not having his daughter with him for part of the holiday. He asked if he might collect Olivia when she was ready.

'No, no. I'll be pleased to bring her, Mr Fawcett – erm, Newby,' Joseph said. 'I – think I know the house.'

Edward looked surprised. 'Newby is fine, Snowden. Have you been to the house before?'

'Many years ago I brought a gentleman and two ladies to a house which I think might have been yours and collected them again to take them back to Hull railway station, and a couple of times after that I brought the gentleman on his own. Then he must have discovered there was a nearer railway station than Hull so I didn't see him again.

'And if I'm not mistaken,' he went on, 'an old friend and neighbour of ours has a position in your household. Mrs Lily Gordon?'

'Mrs Gordon,' Alice squealed, and turned to Olivia. 'I didn't realise that you knew Mrs Gordon!'

Olivia shook her head. 'I don't,' she said. 'Grand-mère tells me when she has visitors to see her, but I'm always at school. Would this lady visit, Papa?'

'Possibly,' her father said. 'Her mother often comes to see your gran, and Lily – Mrs Gordon – calls whenever she's in Hull.'

They drifted off towards their conveyances then, Joseph and Olivia to the carriage and Edward and Alicia to their trap, both girls chattering happily about their next meeting. They hugged goodbye and their fathers smiled and raised their whips as they moved off in the same direction; Joseph in front, as he made faster headway with his two horses, and the pony pulling the trap following them at a brisk trot.

'I'm so happy that Olivia is able to come and stay,' Alicia said. 'I do hope she likes the countryside – she's very used to town.'

'You'll have to find a spare pair of rubber boots for her,' Edward said. 'Not everyone realizes how muddy it can be after rain.'

'Oh, it won't rain,' Alicia said determinedly. 'It's going to be a glorious summer.'

'I hope you're right.' Edward smiled down at her. 'What we want is a good sunny harvest with gentle rain in the evenings.'

It transpired that that was what happened that summer: glorious sunny days and gentle rain on some nights, and they all looked forward to a good harvest.

'Incredible; perfect weather,' Edward said, one evening after supper. The family had retired to the sitting room, apart from Luke and Isolde, who had gone upstairs for their bath and would come down again to kiss everyone goodnight before Beatrix took them up again to read them a story. 'Alicia, you can give out the weather forecast every summer,' Edward continued. 'Three more days and the corn will be ready if this weather keeps up, and we'll begin to bring the harvest home.'

'Will it be all hands to the decks?' Laurie asked. 'Or have you got plenty of labour? Andrew is coming tomorrow; he says he wouldn't mind giving a hand if it's harvest time.'

Edward nodded. 'As long as he knows what he's doing. Mebbe the pair of you can feed the horses when the lads are having their lowance, or stopping for a break.'

'Olivia is coming on Saturday, so we'll carry out water and lemonade for the men at lowance time,' Alicia broke in, 'and extra rations. Cook always bakes such a lot more food at harvest.'

'That's because so many of the horse lads are related to her!' Edward grunted. 'Aunt Hilda has dozens of kin through her late husband's family.'

'We're lucky, then,' Beatrix said. 'But don't be stealing Aaron; I might need him.'

'Why, where are you off to?' Edward asked. 'You're generally here for harvest.'

'Oh, I will be. I'm not going far, just a visit to Hessle on Tuesday morning. I'd accepted before realizing that harvest would be ready so soon. Rosie is going too and I said we'd collect her and go together.' She turned to Alicia. 'You and Olivia can come too if you'd like to. It's open house to welcome Mrs Highcliffe-Rand's son home. He's been living away for some years.'

'Do I know them?' Alicia asked. She had often made visits with her mother, but not since starting at boarding school.

'No,' her mother said emphatically, shaking her head. 'I was invited when I first came here and we met perhaps only once or twice afterwards. The family became quite reclusive. I heard that there'd been a disagreement within the family and the son left home. They must have patched things up and he's returned.'

'His father died,' Edward added. 'He'd lived in this part of East Yorkshire all his life, and knew most of what went on in farming circles but didn't have a lot of success. He wasn't popular. Most people found him arrogant – the father, I mean. James has probably come into the estate. I haven't heard that he'd been cut out of it.'

'My invitation came from his sister, Amelia,' Beatrix said. 'I've met her at Rosie's and other places. She's nice, but I gather she has a difficult time with her mother, and they haven't entertained guests in a long time.'

'Doesn't sound as if it will be much fun,' Alicia commented. 'Not sure I'd want to go, but I'll ask Olivia if she'd like to.'

'Don't invite me, will you, Mama?' Ambrose broke in. He was sitting browsing over a farming newspaper. He rarely indulged in small talk unless it was about farming issues. 'I'll be far too busy helping Pa with the harvest.'

Everyone smiled, but he didn't notice as his eyes went back to the newspaper. 'Looks as if this is going to be a good year for beef,' he murmured, 'but I think I'll still concentrate on pigs. I'd like to focus on specialist breeds.' He lifted his head and looked at Edward and then his mother. 'When I'm old enough, I mean. No one would take me seriously yet.'

'We would – do,' Beatrix and Edward answered simultaneously, and Edward continued, 'Would you like to go to farming college when you're old enough, Ambrose? It would mean that you'd have to work hard on other subjects to get in, of course.'

'Well . . .' Ambrose pondered. He wasn't keen on subjects like history or science. 'Couldn't you teach me?'

'No, I couldn't,' Edward said. 'I don't know enough about specialist breeding. I'm a farmer and know about corn and growing different crops, and cattle too, but not pigs. If you want to specialize, you'll need more advice than I can give you.'

Laurie leaned forward. 'When Ambrose is old enough and is ready for further education' – he turned to his younger brother, and then looked at his parents – 'if he's still in the same mind about pig breeding, could we open up a separate enterprise within the Fawcett-Newby estate? You know, give it a different name but still be part of the whole?'

'That's a *brilliant* idea, Laurie,' Alicia said. 'Maybe we should diversify. Then if one part of the holding does badly, say we have a wet summer and the harvest fails, we can rely on the cattle or pigs to keep us in funds.'

Beatrix and Edward glanced at one another and their lips twitched. Here were their children organizing their futures.

'Actually, we do that already,' Edward explained. 'Every farmer has to; rotating crops and so on is part of farming life if we're to be able to deal with the uncertainties of the English weather, and the resting and renewing of the soil. It's also a question of money: whether we can afford to invest in a completely different enterprise.'

'We'll save up,' Ambrose declared. 'I'll give up my allowance. I don't always use it anyway.'

'Can I look after the accounts?' Alicia asked. 'I'm *brilliant* at mathematics; Miss Dennison, our maths teacher, said I was.'

Beatrix laughed. 'I think Papa and I will start planning our retirement.'

There was an overall groan from the three young people. 'Oh, I didn't mean that we should do it without you,' Laurie protested. 'We'll always need you.'

'That's good to know,' his mother laughed, and felt a sudden stab of love and pride that Laurie was getting through the difficult period of anxiety and uncertainty that had lingered for so long. With Edward's constant reassurance and encouragement, he was at last building up confidence in himself.

CHAPTER SIXTEEN

Olivia was brought over by her father on the Sunday morning and with her in the open landau was her aunt Lucille.

'Oh, *look*!' Laurie breathed. He and his friend Andrew had turned to the window when they heard the sound of hooves on the drive.

'Canoe landau!' Andrew murmured. 'I love that dark red. I've seen them in London. Would it be rude to go and have a closer look at it?'

'No, of course not.' Laurie grinned. 'It would be rude not to greet guests.' He hadn't been referring to the carriage at all, but to the lovely dark-haired young girl sitting in it, beside an older woman. Andrew, clearly, was more interested in the vehicle. Laurie went into the hall and called up the stairs. 'Alicia! Your friend has arrived.'

Alicia appeared at the top of the stairs and ran down, followed more slowly by her mother, who was holding the hands of the twins. Luke would otherwise have tried to climb on the banister and slide down as he had seen Ambrose do, and whatever Luke did Isolde would follow suit.

'Open the door, then,' Alicia said to her brother. 'Don't keep her waiting.'

Dora scurried up the stairs from the kitchen. 'I'll do it, Laurie,' she said, and grasped the door knob, pulling it open.

'Oh, Olivia!' Alicia squealed when she saw the landau. 'What an entrance! What a lovely carriage!' She saw Olivia's aunt sitting in the vehicle and dipped her knee. 'Good morning! Please come in. Hello, Mr Snowden.' She waved her hand to him as he sat up on the driver's seat. 'Won't you come in too? My brother and his friend will be simply dying to inspect your carriage! It's a landau, isn't it? I've seen them in York.'

Joseph touched his hat. 'Good morning, miss. Yes, it is, and thank you, I'd be pleased to come in.'

Lithely he jumped down from the driving seat, opened the carriage door and put out his hand to help Olivia and then her aunt; he nodded to the two young gentlemen, indicating they could look at the landau, and muttered 'Stay' to the horse.

Laurie and Andrew both put their hands to their chest and accomplished a perfect nod of the head, murmuring a polite 'good morning' to the most fashionable woman they had ever seen and another to Olivia. Although Andrew's eyes swivelled back towards the landau, Laurie was immediately smitten by the sight of his sister's beautiful young friend, and knew that he would be completely tongue-tied in her company.

Beatrix came slowly down the stone steps, giving herself time to appreciate the elegant woman stepping out of the carriage. As the visitor bent her head to negotiate the step, Beatrix saw the petite hat atop her chignon, trimmed with small cream pearls and long pale and dark blue feathers which touched the back of her neck, and held in place by cream silk ribbons tied beneath her chin. Beatrix, who often made her own and Alicia's dresses, saw that their visitor's pale blue gown was cut with the bodice and skirt in one piece, the skirt drawn into a bustle at the back, accentuating her tiny waist.

Oh, she thought. I didn't know that bustles were in again. How behind the times I am. But then she bethought herself that Olivia's aunt was a Frenchwoman, and the French always seemed to be ahead of the English in fashion.

Alicia introduced Olivia to her mother. 'It's very kind of you to invite me, Mrs Fawcett-Newby,' Olivia said. 'May I present my aunt, Mademoiselle Lucille Leblanc?.' She turned to her aunt. 'I've told you about Alicia, Tante Lucille, and here is Mrs Fawcett-Newby. Papa,' she added to her father, who was standing behind her aunt, 'may I introduce you too?'

The subtle and perfect introductions were not over until Edward came hurrying across the lawn to meet the visitors with Ambrose scurrying alongside him, but at last Beatrix smiled and said, 'I think that's everyone. Won't you come inside for coffee and cake, mademoiselle? You won't be working today, Mr Snowden?' she added, and he shook his head and murmured, 'No, ma'am.'

'Good! We'll serve it inside as the harvest is under way and the harvest bugs will descend and eat us!'

Joseph Snowden seemed a little uneasy, Beatrix thought, and was pleased that she had decided to invite their guests into the cosy downstairs sitting room with its cushioned sofas and chairs, rugs in front of the ready laid but unlit fire, and books scattered about on the wide window sills where the family spent most of their leisure time, rather than the elegant but formal drawing room on the floor above.

'This is a lovely room,' Lucille Leblanc murmured. 'So very comfortable; yet stylish too. I detect a woman's touch, madame.'

'Yes.' Beatrix smiled. 'I was given total freedom to design the house as I wished when I first came here after my marriage.' She flushed slightly. 'My first marriage,' she explained. 'I was very young and had no idea about design, but I knew what I liked. After I was widowed and then married Edward, we changed it only a little as it suited Edward perfectly.' She gave a little laugh. 'He likes comfort above all else.'

She paused as the coffee and cake arrived and saw that Cook had excelled herself this morning with a choice of two different cakes as well as scones, with cream and strawberry conserve in small dishes. Had she heard that we might have a French pastry cook visiting?

'If you are interested, mademoiselle, after our coffee you might like to see the rest of the house?'

'I would, very much,' her visitor said fervently. 'If Joseph is agreeable. On Sundays he works on his account books, and mine too. I am a *pâtissière* – a pastry chef – and run a shop and café; perhaps Olivia has said? And if . . .' She hesitated. 'If I am not being presumptuous, perhaps you might prefer to call me Miss Leblanc? Olivia likes to use mademoiselle always on introduction.' She gave a Gallic shrug. 'She says she likes to practise her French, but she has a perfect accent in any case; she doesn't need to practise. She uses a Parisian pronunciation like mine, of course; it is the only one she knows, as I taught her. I spoke only in French when she was an infant.'

'Was her mother also French – she was your sister, I'm assuming?'

'*Non.*' She gave another shrug. 'People think that she is my niece, although she is not my colouring, but no, her mother was not my sister. It is a very long story and not mine to tell but Olivia is like family to me, even though she is not.'

The two of them were chatting side by side on a sofa. Alicia and Olivia were sitting in the window; Edward and Joseph were at the other end of the sitting room, deep in conversation, whilst Laurie, Andrew and Ambrose were chatting by the other window, with Ambrose giving forth about something and young Luke nodding as if he understood what they were talking about, whilst Isolde was sitting on the rug having a private conversation with one of her dolls.

'Of course,' Beatrix said. 'I beg your pardon, I didn't mean to pry; families have intertwined lives. A lot of people think that Ambrose is Edward's son; he has the same colouring, with his reddish hair, but only the twins, Luke and Isolde, are his. Although,' she glanced at Edward tenderly, 'he loves all of them equally.'

'I didn't know that,' Lucille Leblanc said frankly. 'I don't think your daughter has mentioned it. She obviously considers your husband to be her father.'

'She does,' Beatrix said contentedly. 'They all do.'

After they finished their coffee and cake, Miss Leblanc

describing the latter as excellent, Beatrix took her on a brief tour of the house, showing her the drawing room and dining room, until she became aware that Joseph Snowden was anxious to be leaving.

'I beg your pardon,' he said, giving a little bow. 'Sunday is a day of reckoning, not driving or giving my drivers their time-tables but looking at my accounts for the week, and assisting Lucille with hers too.'

He thanked Beatrix for her hospitality, shook hands with Edward and kissed his daughter. 'Be good,' he joked. 'And send me a note to say when you want me to pick you up.'

'Oh, but we can bring her home,' Alicia rushed in to say. 'It won't be a problem, will it, Papa?'

'It won't,' Edward agreed as they went down the steps. 'Aaron can drive in if I can't.'

He stopped to inspect the landau whilst Laurie went to look at the horse, which he greatly admired. 'What is he, sir?' he asked Joseph. 'He's magnificent.'

'He is, isn't he?' Joseph was pleased to have an admirer of his rare breed. 'I can't tell you exactly, because his foresires were bred in America and there are few records, but he's of 'Morgan progeny with some Arab and Dutch Gelderland and possibly Welsh cob, which makes him a good carriage worker; not that I use him for pulling a heavy carriage. He's mine,' he said proudly, gently stroking the horse's neck, 'and he's also a steady ride – Olivia rides him in 'new park. Pearson Park,' he added, in case Laurie didn't know of the Hull public park, which he didn't. 'Do you like to ride?'

'Oh, yes,' Laurie enthused, 'although I'm only able to at weekends since I'm away at school during the week. I had my first pony when I was about eight; we've still got him. We're already teaching Luke and Isolde to ride ... but, oh!' He turned back to the steed. 'He's *perfect*!' And he too patted the horse's neck. 'What's his name?'

'I call him Captain.' Joseph grinned, and then hesitated, as if not wanting to be presumptuous. 'Maybe some time, if your sister should come to visit Olivia, you might like to come with her and see my stables, try him out if you wish? Not that he's for sale,' he added quickly. 'Never.'

'I'd like that, sir,' Laurie said fervently, and thought that he would also like to know Olivia much better. He only hoped that he didn't make a fool of himself whilst she was here.

CHAPTER SEVENTEEN

'Trot on.' Joseph gave the command as they pulled out of the drive and turned down the hill.

'Didn't we come in from the top of the hill?' Lucille asked. She was sitting up beside him with a blanket over her knees.

'We did,' Joseph concurred. 'But I thought you might like to see the estuary from here, and we can drive most of 'way along the bank, if it's not too wet, and through to Hessle.'

Lucille pondered for a second and then nodded her head. 'Lovely,' she said, wondering what had prompted the change of heart, when he had said he wanted to spend the afternoon on his accounts as usual. Something had changed his mind.

The tide was out and the estuary calm, with only a few gulls wheeling over the water. 'The wading birds will have gone up on to 'moors,' Joseph remarked. 'It's breeding time.'

'It's lovely, isn't it?' Lucille said softly. 'So peaceful; and look.' She pointed ahead to where a sandbank jutted out of the water and on it stood a still and solitary heron.

'He'll fly off when we approach,' Joseph murmured, and he was right, for as they drew abreast it stretched its hunched neck and rising on ungainly legs spread its wings and silently took off in graceful flight.

Further down the estuary they pulled in at the edge of Hessle foreshore, where a few parents with barefoot children were poking about with sticks in the water. Joseph took off his top hat, placed it on the seat between them and ran his fingers through his thick brown hair, giving a deep sigh.

'I've sat here a few times in the past,' he mumbled. 'When Olivia was a bairn, wondering if I'd done right by her.'

I knew there was something, Lucille thought. I can read this man through and through. 'Why come here?' she asked softly, not wanting to disturb his reflective mood. 'Why not at the pier, if you want to sit by the estuary?'

He was silent for a few minutes, gazing out across the water towards the low-lying Lincolnshire Wolds.

'This is where she – Olivia – is from,' he murmured. 'By rights she should be living in a grand house like the one we've just visited, not in an old three-storey town house in Hull.'

'It is her home! She is happy there,' she protested. 'She's happy with her family, which is what we are! Your mother is her *grand-mère*, I am her *tante*, and you are her much loved papa.'

'But it's a sham, Lucille,' he said, pressing his fingers and thumb hard on his temples. 'It's not right.'

She gazed at him long and hard. 'You're regretting you didn't send her to the workhouse?' she said sharply. 'I seem to recall you said her family said they didn't want her; that they said the child would have brought shame on their honour.' She sniffed. '*Pff!* As if they had any! Refusing to accept that their daughter had fallen in love with someone below her station! Poor girl,' she whispered. 'For that is all she was.'

He nodded. 'She was!' he murmured. 'A slip of a girl. No more than seventeen or eighteen. She didn't deserve to die; and no,' he added, 'of course I've no regrets about accepting Olivia. It's her family who anger me and always will.'

Lucille remained silent, but she took Joseph's hand and gently held it. It was fifteen years since Joseph had brought the young woman and her paramour to his mother's house, where she and Margot were lodging, having arrived six months before following a long and arduous journey from Paris. As he and the young man helped the girl up the steps and through the door, he told his mother and Lucille that he'd had a booking to pick up a passenger in Hessle and take him to Hull, but when he arrived at the designated place there was not one passenger but two, and he straight away realized that this was a runaway marriage. The young woman, dressed in a voluminous cape and hood, had seemed nervous, constantly looking over her shoulder as if unsure what to do before climbing into the carriage.

He hadn't seen her face, Joseph had told Lucille later, and when, halfway to Hull, the young man had hammered on the carriage roof and told him his wife was in labour, he had driven at top speed to the Hull Infirmary; there he had been told she couldn't stay as they had cholera patients on the wards and it wasn't safe for her or the child, and to take her to the workhouse hospital.

The young woman had begged him not to take her there. 'Please, find me a midwife,' she'd wept whilst the young man seemed unable to come up with any suggestion and it looked as if he wanted the earth to swallow him up.

'He was so young too,' Lucille reminisced. 'So unworldly, totally unable to comprehend the enormity of what they had done.'

She too had been young at the time, but would never have been so unenlightened as to find herself in such a situation; except, she considered, I had been persuaded by Margot's mother to accompany Margot to London. She had been astonished when Madame Dupont presented her with tickets not from Calais to Dover as expected, but for a slow train from Paris to Holland and a ship across the German Ocean to arrive at the Hull docks. She sighed. That was another story altogether.

'My poor ma,' Joseph muttered, linking Lucille's fingers through his own. 'I didn't know what to do; I only thought that Ma would know of somebody who could help, and she did, as you remember. There's not much goes on in Hull without my ma knowing about it.'

'Why are you thinking of this now?' Lucille demanded. 'It is in the past. What is your English saying – there is too much water . . . ?'

He gave a splutter and, removing his hand from hers, put his top hat on again. 'Water under 'bridge. You're quite right. It means that it's gone, it's in the past, the water has flowed away.' He shook the reins. 'I hardly ever come this way nowadays, although I used to. Mrs Fawcett-Newby won't remember me, but I brought her here a lot o' years ago on a short visit with a gentleman and a lady I assumed was her mother. I'd guess it was before her first marriage. I picked them up at Paragon station, brought them to the house and collected them again a couple of days later.'

'Imagine you remembering from so long ago,' she said. 'Her eldest boy must be seventeen or so?'

He nodded. 'I'd seen 'posh gent before; picked him up at 'railway station once or twice and brought him up to 'house; but not her, not until that night, cos I don't forget a face, especially not one as lovely as hers. They were resting at 'Station Hotel after their journey and it was dark when they came out so I only saw her briefly, but the gent arranged for me to pick them up for the return journey and I saw her then. She's hardly changed.'

She waited for him to continue, for there was surely more he had to say, and there was. After a slight pause, he went on in a great rush. 'I'm bothered that if Olivia's friendship with her daughter continues, then there might be a possibility that Mrs Fawcett-Newby knows the other family, the ones who turned away from their wronged daughter, and that Olivia might meet her blood relations.'

'Nonsense,' Lucille said. 'How would they know? And they wouldn't recognize her in any case.'

He shrugged and urged his horse to walk on, remembering that other time when he had travelled back down the Hessle road into Hull at breakneck speed to save a life – two lives: a mother and her unborn child – but only managing to save one, his own beloved Olivia.

He parked the landau under cover and asked the young lad who helped in the yard to brush Captain down before stabling and feeding him. It was a job he used to do himself. He'd learned a lot from Tom Henderson, who had taken him under his wing and taught him everything he knew about horses and carriages, and while he was explaining to the lad exactly what needed doing Lucille called to say she'd walk on.

'No, wait, I'm coming,' he said, and with a few last words to Jack he rushed after her. 'I just wanted to say, not a word to Ma. She doesn't know where Olivia's family live and I don't want her to be worried.'

'I won't,' Lucille said. If Joseph's mother was worried she would not say she was, she considered. 'Your mama does not display her emotions. What is it that the English say?'

'She doesn't wear her heart on her sleeve,' he grinned. 'No, she doesn't, but *I* don't want to worry that *she's* worried.'

She gave him a playful slap on the arm and then tucked her hand into his. His mother was a wily elderly woman and she had known Mrs Gordon, the housekeeper at the Old Stone House and the daughter of one of her oldest friends, for many years, even before she left Hull for London; if she had wanted to know about the family living in North Ferriby she had probably found out everything already. But Joseph was not talking about them; he was talking about the other family, who lived in nearby Hessle, where Olivia's young mother had disgraced her family by falling in love with the wrong man: a very young man without money, family or pedigree, who by his passion and hers had produced a child he couldn't look after following his lover's untimely death.

He had pleaded with Joseph not to take the child to the workhouse. 'Can you find someone willing to take her? Perhaps someone who has lost a child? A wet nurse would know, or maybe take her herself. Please! I beg you. Or will you ask Clara's family? They won't speak to me,' he had wept. 'They banned her from seeing me, which is why we ran away. They said that they would give our child to an orphanage.'

Joseph did go to see the family; he went to tell them that their daughter had died in childbirth but that the child lived and was in the care of a wet nurse at his own home.

They refused to believe it at first, but when he said that their daughter was lying in an undertaker's restroom Clara's father, accompanied by his schoolboy son James, reluctantly agreed to go with him to confirm it.

Joseph had driven them there and waited outside the undertaker's premises; when they came out, Joseph saw that the younger man was shaking with grief whilst his father's face was white and etched with anger.

'Where is the person who did this to my daughter?' he'd barked at Joseph. 'I shall report him to the authorities; he will face prison for his crime!'

'I don't know where he went, sir,' Joseph had replied. 'He was a passenger in my vehicle; I merely picked him up as previously arranged. The young lady was with him. She didn't appear to be under any kind of duress. I would have known, sir, had she been.'

'How would you have known?' Clara's father had raised his stick threateningly at Joseph, who took a step back.

'Would you kindly put your stick down, sir?' he'd responded mildly. 'I'm a man of the world; I meet many people in my way of business and I can tell you that the young lady was not coerced into entering my carriage but entered willingly. I was taking them to the Hull railway station for a journey to Scotland.'

'And where is he now?' he'd shouted. 'Skulking somewhere in an alleyway?'

'That I couldn't say, but I can tell you that he was extremely distressed by the loss of your daughter. In great anguish at her death. He asked me to ask you if you would take care of their child, who was conceived in love.' Joseph had known before he asked the question what the answer would be.

Lucille paused at the bottom of the steps, and again took his hand. 'You did what you could, chéri,' she said softly. 'We all did. We could not have done more; and we gave the child love.'

CHAPTER EIGHTEEN

'Darling Bea!' Beatrix's friend Rosie came the next day, driving a battered old governess cart. 'I've called to say that Mrs Highcliffe-Rand's welcome-home party for her son has been cancelled. The word is that he has put his foot down and refuses to attend. I've heard this first hand from Amelia's personal maid, who brought a note from Amelia to say it was off. She explained in the note that her brother was in a huff because he said it was nothing to do with anyone else that he had come home and he was not going to pander to tittle-tattle!'

'Oh, bravo for him,' Beatrix said warmly, and rang the bell for coffee. They had the sitting room to themselves as Alicia and Olivia had taken the twins to see the harvest being brought home. 'I like the sound of him. Or is he an ogre?'

'Well, he never used to be,' Rosie said. 'I recall him as a most kind and pleasant boy.' Her face saddened. 'But that was before – before tragedy struck.'

'A tragedy? Oh, what was that? I don't remember one.'

Rosie put her feet up on a footstool, making herself at home as she always did. 'No, you wouldn't. You'd have been busy with your new infant and keeping Charles at bay.'

Beatrix considered wryly that Rosie had no compunction about discussing personal matters, providing she could trust the person she was talking to or about.

'It was all very sad,' Rosie went on. 'Amelia's younger sister, erm . . . Clare? Clarissa – no, Clara! She became suddenly ill; influenza, I think it might have been, or was it measles – or whooping cough? She must have died very suddenly, for we heard nothing until we were told of her death. She was just a girl, so pretty and lovely, maybe seventeen or so. Her parents thought that she'd make a good marriage; not like Amelia, who had told them that she'd choose her own husband, thank you very much. Though the dear thing hasn't yet chosen one, and I doubt that she will.' She gave a nonchalant shrug. 'She's about our age, so there won't be much choice left, I'm afraid.'

She pondered for a moment, and then said, 'It was all quite odd. Clara's funeral was very quick, because of infection the family said, and no one was invited. Amelia didn't attend – she was sick with grief – and nor did her mother, but then she wasn't expected to, being of the old school brigade who believed that women shouldn't attend funerals; but my mother decided she should be there and dragged Papa along for form's sake; she said it wasn't right that such a young girl should be buried without anyone to see her off on her journey. I wished afterwards that I had attended, but I was pregnant with one of my boys.'

She looked vaguely up at the ceiling and said, sighing, 'I can't remember which one it was. Five boys and I can't always recall their names, or which is which!'

Beatrix laughed; not at the subject matter, for a young girl's death wasn't in the least amusing, but at Rosie's inability to remember her sons' names. Rosie, she thought, gets more and more like her eccentric mother.

'Was it Edwin?' she asked. 'He's younger than Alicia, isn't he? My one and only visit to the Highcliffe-Rands' was shortly after – not long, in fact, after I – we – Charles and I came to live here after our marriage. I don't recall meeting anyone else from the family subsequently, apart from Amelia and her mother.'

Rosie shook her head. 'No, perhaps not,' she said vaguely.

'Mr Highcliffe-Rand was extremely arrogant and his wife a very pompous woman; they were not well liked, and few people accepted her invitations. She would have invited you and Charles to calculate your worth, Beatrix. Amelia says her mother only asks my mother and me because she thinks we're outlandish and she can talk about the things we say and do to her confidantes afterwards.' She took a sip of coffee. 'I can't think why she has that opinion of us; we're perfectly normal, I'm sure, unlike her.'

'So what happened to the boy?' Beatrix asked. 'Where has he been since all this happened?'

Rosie shrugged. 'James? Don't know; his name rarely crops up. I rather think he left home – didn't get on with his father or something. Amelia doesn't discuss him, only her mother, who drives her scatty.'

Alicia and Olivia, each holding hands with one of the five-year-old twins, were making their way towards the fields that were being harvested; they could hear the sounds of the workers, the horse lads calling to their teams, the thatchers working methodically to make the stacks watertight, and as they approached they could see the enormous crowd all busy with their designated tasks. Some of the fields were already harvested and wagons trundled back to the farmsteads pulled by teams of heavy horses.

'I love to see the harvest being brought home,' Alicia enthused. 'Everyone works together, even the children, look.' She pointed to a scattering of boys wearing flat caps like the men and the little girls wearing cotton bonnets to keep the sun off their faces and the backs of their necks as they raked with hay rakes bigger than themselves and tied the cut corn into sheaves.

'I've never seen it being brought in before,' Olivia admitted. 'Do the children receive a wage for harvesting or are they here because their parents tell them to be?'

'Both,' Alicia said. 'At least, Papa always pays them. He says it's only right if they're doing a job of work they should be paid for it.' She frowned a little. 'And Mama says that the families depend on the extra money; to have an extra shilling or two at the end of the week can buy them a little comfort. And we always feed everybody, which we can help with, Olivia, if you'd like to?'

When Olivia said yes, she would, Alicia said she would lend her an old dress and a bonnet as otherwise hers would get very dusty, even just carrying food and drink to the hayfields.

'It will soon be lowance time,' she said. 'That's when the men stop to eat and drink. Cook makes meat or chicken pies and bakes piles of bread to eat with cheese or meat paste, and we can help by carrying the baskets and water bottles up to the fields.'

'I'll enjoy that,' Olivia said cheerfully. 'It will be a new experience.' She glanced back at the fields. 'Who's that at the far side of the field? Is it your brother and his friend?'

'Laurie and Andrew? Yes, it is. Laurie must have roped him in to help with the horses, though I rather think Andrew's a city boy.' Alicia frowned as she watched. 'He doesn't seem to be managing the plough horses very well.'

'I could do that,' Olivia said confidently. 'When we come back with lunch—'

'Lowance, pronounced looance round 'ere, miss.' Alicia assumed a mock country accent. 'You'm not from these parts, I reckon?'

Olivia shook her head. 'No,' she said, following Alicia's example. 'I be from 'ull, ma'am. Born 'n' bred.'

They both fell about laughing. 'You don't sound like 'ull,' Alicia told her, dropping the aitch as Olivia had done, while Olivia stressed that she was and repeated, 'Born 'n' bred and proud of it.'

They turned towards the gate to go back to Old Stone Hall, the reluctant Luke and Isolde declaring that they had only just come out, which was true. Olivia turned to look back at Laurie and Andrew; both boys had their sleeves rolled up to their elbows, and whilst Laurie looked perfectly at ease with the lumbering plough horses he was leading, Andrew seemed most uneasy with his team, stepping away from them as if afraid they might tread on him with their great shod hooves.

'Alicia!' she said. 'Would you mind if I run back and give your brother a hand first? I don't think Andrew is coping.'

'Oh, yes, can you do that? I'll take the children back. Ask Andrew if he'll come and help me with the food.'

'I'm not a children,' Isolde complained. 'I'm a girl.'

'Of course you are, darling,' Alicia smiled at her little sister, 'and Luke is a boy.'

'No, he's not; he's my bruvver.'

'I know, and mine too,' Alicia agreed, and was met with a scowl from Isolde, who complained that he wasn't. Alicia decided that here was a conversation for some other time and ushered them both in front of her.

Olivia lifted the hem of her skirts and ran back through the stubble; behind her she could hear Alicia coaxingly explaining to Isolde that they were going to fetch the food for the workers and she needed them to help her, while Luke was whining that he didn't need to hold her hand and was going home on his own. I've often wondered what it would be like to have brothers or sisters, she mused as she neared Laurie and Andrew; it would be nice to have a sibling like Alicia or Laurie, but I can see that a lot of patience is needed for younger ones.

'Hello, Laurie, hello Andrew,' she called. 'I've come on a mission. Alicia asked if Andrew could possibly help with carrying the looance back for the harvesters.' She gave Laurie a mischievous grin when he raised his eyebrows in astonishment.

'I didn't know you spoke the language, miss,' he teased.

'Oh, I'm a linguist, sir.' She dropped a mock curtsey.

'Well, I'll be glad to,' Andrew said in a relieved manner, pulling a handkerchief out of his pocket and wiping his forehead. 'But who's going to help Laurie?'

'Oh, I can manage—' Laurie had begun when Olivia broke in.

'I will,' she said. 'I'm used to horses, although not ones as big as these lovely Shires.' She ran her hands over the back of one of them. 'I'm not afraid of their size.'

'No?' Laurie asked. 'Well, if you're sure!'

'Alicia has gone back to the house,' Olivia told Andrew, 'but you'll catch up with her if you're quick.'

Andrew didn't require any persuasion. He took a cap from his trouser pocket, rammed it on his head and turning on his heel sped off, calling back, 'I'll see you later.'

Laurie heaved a breath. 'I could have managed better without him, to be honest,' he told Olivia. 'He was really keen to help, but I think he was scared of the size of the Shires, even though I told him they were gentle beasts. Somehow his feet got in the way.'

'I suppose the horses know what to do and where to go in any case,' Olivia remarked, running her hand over the neck of the nearest. 'They'll have been doing the harvesting for a long time?'

Laurie nodded. 'Pa says they used oxen when he was a lad at Home Farm; I expect they were especially good for ploughing on the heavy clay soil, but mebbe horses are suitable for more jobs; they can be used for mowing grass, carting, or reaping, as much as for ploughing or pulling the hay wagons for the men waiting to stack.'

They were moving towards the field gate as they were talking, and Laurie pulled his hat over his face. 'Phew!' he breathed out. 'It's hot!'

'You must burn easily?' She was opposite him, her hand on the reins of the nearest lead horse. 'Being so fair.'

'Yes,' he agreed. 'We all do, except for young Luke; he's a bit darker, more like our grandfather, Gampa Luke – Pa's late father. He ran Home Farm before Pa took it on after our grandfather had an accident.'

'Gampa?' She smiled a little wistfully. 'That's a nice name

for a grandfather. I don't have one, never have, though I have a *grand-mère*, Pa's mother.'

'I think it was Ambrose who named him. He couldn't say Grandpa.'

He was silent for a moment as they negotiated the gateway and the team, without halting in the least, pulled out and turned to go up the hill.

'Don't you have maternal grandparents?' Laurie asked as they walked either side of the team.

'No,' she answered. 'Nobody; or at least, not as far as I know. I became Pa's ward when I was a baby, his and his mother's, my *grand-mère*. He's told me some of the story of my birth, but not all of it.'

He turned to her. She wasn't in the least red-faced or perspiring, as he was; beneath the bonnet which hid her black hair her face had a healthy glow.

'But you have an aunt . . . Lucille? She's not your father or mother's sister?'

She smiled and shook her head. 'No, neither, therefore not my real aunt. But it doesn't matter. I'll find out when Pa's ready to tell me. I'm loved, and that's what's important.'

CHAPTER NINETEEN

'I really like Olivia,' Laurie said, his hand on Alicia's shoulder as two weeks later they waved goodbye to her friend as she drove away in her father's carriage; not in the landau this time, as Olivia's grandmother Irma Snowden had come along for the drive and preferred the covered brougham. Olivia had climbed up into the driving seat next to her father.

The two girls had enjoyed their time together away from the constraints of school. They had helped out for several days during harvest, Alicia organizing the lowance for the workers and supervising Andrew, who excelled at wrapping up packets of bread, cheese and pies, making bottles of cold tea and packing everything into baskets before carrying them into the fields when the harvesters stopped for a break, while Olivia stayed with the horses, gently brushing down, feeding and watering the ones that were resting whilst Laurie took the next team out again.

'It's non-stop, isn't it?' she'd said, when he brought in another team of three and exchanged them for the horses that had been rested.

He nodded and put his head under the tap to wash off the dust. 'You can stop any time you want,' he told her, shaking his head to disperse the water. 'This is supposed to be a holiday for you, isn't it?'

'I can't stand around watching whilst everyone else is

working,' she insisted, picking up a soft brush to clear the dust from the first horse and then using a cloth and bucket of water to clean his hooves before leading him to the water barrel and to feed. 'Besides, I like to do it. I help in Pa's yard whenever I can.'

'We can stop soon when the men have their looance,' he said, 'and then we can swap over if you like and you can bring the teams in whilst I clean them up.'

'All right,' she agreed. 'How many horses do you have? I seem to have lost count.'

'We've twelve of our own but we also share with other farmers at harvest time; it's important that everybody helps each other whilst the weather holds, so we've been leading one of our neighbour's teams as well as our own.'

'There was a pregnant mare,' she told him. 'Is she one of yours?'

'Possibly,' he said. 'She'll be working until she foals.'

'Poor mare,' she murmured lightly.

'Not really. They're very strong, but we'll keep an eye on her if she's one of ours. We take great care of our animals,' he said. 'We couldn't manage without them; even though machinery with engine power is coming in we'll always need our horses.'

'I know.' She laughed. 'That's what my father always says.'

Laurie stopped for a moment as if contemplating something, and then seemed to give himself a mental shake and continued with what he was doing.

For the rest of her holiday, she and Alicia rode out every day, Laurie lending Olivia his horse as he said he had some schoolwork to do now that Andrew had returned home to York. They rode the lanes around the village and to the village of Swanland, where Olivia admired the pond and the ducks, and then on to busy Hessle, returning along the towpath by the swift-flowing estuary to North Ferriby and home.

'It's strange that this part of the estuary seems to have a different atmosphere,' Olivia said. 'I often walk to the Hull pier, and there it seems like a working river, which of course it is: there are always coal barges or steamers and trading luggers crossing over to Lincolnshire, and the bigger ships heading out towards the sea. Here, the estuary seems more leisurely.'

'It isn't always,' Alicia said. 'It can be dangerous, with flood tides and rip tides; people have drowned up here, stepping on to the saltmarsh and not being able to get out. Papa says this is the inner estuary, so it shows a different face, but it's still dangerous water; it's . . .' she paused in thought, 'something to do with the saline, I think, that comes in from the sea, and also because of land reclamation in Holderness, which is where Pa's sisters live, and the sediment and industrial waste from Hull. There used to be an ancient ferry crossing somewhere here too,' she added, 'to take travellers to Lincolnshire and then on to London.'

Olivia nodded. 'Just like Hull,' she said. 'It's always been an important estuary.'

Alicia showed her the garden with its beds of fragrant roses, and the orchard where some of Ambrose's pigs were snuffling beneath the fruit trees and chomping on fallen fruit; they walked down the front lawn, past the statuary and fountain that Beatrix had designed and brought in workmen to build for her when she was a young bride and new to the house, and then on to the woodland path that she had had cut through so that she could see the glint of the estuary from the house windows, and where she had planted sweet-smelling climbing honeysuckle and roses which now reached the tops of the trees.

Edward had said that he would drive Olivia home whenever she was ready to leave, but she never had been ready, until her father finally sent a postcard at the end of a fortnight to say he would collect her on the Sunday, bringing his mother with him if it was all right to do so.

Mrs Snowden had told Joseph she was astonished at the size of the house as they trundled up the long road towards it and she caught sight of the mansion through the trees, but no one would have guessed, as she walked through the front door, that it was the first time she had entered such a large establishment. She calmly took a seat in the sitting room, and sat with a straight back and her hands folded over the top of her walking stick as Olivia introduced the family.

Mags Newby came in to meet her, sitting comfortably beside her as they drank tea and ate cake, and in quiet conversation told her that she had returned only the day before from a visit to one of her daughters in the district of Holderness, east of Hull.

'It's very nice to see them,' she told Irma Snowden. 'And I could take 'whole of 'year visiting all my daughters and their families, but it's lovely to come back home. I'm a widow, you see, as I believe you are too, and I need to be settled. I'm thinking of asking Edward if I can have back my old house where all my bairns grew up.'

'Why, is someone else living in it?' Mrs Snowden asked, astonished that anyone could have more than one house.

'Yes, Mr and Mrs Hallam. He's 'estate manager and Dora is, or was, Beatrix's personal assistant. She's not needed so much now, but she's always ready to help if she's asked. Luke and me moved from 'old cottage when we bought Home Farm from Neville Dawley . . . oh, a lot o' years ago, and Edward moved into it. He was a young man by then and it was long before Beatrix came to these parts; he wanted to live on his own. He did it up, made alterations, you know; made a bigger sitting room and put a porch on 'front where he could sit and look out over 'fields.' She sighed. 'And although 'farmhouse is all right, I don't need so much space and I thought it would be nice to go back to 'old one and rekindle memories. I could still walk down here to Old Stone Hall if I wanted some company: my sister is 'cook and spends most of her time here, even though she has a cottage in Hessle, and I could give her a hand in 'kitchen like I used to.'

'Mm,' Mrs Snowden murmured. 'Why don't you stay where you are and ask your sister to come and live with you?'

Mags raised her eyebrows. 'I hadn't thought of that, I must admit. But I think we'd both like to have our own place.'

'Well,' said Mrs Snowden, 'I'm still in 'same house that I came to as a bride over forty years ago, and after Mr Snowden died it was just me and Joseph and an occasional lodger that I took in, cos it's a tall town house and we didn't really need all of the rooms; then suddenly I had two young Frenchwomen living with me! Our Joseph is so soft-hearted. They'd arrived on 'ship from Holland and asked him if he knew of decent lodgings, so he brought them to me and they got really settled for quite some time, especially Lucille; she said she'd like to stop, and then Margot . . .' She pursed her mouth. 'Well, she eventually hightailed it to London to stay with an aunt, and I was right glad to see 'back of her cos I didn't care much for her if I'm honest, and,' she nodded confidingly, 'I think she had an eye on our Joseph and that wouldn't have gone well; she wasn't his sort at all. Lucille took her to London as she hadn't the wit to go by herself, but happily Lucille came straight back to Hull, which was a great relief because we had Olivia with us by then, and I couldn't have coped with an infant on my own.'

Mags's jaw dropped as she tried to assimilate this conversation and found that she couldn't. A quiet knock came on the door and a maid entered to clear some of the crockery and ask if anyone would care for more tea or coffee; Edward, who was in conversation with Joseph, said yes he would, but Joseph declined, and then the door opened again and Mrs Gordon came in and Beatrix called out to her to say hello to Mrs Snowden and Joseph, as she understood that she knew them.

Mrs Gordon said that yes she did, from many years before, and how nice it was to see them both again. 'I've met Miss Olivia since she came to visit,' she told Mrs Snowden. 'She's a lovely young lady, and she and Miss Alicia are such good friends. I hear that she's proved very useful during 'harvest.'

Olivia, who was chatting with Alicia, and both of their fathers, turned her head and raised her eyebrows at the mention of her name, and, excusing herself, stood up to come across to the housekeeper and her grandmother.

'Such a coincidence, Grand-mére, that your friend Mrs Gordon should be here! I heard you mention the harvest, Mrs Gordon. I've had such a wonderful time helping with the horse teams; everyone works so hard and no one complains in the slightest.'

'I'm sure they don't,' Mrs Snowden said primly, turning to Mags. 'I've known Mrs Gordon, or Miss Gordon as she was then, since she was a girl, afore she went off to London to work. Her mother is a good friend and neighbour of mine. It's a small world, isn't it?'

They all agreed that it was, and during the slight pause that ensued Joseph stood up. 'We'd better start making tracks for home,' he said, glancing at Olivia and then at Beatrix. 'It was very kind of you to invite Olivia to your lovely house, Mrs Newby.' He had decided to use just the one name rather than get into a taffle with Fawcett-Newby, and was gratified to see her smile in acknowledgement.

'Olivia is welcome at any time, Mr Snowden. It's been lovely to meet her, and you and your family too.'

Then Edward was on his feet as well, echoing the invitation, adding, 'I'm quite sure our daughters will make the arrangements to suit themselves.' He grinned. 'They seem to have much in common.'

'We do, Pa,' Alicia broke in. 'We've already been making plans for the next term break.'

Edward and Joseph Snowden glanced at each other, each raising an eyebrow, and both of them shrugged and smiled. 'It seems that we might soon be made redundant,' Edward said, glancing at Alicia. 'Our little girls are growing up.'

Olivia helped Mrs Snowden up from her chair and led her towards Joseph, then came back and tucked her arm under his. 'We are,' she said softly. 'But we'll always need our fathers, come what may.'

CHAPTER TWENTY

Lucille gazed out from her top-floor bedroom window as she sipped her coffee. The Hull street below was quiet, being a Sunday, although earlier she had seen people turning towards Charles Street and guessed they were going to St Charles Borromeo church.

Her mother had been an ardent Catholic and attended many of the vast number of churches and cathedrals of Paris in turn, as if to be sure of a punishment-free afterlife, and although Lucille had followed the same path of religion until she was thirteen, she had then decided that she could pray just as well wherever she was, without getting up early to go to church and listen to a priest droning on, especially when he spoke in Latin, which she didn't understand.

Lucille's father had died leaving his family in poverty, having been an artistic man without enough talent to make a living; her mother had spent a lot of time on her knees, scrubbing floors or polishing table and chair legs belonging to rich Parisians who could well afford to pay more than the pittance they gave her.

Lucille had loved her father in spite of the names her mother had called him. She had siblings much older than her and was born at a time when her mother had thought she was done with all that nonsense; her father had gloried that here was a last chance to make something of an offspring who might keep him in cigars and cognac when he had totally failed with the others. His eldest son had become a priest and was therefore lost to him as he was an avowed atheist himself; one daughter went to the bad, as he put it, and the others had just drifted away out of his reach.

This youngest daughter he taught to read and write when she was very young, and he had great plans for her further education; he taught her to think for herself and to develop her own opinions and not copy the sentiments of others, particularly those of her mother.

She had attended school and was considered to be a star pupil, so her teachers were saddened when after her father's sudden demise her mother told them, and Lucille, that now was the time to put away dreams, understand real life and start to earn a living. It was a living that meant joining her mother on her knees, not praying but scrubbing floors and polishing table legs as she did.

Lucille stretched backwards in her chair as she saw Irma Snowden's friend and neighbour Ruby Gordon walking along the street; she liked her, but didn't want to indulge in conversation, not today, and Ruby would be sure to knock if she should see her. These few hours were a precious time in which she could be entirely alone, as Irma had gone with Joseph to collect Olivia from her friend's house.

She had much to thank Irma for, and Joseph too, of course, for he was one of the cabbies waiting on the dockside to collect passengers from the ship that had brought her and Margot to Hull. She'd seen him quietly waiting with the other cabbies, his whip raised to indicate that he was free, but not shouting out as some of the others were doing. She'd raised her hand to him, indicating that he should come across, and he had touched his hat and given the reins to a small boy standing by his elbow.

Lucille was badly in need of assistance; Margot was useless and apparently incapable of carrying one single piece of luggage from the large number she had brought with her. She

115

had also been terribly sick on the way over, even though it wasn't especially rough, although probably more so than the Channel would have been. That was the crossing Lucille had thought they would take, but Margot's mother had obviously had her own agenda when she sent Margot and her companion by train across to Holland, and then by ship from Rotterdam to Hull, from which port they were expected to make their own arrangements to get to London, where Margot's aunt, she said, was expecting them.

Which turned out to be totally untrue, Lucille mused wryly. After so many years, she had lost the frustration that she had felt at the time, and was no longer interested in Margot or her mother, for she had guessed why Margot's mother wanted rid of her daughter and why Margot had spent so much time in the ship's latrine. Lucille was almost sure that the other girl had miscarried.

She had put the episode out of her mind when, at the end of that first dull and dreary English winter, that unhappy and wretched young man and his exhausted wife-to-be had been brought to the house by Joseph and had begged to be allowed to stay as the girl was about to give birth.

Lucille had been offered little comfort or concern in her own young life and heard none expressed for others, but she saw it then in Joseph and his mother as they cared for these strangers and it had touched her enormously, so she had rolled up her sleeves and scrubbed her hands under the cold tap before making the young woman more comfortable by removing her undergarments and stays and helping her on to the sofa. Irma Snowden had heated the kettle and found old sheets, then sent Lucille racing off to a nearby street to fetch a midwife whilst Margot had turned her back and silently crept upstairs to the room they had then shared.

It had been to no avail; the young girl was already running a high fever, probably with influenza, and although the child was safely delivered the midwife couldn't save the mother. Lucille gave a pensive sigh. 'So that is what I became,' she murmured aloud. 'Olivia became my daughter, although she doesn't know it, and nor does Joseph. I couldn't love her more if I had given birth to her.'

She heard the front door open and Olivia's voice calling up to her. 'Where are you, Tante Lucille? I want to tell you everything!' Lucille heard her running up the stairs and a quick knock on the half-open door. 'May I come in?'

She looked flushed and beautiful, and Lucille smiled. 'Of course, chérie. You have had a lovely time, yes?'

In French, Olivia described bringing in the harvest and how she and Laurence had worked the teams of Shires together. 'So you want to be a country girl now, do you?' Lucille teased her.

Olivia beamed, dimples appearing in her cheeks. 'It's hard work,' she admitted, 'but Laurie is so good with the horses, although I think they know what to do; I'm sure they could almost follow the route back to the farmstead without anyone driving them. Grand-mère is boiling the kettle for tea,' she added. 'Would you like some?' She glanced at the empty coffee jug and cup.

'No, thank you, but I'll come down. Your papa will be so happy to have you home again; he's missed you,' she said. 'He's only just become used to your being away at school, but a whole fortnight without seeing you . . .' She smiled, and lifted her eyebrows and her shoulders.

'Yes, I know.' Olivia dropped her voice. 'But before we go down I want to tell you that Alicia and I have come up with a plan; not for this year, but for next: we'd like to go to Paris to finish our education. Would it be possible, do you think? Would Papa give me permission?'

Olivia brought up the subject again that evening, when they were relaxed and sitting quietly chatting, after the supper dishes had been washed and put away, and it was no surprise to Olivia or Lucille that Joseph was startled.

'I wouldn't be happy about it,' he protested. 'Is 'French

education system any better than ours? I thought that 'York school was one of 'best.'

'It is. But it's not about that, Papa,' Olivia explained. 'It's about learning about another country's culture and expanding our minds, and it's especially rewarding for young women who might never experience such things otherwise.'

'Lucille is French,' he grunted. 'And she came to England!' Thus he defeated his own argument.

'It was not the same for me,' Lucille said quickly. 'I would have gone practically anywhere to get away from my life in Paris; I was nothing but a drudge and I wanted to leave home and make my own life. Margot's mother gave me the chance of freedom, although that wasn't her intention: she was more resolved on getting rid of her irresponsible daughter and gaining her own liberty.'

She glanced at Joseph's mother; the older woman knew what she meant. Only Irma Snowden had seen through Margot's performance, and didn't want her anywhere near her only son with her coy manner, teasing eyes and demure pouting mouth. Margot with her pampered behaviour would have led trusting Joseph astray and bled him dry; and she almost did. But for the fateful arrival of the tragic young couple who desperately needed help, he might have succumbed to her wiles.

'I don't remember Margot,' Olivia remarked. 'Or at least I don't think I do.'

'No, you wouldn't,' her grandmother said. 'She left for London when you were just a little bairn. She wanted a glitzy life.'

Joseph shifted in his seat. He always felt uncomfortable talking about Margot. She had almost ensnared him; she was bold and beautiful and most definitely on offer, but she would not be the kind of wife who would want to bring up a family. He had seen her expression when he had brought the young couple inside; her lovely mouth had turned down in disgust, and she promptly went up to her room and stayed there whilst Lucille and his mother endeavoured to help the midwife save the girl and her child.

He disguised a small sigh; in spite of being besotted by her, he had been relieved when she finally packed her bags and left, tired of having to compete for attention with a motherless baby, for he, his mother and Lucille had no intention of giving the infant to the workhouse and thus condemning her to a dark and unknown future.

As he mused on the past, Olivia slipped out of the room to get a book from her bedroom.

'I think she should be given the chance,' Mrs Snowden announced as the sound of her footsteps faded.

Joseph, startled, jerked up his head to look at his mother, and Lucille too gazed at her in astonishment.

'She deserves it,' Irma said softly. 'She was lucky enough to be born here with us. It was meant to be, so why would we deny her now? I don't know what it will cost to go to a school in France, but Lucille can find out and you can have my savings if there's a shortfall. I want for nothing as long as I have a roof over my head.'

She glanced at Joseph, and then looked away as if consumed with emotion. 'There was a purpose in her being here. Not what her poor mother had planned for, or her father either I should say, thinking back to his grief; but here she is and we must do what we can to give her what her own blood family denied her.'

CHAPTER TWENTY-ONE

'So have you given it any thought, Mama?'

Alicia gazed anxiously at her mother, who had her eyes fixed firmly on the sewing in her hand. Ambrose always needed a button sewing on a jacket or had a hole in his socks which required darning. Dora used to do these things for them all, but at present she only came in three days a week to help out with delicate washing or letting down the hems on Isolde's dresses now the little girl was shooting up and out-stripping her twin Luke. But Beatrix didn't mind in the least doing these homely jobs; it reminded her of when she was a girl and would make her own gowns.

'Given what some thought, dear?' she murmured, not looking at Alicia.

Alicia dropped to her knees at her mother's feet and gazed up into her face. 'You know very well, Mama!' she said, and Beatrix couldn't keep a smile from her lips; she had never been any good at subterfuge or dodging a question.

Edward, who had come in for lunch and was taking a short break before going outside again, had heard what Alicia had said and carefully raised the newspaper he was reading in front of his eyes, so that he could pretend he wasn't listening.

'About Paris!' Alicia gently nudged her mother's knee. 'Because if you don't agree, Olivia's papa won't let her go either.'

'So you want to go to a French finishing school just to help Olivia?' her mother said disingenuously.

'*No!* Don't tease,' Alicia pleaded. 'You know that it was originally my idea.'

Beatrix smiled and put down her sewing, and then looked surreptitiously at Edward, who had lowered his paper and was peering over the top of it. She saw by the way his eyes creased that he was smiling.

'You should ask your papa,' she told Alicia. 'He knows a lot about Paris. Much more than I do; how busy it is, and the pickpockets, and the criminals who entrap women, young and old.'

'I never said anything about criminals,' Edward remonstrated, putting down the paper. 'Pickpockets, yes, but not criminals!'

Alicia looked from one to another; she knew they were sparring, but didn't know why.

'Pickpockets!' Beatrix had caught him out. 'Oh, I know them well. Especially being a London gel. We were constantly besieged by pickpockets. They were forever stealing our purses, our silk handkerchiefs – just like a Dickens novel!'

'All right, all right.' Edward put away his newspaper. 'I give in.' He gave Beatrix a rueful grimace. 'You know what, Alicia? I promised your mother on our wedding day that I'd take her to Paris one day. And I will! We could have gone on our honeymoon.' He shook his head. 'But no, she didn't want to leave her – *our* – precious children behind.' A tender smile touched his lips and he added softly, 'Always afraid that someone would run away with them if she wasn't here to look after them.'

Alicia saw her mother lower her eyes, and knew that she shouldn't ask questions as it was something private, and of course there never had been time for a trip to somewhere like Paris because the twins had come along, and the holidays they all had were a few days in a rented house along the coast where they played on the beaches in places like Scarborough, Bridlington or Filey, or once a memorable trip up to the

North Yorkshire moors when both she and Laurie had realized what a large county Yorkshire was.

'But if I went to finishing school in France,' she dared, 'you could come to visit me or bring me home for the holidays?'

She wondered if Olivia was having the same difficulty in persuading her father to allow her to go away to school. He seemed afraid to let her go very far at all; according to Olivia, he had even had doubts about letting her come to North Ferriby. Alicia sighed. Whatever was he worrying over? She wasn't sure how Olivia's grandmother, her *grand-mère*, would react. Perhaps she would worry, being so old, but at least *Tante* Lucille wouldn't object; and, Alicia thought excitedly, perhaps she would take us and Mama could come too.

'You're not yet sixteen, Alicia,' Edward was saying when the door opened and five-year-old Luke wandered in, wearing a battered top hat and carrying a walking stick.

Alicia glanced at her young brother, and answered, 'But if we went for the September term next year, I'd be nearly seventeen! Who are you, sir?' she asked, turning to Luke. 'Do we know you?'

'I don't think you've had that honour, miss,' Luke replied. 'I'm Luke the Duke.'

Edward smiled. 'I remember that top hat! Where's it been all these years?'

'It's mine.' Luke pulled the hat even further down over his head so he couldn't see without stretching his neck backwards. 'It was in the toy box and it doesn't have anybody's name on it, so it's mine now.'

'We've all worn it,' Alicia chipped in.

Edward signalled for Luke to come near and the boy stood up straight in front of him. 'Isolde wanted it, but I told her that ladies don't wear hats like this and she'll soon be a lady.'

Alicia saw her parents exchange a glance and both gave a wide smile.

'The first time I met your mother,' Edward said, his conversation directed at Luke, but meant for Alicia, 'She was wearing this very same top hat.'

Luke opened his mouth to speak and then closed it again.

'Really?' Alicia exclaimed as if she hadn't heard the story before, and her mother gave a laugh.

'I'd only just arrived at the house,' Beatrix said, 'and was exploring. I'd wandered into the barn and found all kinds of old things, including the hat, and I'd put it on my head when . . .' she paused in remembrance, 'when . . .' She glanced at Luke and held out her hand and he took off the hat to give it to her. She ran her fingers round the brim and handed it back it to him. 'And that was when your papa came in looking to see who it was poking about amongst all the old odds and ends and found me wearing this hat.' She patted Luke's cheek. 'It's yours now,' she murmured. 'It belongs to Luke the Duke.'

There was something, Alicia thought as she sat and listened and watched; something emotional or secret that is nothing to do with me, or anybody else, but only with her parents. She didn't want to ask what it was, but she had a happy sense that it was something good.

Ambrose hadn't had lunch with the family that day. He'd been feeding the pigs and scattering some grain for the hens, and then just wandering round, checking fences and gates as his father had taught him to do.

'Every time you come out,' Edward had told him when he was quite young, as he'd taught Laurie too, 'don't come for just one purpose, such as checking your pigs, but look about to see if anything has occurred overnight; for instance if a gate has blown open, which means the lock has come loose and needs fixing, or if an animal, say a horse or a cow, has leaned too heavily on a fence rail to reach over it for some fresh grass, and broken or loosened it. Or even if a water bowl has been knocked over and emptied out so the animals can't get a drink.' Ambrose had listened and taken notice, and each weekend or holiday he did just that so that it became second nature to him.

Everything seemed to be in order, so he wandered to the back of the house to put away a fork, and smelled food cooking. He wrinkled his nose: stew, or maybe steak and kidney pudding. He headed for the kitchen door, leaned the fork against the wall and scraped his boots on the metal scraper. He pushed the door open, eased off his boots in the boot room and went into the kitchen.

Cook was by the range and the staff, apart from Janey the kitchen maid, who was dishing up from a big pan of potatoes, were just about to sit down at the long table, with Aaron at the far end, Mrs Gordon in the middle next to Cissy the upstairs maid, a place set for Janey on the other side, and at the head a place for Cook.

'Ooh!' Ambrose said, salivating. 'Sorry, I didn't realize it was dinner time.' He gazed towards the table, where a deep dish of huge Yorkshire puddings was being handed round, and licked his lips. 'Are we having this upstairs?'

Cook turned her head and smiled. 'No. Cold meat and potato salad was requested, Master Ambrose. I'm cooking a joint o' beef for later. This is pork casserole left over from 'pork you had yesterday.'

She saw the disappointment on his face. 'There's ample if you'd rather have this,' she said, 'and there's plenty of mash and Yorkshires.'

'Yes, please,' he said, and rushed to the deep sink to wash his hands. Aaron and Mrs Gordon exchanged a smile and Janey set another place next to hers.

'Proper farmer's lad, aren't you, Ambrose?' Aaron passed the Yorkshire puddings up the table as Ambrose sat down.

'I would guess I am.' Ambrose grinned as he helped himself. He and Aaron got on well; Aaron now collected him from school every Friday and mostly took him back again each Sunday.

At thirteen, Ambrose reminded Aaron of himself at the

same age; he'd been thirteen and willing to work when he'd come to stay with Miz Beatrix when her first husband had to return to London on some urgent matter. Aaron's boast from then on was that he had known Miz Beatrix longer than anyone else apart from his mother, Mags and Edward.

'So what's on for this afternoon?' Aaron asked Ambrose as they finished lunch and Janey got up to clear away, and Mrs Gordon excused herself.

'There's no pudding today, Master Ambrose, unless you'd like leftover Yorkshires with jam or syrup?' Cook told him.

'No, thank you, I'm full up. It was lovely,' he answered. 'I'll last now until suppertime.' He turned to Aaron. 'I've got some studying to do,' he said. 'Boring things like history.'

'Aah,' Aaron was about to say something else, when there was a quiet knock on the inner door which heralded the arrival of Alicia. Aaron immediately stood up.

'I said you'd be here,' she said triumphantly to Ambrose. 'Mama was bothered that you'd miss lunch, but I said there was no chance of that, and you'd be filling your face in the kitchen. I hope you didn't eat anyone else's portion.' She smiled at Cook, who was shaking her head. 'What have you had?'

'Pork casserole with massive Yorkshire puddings,' Ambrose gloated. 'I'm coming up now.'

'Ooh,' Alicia said. 'Could we have Yorkshires tonight, Cook? Please? We all love them.'

Cook raised her eyebrows. 'They're on the menu, Miss Alicia, don't worry.'

When they had gone, Cook turned to Aaron. 'Don't forget your Ps and Qs,' she said quietly, just as she'd done when he was a boy.

'What do you mean, Ma?' He frowned.

'It's *Master* Ambrose to you and me,' she said.

'He's just a lad,' he protested. 'And Edward's my cousin! I *never* step out of line and they know that. When Ambrose is older and probably running this place, he'll be *sir*, or whatever he chooses to be, and I'll mek sure that's what we'll all call him; but until then or even sooner, he's just Ambrose for now.'

'You're respectful to Master Laurie,' she insisted.

'Laurie is different entirely from Ambrose,' Aaron explained, 'and he's already asked me to call him just Laurie; but Master Laurie, or Laurence, suits him; he'll be a proper gent, one day, will Laurie; just as his mother is a proper lady, even though she wasn't born to it.' He pursed his lips. 'They've got a gentleness running through their veins,' he said. 'Something in their blood that makes 'em different.'

CHAPTER TWENTY-TWO

'Alicia!' Laurie called upstairs to his sister. 'Mr Snowden said if I'd like to have a look round his stables I could go whenever I want, but I'd rather ask beforehand in case he's busy; I was thinking of tomorrow, if he's free,' he went on as she came down. 'And I wondered if you'd like to come too, to visit Olivia?'

'Oh, yes, I would.'

'I'm sending him a postcard to ask if it's convenient.' He pulled a card out of his jacket pocket and waved it at her. 'If I go down to the box now, he'll get it by this afternoon's post. I thought we could travel in by train, save bothering anyone.'

'Yes, that would be lovely,' Alicia enthused. 'The holidays are just flying by; we'll be back at school before we blink.'

'I know,' he agreed, and paused by the table in the hall to add a postscript to the card before he opened the front door and they walked down the steps. 'And I've done very little studying.'

'Nor me,' she said. 'I'll walk down with you as far as the estuary. Are you going through the wood?'

He nodded. 'Yes, it cuts off a corner and I like to listen to the birds in there. I saw a sparrowhawk the other day and when I stopped to watch him I saw treecreepers too.'

'Why are you going to see Mr Snowden's carriage horses?' Alicia asked as they walked down past the statuary and the rose beds towards the wood at the end of the lawn and the long grassy area where their mother had planted snowdrops and daffodils and let wild flowers grow in profusion. 'We're surrounded by horses.'

'We are, but not like that Morgan of his – Captain. Don't you remember when he drove him here to bring Olivia? I wondered where he'd got him and how much he cost.'

'Why? Would you like one like him?'

'Mm, I would. But not yet,' Laurie murmured. 'Not while I'm still at school.'

They walked through the avenue of trees, neither of them speaking, knowing that by being quiet they would see many more birds. Alicia silently pointed a finger towards a pair of treecreepers on either side of an oak, both probing the bark with long, sharp bills to capture insects beneath it, then moving slowly up the trunk again. They heard a rustling amongst the leaves and a clacking *chuk-chuk* and looking up saw a red squirrel on a branch above them. They both smiled.

'What would you do with him if you had one?' she whispered as they walked on, coming out of the gated wood on to the road. Opposite was the estuary, and they walked towards it. 'A Morgan, I mean. Race him? And where?'

'Not sure. Beverley, Malton, Doncaster. Yorkshire is the best place in the country for horse racing, but . . .' He hesitated to commit himself, knowing how enthusiastic Alicia could be, whilst he was steadier, and not yet ready to be tied down. 'Well, good horses have to be bred from good stock.'

She turned to him, her eyes open wide. 'A stud farm? But – how would you start something like that? That's a very long apprenticeship, surely.'

'I know,' he nodded. 'That's why I said not yet.'

Laurie was so balanced, she mused. Not like her; she would rush into a project that seemed like an excellent choice at first hearing, whilst Laurie would research and study all aspects of whatever took his interest.

He glanced at her as they stood close to the edge of the

water; it was low tide and calm, but they had seen it at its highest, when the saline waves washed over on to the road and great care had to be taken. People had drowned in the estuary through not taking proper precautions or not realizing the power or the strength of the breakers.

'I'm not seriously thinking of a career in horse breeding,' he said, 'but . . .'

Alicia put her head to one side. 'You can tell me if you like,' she responded. 'But you don't have to; not until you're ready. I won't tell anyone if you want to confide, or if you're not sure.'

'It's just that I don't know if I'd be good enough for what I have in mind,' he murmured. 'I've been interested for a long time.'

He thought of when he was very young, five or something; his mother had asked his father – Charles, not Edward – if he might have a pony and Charles had refused, saying no, he had to wait, he couldn't have everything he wanted. But then two or three years later he had changed his mind and taken him off to Beverley without his mother, not saying why, and bought him a Shetland pony and all the gear that he would need. He'd called him Hardy and he had been so excited; but he realized as he got older that it had been a sop, an inducement, for an agreement: his father wanted him to go to his old school and his mother thought him still too young, and it was Charles's way of saying that *he* was in charge, even though he was hardly ever at home, and that the children and their mother would have to do as he said.

But now, very soon he would be an adult, and his mother and Edward already treated him as such, even though they were always there to advise on issues that he couldn't quite make out, and guide him in the right direction.

'I'm going back now,' Alicia told him, intruding on his thoughts. 'I'm going to practise my French. I'll see you at lunch. Enjoy your walk.'

He lifted a hand and walked on by the foreshore, where presently he stopped to watch a sloop sail past and then a coal barge chug by. He wondered what the land looked like from the middle of the river. A different perspective entirely, he guessed, and then his gaze crossed the estuary to the village of South Ferriby on the opposite shore.

There must have always been a regular crossing from Ferriby to Ferriby, and perhaps even now travellers might pay a boat owner to take them across, he considered; it would save the journey into Hull. Brough, of course, would once have had a more regular ferry service, being a principal Roman town. There have been so many changes, and the railways have made so much difference to everyone's lives. But it's still a long way round to reach Lincolnshire; why has no one ever thought of building a bridge? Or maybe they have, and nothing came of it.

He posted the card to Joseph Snowden in the village, stopped to gaze up at the All Saints church steeple and the windows which were sparkling in the sun, took a wander around the lanes, and stopped at the smithy to look in but there was a horse in there and the farrier was bent over shoeing, so he retraced his steps through the village to return home.

'Morning, Master Laurie,' a voice called, and he looked up to see Aaron driving the single-horse dog cart. He crossed the road to speak to him.

'Where are you off to, Aaron? Going home, by any chance?'

'Aye, I am.' Aaron casually touched his cap. 'Can I give you a lift, young sir?'

Laurie nodded. 'Please. I've lingered long enough.' He walked round to the other side of the cart and jumped up by Aaron's side. 'I needed to post a card and came along the foreshore; it's such a lovely morning I wandered round the village, went to look at the church and the smithy and explored a bit and found a pond just brimming with pond life.'

'The reed pond, was it?'

Laurie nodded. 'Yes, probably, though I'm not sure if that's the name.'

'Used to be used for sheep dipping when I was a lad,' Aaron told him.

'How old are you now, Aaron?' Laurie said curiously. 'I feel as if I've known you for ever.'

Aaron grinned. 'That's because you have. I'd just left school so I must have been about thirteen when Edward came to ask my ma if I'd come to Old Stone Hall and stay with Miz Beatrix. And you're how old now?'

'I was seventeen in May. So that makes you, what? Thirty or something?'

'Crikey!' Aaron muttered. 'I'm practically an old man.'

'Have you never met anyone – erm, a young lady that you might want to marry?' Laurie blushed slightly, wondering if he was asking about something too personal and shouldn't. He and his friends at school often talked about the kind of young women they would like to court. Some of them claimed they had already kissed someone, friends of their sisters perhaps.

But he thought that Aaron might not mind the question and he glanced surreptitiously at him and saw him chewing on his lip as if pondering.

'Or have you ever kissed someone?'

'Apart from my ma, do you mean?' Aaron blew on his lips. 'Oh aye, when I was at school. Lads were allus chasing lasses, trying to steal a kiss. But not since. I guess I'll allus be a bachelor. You see, Laurie,' he glanced swiftly at him, 'is it all right to call you Laurie?'

'Of course it is!' Laurie laughed.

'Well, 'fact is, I fell in love with somebody when I was very young and I've nivver got over it. She was far too good for me, and married already in any case. She was just perfect in every way; kind, beautiful, not just in looks, but in her whole being.' He clicked his tongue at the pony to get a move on and gave a big sigh. 'So there'll be no one else in the world to match her.'

They pulled up the hill and in through the open gate to the front drive and the door. 'Here we are, young sir,' he said.

'You could have gone to the kitchen door, closer to the stables,' Laurie pointed out.

'What? And let my mother see me bringing 'young master

to 'servants' entrance?' He gave Laurie a wink and then grinned. 'I'd nivver hear 'end of it.'

Laurie chuckled and jumped down. 'Thanks, Aaron.' He ran up the steps to the front door and then turned to watch Aaron flick the reins and continue on round to the rear of the house. He paused for a minute before opening the door.

I do believe, he considered as he stood there, in fact, I'm sure, that Aaron was talking about my mother.

CHAPTER TWENTY-THREE

Laurie and Alicia caught an early train, though they had to ask Aaron to drive them to Brough as that train didn't stop at North Ferriby. Laurie was hatless and wore a plain grey sack coat with grey trousers, a casual style that he wore for home, contrasting with the dark cutaway coat, trousers and top hat that he wore for school. Alicia had dressed in a pale blue cotton gown and jacket and wore a brimmed bonnet, as the weather was warm, but as Edward had said there might be thundery showers later she also took an umbrella.

When they arrived at Paragon station half an hour later, she murmured that it was much more convenient than driving in. 'Though rather sooty.' She showed her gloved hands to her brother, who raised his eyebrows at the black marks where she had grasped the carriage handrail.

Outside on the concourse, there were one or two beggars sitting on the pavement, who merely looked up at the brother and sister and didn't approach them. Carriages were waiting for fares and drivers were standing by them. Laurie noticed that two of them had the Snowden insignia on the doors and both drivers had their heads turned towards them. The lads looked at each other and then one of them walked over to them.

He tipped his forefinger to his top hat at Laurie, who appreciated the fact that Joseph Snowden supplied a smart uniform for his drivers. 'Good morning, sir – miss.' He inclined his head towards Alicia. 'Would you be Mr and Miss Fawcett-Newby?'

Laurie answered that yes, they were, but they hadn't expected to be met.

'Miss Olivia's instructions, sir,' the driver said. 'I believe she has made plans.' He raised a quizzical eyebrow as if to say *You know what ladies are like.*

'In that case,' Alicia said, 'we'd better come with you. We don't know where Mason Street is anyway.'

'Easy enough to find, miss.' He held the carriage door open for her. 'But a bit of a stretch if you don't like walking. I've been asked to take you to 'stable yard.'

She giggled at Laurie as they set off, and said in a languid little voice, 'And I'm only used to walking from one carriage to another in my tiny little shoes.'

Laurie smiled. 'He's not to know how often we tramp round the estate; you're dressed like a young city woman. A London gel,' he mimicked. 'As Mama says she once was.'

'Should we give him a gratuity?' Alicia said. 'He might be missing out on a fare.'

'Oh, yes. I suppose we should.' He fumbled in his trouser pocket and brought out a sixpence. 'Is that enough, do you think?'

She gave a little shrug. 'Probably. I don't know. Aren't we lucky to be innocent of worldly affairs?'

'Town and city affairs yes, but we know the price of grain and dairy products and the cost of a loaf of bread.'

'True,' she nodded. 'Of course we do.' She leaned forward. 'Do you know what? I really hope that Olivia takes us to see her aunt's bakery and café. Maybe we could have a cup of coffee and slice of cake with her.'

'I can't imagine Mademoiselle Leblanc in a cap and apron,' he said. 'She's so very elegant. Do you think most Parisian women look like her?'

'I don't know, but I'm hoping I'll find out next year.'

'Oh, you still want to go to school there! I didn't realize that you were so serious.'

'We're deadly serious,' Alicia told him. Glancing out of the window, she murmured, 'I think we're nearly there; we've just passed the church that Olivia told me about. That didn't take long, did it?'

The driver passed a gated garden on the left, turned right at the top of Jarrett Street, then immediately left into a narrow street with a metal sign that announced it to be Charlotte Street Mews.

The driver pulled up outside a large gate that had a wooden board above it bearing the same insignia as on the carriage doors. He put out a hand to Alicia, who took it and smiled. 'Thank you.' Laurie, following her down from the carriage, surreptitiously slipped sixpence into the driver's hand and was surprised when he gave him a knowing wink.

'Just through the gate, sir, miss,' he said. 'Mr Snowden'll be in one of 'stalls, I should think. Ah, here he is,' he added as Joseph came out into the yard, followed by Olivia, who wore a plain brown cotton dress with a sacking apron over it, and a pair of rubber boots on her feet. In her hand she carried a sweeping brush.

'Here I am in all my finery,' she called gaily. 'Do excuse me,' adding a 'Thank you, Parker' to the driver, who touched his forehead to her.

She looks lovely, Laurie thought. It wouldn't matter at all what she wore, she'd still be beautiful. He smiled and raised his hand in greeting.

Joseph shook his head and said jocularly, 'I said to Olivia that she'd be caught out if you were early, and now she has been. What a beggar girl she looks.'

'These are my friends, Papa.' She pretended to punch him. 'I've seen Laurie in his working clothes, and Alicia too when we were helping with the harvest. Perhaps you could come too if we're invited again. You'd enjoy it.'

135

'Manners to wait until asked,' Joseph teased her. 'Now, young man, would you like to come along in and look at 'rest of my hosses? I've got some here at 'livery which aren't mine, and I know you'll want to see Captain again. Are you staying, Olivia, or taking Miss Alicia to see Gran?'

'Just Alicia, Mr Snowden, not Miss,' Alicia pointed out. 'We're not used to formality, except with grown-ups.' She smiled, her cheeks dimpling.

'Then I'm overruled,' Joseph joked, 'cos I'm not yet a proper grown-up. Come on then, lad,' he said to Laurie. 'Let's show you our team. We'll be over for a cup of tea in half an hour, tell Gran.'

'We're just round the corner,' Olivia said to Alicia, tucking her arm into hers. 'Just a step, as my *grand-mère* would say.'

'Your *grand-mère*,' Alicia said. 'What does she think of her French title?'

'She doesn't really like it,' Olivia said. 'I really only say it to tease. She likes me to call her Gran, says she feels like a proper grandmother then, and I tell her that she is. She's the only one I have.'

'Mm.' Alicia contemplated. 'Well, I call my mother's parents Grandmama and Grandpa, and Papa's – Edward's – mother is Granny Mags. I think we've always called her that.' Then she added regretfully, 'Gampa Luke died a while ago. We still miss him.'

'And what about your . . . natural father's parents? What names do you give them?'

Alicia lifted her shoulders in a shrug. 'We never see them. They don't visit or write. They've cut us out of their lives since Charles's death and Mama's remarriage. Mama says she doesn't think they like children, they didn't even like their own son or daughter.' She paused for a second. 'I'd almost forgotten about her: my aunt Anne. She came to visit us once when we were small. She scared Laurie and me; she seemed angry about something and yet triumphant too. How odd! I haven't thought about her from that day to this and it must be . . . maybe ten years ago. I wonder what happened to her?'

Olivia paused, grasping a cast-iron handrail at the bottom of steps leading up to a town house with a solid front door and a shiny door knob. 'So even with conventional families, nothing is ever straightforward,' she said, 'and I thought that it would be.'

Alicia laughed. 'There is nothing conventional about our family, Olivia. I don't think there is such a thing.'

Olivia opened the door and invited her friend in. There was a smell of polish and another one of something baking too.

'Lovely smell,' Alicia breathed in. 'Bread? It smells like our kitchen.'

'Gran said she was baking scones, even though I told her I was going to take you to *Lucille's Pâtisserie & Petit Bistro* for lunch.'

'Oh, how lovely. I was hoping to see it. Laurie said he couldn't imagine Mademoiselle Leblanc in an apron and cap because she's so elegant.'

'She is, isn't she?' Olivia smiled. 'I hope I look like her one day. We'll get that aura when we've been schooled in Paris.'

'Do you think so?' Alicia followed Olivia down the long hall towards a door that she thought might lead to the kitchen.

Olivia nodded and whispered, 'I've got Grand-mère on my side as well as Tante Lucille; now we just have to work on Papa!'

The door opened and Mrs Snowden stood there, holding a tea towel. 'I thought I could hear whispering. Olivia, take Miss Alicia into the sitting room, not bring her into 'kitchen! Good morning, miss,' she added to Alicia, and shook her head disparagingly. 'That girl!'

'Alicia commented on the lovely smell of baking, Gran; that's why we headed this way,' Olivia said, and sighed. 'Come on then, Alicia, about-turn.' She gave a wicked grin and said over her shoulder, 'Pa said they'd be here in about half an hour for a cup of tea.'

Mrs Snowden flapped her tea towel at her. 'Go on then. The scones are just about ready.'

A table in the front window was already set with cups, saucers and plates and spotless, beautifully ironed table napkins. Alicia sat down and looked out. 'You have a good view of people walking by,' she said, and pointed a finger opposite. 'That's the street we came up. Jarrett Street, isn't it? We passed a garden, and the church that you told me about as a landmark.'

'Yes, I thought if you were walking you could ask for directions to St Charles. It's a lovely church, with fabulous hangings. It's so called because of Charles Borromeo, who was Archbishop of Milan and later canonized, so there are churches named after him all over the world. But then Papa said one of the drivers could pick you up.'

Olivia slipped out of the room to wash her hands and change her dress. Whilst she was gone Mrs Snowden came in carrying a tray holding a teapot, a jug of milk and a plate of scones. Alicia got up to take the things from the tray and put them on the table.

'Thank you, m'dear,' Irma Snowden said. 'Not used to being waited upon?'

'We're all taught to help,' Alicia said as she arranged the plates on the table. 'Mama says we must learn what the housekeeping staff does for us and we'll appreciate them all the more; besides,' she added with a mischievous smile, 'our cook is Papa's aunt, her son Aaron, who is head groom, carriage driver and general factotum as Papa calls him, is his cousin, and including Mrs Hallam and Mrs Gordon they've all been at the house since before Laurence and I were born, so there's absolutely no chance whatsoever of any of us getting above ourselves!'

Mrs Snowden held the tray with one hand while the other she put on her hip and gazed at Alicia. 'Well, I never!' she said, astonished. 'I'd never have guessed.'

Alicia dropped her voice to a whisper. 'And the reason is that all the female staff absolutely adore my father, and although Aaron doesn't know that we know, *we* know that he loves my mother and always has done.'

Mrs Snowden opened her mouth to say something, but before she could think of a suitable response Olivia came back into the room wearing a clean lemon-coloured summer frock which just reached her ankles. She had undone her plait, and her black hair, brushed and shiny, hung down her back to her waist.

They'd finished a pot of tea and eaten a scone each, and Mrs Snowden had come back to sit with them and listen to their chatter, when Laurie and Joseph came in. They washed their hands before sitting down at the table.

Laurie looked animated. 'Such good stock, Alicia,' he murmured. 'And Captain is just splendid.'

'Twenty-first birthday present, then?' she suggested. 'Where does he come from?' she asked Joseph.

'I'd been looking for some time,' he told her. 'I'd read reports in several journals and it took a couple of years before I heard of a set-up in North Yorkshire which was breeding them, so I wrote to them and took a ride out to have a look for myself.'

Laurie was unusually animated, asking questions of Joseph Snowden about the Morgan breed; he drank a cup of tea and ate a scone, but Alicia saw Olivia glancing at the clock. 'Do you wish us to be going out, Olivia?' she asked.

'Well, if we want to have lunch at Lucille's *Petit Bistro*, I think perhaps we should. She does get very busy across lunchtime.'

'Indeed,' Mrs Snowden said. 'You should be making tracks now! Let me re-plait your hair, Olivia, and then wear your bonnet, and you'll pass all right for lunch out.' She was her usual practical self, but Laurie and Alicia saw how proud she was of Olivia, and thought how blessed she must feel to have her in her life.

CHAPTER TWENTY-FOUR

Olivia led them in a different direction, towards the centre of the town and the town docks. They walked from the Queen's Dock, which was crammed with shipping from many countries, and crossed the road to cut down the side of the warehouses at Prince's Dock waterway, where they saw local shipping as well as the ferry from Rotterdam, before turning into a side street with many old buildings which brought them out into the Market Place.

There wasn't a market that day, but Holy Trinity church right in front of them had its doors open wide in welcome. They didn't go across the square, however, but with Olivia in the lead turned right towards a variety of shops and businesses, and finally stopped at a café and bakery where tiered cake stands in the window displayed the most appealing pastries: croissants, canelés, éclairs filled with chocolate and cream, and other tantalizing confections that made their mouths water.

A wooden sign extended over the window and above the door with a sketch of a bridge over the River Seine on which the words *Lucille's Pâtisserie & Petit Bistro* stood out in attractive gold lettering.

'Goodness,' Alicia gasped. 'Does your aunt make all of these?'

Olivia nodded. 'She does. Isn't she wonderful? I've tried most of them and they simply melt in the mouth.'

'We'd better go in, then,' Laurie said. 'My treat.'

Of course he wasn't allowed to pay. The young serving girl, who was dressed in black with a white apron and cap, brought them a jug of coffee, a large plate bearing an assortment of cakes and pastries, and large snowy white napkins to cover their clothes. Laurie tucked his under his chin and invited Olivia and his sister to choose first.

The café was busy, some ladies eating dainty sandwiches filled with salmon and cream cheese whilst greedily eyeing the plates of canelés and cream-filled choux pastries in front of them; some men, who were eating alone, had baskets of various types of bread, baguette and brioche wrapped in more white napkins set on the tables before them, along with hunks of ripe Camembert and jugs of steaming coffee.

Lucille, dressed in crisp white cotton under her dark navy pinafore, wore a tall white pleated chef's hat and spoke briefly to everyone sitting at the tables. Alicia noticed that she had not one spot of flour on her face or immaculate clothing, unlike Mrs Parkin, who almost always had a dusting of flour on her nose or eyebrows.

'I am in awe of you, Mademoiselle Leblanc,' Alicia said softly, when she came to speak to them. 'My goodness, what a gift you have for producing beautiful cakes. A delight to the eye as well as being delicious.' She clutched her middle. 'I've been so greedy! Thank you – *merci*,' she added, thinking that just thank you wasn't enough for such a treat.

She wanted to ask who had taught Lucille to bake such wondrous cakes and pastries, but the shop door kept opening and closing, and even though it seemed that there was also a room upstairs they thought they should leave to make room for paying customers.

Laurie asked the serving maid if she would make up a box of cakes for him and Alicia to take home for their family, and she did so, putting them in a pretty cardboard box and tying it with blue ribbon.

They thanked Lucille again when they said goodbye, and

141

Laurie gave a gratuity to the young maid as well as paying for the extra cakes, so she dipped her knee to him as they left.

Olivia led them out of the market area and turned left into Whitefriargate. 'This is Hull's renowned shopping street,' she announced proudly, turning slightly and pointing in the opposite direction. 'The street at the top is Silver Street and is where jewellers have their shops and silversmiths work on beautiful items: jugs and plates and candlesticks, rings and brooches, and all manner of insignia too, whereas Whitefriargate has the best of gowns, hats and shawls and anything else that a lady might covet, and shops with gentlemen's attire too.'

Whilst Alicia and Olivia stopped to admire a pretty hat in a milliner's window, Laurie walked slowly on. He paused to look idly at a window display of gentlemen's clothing, and heard a soft voice at his elbow.

'Buy a bunch of violets for your ladies, sir?' A very young girl of perhaps twelve, dressed in a ragged though clean skirt and thin blouse with a shawl over her shoulders, stood behind him. She carried a wicker basket holding a few drooping bunches of violets over a thin arm, and one bunch in her hand. 'Your sisters, or sweethearts?'

He smiled at her. 'My sister and her friend,' he murmured, and put his hand in his trouser pocket for change. His pocket book was inside his jacket, as advised by his tutors when visiting York, and by his father before he came out, who had suggested he put a few coins in his pocket for beggars. Laurie had nodded at him as he warned him that there were always pickpockets in every town and city and wondered how he knew, for Edward hardly ever visited such places.

He dropped coins into the girl's hand and she closed her fingers over his, trapping them in her palm as she whispered, 'A penny for a kiss, sir.'

He was startled by her bold comment, and blushed. Though he had often given coppers to beggars, children in York especially, they had usually scampered away with the coins clutched in their fists as if they feared he might change his mind and snatch them back.

He laughed, shaking his head, and said, 'I'm saving that for—'

'Your future sweetheart, sir?'

He didn't answer her question, but said, 'I'll have two bunches of flowers, then. One for my sister, and one for—'

'Your future sweetheart,' she murmured again. 'You couldn't do better than . . .' She paused, and dipped her knee to Alicia. 'Good day, miss.' Turning to Olivia, who smiled at her, she dipped her knee again. 'Good day, Miss Olivia. I hope you're well on this fine day?'

'I am, thank you, Trixie. I hope you are too?'

'You know her?' Laurie asked as they walked on, Laurie handing the wilting flowers to Alicia to put in her basket alongside the box of pastries.

'Yes. She comes to the *pâtisserie* at closing time, and if there's any bread left Tante Lucille lets her and the others have it for coppers. She says she charges them as it encourages them to try to earn a living rather than begging. But I've seen her give it to older vagrants who can hardly walk, let alone work.'

'What a nice person she is,' Alicia murmured.

Olivia nodded. 'She says she knows how hard it is to be without money. When she was a child, living in Paris, her mother cleaned other people's houses for her livelihood.'

Miss Leblanc is so fashionable and elegant, Alicia thought, no one would ever guess that she had been poor. Had she considered the matter at all, she would have imagined that Olivia's aunt had grown up in comfortable circumstances, but now she viewed her in a different light, wondering how she had managed to pull herself out of that dire situation.

They had walked a circle, as Whitefriargate finished or began by Prince's Dock, and Olivia told them this was where Hull's ancient town walls once stood: they looked over the bridge at the cargo ships and up at the Wilberforce monument before moving on to the red brick church of St John,

143

the first church to be built as the town began to expand beyond the walls.

'Now I'm going to show you Albion Street,' Olivia said, pointing out the Hull Infirmary at the end of the road, 'unless you are bored and would like to go home for a cup of tea?'

'I'm not in the least bored,' Laurie said, 'and I'd like to see more of the splendid buildings that I noticed as we were driven here; but I'd like a cup of tea too,' he added quickly, in case he was being rude by refusing the offer of tea. 'And we mustn't forget the time of our train, Alicia.'

'No we mustn't, but we still have plenty of time,' she said, and so they walked slowly along Albion Street, admiring the grand buildings and elegant Georgian houses, until they came to the church of St Charles Borromeo, but as the doors were locked they couldn't enter, and continued to walk on towards Mason Street and Olivia's home.

'Have I tired you out?' Olivia asked as they mounted the steps.

'Not a bit,' Alicia declared, 'though my feet ache. I should have worn sensible shoes rather than these sandals.'

'They're nice, though,' Olivia commented, and the two girls chatted about shoes for a few minutes before Olivia opened the door. She held it open for Alicia and Laurie to enter and glanced out at the passers-by, waving a hand at an elderly neighbour and noticing a man and woman and small child walking slowly past on the other side of the road and looking up at the houses before she closed the door.

'Thank you, but we had better be on our way, Mrs Snowden,' Alicia said, after they had drunk the teapot dry and been asked if they'd like a fresh pot. 'We've had such a lovely day, haven't we, Laurie?'

'Splendid, thank you,' Laurie agreed. 'And thank you for showing me your stables, Mr Snowden, and especially Captain. He's very handsome and well mannered; I love him!'

Joseph had come home for something to eat and drink but

was still in his working clothes, as he intended to go back to the stables. 'Perhaps I could bring him up to Beverley some time and you could ride over and try him out?'

Laurie beamed. 'I'd really like that,' he said. 'But I'm back at school shortly so there's only this coming week left.'

'Well,' said Joseph, 'I'll see how things are, and if I'm free on any day I'll drop you a postcard, shall I? It would be good to give Captain a longer run than usual, and especially on grass.'

'He could come on to one of our paddocks, sir, rather than going up to Beverley. It's a couple of miles nearer.' Laurie stood up, and Alicia followed suit. 'Unless you'd like to give him a gallop on Westwood.' He put out a hand to shake Joseph's. 'Whatever you decide.'

On the doorstep they thanked the Snowdens again for their hospitality, and after Alicia and Olivia had excitedly said they'd be meeting at school again soon, they waved goodbye. Laurie glanced back at Olivia in the doorway and then turned to his sister. 'She's lovely, isn't she? As a person, I mean,' he added quickly when he saw Alicia raise her eyebrows ironically. 'Nothing more.'

'Really?' she said. 'She's beautiful.' She tucked her arm into his. 'What did the little flower girl say to you?'

He glanced down at her. 'Never you mind, nosy parker!'

CHAPTER TWENTY-FIVE

Joseph rose from the table where he had eaten a ham sandwich and drunk several cups of tea, and stretched his arms above his head. 'I'd better get back,' he said, looking at the clock on the wall. 'It's time for the changeover of drivers.'

'I'll clear away,' his mother said. 'Lucille'll be in soon. What a nice young couple, aren't they? The brother and sister. Proper gentry, but no side on them. None at all.'

'Aye, very,' he answered. 'Olivia's found some good friends there.' Her class, he thought, but didn't say.

The doorbell rang, making them both jump. 'Lucille forgotten her key?' he prompted, but his mother shook her head.

'No, she never forgets it. Shall I go or will you?'

'I'll go. I'm on my way out anyway. I'll be back at about six o'clock.'

He stepped into the hall, picked up his jacket from the hall stand and opened the door.

A tall man a few years younger than him, with dark curly hair and dressed plainly though stylishly, stood on the top step. 'Mr Snowden? Erm, I – that is . . .' He cleared his throat. 'Do you remember me, sir?'

Joseph stood transfixed. Someone he had thought he would never see again faced him. 'Aye,' he croaked. 'Never forget a face, nor 'last time I saw you.'

'I've seen you over the years when I've passed through Hull, Mr Snowden, but never dared approach you.'

'Why have you come now?' Joseph didn't mean to sound brusque but that was how he feared it came across simply because he was shaken to the core by the fear of what this visit might imply. 'Why haven't you called before?'

'May I come in? I need to explain.'

Joseph gave a half glance up the stairs Olivia had climbed not five minutes before. He opened the door wider; he had to know why this man was here now.

The caller followed Joseph into the front sitting room where they had just taken tea; his mother had cleared away and put back the lacy runner on the table with the brass and glass table lamp in the centre. The visitor looked round and his mouth trembled. 'It's as I remember it,' he murmured. 'Just the same. How – how is your mother?'

As he voiced the words, Irma Snowden came back into the room. Seeing their caller, she clutched her throat and then grasped the back of a chair. 'Why – why are you here?' she stammered, asking the same question as her son.

The man took a breath, clearly overcome, and without being invited pulled out a dining chair and sat down. With his elbows on the table, he clutched his head in his hands and shook with sobs.

Mrs Snowden moved towards him and put a hand on his shoulder. 'Now come come, Oliver. Time's passed, and life has moved on.'

He sat up. Reaching for a pocket handkerchief, he took a deep breath and wiped his tears, saying, 'I'm so sorry. So sorry. I thought that I would be all right, but seeing this room brought everything back as sharp as if . . . only yesterday.'

He stood up and pushed the chair back to the table. 'I do beg your pardon, Mrs Snowden. And yours as well, Joseph.' He looked at Joseph, whose eyes were moist too. 'I really didn't want to upset anyone, but . . .' he took another breath,

'I'm leaving the country and couldn't go without – without coming to see you and asking about my daughter.'

'Please sit down.' Joseph's voice trembled as he pointed towards the sofa. He saw the hesitation. 'Not 'same one,' he said roughly. 'We bought new.'

Irma shook her head. She thought the vision of the blood-stained sofa had gone from her memory, but it hadn't. In spite of her best efforts with old sheets and towels, the sofa was ruined and had had to go. Joseph had hauled it to the stable yard and, venting his anger and despair at the young woman's death in his own home, he had smashed it to pieces and then set fire to it.

'I wrote,' Oliver Rushton murmured. 'After I left Hull. I couldn't leave a forwarding address as I was wandering from town to town looking for work, looking for lodgings. I was desperate after Clara's death. I couldn't believe it; it was like a living nightmare. I'm sorry, I know that I left you with the burden of taking care of the child, but,' he shook his head, 'I didn't know what to do.'

He didn't, Irma thought. He had no idea. He was too young for the responsibility, and so would the girl have been, had she survived. She held in a sigh. But that is what young love is like and they don't listen, because they think that older people don't understand, that no one has felt the emotion that they feel. But anger crept into her thoughts too; the girl's parents had ignored the young couple's pleas; because he wasn't of their class they had simply dismissed him, not seeing that he was a good and honest young man who loved and would have taken care of their daughter.

She glanced through the window; a woman with a child, a boy, of maybe three or more were standing across the road. Then she saw Lucille come round the corner, glance at the woman and cross the road towards their house.

'Where are you planning on going?' Joseph asked Oliver.

'To America. I met a woman who saved my life.' He looked up at Joseph and a tear trickled down his cheek. 'I thought I would never love again and I was ready to give up on life, but I – well, my father had been a tailor and my mother a dress-maker, both long gone by then, but they had taught me something of their trade and I went to London and found work with a tailoring company. I seemed to fit in and my skills came back; and then I met Mary. She's a milliner, the kindest of women, and she saw how my distress had all but ruined my life.'

They heard the front door open and Lucille called out, 'I'm home, and I've found someone on the doorstep.'

The sitting room door opened and Lucille came in holding hands with a small boy, with a woman following behind her. Lucille looked stunned when she saw Oliver standing there. The woman on the doorstep had only mentioned 'a caller'.

'Mary.' Oliver stood up. 'I'm so sorry, my dear. I left you standing there.' He gave Lucille an awkward bow. 'Lucille,' he said, and the tears ran down his cheeks again. 'I've never thanked you. Can't ever thank you enough.'

She shook her head. Like Joseph and his mother, she was instantly back in that terrible night.

She hadn't known the district well back then, but Joseph's mother had told her where to find the midwife in Sykes Street before she was to cut down King Street and across Charles Street – she would know it by the shops that would be open, Irma had said – and that would bring her out on to Albion Street where the doctor lived.

She remembered how, as she ran, she kept repeating the street names over and over so that she wouldn't forget them. At the midwife's house she gave her the message to go immed-iately to the Snowdens' house where there was a woman about to give birth.

'Is it one of them Frenchies?' the woman asked.

'No,' she'd replied. 'I am one of the Frenchies. It is an Eng-lish woman and she is very sick. There is much blood.'

The woman had put on her coat. 'Mrs Snowden, she teks in all 'waifs and strays that nobody else will have,' she'd said, and

Lucille remembered that she hadn't known what she was talking about.

'I beg your pardon,' Oliver Rushton said apologetically, bringing her back to the present. 'May I introduce my wife Mary? And this is our son, Jamie. We have been married these last five years.'

He paused. Someone was singing, out in the hall or on the stairs. It was a joyous sound: a young clear voice reciting the popular ballad 'Over the hills and far away'. *Tom he was a piper's son . . .*

The door opened and Olivia came in. She had changed into a light blue flimsy cotton dress that floated about her ankles; she had brushed and smoothed her long hair and left it loose to fall to her waist. She stopped as she saw the strangers, and dipped her knee.

'I do apologize!' She gave a surprised smile. 'I didn't realize we had visitors. Please excuse me.' She saw the little boy. 'Hello! What's your name?' The child rushed towards his mother and hid his face in her skirts, but turned one eye shyly back towards Olivia.

'Olivia,' Joseph said, clearing his throat, and Oliver Rushton gasped.

'Olivia! You gave her my name!'

Olivia's gaze went from Joseph to the stranger and her face paled. 'What?' she breathed, and Lucille stepped towards her and took her hand.

'It is all right, chérie. There is nothing wrong. Joseph!' she said. 'You must explain.'

'Olivia,' he tried again, his voice hoarse. 'This is . . . your father, Oliver Rushton, his wife Mary, and their son Jamie.'

With great restraint, for she felt as if someone had struck her, Olivia stepped towards the stranger and dipped her knee, but reached for Joseph's hand and clutched it. She swallowed and breathed hard. 'I am Olivia Clara Snowden,' she said, and looked towards Joseph before turning again to Oliver. 'I knew I was named Clara after my mother,' she said softly, 'but not – not that I was named after my – birth father. I'd like to sit down.'

'P'raps we all should,' Irma said. 'Please, everyone take a seat; don't stand on ceremony. I'll make us a pot of tea.'

'I must slip out,' Joseph said hurriedly. 'I'll be only five minutes, but the men will be waiting. Lucille, will you . . .' He ran out of words, but she knew what he wanted. She would ask the questions and they would listen to the answers.

For the benefit of Olivia and Lucille, Oliver Rushton explained again where he had been: his travels across the country to find work before arriving in London, meeting and marrying Mary, and their planned voyage to America, where she had relatives.

'We are setting up in the tailoring and millinery trades,' he said. 'There are many opportunities, and I've managed to save enough money to be able to open a shop. British tailoring is valued over there.' He gazed at Olivia and said huskily, 'But I couldn't leave without first finding out what had happened to my daughter. I had trusted Joseph to do whatever he could for you, rather than sending you into a workhouse orphanage, which was the only option open for me.'

Olivia put her hand to her chest and her mouth dropped open. 'I – didn't know,' she whispered. 'I only knew that my mother had died at my birth and her husb— that is, my – the man who had sired me couldn't keep me, for he had no work and no means of providing for me.'

Her unseeing gaze travelled around the room before resting on the small child. 'And – this is my brother?' She smiled, though a tear ran down her cheek. 'Hello, Jamie,' she said softly. 'I'm so very pleased to meet you.'

Irma Snowden brought in a tray of tea things and placed them on the table and Lucille hurriedly went to fetch a box of cakes that she'd brought home. These were opened just as Joseph came back.

'I should have written to say I was coming,' Oliver said, still overcome with emotion, 'but I was so afraid of what might have happened, although I trusted you, Joseph. I thought that you might have found someone willing to take her and bring her up as their own. I had such fanciful ideas, and instead I find that here she is, still safe with you – and looking so much like her mother.'

Joseph shook his head to the offer of tea, and said, 'We couldn't part with this precious child. Lucille and my mother visited wet nurses on 'recommendation of 'midwife and one fed her for three months, and by then she was part of our lives.' He smiled tremulously at Olivia, pleased to unburden himself at last. 'Olivia is officially the ward of me and my mother; Lucille was too young for the role then, but she has been a true mother to her. Olivia belongs to us, and we love her as our own.' He began to weep. 'We could never part with her.'

Olivia went to his side and put her arms about him. 'Papa, you never will. You have cherished me as no one else ever could.'

Mrs Snowden wiped away a tear, and Lucille gazed at Oliver Rushton. She nodded at him and looked at the child Jamie, who was gazing curiously at them all in turn as he stood close to his mother, who looked at everyone with tender eyes.

'It was meant to be,' Lucille murmured. 'Ordained.'

CHAPTER TWENTY-SIX

At five o'clock the following morning Lucille was briskly walking to the café in Hull's Market Place to begin her baking. She had barely slept the previous night, tossing and turning and reliving the evening's events.

Oliver Rushton and his family had left after a further hour, but before they did Oliver had dipped his fingers into his top pocket and brought out a small box. He'd turned to Olivia and said softly, 'I bought this ring for Clara. We had planned that if we couldn't gain permission to marry then we would run away to Gretna Green in Scotland, where the law would allow it. Clara was seventeen and I not yet twenty-one. But' – he looked away – 'we were very much in love, and our passion had overtaken us. Clara told her parents that she was with child, and that made them even angrier. They said the child, if it lived, would be given away, and so we brought our plans forward.'

He put his hand over his mouth for a second. 'Clara hadn't felt well and we thought it was because of the strain and anxiety, but in fact she had influenza with a fever. It was that which killed her, not giving birth, even though she was a slender young woman.'

He had opened the box to show a plain gold wedding band, which he held out to Olivia. 'I would like you to have this, and perhaps one day you will wear it at your own wedding.'

She took it from him, and with tears glistening she leaned forward and kissed his cheek. 'Thank you,' she'd whispered. 'I will treasure it for ever.'

So that is the happy conclusion, Lucille reflected. All's well that ends well. Joseph is happy that he won't lose his precious girl, which I know is what he must have feared most of all when Oliver Rushton arrived on his doorstep, especially when he said that he was leaving the country.

She gave a little smile: as if Olivia would leave him! She so clearly adores Joseph, and her *grand-mère* too, but what of me? She cares for me, I know, but what am I? I was a surrogate mother to her when she was a child even though so young myself, but I was afraid too, afraid that my so-called friend Margot with her seductive eyes and soft mouth would make a play for Joseph. It had been her intention from the beginning when we arrived in England. She had the power of seduction and she wanted a man to take care of her.

And she almost had him. I knew that. I'd already noticed how his eyes followed her, and but for that night when he carried Clara into the house where she would give birth, and Margot ran upstairs to our room and put pillows over her head to muffle the cries, she would have ensnared him.

Joseph hadn't seen a newborn child before; what man does? But Oliver Rushton stayed by Clara's side the whole long night, and I think that is when Joseph knew what real love was as he waited, sitting on the stairs out in the hall.

She was nearing the Market Place and hoped that she would have a busy day and could concentrate on what was now important to her, but Margot kept intruding on her thoughts and she knew that she must think it all through before erasing the memory of her.

As Olivia grew in those early months, Margot was deprived of attention. Joseph was intoxicated by the child and had spoken to his mother about applying to the courts to become her guardians. Irma Snowden had discussed it with her at length, but not with Margot, whom she disliked intensely. But Margot had overheard and had said to Joseph, 'Shouldn't the child be adopted, Joseph?' in that pretty way she had, which I knew so well could turn any man's attention to her. 'But you could only do that by marrying,' and she'd smiled and shrugged her shoulders. 'The courts won't allow it otherwise. A single man can't look after a child alone.'

'But I'm not alone,' he'd said. 'I have my mother, and—'

What else did he say? Lucille unlocked the shop door and stepped inside, and breathed in yesterday's baking. I can't remember because I was too afraid of losing both Olivia and Joseph, and Irma too, if I'm honest with myself; by then they were my family.

In the kitchen behind the shop, she opened the door of the range and breathed in a sigh of pleasure as she saw the coals were still red. She put on a few pieces of wood to bring it to life, closed the door again, and shook the kettle to check there was enough water for her coffee jug.

She sat on a stool and continued her reflections as she waited for the kettle to heat up. It was then, she recalled, that Margot had decided she would go to London and stay with her aunt after all, which had been her mother's intention all along: to pass the responsibility of her daughter to someone else.

'You must come to London with me, Lucille,' Margot had said. 'That is why my mother paid for your journey from France. To accompany me!'

But we have been here all this time; over a year, I told her. I have work here at the bakery. I am earning my living and paying rent for both of us whilst you – I recall how angry I was – you do nothing all day; you don't even help Mrs Snowden with the dishes. And Margot simply shrugged, and said she was a guest in the house.

She sighed and made her coffee. It was so long ago that I can barely recall the details, but I do remember that I told Mrs Snowden and Joseph that I had to accompany Margot to her aunt's, even though I would lose a day's wages at the bakery, but I would come straight back. I liked this town and had plans of my own, though I hadn't told anyone about them then.

Joseph was horrified that I could even consider it; we had settled as if we were family, he said, though I think his mother was relieved to see the back of Margot. 'You'll come back, Lucille?' she whispered to me. 'You must. We can't manage without you.'

Lucille smiled to herself as she drank her coffee, then got up from her stool and put out her baking bowls and her salt and sugar pots on the large wooden table; put the yeast in a small bowl above the range with a pinch of sugar to make it warm and bubble.

And then, she thought, her recollections returning, I took Margot to London, for she wouldn't have found her own way there. I asked if she'd written to her aunt to say she was coming and she said she had not. I bought a London map and found the street and I knew the house number. I paid for a cabriolet to take us from the railway station and drop us outside the house: it was a tall building with steps to the front door which I ran up to ring the bell and then ran down again to where Margot was standing with her trunk and other luggage, waiting for me to assist her.

I kissed her cheek. 'Goodbye, Margot,' I said. 'Enjoy your stay. I hope you have a good life.'

Lucille stood stock still in front of the range, remembering. She began to laugh. And then I turned tail and didn't turn back, even though she was shouting, 'Wait! Wait!' and I ran and ran back the way we had come, heading towards the railway station and home to Hull. We never saw or heard from her again. *Friponne ingrate.* Ungrateful minx.

She took a deep breath and tipped the flour into a warm bowl and made a hole in the centre, scattered in a pinch or two of salt, then poured the yeast mixture into it and put it in a warm place.

'Now, what shall I bake whilst waiting for the yeast to froth?'

'Are you asking me or talking to yourself?'

156

She jumped. She thought she'd locked the door, her habit whilst she was alone, until her assistant Molly was due.

'Joseph! What are you doing here?'

Joseph looked at her empty coffee cup. 'Called for a cup of coffee, but I see I'm too late.'

'No, no. I can make more,' she said hurriedly, and reached for the kettle to refill it.

He took it from her. 'Let me. I don't want to hold you up. What are you making this morning?'

'I'm, erm, going to make white loaves and bread cakes first as they take longer to prove, and then croissants and maybe brioche. Then something sweet like canelés.'

'Are they the ones shaped like little puddings, with rum in them?'

She nodded. 'Sometimes I mix in rum, yes, but not always; sometimes vanilla.'

'I like those.' He made another pot of coffee and poured them each a cup. 'Why did you run off so early this morning?'

She looked at him. 'I didn't run off,' she said. 'I'm always up early.'

'You usually have a cup of coffee before you leave. I wouldn't see you until the afternoon if you didn't.'

'Oh, I didn't sleep very well and I was meditating about yesterday, so I got up earlier. I was thinking of Oliver Rushton arriving after so many years. I'm pleased he found someone to make him happy again. Mary seems very nice, yes? And Olivia, she behaved so well, so grown up and sensible.' She took a deep breath. 'Did she say anything after I went up to bed? Her thoughts on meeting him?'

'I think she was pleased,' Joseph said. 'She said, that – erm, what was it? Oh, that it closed a chapter and she needn't wonder what he was like any more; and that he seemed like a kind man who really had loved Clara.' He paused. 'I thought it was significant that she didn't say her mother.'

Lucille nodded thoughtfully. She was still mixing and shaping her dough, even though she was listening. 'Because she never knew her,' she murmured, 'and never will. But now she has seen the man who created her.' She looked up at him. 'How does that make you feel?' she asked softly.

He smiled. She thought he looked happy.

'Olivia said that she considered that she and her friend Alicia had things in common, and I asked what she meant. She said that Alicia had hardly known her natural father; that he had a house in London and spent most of his time there.'

Lucille's lips drew in in astonishment, but she didn't comment.

'And that after he died and her mother married Edward, everyone was happy and felt loved and cared for.' Joseph cleared his throat, for it had suddenly gone husky. 'I've been anxious sometimes, over the years, wondering if we'd really filled the gap left after Olivia lost a mother and father.'

Lucille stopped what she was doing for a moment and wiped her floury fingers on a clean cloth.

'And then,' he went on, 'I realized that she hadn't actually lost them because she'd never known them; that *we'd* replaced them, seamlessly. You and I had become her parents and my mother her grandmother. We were a normal family, except . . .'

'Except?' she queried.

'That you and I weren't married. If we had been, no one would have noticed the difference, especially not Olivia.'

'So there is a difference?' she said, vigorously beating up a batter.

He put his hand over hers to stop her. 'There's no reason why we shouldn't rectify that. I'm a bit slow on the uptake, and to begin with I thought that you were too young to be married – and that you might think I only wanted marriage to secure Olivia.'

She stared at him; that thought had occurred to her. She swallowed. 'And . . . ?'

'And then you opened the bakery and café, so you obviously wanted to stay.' He looked round at the kitchen. He'd put up shelves and cupboards for her equipment and found a large baking table that he'd stripped and scrubbed. 'I helped you secure a loan; you wouldn't accept one from me, and you seemed happy to be doing something for yourself.'

She nodded. She was. She had been.

Joseph gazed at her. 'But I would dearly love to have you as my wife, Lucille,' he said softly. 'Olivia is grown now and needn't be 'full focus of our attention. I love you,' he murmured. 'I always have; I love your accent, your shrugs, your style and most of all your capacity to love a child who came into your life in the way that Olivia did; and I'd like to have some of that love too.' He dropped his gaze and fiddled with his hands and said sheepishly, 'That must be 'longest speech I've ever made.'

The doorbell rang. Molly called out, 'It's onny me. You left 'door open.'

CHAPTER TWENTY-SEVEN

Alicia and Olivia looked for each other as carriages and traps drew in at the school entrance. The arrivals had been staggered; the new and younger pupils had come the previous day so that they would not be overwhelmed while still finding their way about the building, and for this they had the help of some of the senior students who also came in a day early to show them their dormitories and classrooms. For Alicia and Olivia, this would be the last year before they made their final decision on what to do next.

Edward and Joseph arrived at the gates within a few minutes of each other. 'Oh, we should have had a race,' Olivia exclaimed as the two girls hugged each other. 'But we would have won if Pa had raced Captain!' She dipped her knee as Alicia's mother stepped down from the carriage. 'Hello, Mrs Fawcett-Newby. It's nice to see you again,' she said.

'And you too, Olivia. You're looking very well,' Beatrix answered. 'Ah, Miss Leblanc, how are you?' She made a half-turn to greet Lucille, who, as always, was impeccably dressed, and looked particularly vivacious today.

Lucille bent her head in greeting. 'I'm exceedingly well,' she smiled. 'I hope you are too. The summer has been glorious, hasn't it?'

'It has. We had a splendid harvest. I think that Olivia

enjoyed her time with us. She was a great help with the horses; Laurie was most impressed.'

'Ah, well, she has Joseph to thank for that. He put her up on horseback before she could even walk.' Lucille paused. 'I think,' she said hesitantly, 'we have something to discuss – about schooling for our daughters next year?'

'We do,' Beatrix agreed. 'Alicia has brought up the subject of finishing school in Paris several times. You will know of them better than I; I would value your opinion. Could we meet?'

Lucille paused for only a second. 'Of course. That would be lovely. Do you come into Hull often? I could come to you, but possibly only on a Sunday – the bakery, you know, takes up much of my time during the week.'

'Then I'll come to you,' Beatrix said, and again thought how animated Miss Leblanc seemed to be. 'If you choose the day I will come on the train, and perhaps bring Mrs Gordon with me so she can visit her mother? She'll be happy to do that, I'm sure.'

So it was agreed, and whilst Lucille and Beatrix discussed the best day for the planned meeting, Edward and Joseph took their daughters' luggage into the great hall for the porters to take upstairs to the room they were to share for the coming weeks. Beatrix and Lucille followed them, to be greeted by the headmistress, who said she'd been hoping to have a word with them.

It seemed that the previous term Alicia and Olivia had already discussed with their form mistress the possibility of going to a finishing school somewhere abroad. The teacher had said that she didn't know enough about such institutions and advised them to speak to the headmistress, which they had done separately.

'I have had a conversation with Alicia and Olivia about the type of school they thought they might attend abroad, in Paris or Switzerland.' Miss Jenkinson folded her hands precisely in front of her. 'We would be very sad to lose them if they do decide to follow that particular path. They have been a credit to the school and we were looking forward to continuing with them until they leave full-time education. They both have much to offer, and would be fully rounded young women when that happened, much more so than if they should be, erm, *finished*, or tutored only in the refinement of social graces, to be ready if suitable husbands come calling. Not that there is anything wrong with a happy and congenial marriage,' she added hastily.

'Indeed there is not,' Beatrix agreed, wondering if the head-mistress was happy in her own single state. It was worthy, she thought, that she was teaching her students to have ambitions of their own rather than following only what their parents wanted for them. But what was she implying? That their daughters were going to do nothing except wait for dashing young blades to come along? She certainly didn't want that for Alicia, and was fairly sure that Lucille and Joseph wouldn't want that for Olivia either.

Agreeing with Miss Jenkinson that they would give the topic more thought, they walked back out into the autumn sunshine where Joseph and Edward were waiting, and Lucille gave a sudden laugh. 'Miss Jenkinson did not have a mother like mine; she wanted more than anything for me to find a rich husband who would keep her in luxury for the rest of her days.' She turned her gaze to Joseph and tucked her arm in his. 'You will be glad, I think, Joseph, that you won't ever meet her.'

'Oh, Tante – *Mama* – have you told Alicia's parents?' Olivia said in astonishment. 'I've said nothing!'

Beatrix, Edward and Alicia looked from Olivia to Lucille and Beatrix lifted her fine eyebrows questioningly at seeing Lucille and Joseph now arm in arm.

'*Non?* Then you may now, chérie!' Lucille gave a radiant smile. 'But only to people who matter. We don't want a fuss.'

Olivia turned to them, her eyes bright and joyous. 'Papa and Tante Lucille are to be married,' she exclaimed, 'and I can now introduce her as my mother, which is what I have always longed to do, as that is how I think of her.'

'What wonderful news!' Beatrix said warmly, and put out a graceful hand to clasp Lucille's as Edward shook Joseph's hand firmly.

'I always thought you looked married,' he said. 'You seem right together.'

'And my *grand-mère* is deliriously happy,' Olivia went on, 'but I will tell you how it came about when we go to our room, Alicia. It's quite a long story!' She turned again to Edward and Beatrix. 'And I'm to be an attendant,' she said excitedly. 'I've never been to a wedding, although I've seen brides arriving at Holy Trinity and often at St Charles.'

'I'm so thrilled for you.' Alicia dropped a neat curtsey to the couple and then turned to Olivia. 'I was a flower girl for Dora, Mama's assistant, when she married Hallam, and then at Mama and Pa's wedding when it was allowed after Charles's mourning period was over. But that was ages ago.'

More questioning eyebrows were raised and even more smiles. More enquiring too about when and where the marriage would take place, and Lucille and Joseph both said not yet, with Joseph sheepishly explaining that he had only just asked for Lucille's hand in marriage. 'We've had a few topsy-turvy days,' he grinned, 'and to be honest I can hardly believe that it's happening – or what took me so long.'

'And,' Olivia's voice dropped to a murmur, 'I've met my biological father, who turned up on our doorstep. I didn't know him, of course, but Papa and Tante Lucille recognized him immediately, as did Grand-mère.'

She gave a little shrug of pleasure and Beatrix thought she looked very much like Lucille in her mannerisms, even though she had not one drop of French blood as far as she knew.

'He has a wife and a young son, so I have acquired a half-brother called Jamie,' she chatted on. 'I probably won't ever see them again as they're going to live in America where his wife has family, but I hope that they write occasionally.' She pursed her lips and lowered her voice. 'The only people we don't know anything about are my mother's family. Perhaps they were ashamed of their daughter, yet I don't understand why they should have been; Oliver wanted to marry Clara, he told us so, but' – she shook her head – 'they wouldn't allow it.'

There was nothing further anyone could discreetly say on the subject, and after a little more conversation about the summer and the coming autumn, the talk turned to setting off on the return journey. 'Tomorrow we see Laurie and Ambrose off to Pocklington,' Beatrix said. 'The house is going to be quieter with just the twins at home; they have each other for company and rarely need any entertainment.'

Alicia and Olivia then kissed their parents goodbye and drifted off to greet their friends, turning back to wave their hands and blow kisses as the carriages drove away.

'What was that all about?' Edward asked as he and Beatrix followed Joseph's carriage out of the drive and on to the road home.

'What?' Beatrix said.

'Olivia's family? Did I know about that? And what was it you and Miss Leblanc were discussing about the girls and schools?'

Beatrix gave out an exasperated breath. 'You know about *that*.' She reached out and nipped his thigh with her fingers. 'We talked about it when Alicia came home for the summer holidays.'

'Ow!' he said, and grinned. 'I've brought in a harvest since then. How do you expect me to remember such things?'

'Maybe you had your mind on something else,' she said. 'We've had a busy summer.' She put her hand to the brim of her bonnet and pulled it down to shield her eyes from the bright sun as it slipped lower towards the horizon. 'The head-mistress wasn't very happy about Alicia and Olivia leaving to go to a finishing school; she implied that they were too clever and intelligent, and obliquely suggested that some of the schools abroad were only there to train up young ladies in the arts of speaking French, which they do already, flower arranging and conversation . . .'

164

Edward laughed. 'Hah,' he chortled. 'I'd say that neither of them requires lessons in the latter. They are both quite gifted!'

'. . . Particularly in relation to young men,' she finished.

He groaned and looked at her. 'You mean with a view to an advantageous marriage?'

Beatrix didn't answer but only nodded her head and waited for a tirade which didn't come, but she felt the simmering tension as old memories came to the fore.

'You're not seriously considering it, Bea? Surely Alicia is intelligent enough to want more than that? We don't want her going along that well-trodden path.'

'Of course we don't; it isn't a requirement, not for us, and I don't think Miss Leblanc wants that for Olivia either. I don't think she – Miss Leblanc, that is – is as worldly as she appears to be. She had a poor childhood, from what I understand. But what she does want, and I would imagine that Joseph wants it too, is the very best for Olivia.'

'If they are considering that Olivia has been deprived of a better life than they have given her simply because she was born out of wedlock,' Edward said quietly, 'then they are very much mistaken. As far as I can tell she's been given love and kindness all her life by people who didn't even *know* the couple who conceived her.'

Beatrix nodded. 'I believe that is probably why they still want to do their best for her.' She smiled. 'By giving her the compassion and love she deserves rather than sending her to an orphanage when she was just a baby, where she would have had an entirely different life, they have ensured that she has grown up to be a well-rounded young woman. A joy to know.'

CHAPTER TWENTY-EIGHT

'How is it that all our children are leaving us?' Edward said the next morning, looking at the trunks and valises littering the hall as Laurence and Ambrose prepared for their journey back to school, where they were going to be full boarders for the first time.

'Not us, Pa, we're not going,' Luke said earnestly. 'Not me or Izzy. We won't leave you.' He clung to his father's leg and immediately Isolde clung to the other one, whereupon Edward attempted to walk round the hall with a twin stuck on each foot.

'Are you sure?' he said, pretending to dislodge them. 'Ambrose is going too.'

'I'll stay at home if you like, Pa,' Ambrose frowned. 'I've plenty to do here.'

'Oh, yes, please do.' Isolde jumped off her father, ran to Ambrose and clamped on to him like a limpet. Ambrose had grown considerably over the summer, both taller and broader. 'We can help you with the pigs, or Luke can, cos he doesn't mind the mess.'

'Well, maybe when you're a bit bigger,' Ambrose said decisively. 'Looking after a special breed is very important, and besides, you do seem to end up in the sh— mud, don't you, Luke?'

Edward raised his eyebrows significantly. Expressive farmyard

166

language was not allowed inside the house, he had explained to Ambrose when he was still very young, as the boy had a habit of listening to the estate workers and then repeating their sometimes fruity expressions at home. But Ambrose had remembered just in time, probably because his mother was coming down the stairs.

'What's this?' she said. 'Why are all of our children leaving us?' she echoed. 'Pa? Have you been beating them again?'

'No, no!' Luke and Isolde spoke up in unison, as they so often did. 'We're not leaving; it's only Ambrose and Laurie going back to school. I'm going with them, and then I'm going to look after Ambrose's pigs,' Luke added. 'Pa will show me how, and then when I'm old enough I can be second in command, can't I, Amby?'

Ambrose is growing up so fast, Beatrix thought. It's not so long ago that we were all calling him Amby, and now it's only the twins.

Behind her Laurie ran down the stairs; her precious boy who was almost a man. He had been her salvation during the turbulent life she had had with Charles; the child who had given her the courage to remain strong throughout her difficulties.

He put his arms round her and gave her a hug. 'I think I know what I'm going to do with my life after school, Mama,' he whispered. 'I've been thinking about it during the holidays. I want to discuss it with my form teacher first and find out what will be involved, and what studying I'll need to do and how long it will take to achieve the qualifications, for I know nothing about it; and then I'll go through it all with you and Pa.'

She kissed his cheek. She could smell the soap that he used and saw the slight shadowy down on his upper lip and chin. Her son was growing up.

'You must do as you think best,' she whispered back. 'You know that we will support you in whatever decision you make. Take your time; there's no hurry.'

He smiled down at her. He was a good head and shoulders taller than she was. Darker hair too, not the blond he once had. 'Thank you,' he murmured. 'I want to make you both proud.'

'Right, then.' Edward clapped his hands. 'Who else is coming? We'll take the old clarence, plenty of room in there for the luggage and an extra child. How many boys have we got?'

'Three at the last count,' Beatrix said, and Ambrose asked, 'Who's sitting on top? Is Aaron driving, cos I'd like to sit next to him if he is.'

Beatrix glanced down at Isolde and saw her bottom lip quivering. 'Would you like to go too, darling?'

'Yes, please,' the little girl said in a tearful whisper. 'Are you coming, Mama?'

'Shall we both go?' Beatrix asked her. 'I will if you will.'

Isolde jumped up and down. 'Yes, please, or I'll be the last one here.'

'We're not leaving Luke there, sweetheart,' her mother assured her. 'We'll be bringing him home again; he's not ready for school yet. Perhaps in a year or two we'll have a look again at schools for both of you? But I'm not sure if I'm ready to lose my babies yet. Come on, let's fetch our coats and bonnets.'

They all piled into the carriage. Edward had said he would drive and had given Aaron the afternoon off to do whatever he wanted, though he knew that the younger man would find a job to do. His work was here, and although he sometimes drove into Hessle to catch up with people he knew, and always drove his mother home in the evening after her duties in the kitchen were finished, he considered his place was at Old Stone Hall, where he had two very comfortable rooms above the stable block which had a window with curtains that his aunt Mags had made and two comfy chairs and a bed that Beatrix had given him, and ate his meals in the kitchen with the other members of staff.

Ambrose and Luke sat up in the driving seat with Edward. Ambrose couldn't wait to learn to drive the carriage, especially now he'd reached thirteen; he was allowed to drive the single horse trap about the estate or even down to the village, but not two horses. Edward was always concerned about their children's safety. Laurie sat at his mother's side and Isolde sat next to the window so she could look out and wave to people she saw.

'It's like an adventure, isn't it?' Isolde spoke up as they set off, and Laurie smiled, and said it was.

'What would you like to do when you're as old as Alicia?' he asked her. 'I know you're very good at reading.'

'Yes, I am,' she said, without any trace of modesty. 'And numbers, but I'm going to be an artist, like Esmond, Aunt Rosie's husband. Or else I might be a pianist and play in concerts for people; for money,' she added, and her mother hid her smile behind her glove.

'I wish I could have been so sure when I was Isolde's age,' Laurie murmured.

'You weren't so very much older than she is when you inherited the estate,' his mother said softly.

'I remember,' he nodded, 'and I remember feeling scared about the prospect of it; I simply didn't understand what it meant. I thought I'd have to work in a bank like my father – Charles – and only come home now and again.'

'You were only eight.' She squeezed his hand. 'How could you be expected to know? But you have a choice now, and there's still no urgency for you to decide.'

'Some of my school friends have already decided. Jonathon is going to teach history, and a few of the others have decided on teaching too, but I don't want to do that.' He opened up his hands and stretched his fingers wide. His hands were broad and strong, and she thought that he could become a farmer if life took him that way.

'Have you thought any more about horse breeding?' she asked. 'You fell in love with Mr Snowden's horse, didn't you?'

'I did.' He laughed. 'But then I realized that horse breeding was a career for someone older; someone more experienced who had perhaps made some money and was able to afford to do it. But what I have in mind now will give me experience and a good vocation if I have the aptitude and ability.'

Beatrix put her head on one side. 'Yes?'

Laurie hesitated. If he spoke of it too early, would it come to pass? Would he be clever enough or competent enough to complete the long study?

He took the plunge. 'I'd like to become a veterinary surgeon, specializing in horses and probably cattle too.'

Beatrix breathed out. She would never have guessed, but of course it made sense. When Laurie was given his first pony, he was meticulous in caring for him, running his hands down his back and legs, checking his feet and hooves; in fact, Charles on one of his rare visits had once laughingly called him the horse doctor, and Laurie had been embarrassed and didn't do it again in front of him.

'How wonderful,' she said. 'That would suit you so well!'

'Do you think so?' Laurie looked at her eagerly. 'Do you think I'd be up to it? I'd need to get excellent results in my exams to qualify for the college; there are two, one in London and one in Scotland. I've looked them up in the school library and there's been a Royal Charter for about twenty years, but the veterinary profession itself has been established for over a century.'

Beatrix felt a warm glow as Laurie spoke eagerly and enthusiastically about what he had learned about the profession and said that if he passed the entrance exam he'd like to go to London and maybe he could stay at his grandparents' house – his mother's parents, that is, not his Dawley grandparents, as they never saw or heard anything of them and they could be dead for all anyone knew.

Beatrix had nodded or shaken her head as she listened. He had obviously been considering this for some time but hadn't been willing to talk about it until it was clear in his mind. Now he was driven by enthusiasm at the prospect that his expectations could be realized, and she was sharing in those hopes.

As for the Dawley grandparents, Charles's parents, it was

true that they never wrote, not even to ask about the children. That hurt her; she didn't expect them to be interested in her, not since she married Edward, but Laurence, Alicia and Ambrose were their kin. It would be Charles's mother, she suspected, who would have decided to cut them off. She was a spiteful, vindictive woman who hadn't cared for her own son, let alone his children.

She gave herself a mental shake; why was her former mother-in-law still a thorn in her side? Forget her, she thought, and Alfred Dawley too. He, she imagined, had probably taken offence when they had changed their name, for he would almost certainly have heard about it.

Some years before Charles died, his sister Anne, well over the age when she could have expected to marry, had come into an inheritance and run away from home, seeking refuge with Beatrix for one night only as she fled to France, taking the long route via Hull to Holland and across the continent in case her parents should search for her. Beatrix had received one postcard from her to say she had arrived at her destination; and then silence.

She sighed. As Edward would say so succinctly, *We're well rid of them.*

CHAPTER TWENTY-NINE

Edward trundled into Hessle to the blacksmith's in a lopsided cart pulled by a single horse, hoping the loose cartwheel wouldn't fall off before he got there and tip him out.

He pulled up safely outside the smithy a few minutes later and was relieved to see that the fire was lit and the smith in his leather apron was forging something on his anvil. Behind him, above the red-hot furnace and very neatly set out on the stone walls, were racks and hooks and shelves of equipment, the tools of his trade: hammers, tongs and chisels, and various other iron implements the use or name of which was unknown to him. Nothing seemed to change here; he remembered coming on errands as a boy for his father and Neville Dawley.

'Morning, Edward.' The smith had barely looked up, but clearly he had seen him pull up outside. 'What can I do for thee?'

'Lost a linchpin,' Edward said. 'The wheel's hanging off. Can you fix it while I wait?'

The smith took a step back and carefully laid down the tool he was using before coming towards him. 'Is this 'same cart that young Aaron uses?'

'Aye, Jack, it is. It's a very useful little cart,' Edward said, 'and nice and light for old Harry to pull, but the wheel's been wobbly for a while.'

Jack bent down to take a look. 'Aye, I thought so. I've fixed it several times. I 'ave a mind that you sh'd think on spending some brass and get a new wheel fitted. This is done for; 'wheel's completely cracked and 'd be better use on 'bonfire.' He straightened up. 'You'll need to step over to 'wheelwright and give him a bit o' work.'

Edward shrugged. 'If that's your expert opinion then that's what I'll do. Will it get me across to him before dropping off?'

'I reckon so, but you'll do better pushing it over while I tek a look to see if yon old hoss needs shoeing.'

Edward thought that it wasn't long since the aged animal had been shoed, but he was quite willing to let the smith take a look and do what was necessary, because he knew he'd give old Harry a nosebag of oats whilst he was doing it.

'I saw your lad not long ago,' Jack went on, as he uncoupled the horse from its traces. 'Your eldest. He passed by, but I was busy at 'time, so couldn't stop to talk. Fine-looking lad. Teks after his ma, I reckon.'

Edward smiled. People had almost forgotten about the Dawley connection; they only knew that he, born and brought up in North Ferriby, had married the young London widow, and as few of the village people had ever even seen Charles it was assumed that all the children were his. He was perfectly happy with that perception.

He trundled the cart across the street and round the corner towards the wheelwright, hoping he'd be able to accommodate him; otherwise he'd have to lead Harry and walk home as he was too heavy to ride on the horse's old bones. He only kept him as he was sentimental over the animals, which was not a usual trait amongst farmers.

'Well, this is a comedown.' He heard a voice behind him. 'Hard times, old boy?'

He turned to view the speaker and saw someone, younger than him, whom he didn't recognize. He dropped the cart and waited. 'Sorry – I don't . . . ?

'You don't remember me? Well, it has been a long time. James Highcliffe-Rand, though I only use Rand nowadays.'

'Good heavens.' Edward put out his hand. 'A voice from the past.' Edward hadn't seen James Rand for many years; he'd been only a boy when he dropped out of view following a family altercation, or so Edward had been told by his mother. He'd hardly known him, as he was much younger than he was, although he knew his sister Amelia.

'How are you?' he asked. 'Back in the district, or . . . ?' He tried desperately to recall what Mags had told him, but the details escaped him.

'I'm well, thanks,' James said, and joked, 'Faring better than you are, by the look of your broken-down old handcart. I'd heard you'd married a rich young widow!'

James's eyes looked red and swollen, and Edward noticed that he didn't look well, even though he said he was. 'I did,' he answered. 'Where are you living these days?'

'York,' he mumbled. 'I say, have you time for a beer?'

'Erm, yes. Can do. I'm just taking this into the wheelwright's; hang on a minute, will you?'

Edward went into the wheelwright's shop and left the cart with him after asking if it could be repaired or a new wheel fitted. He was told something could be done and to come back in half an hour.

'That's a relief,' he told James, as the two men crossed over the square to the Admiral Hawke inn. 'I didn't want to walk home.'

Inside, both men ordered a glass of stout. 'I heard some time ago that you were back in the district,' Edward said. 'Was that after your father died? I thought you'd come back to run the estate, but I've never seen you.'

James Rand first nodded and then shook his head. Each man was wearing a frothy moustache from the creamy head of the stout.

'I left home. Gave up school – I was sixteen and I couldn't bear to live at home any longer, certainly not whilst my father was alive. I did all kinds of work, odd jobs, clerking mostly, just to pay for board and lodgings, although Amelia sent me money now and again, even though she didn't have much herself. Our father always kept us short, miserly beggar!

'Then I started as a solicitor's clerk and eventually became senior clerk; I only came back to Hessle once, to sort out the estate after my father died. I'd kept in touch with Amelia and I knew that one day I'd have to come home and deal with it. Everything was in chaos after my sister died. Father just gave up. He couldn't cope, ignored everything; and my mother wouldn't even speak of her.'

Edward had lost the gist of what he was talking about; he seemed to be rambling. He shook his head. 'Hang on. I don't know anything about another sister,' he said. 'She died? I'm sorry, but I can't say I remember her. I only knew Amelia.'

James sighed. 'Poor Amelia. She's taken the brunt of it all, coping with Father's bitterness and anger and Mother's disapproval of everything and everybody. Amelia has no life of her own, and I'm sorry to say I don't really help her, although I did give her a hand with sorting out Father's affairs after he died. Otherwise, I only come back once or twice a year and Amelia and I keep in touch by letter.'

'I'm sorry,' Edward said again. 'I didn't know. I haven't seen Amelia for some time. Beatrix has met her once or twice through Rosie Stokes; and I think your mother invited her to call when she first came to live here. Beatrix was a Londoner, born and bred, though you wouldn't know it now; she's a dyed-in-the-wool country woman! Tell you what, why don't I ask her to invite you and Amelia and Rosie and Esmond over for supper – or perhaps you're married . . . ? I don't really keep up with social chatter.'

James took a breath. 'Between you and me, Edward, I've been married for five years. Amelia knows, but I haven't told my mother. Ellen and I live in York and she has never once been here; she never met my father and hasn't met my mother – or Amelia, who is longing to meet her. We have a son, and another child on the way. Amelia begged me not to tell my mother in case it sets her back to how she was when

Clara died. She was totally deranged, and is still unable to comprehend that we were devastated by her loss too. Mother thinks that she's the only one who suffers, and blames everyone but herself or our father for what happened.'

Edward glanced at the clock above the bar. He'd have to leave soon. There were jobs waiting for him and his half-hour would soon be up.

'Clara was your other sister? Do you mind my asking what did happen, or would you rather not talk about it?'

James looked across at him. 'You really don't know, do you? Maybe it's only women who hear the gossip. The village tom-toms have been silenced. Well, she might have had influenza – at least that was the story my parents put about – but she died following childbirth. She and her . . .' he paused, 'her lover were running away to Scotland to be married, because our parents wouldn't allow it. She was only seventeen.' Edward heard the break in his voice and saw how his eyes became moist. 'About the age the child will be now. The child we never saw.'

'It?' Edward said. 'You don't know if it was a boy or girl?'

James shook his head. 'No. Clara had begun in labour as they were being driven to Hull's railway station, and the cabbie took them to his own home and sent for a midwife. That's where she gave birth – in this fellow's house – and then this same fellow drove back from Hull and came to tell us what had happened and ask if we would take care of the child. My father's response was unrepeatable, although in the end he did agree to arrange to have Clara's body brought home for burial. I wish I could remember the name on the carriage; the cabbie was so concerned.'

His face was awash with tears. 'You see, Edward,' he brought out a large white handkerchief and wiped his face and blew his nose, 'this is why I rarely come back; I just can't bear it. I'm so sorry,' he muttered. 'I've just been to visit her grave, and it's so hard, and yet I know that I must talk about it to those I can trust, just to clear my own head, or I'll never have a life of my own.'

There was nothing that Edward could say. How hard it must

have been to be put in such a dreadful position when he was too young to stand up to his father or help his sister. There must be so much more to this wretched story of young love – and somewhere the child at the centre of it, abandoned by its family and put out to strangers.

CHAPTER THIRTY

'We were going to start without you,' Beatrix said as Edward bounded up the kitchen steps to the hall.

'Sorry.' He kissed her cheek. 'I've told Aunt Hilda I'm back. She says that everything is just about ready for serving.'

'Where have you been? The house is quiet enough without you being absent.'

'Luke and Isolde?' he asked. 'Where are they?'

'They'll be down in a minute. Isolde has been practising the piano and Luke has been boring his tutor with details of pig breeding: the poor man's only just managed to escape after making the excuse that he would miss his train. So where have you been?'

They heard the luncheon bell and Edward turned towards the stairs to go up and wash his hands and face and change his shirt. 'To Hessle,' he called over his shoulder. 'I was coaxed into buying two cart wheels instead of one, and then I met someone. Tell you about it shortly.'

When he came back down, followed by the twins, he had a question to ask. 'Beatrix,' he said, 'would you mind if we just had a sandwich or a piece of pie at lunchtime – lowance,' he grinned, 'seeing as there are just the four of us? I need to work in the afternoons, and having a hearty lunch doesn't put me in the mood for it.'

'Today, do you mean?' she asked. 'Or on most days?'

He nodded. 'On most days. Or if you and the children want to eat more substantially then you should, and I won't mind eating in the kitchen, or from a tray. It's what I used to do.'

'Not for a long time you haven't. What's brought this up?' she queried. 'We've always had lunch together.'

'I know we have,' he agreed. 'It's just that I've spent time chatting to people in Hessle this morning and now I'll be late for my afternoon jobs after having lunch, whereas just a plate of bread and beef—'

'You need more help, then,' she interrupted. 'You're supposed to be in charge, not to be doing jobs like driving into Hessle with a wobbly cart wheel. Where was Aaron?'

'Doing something else. I didn't realize just how much I relied on Laurie and Ambrose during the holidays. Especially with the pigs and the horses.'

Beatrix began serving up lunch that Kitty brought in. 'If they go away to university or farming college they won't be here much at all,' she replied sensibly. 'So you need a second Aaron, don't you?'

'My father always managed on his own, even after I'd gone away to college.'

'That was quite different and you know it,' she admonished him. 'He didn't have the acreage we have, or the number of animals. Where's Hallam?'

'He's gone over to see one of the tenants. Anyway, he isn't hands-on, he's the manager.' He changed the subject. 'Dora looked a little peaky when I came through the kitchen. Is she all right?'

'Dora? Is she here? It's not her usual day for coming in. I'll pop down when we've finished. We've got an under-cook coming for an interview today.'

'Under-cook? Really? Why? What does Aunt Hilda think of that? Not much, I shouldn't think!'

'On the contrary; she was the one who asked. She didn't want a kitchen maid; she asked if she could have someone who could take over the cooking if she couldn't do it.'

'Is she not well? She hasn't said, has she? Ma will know.'

'She said the days were long. She walks in from Hessle in a morning; she won't let Aaron pick her up, as she says it takes him from his duties, though he does drive her home at night.'

'I keep thinking,' he mused. 'If Ma moved up into my cottage . . .'

Beatrix smiled. 'Your bolt hole?'

When she had first met Edward he was living in the original Home Farm cottage where he and his sisters had been brought up, and his parents had moved down to another nearer to Old Stone Hall so that they could look after Neville Dawley as he became older and more infirm. Edward had then built on to the original cottage, making a substantial family home despite living in it as a single man.

'Not any more it isn't,' he laughed, 'but it's always been a special place.'

'It has, hasn't it?' Her eyes sparkled, and Edward leaned towards her and squeezed her hand. The cottage had been special to both of them, for Beatrix had been invited to visit with her three children when she was almost out of mourning for Charles, and it was there that she and Edward had declared their love for each other.

'If Ma moved up then Aunt Hilda could move in with her,' Edward said after a moment, reverting to the matter on hand. 'They are sisters after all, and they'd be company for each other.' He finished his meal and rose from the table. 'Shall I mention it or will you?'

'I will,' she said. 'I'll ask your mother first. She's the one who would be offering to share her home.'

He nodded and turned to the twins. 'All right, you two. What's on the agenda this afternoon?'

'Pigs,' they chorused. 'I promised Amby we'd look after them,' Luke added.

Isolde nudged him in the ribs. '*Ambrose*,' she said. 'We haven't to call him Amby now he's at school. Excuse us, please?' she said, getting up from her chair. 'Thank you, Mama.'

'Rubber boots,' their mother called after them, 'and old coats.'

They both nodded and dashed away. 'We seem to be turning into pig farmers,' Beatrix said, as Edward too went out of the door. 'Was that our intention?' As he left she realized that he hadn't said who he'd seen in Hessle.

The door had no sooner closed behind them than a maid came in to clear away the dishes, closely followed by a rather pale-faced Dora.

'Are you all right, Dora?' Beatrix said in concern. Dora was usually energetic and always busy, and Beatrix was anxious that she seemed so lethargic. In any case, this wasn't one of her working days. 'Let's go in the sitting room.'

'I'm a bit out of sorts,' Dora said, as they went next door. 'Maybe there's something going about. Cook doesn't feel well either, but I think she's just tired. She never takes time off.'

'There won't be so much cooking to do now that half the family has temporarily left home,' Beatrix said. 'Come and sit down. Have you had lunch? Would you like some coffee or tea?'

Dora gave a shudder as she took a chair. 'I can't face either at the minute,' she said. 'It just turns my stomach.'

Beatrix turned slowly towards her. 'Dora!'

Dora lifted her head, a questioning look on her face.

'Have you, erm, have you seen the doctor?'

'No. I'm never ill. It'll just be a bug that's going around, I expect. The new under-cook has arrived; that's why I came up from the kitchen. Cook asked her to come after lunch when she'd have a bit of time to talk to her. She seems all right. She's not a girl, but she's not all that old either. Middle twenties, I should think. A young widow.'

'I haven't met her yet,' Beatrix said. 'I wanted Hilda to be comfortable with her understudy, so to speak. I still haven't quite grasped why she wanted any help, it's not like her. She can have time off whenever she wants, surely she knows that.'

Dora nodded. 'I'm sure she does. But she won't ask. She says she doesn't like to be a bother.' She suddenly stood up and grasped the back of the chair to steady herself. 'I came in today to see if there was anything to do, I was that bored with my own company, but I think I might go home if you don't need me for anything, ma'am?'

Beatrix smiled. 'I don't for the moment, Mrs Hallam,' she said drily. They had known each other for so long and yet Dora never forgot her place, and sometimes Beatrix wished that she would. She owed so much to her; she couldn't have had anyone better by her side in some of her past dark days.

'You'll see the doctor, won't you, if you don't feel any better?' she said, as Dora turned for the door. 'And tell Hallam. Don't hide anything from him if you're feeling unwell.'

Dora paused. 'Tell Hallam?' Her eyebrows lifted and then she gave a little frown. 'What should I tell him? It's only a touch of – of – nausea.' She put her hand to her mouth and her eyes widened. 'Do you think . . . ?'

Beatrix lifted her hands and shoulders in a shrug. 'I don't know,' she said. 'But I thought you might.'

Dora eased her way back to the chair and sat down again. 'I never check,' she whispered. 'I've never thought I'd need to, it's been so long.'

Beatrix stood up. 'Come along,' she said authoritatively. 'Let's find Aaron and he can take you home.'

Aaron was driving down the hill. The pig unit was halfway down one of the fields and he could see Luke and Isolde within the enclosure, running about trying to catch one of the piglets. He drove through a gate into the field towards them and saw Isolde slide and trip and heard her shout.

'Oh, great heavens,' he moaned out loud. 'What a pair!' He gave a laugh and then saw Isolde get up and immediately fall down again on to her hands and knees and Luke doubling over with laughter.

He jumped out of the trap and fastened the reins to a fence post. 'Hey, come out of there, you young varmints.'

The children looked up and Isolde held her hands wide apart. They were brown with something and it might or might not have been mud. Aaron ran round to the gate and into the field pen. 'Come on, 'pair of you. Let's have you home for a swill down afore your ma sees you, and for heaven's sake don't you dare touch me.' He shook a threatening finger at them. 'Back door for a swill down under 'tap.'

'*No-o!*' Isolde shrieked. 'The water's cold!'

He took the pair to the back door. Isolde was in a far worse mess than Luke. Aaron put his hand on the pump handle and grabbed her with the other so she didn't run away. 'Open 'door, Luke,' he called, and the boy did so, almost hysterical with laughter at the state of his sister. Aaron began to unbutton her dress down the back to take it off and bellowed through the open door, 'I've got a child here covered in pig shit. Can someone give us a hand?'

A face appeared at the window and he heard a voice he didn't recognize say in a shocked tone, 'Cook! There's a man outside taking a frock off a little girl!'

His mother came to the door and behind her a young woman stared out at him; he stared back as if he had never seen the like of her before. Her eyes were sky blue and her hair as red as a sunset. He took a breath, then blew it out and pushed Isolde towards the pump, holding her arms under the water and then her body whilst she shrieked and pushed against him.

His mother tutted and went back inside, while the young woman took her place and leaned against the door frame, folding her arms in front of her.

'Well, come and help me then,' he said. 'Don't just stand there, whoever you are.'

'No fear,' she said, and he saw a trace of the grin that she was trying to contain. 'And you'd better get under 'pump yourself, cos you're not coming into this nice clean kitchen in that state.'

She turned suddenly as someone appeared behind her, and he saw her dip her knee.

'What's happening?' Beatrix came to the door. 'Oh, my goodness. Isolde! Whatever have you been up to?' She dissolved into laughter. 'Don't let her inside, Aaron! Will someone go and rummage for an old sheet or towel, please?'

CHAPTER THIRTY-ONE

'Who was that?' Sally Hawke asked as Cook invited her to sit down at the kitchen table and poured tea from a large brown pot into two large cups. From where she was standing, she could see Aaron handing Isolde over to Beatrix.

'That's 'mistress, Mrs Fawcett-Newby,' Cook said. 'And next to her is Mrs Hallam – Dora, we call her – who came down wi' big sheet to wrap Isolde in. Dora's 'wife of 'estate manager and 'companion to 'mistress. She's been here ever since 'mistress came from London to live here.'

'Ah!' Sally Hawke murmured. 'And the man who brought the little girl into 'yard and put her under 'pump? Is she his daughter?'

Cook looked at her, noticed her wedding ring, and sat down and cradled her cup. 'That's Aaron, my son. He's been here since he was thirteen; first person Miz Beatrix took on, on 'day she arrived after her wedding.'

Sally frowned. 'Whose wedding?'

'Mrs Fawcett-Newby's.' Cook frowned. 'Her first marriage, to Mr Dawley. Are you not from round here?'

Sally shook her head. 'No, I'm not. I'm originally from Cottingham, near Beverley, you know?'

'Heard of it,' Cook said. 'Never been. Allus lived round here. Born and brought up in Hessle. I still live there.'

'I worked in a big house in Hessle a year or two back. I went as cook, but 'mistress was a nightmare to work for. I couldn't do a thing right. It wasn't just me; she could never keep staff. Pity, though, cos her daughter was lovely.'

'Who was it?' Cook asked.

'Mrs Highcliffe-Rand. Even her son had left home, so I was told.'

'Oh, aye. She was allus known to be difficult. So how did you find us?'

She used *us* in a familiar way, as if everyone was part of the family.

'Someone I know works at a house nearby and told me you were looking for temporary help in 'kitchen, so I thought I'd apply.'

'Ah, do you mean Rosie and her mother?' Cook smiled. 'Rosie – her mother is Mrs Stokes, can't remember Rosie's married name, but everybody calls her Rosie – she's a friend of Mrs Fawcett-Newby.'

'So is there a Mr Fawcett-Newby?' Sally asked.

'Oh aye, course there is; he's my nephew Edward. My sister Mags Newby's son. Edward is Aaron's cousin.'

Sally took a deep breath and was about to ask another question, but then changed her mind. This was the most unusual household she had ever come across. If she was accepted as under-cook, and she hoped that she would be, then she would find out about all the relationships. 'So did you say that the little girl was Aaron's?' she couldn't help but ask.

Cook gazed at her. 'No, I didn't say that. That's Isolde, and 'little lad is her twin brother Luke, and they're 'youngest children of Mr and Mrs Fawcett-Newby. Our Aaron isn't married.' She leaned forward and put her cup on the table. 'So, Mrs Hawke, now you know all about us, what can you tell us about you?'

'There's not a lot to tell, Cook,' Sally answered, casting a glance out of the window behind the cook's back. Mrs Fawcett-Newby had disappeared with the children and Aaron was pulling his wet shirt over his head.

He had a broad back, she noticed, and muscular arms which were not apparent when he was wearing his outer clothes. He opened the back door and dropped the shirt into a basket in the lobby and then turned back and walked away as if he were going round to the side of the house; probably towards stables or barns, she thought. Then he turned and saw her watching and gave her a sly wink.

'Are you owt to do wi' the Admiral Hawke inn?' Cook asked her. 'The one in Hessle?'

Sally shook her head. 'I wish I had sixpence for every time anybody asked me, but no, not as far as I know. Hawke was my husband's name. My name was Brown. There are quite a few Browns in Cottingham. I'm a widow, I might as well tell you now. I met Mr Hawke when I was nineteen. He was a widower and needed a wife to look after him. My ma and me didn't get on and I wanted to leave home but she said she needed me for doing chores. Then Mr Hawke asked her if he could marry me and he'd make sure that she – Ma, that is – wanted for nothing, so they agreed it between them.'

'How old was this man?' Cook asked, affronted by the idea. 'It sounds very odd, it's like selling your own daughter.'

'He was nearly forty,' Sally said, 'but I wasn't against the idea. I thought him a better option than staying with my ma.'

She looked sideways at Cook, and lowered her voice so that no one else could hear if they should come in. 'As it happens, he didn't need much from me, only cooking and cleaning, and I liked cooking.' She gave a little smile. 'It turned out that he didn't have much money either, so he could only give Ma a pittance, which didn't please her, but I got to have my own roof over my head and do as I pleased, more or less, but then he popped his clogs just over two years later. There wasn't enough money left for me to live on, not even after I'd sold all his belongings, and it was a rented house, but I was over twenty-one so I could please myself and didn't have to go back and live wi' Ma, so I looked for work as a live-in cook . . . and that's my story.'.

She sat back against the cane chair and pressed her lips together. 'I'd like to find somewhere permanent so I can get settled, you know? I'm twenty-five now and I'm not one for going from place to place. I'm a plain cook, but a good bread maker, my fruitcakes are full o' fruit and I can make a roast dinner and Yorkshire puddings that float on air!'

Cook smiled. She liked this sharp, lively young woman and thought she would do. She'd have to talk to the mistress first, of course, but she'd tell her she thought her suitable.

She called for Kitty, and from behind the staircase door asked her to ask the mistress whether she would see the applicant for the under-cook position and, in a murmuring whisper, to tell her Mrs Hawke was suitable.

Sally wandered outside as she waited for the maid to return, so was there when Aaron reappeared wearing a clean shirt and trousers, on his way to bring the horse and trap down from the field where he'd left them.

'Hello,' he grinned. 'You're still here. Are you waiting to see somebody?'

She nodded. 'Mrs Fawcett-Newby. I'm applying for work as under-cook, under your ma,' she added.

'How do you know she's my ma?'

'She told me. Told me you'd been here since you were thirteen and were 'first employee Mrs Fawcett-Newby ever had.'

She appraised him, looking him up and down from his boots to the top of his head, and with an ironic grin he turned round and held out both arms so that she could look at him from behind. Then he turned back to face her and folded his arms in front of him. 'So what's your name, miss?'

'Sally Hawke,' she said, lifting her chin, 'and it's Mrs.'

She waited for the disappointment to show on his face as it had on so many other men's when she'd told them, but she had to wait a little longer with Aaron, who said, 'He couldn't tame you then? Upped and left, did he?'

A slow minute passed before she said, 'Yeh! Wore him out.' But a twitch of her lips betrayed her and she said truthfully,

'Died from a lifelong illness. Poor Arthur. He wasn't a bad sort.'

'Widowed, then?' She lowered her eyes and he saw the golden lashes. 'Need someone to look after you?'

She hesitated and then shook her head. 'No,' she whispered so quietly that he could barely make out her words. 'I can look after myself; but I'd like someone to care for me.'

He nodded towards the door. 'Maid's looking for you,' he murmured, and she turned away and went inside.

Shall I wait, he wondered? Would I seem too eager? Aye, I would, he thought. I'll do what I was asked to do and take Dora home. He set off up the field whistling, and the mare fastened to the fence whinnied back at him. 'I'm coming, I'm coming,' he called to her. 'I do have other fish to fry, you know.'

Sally Hawke waited in the hall. Kitty had said that Mrs Fawcett-Newby would be down in a minute, and within moments Beatrix appeared on the landing and came down the stairs.

'I'm sorry to keep you,' she said, smiling warmly. 'There's never a dull moment in this house. Isolde is soaking in a bath, as she didn't smell very savoury, and I won't say that the house is generally more peaceful than this, because it wouldn't be true!' She opened the door into the sitting room. 'We have three other children who are presently at school; they're older than the twins, but nevertheless we are still quite a rowdy household. I always warn potential staff so that they're aware that this is a family home above all else.'

'How lovely,' Sally said, without thinking. 'I've worked for people in grand houses before and 'servants have always had to creep about so as not to disturb anyone so 'family can pretend they're not there.'

'It isn't like that here,' Beatrix told her, 'not in the least. So come and sit down and tell me about yourself.'

CHAPTER THIRTY-TWO

Beatrix had not yet made the journey into Hull to meet Lucille so that they could discuss the girls' future plans. The week after they had gone back to school she wrote a postcard to Lucille, suggesting she could call the following Sunday if it would be convenient. Mrs Gordon had said she would travel with her on the train, which would be sensible, Beatrix thought, even though fretting that it was ridiculous that it wasn't considered proper for her to travel alone, even on a Sunday, when it would be quiet. But it would at least save Dora the journey. Dora was still rather unwell, and although she hadn't told any of the staff that she was pregnant most of them had guessed and were thrilled for her, as was Hallam, she'd told Beatrix.

'When are you going to start calling him Simon?' Beatrix had said. 'Or perhaps you do,' she'd added.

'I do, at home,' Dora had said. 'But it's easier if I say Hallam in front of everyone else or they might wonder who Simon was!'

Lucille replied that Sunday would be perfect, and although the town would be quiet and there wouldn't be any shops open they could sit in her café and have coffee and cakes without being disturbed. She added that Joseph would meet Beatrix at the station and drive her to the café.

The weather, although sunny and bright, was becoming

colder, and Beatrix dressed in a warm coat and hat for her visit to Hull. Isolde had begged to be allowed to go with her, but she said no, not this time. She knew the child would become bored and fidgety, and she told her that there would be no shops open for her to look at.

'You could go to the church service, of course,' she murmured, 'but you'd have to stay until the service was over whilst I speak to Miss Leblanc, and it isn't like going to Sunday school.'

Isolde immediately changed her mind and said she would ask Papa if she could help him instead; he was going to take out some of the old trees in the orchard.

'Be sure to remind him that he mustn't take down the trees with mistletoe on them, won't you?' her mother said, even whilst knowing that Edward wouldn't. He had been the one who had pointed out to her the massive bunches that grew so thickly in the trees when she had first come to live in the house, so many years ago. She only mentioned the mistletoe now to make Isolde aware of it.

The journey was quick and uneventful, and true to their arrangement Joseph Snowden was waiting outside the station concourse. Whenever Beatrix came to Hull by train she always glanced at the rear of the hotel where she and her mother, coming from London for the very first visit with Charles to look at her prospective home, had rested and enjoyed a welcome pot of tea before continuing on their journey to North Ferriby.

Mrs Gordon set off to walk to her mother's house, saying she would meet Beatrix back at the station for the two o'clock train, and it was barely five minutes before Joseph's carriage arrived at Holy Trinity, the oldest parish church in England, where the bells were ringing out to encourage the worshippers who were hurrying towards it. Joseph pulled across the square towards Lucille's teashop, where the blinds were drawn to show it was closed, but she opened the door just as Joseph was reaching up to hand Beatrix down from the carriage, as if she had known exactly when they would arrive.

'I'm sorry it is only a short visit,' Lucille said, taking Beatrix's coat and hanging it on a peg. 'Life is always so busy, I'm sure you'll agree. But we can have a nice chat, and as it is almost time for luncheon I have made some savouries and cakes that we can eat as we talk, and of course there is always coffee. You will excuse my mode of dress?' She described with her hands the cap on her head and the long apron she was wearing over her clothes.

Beatrix smiled. 'I can't work out how you remain chic even when you are working. It's a French flair, I'm sure of it,' she said boldly, having been taught by her mother that it wasn't polite to comment on someone's appearance. It's strange, she often thought, how our mothers' teaching always rings in our ears – those of us who choose to listen, that is. I always did, and I hope that my children do too.

'Thank you,' Lucille said. 'You are kind.'

Beatrix shook her head. 'Truthful!'

Lucille brought in a glass tray of savouries and pastries and a steaming pot of coffee, and then took off her apron and cap.

Beatrix's mouth watered. She had eaten an early breakfast with Edward as she always did, and sometimes she had a small second breakfast with the children, but never anything like the one in front of her.

As Lucille poured the coffee, she chose a pain aux raisins but also eyed her absolute favourite, canelés, caramelized pastries with a hint of vanilla which melted in the mouth. When pressed to have one, she regretfully refused, saying it would be far too greedy, and Lucille said she would pack some for her to take home. Then they began the discussion which was the reason for the meeting.

'I must tell you, Mrs Fawcett-Newby—'

'Beatrix, please!'

Lucille nodded. 'I must tell you, Beatrix, that I know very little about finishing school, as the English call it. When I finished school it was because my mother said that I must. My father would have said that I must stay on to complete my education, for I was intelligent,' she said frankly, 'but, alas, he died and so my mother made the decision for me. We had little money, so I must work.' She gave a little shrug. 'But not as a pastry chef. That was not an option for me.'

'I do understand,' Beatrix murmured. 'Girls and young women are not generally asked what they would like to do with their lives. It's assumed that they will either work' – fortunately that wasn't a necessity for me, she thought – 'or marry and be kept by their husbands. It's the usual thing for most of us, I think, no matter where we live in the world. I went to boarding school for a short time,' she added, 'as Olivia and Alicia are doing at present.' There is really no need to mention my early marriage to Charles, she considered. That is for some other time.

'I see,' Lucille said quietly. 'We have come from different worlds, I think.'

'Different, and yet in some ways very similar.' She took a quick breath. 'After thinking over what the headmistress said, I am reassessing the idea of Alicia's moving abroad to finish her schooling. You and Mr Snowden will have your own opinions and decisions to make about Olivia, of course, but some of Alicia's letters home have given me an inkling that perhaps she has changed her mind!'

'Olivia too,' Lucille exclaimed. 'They have talked about this together, I think. Olivia is already a French speaker so does not require that study, and if she chooses to marry she will also choose her own husband. No one will force her in that direction. She knows her own mind.'

'Good, so we are both of the same opinion,' Beatrix agreed. 'I have, however, been making some enquiries, and if Alicia or Olivia should want to continue in one of the professions or some other vocation it might be possible to take examinations for university.'

'If that is what they want to do,' Lucille said slowly. 'Olivia, at least, will want to choose for herself.'

Beatrix nodded. 'Alicia too.'

On the train journey home Beatrix was quiet, preoccupied by the discussion with Lucille.

'Is everything all right, Mrs Newby?' Mrs Gordon asked.

'Yes, everything is fine, thank you. I'm contemplating family matters. About the children mainly, they are all growing up so fast.'

Mrs Gordon nodded. 'I expect that Master Laurence will be considering his future.'

It wasn't a question, just an observation, Beatrix thought, but when Laurie did eventually make a decision, what he chose to do might impact on his siblings, although not so much on Ambrose, who had decided to breed pedigree pigs when he was very young and hadn't reassessed that decision in the least. She thought that Luke would probably follow him, for Luke considered that the sun shone out of both his brothers, but especially Ambrose.

But Alicia and eventually Isolde must have a say in their futures too, married or not, she considered. That most surely should be their choice, with a little judicious advice from her and Edward.

'Yes, Mrs Gordon,' she answered. 'He will be, and I expect he will make up his mind soon.'

On the following day, a letter came in the afternoon post. It was definitely from Laurie; she recognized his writing on the envelope. He should be a doctor with that scrawl, she mused.

Dearest Mama, and Pa,

I have at last finished contemplating and dithering and talking to my tutors, and I have decided (I think!!!) that after I have discussed the matter with you again, I'll know what I'm going to do in my life and future career.

It will take longer than I thought, and I will have to complete a degree first, but I will tell all next weekend, when I'd like to come home, if that's all right. If it isn't convenient for anyone to collect me, I can get a lift to York and then catch a train to Hull and another one home.

Your ever loving son,
Laurie.

'Oh my goodness,' Beatrix murmured as she read his letter. 'Has it come at last? The first of my children to leave home?'

When she said this to Edward with tears in her eyes, he kissed her forehead. 'Ridiculous!' he said sternly. 'He isn't leaving home. How can he? *This* is his home. Whatever he decides to do, he'll come back. He was born here, his roots are here, and he'll never be able to pull them up.' He shook his head. 'It's different for daughters: they're more likely to leave home and make themselves another, but not for a long time. Of course,' he said mildly, looking at her quizzically and raising his eyebrows, 'if you're feeling broody we could have more children. You're still young enough, and as beautiful as ever.'

He made to grab her and she pretended to squeal, but the door opened and Isolde and Luke charged in, intent on telling them what they had been doing.

Beatrix suppressed a laugh. 'Possibly not at the moment, Mr Fawcett-Newby.'

CHAPTER THIRTY-THREE

Edward decided that he would collect Laurie. There was nothing pressing to keep him at home and he and Beatrix set off just before four o'clock on the Friday evening. With a bit of luck they would be home before dark. Luke and Isolde wanted to go too, but their father said no as it was more than likely that Ambrose would want to come home too if Laurie was coming and there wouldn't be enough room in the trap for all of them.

'Can't we go in the clarence?' Isolde asked, and again Edward shook his head.

'No, we can get there and back much faster in the trap. We won't be long.' The children stood on the top step and sulked until Aaron came along and said he needed them for something.

'What about this new cook, then?' Edward asked as they drove off.

'What about her?' Beatrix said.

'She's not a relation. Everybody else is – or just about.' He grinned. 'I rather think our Aaron is smitten! He pretends he's not, of course, but Aunt Hilda says he's popping in the kitchen much more often.'

'Really? I thought he was a confirmed bachelor.'

'No! He only put that about cos he's doted on you! And he knows there's no chance there!'

'Mm? Well, he's not much younger than me, maybe five years or so,' she teased. 'But Sally? Does she know?'

'I expect so; you women seem to know, don't you?'

'Yes,' she said. 'We generally can tell, but we're not supposed to notice.'

After they'd put a few miles behind them, she said, 'Has your mother mentioned our talk about her moving up to your old place?'

He nodded. 'She has, and she's discussed it with Aunt Hilda, who I think is warming to the idea. They'd be company for each other, and it's so much nearer for Hilda to come to us, and to go back home whenever she wants.'

'Yes, especially now that she has Sally to help her. But we must let them decide. I don't think Hilda has been well; she's been rather out of sorts. She and your mother should take a holiday. There's no reason why they shouldn't go and see their families for a few days. And then,' she went on, 'if they do transfer up the hill, Dora and Hallam can move into Home Farm in time for the baby.'

'Ah! Is that the plan?'

'It's mine and Dora's plan. She's a friend as well as a companion, don't forget, and I'd like to see her living nearer rather than being down in the village, even if she won't be working here. I'm sure Hallam would prefer it too, don't you think? Handier for work?'

Edward agreed. 'You've got everything and everybody organized, have you?' he asked quizzically.

'Just about,' she said equably, giving him a serene smile. 'Except for you and the children.'

As expected, Ambrose was also waiting to come home. 'I've asked permission,' he said, after greeting them. 'I explained that I'd put a lot of work into looking after the pigs and as they are a special breed I must check them out myself from time to time. My form tutor said I must think about going to

197

farming college when I'm old enough, and I think that's what I'll aim for.'

Laurie shared a look with his parents. 'It must be very satisfying to be so committed and so sure,' he murmured. 'Ambrose will never change his mind. He'll always know that that is what he's going to do.'

'I've only just realized,' Beatrix replied, 'that Ambrose is just like my father. He never rushes into anything, but works out exactly how to deal with a problem and monitors it methodically until it's finished.' She was silent for a moment, remembering her father's calmness after Charles's sudden death and how he organized so much for her so that she didn't have to; everything but the funeral, and Charles's father Alfred Dawley had taken charge of that, much to her distress.

'You're exactly right,' Edward said, as they waited for their sons to pick up their luggage and climb into the trap. 'Ambrose,' he called, 'would you like to sit up here with me?'

Laurie sat in the back of the trap with his mother and their weekend luggage. 'Mostly washing and books,' he said. 'I intend doing some reading tomorrow. Have you heard from Alicia?'

'Yes,' she said. 'She wrote and told us that you'd met in York.'

'I dropped her a postcard,' he told her. 'I wanted to look for a particular book that we didn't have in the school library and there are some marvellous bookshops in York, so I thought we'd get together whilst I was there. Olivia was with her,' his cheeks flushed a little, 'and then quite by chance we saw Daniel Gough, Stephen's son. I haven't seen him for an age. He's studying at York Diocesan College.'

'Oh, really? It's ages since we last saw the Goughs; I must write to Anna and ask them over for lunch when you're all at home. Is Daniel going into the church?'

'No, he's not. We went for coffee in a place by the river and Daniel told us that he wants to read law and will join his father's firm once he's qualified. He's rounding off his education in York at the college before he sits for London or Durham, depending on who'll accept him. Alicia was very interested in what he was saying and asked if there were any women studying law.'

'Really? Last time we discussed careers she seemed interested in accountancy. What changed her mind, do you think?'

Laurie grinned. 'Could it be something to do with Daniel Gough being extremely handsome as well as clever, interesting and amusing?'

Beatrix drew in a deep breath. 'By the time she's old enough for university he will have moved on, surely?'

'He's only about eighteen months older than me,' Laurie laughed, 'so he's not *that* old,' and Beatrix thought how much more light-hearted her son was than he used to be: gone were the old childhood anxieties, and maybe, she considered, it was because he had now decided on his future role. She wouldn't press him now, she'd wait until the matter could be discussed with Edward too, but she hoped above all that he wouldn't choose to move too far away and would remain within reach of home. What a mother hen I'm turning out to be.

The red sun that had slowly dipped down towards the horizon as they drove home had gone, and the lamps were lit during supper. Afterwards Ambrose went off to see his pigs, and Kitty brought a tray of coffee to the sitting room for Laurie and his parents. Edward picked up a sherry decanter and poured Beatrix a small glass. 'Laurie?' He lifted the decanter towards Laurie.

Laurie shook his head. 'No thanks, Pa. I'm not keen. I tried it after supper one night when a few of us were offered it by the headmaster. A bit too potent for me. I've had a glass of Burgundy – Pinot Noir, I think it was – and I quite liked that, but definitely with a meal rather than on its own.'

Beatrix raised her head. Was this her son, discussing wine? It didn't seem . . . but no, it was bound to happen; her boy was almost a man. A sense of loss that he'd grown out of childhood battled with pride that he had the makings of a fine, decent young man for supremacy in her mind.

'Coffee, then?' she offered, and lifted the coffee jug, conscious of the catch in her voice.

'Please,' he said, and in return picked up a plate of shortbread biscuits to hand to her.

She shook her head in refusal; he took one, but before taking a bite, he asked, 'Would this be a good time to talk about potential careers?'

'It certainly would,' Edward said. 'As good a time as any.' He lifted his glass in salute. 'We're eager to know what ideas you have for the future.'

'Thank you, Pa.' Laurie took a sip of coffee. 'It's all in my head at the minute, apart from talking to my tutor, who's been an absolute brick, going through various options with me and discussing what I like most, and talking to the head, who thinks I'm up to it, academically, even though he hasn't taught anyone who's gone into it. I've spoken to Mama about it briefly, but I wanted to sound out both of you for your opinions before I went any further.'

Beatrix cleared her throat and gave a little cough. 'And – you said before that you'd need to get into university first?' she suggested. 'Does that still apply?'

He lifted his head. 'Oh yes, definitely. I wouldn't be considered without a first-class degree in my hand.'

He sat in contemplation for a moment; Beatrix and Edward waited. 'So, here's what I want to do. I've thought about it for a long time and it's the only thing that I really feel excited about. I'd like to be a veterinary surgeon, specializing in horses.'

Edward's eyes lit up. 'Really?'

'That's wonderful,' his mother said. 'You've always loved horses. I'm so pleased.'

'And not only riding horses,' Laurie blurted. 'The Shires that pull the ploughs, and the carriage horses, and, oh, the

Morgan – Captain – that Mr Snowden drives – one day, if I could afford one, I'd love a Morgan of my own. In fact, that day Alicia and I went to visit and I saw Mr Snowden's carriage horses and then he brought out the Morgan so that I could have a better look at him, that was when I knew what it was I wanted to do.'

CHAPTER THIRTY-FOUR

'Seemingly it will cost quite a lot of money,' Laurie told his parents. Beatrix detected a note of anxiety, and Edward glanced at her; she was the one who handled the estate accounts. 'And to be offered a place at veterinary college in either London or Scotland,' Laurie continued, 'I'll definitely need the degree. The course will probably take about four or five years to complete, and then I'll have to work in an established veterinary practice before I can begin to think of setting up on my own.'

'I don't think there will be any difficulty over money for your training, Laurie,' his mother said, 'and before there's any question of setting up a practice you'll come of age, and will be due an inheritance.'

Laurie broke in eagerly, 'I've been thinking about that. It could be used for the fees, and Ambrose's too if he goes to farming college, then we're not breaking into the estate pot. It doesn't seem fair otherwise.'

Beatrix was touched. They had all shared when they were young; there was no greed or avarice amongst her children. With barely a catch in her voice, she said, 'We would be delighted if both you and Ambrose attended university or farming college to study for whatever profession you decide upon; and Alicia too if she has a mind to. You've done a great deal of research,' she added. 'Well done.' She rose from her chair and planted a kiss on his forehead. 'I'm so proud of you.'

'Thank you,' he said, and got up from his chair and gave her a hug, then turned to Edward. 'Pa,' he said, and his voice croaked, 'I couldn't do it without your encouragement as well. I'm going to tell Alicia and Ambrose what I'm planning; they'll be interested to hear, but,' he frowned a little, 'Luke and Isolde? Maybe I should wait awhile? It's a lot to take in at their age.'

'Just tell them you're going to work with horses, something like that,' Edward said. 'How splendid.' He turned to Beatrix. 'Our own vet on hand!'

Laurie told Ambrose, who was astonished at the news. 'You must be very, very clever,' he said. 'All that studying and learning about surgery and delivering foals. Will I have to do that much, do you think? I used to think that with pig breeding you had to just let the pigs get on with it; you know, put the boar in with the sows!'

'I suppose that is the case, essentially.' Laurie gave a grin. 'But you'll need to know which boars to use if you want a special breed. It's about heredity, and qualities that will run from parents to offspring. You'll need to study biology, perhaps.'

'Oh, yes, of course. I'll need to read up a lot more and talk to Pa about it.' Ambrose had a frown running across his forehead. 'I know what to do when I'm with them; it's learning about their weight, and if I'm giving them the right kind of feed and so on, that bothers me.'

'Hmm,' Laurie said thoughtfully. 'Ask Pa if he knows anyone who is into pigs. He knows most of the farmers around here, and maybe you could ask if they might let you work there during half term or some time, or maybe in the next Easter holidays.'

'Won't they consider me to be a threat?' Ambrose asked. 'You know, if I'm going to be in the same business?'

Laurie gazed at his artless young brother. 'Not just yet they won't. They'll think that you're trying out different aspects of farming before you decide on your options. They won't know, and so don't tell them that you're going to be the most successful pig breeder in East Yorkshire!'

Ambrose gave a huge grin and patted his nose as he'd seen Edward do. 'I won't.'

Aaron drove the two boys back to Pocklington on Sunday afternoon in time for school supper. In case they were hungry Cook had left a hamper for them with an apple pie, a round of cheese and a fruit cake each to share with their friends if they wished.

'Your mother is a great cook, Aaron,' Ambrose said, moving the cloth from the basket and taking a big sniff. He was sitting in the back of the trap and Laurie was sharing the driving seat.

'Can I drive, Aaron?' Laurie asked as they drove out of the gate and up the hill.

'Yes, can do. Let's just get on to the main road and you can give Tommy his head; he's in need of some exercise.' Aaron shook the reins. 'Come on, old lad, let's be having you.'

Laurie decided to confide in the older man. He was practically a relation, the boys considered, not that Aaron himself would ever say that. 'I've decided what I want to do after I've finished school.'

'Have you? Already?'

'You left at thirteen, didn't you? So it's about time I thought about it.'

'Yeh, but it's different for you, and it was different for your pa – Edward, I mean. Owd Neville Dawley gave him 'chance of an education and he took it. I took 'chance of working for your mother and I've never regretted it.' He slowed as they reached the main York road and drew in so that they could swap places. 'And I've got 'best job I could ever wish for.'

'Pa says you stayed on because you fell in love with my mother,' Laurie commented lightly as he flicked the reins and the horse tossed his head and whinnied softly as he felt a different pair of hands guiding him.

'Did he now?' Aaron gave a grunt. 'Well, I might have done, but I'd never have told her. So don't you be telling her either,' he said, shaking a warning finger.

'I won't,' Laurie said. 'But aren't women . . . aren't they able to tell? That's what the chaps at school say, that young ladies can always tell if a boy is sweet on them. But . . .' He hesitated. 'How do *we* know the difference between liking someone – a girl – as a friend and, erm, it being more than that?'

'You mean wanting to kiss them, or hold their hand? Yes,' Aaron clicked his tongue and sighed, 'it's a bit of a dilemma, Laurie, I can tell you that much. I mean, well, I never ever thought of your mother in that way. She was lovely, she still is, but when I met her she was already married – just; for onny a couple of weeks, and I was onny a lad out of school, but I wanted to protect her cos there was nobody else. At least, there was Edward, but he couldn't, cos he was a grown man and folk would have talked, so I made it my special job to take care of her when Charles Dawley wasn't here.'

Laurie nodded. 'But Pa loved her. He told me that, and that he had to keep his love hidden because she was married.'

'Aye,' Aaron said slowly. 'That's right.' He was silent for a while. 'I suppose . . . that if there's no reason why you shouldn't declare it – if, for instance, you met somebody and were immediately attracted to them and they were free – then there's no purpose in wasting time, wouldn't you say? Especially if you're well past your youth.'

Laurie glanced at him. 'Are you asking me a personal question, Aaron, or just speaking generally?'

'Erm.' Aaron rubbed his chin. 'I suppose I'm asking a question when I already know the answer.'

'Are you talking about the new under-cook, Aaron? Sarah?' Ambrose's voice carried up from the back of the trap; they hadn't realized that he was listening. 'I think she's lovely. I'm probably not going to get married – well, not for a long time anyway – but I love the colour of her hair. She's too old for Laurie, but she'd probably be just about right for you, Aaron.'

'Sally is her name, not Sarah,' Aaron answered, turning his head to look at Ambrose, who was sitting facing away from him. 'And how would you know anything about it?'

'When I've been in the kitchen I've seen the maids raise their eyebrows or give a sort of smirk when you come in, and Sally goes into the larder or searches in a cupboard or just turns her back as if she hasn't noticed you.'

Aaron blinked in astonishment and glanced at Laurie, who was trying to hide a grin. 'Have you noticed anything like that? She hasn't been working there much more 'n a week!'

'No, but I think she probably has.' Laurie's grin broke out. 'Well, if you're not interested and want to quash the rumour, then you might want to keep out of the kitchen, or else you might find yourself hooked.'

Aaron sat back and folded his arms in front of him. 'I thought *I* was giving out advice here?'

'I thought you were too,' Laurie stuttered, his mouth twitching. 'But I think you're probably not up to it.'

That same weekend Alicia and Olivia had asked their form mistress if they could go into York to buy personal items. The request was granted as they didn't ask too often; they were star pupils and considered to be responsible enough to go into the city without a chaperone as long as they stayed together. The weather was promising, but although both wore the uniform dress of grey shirt and skirt and boater, they each carried the short navy school jacket just in case it rained. It was now October and the temperature could drop.

The school carriage took them in and one of their teachers travelled in too. She asked where they were going and they said to the library, which was true, and to buy stationery to write home. What they didn't say was that they intended to go to the café by the river where they had met Laurie and Daniel Gough.

The café was well frequented by college students, and although they were not meeting anyone this time they liked the atmosphere, and the coffee and biscuits were good. They visited the library first, as was their intention, then browsed amongst the books in various new and second-hand bookshops, of which there were many in the narrow streets of the city.

'Oh, look,' Alicia said, when they were gazing at the window display of a shop in Petergate. 'There's a copy of *Alice's Adventures in Wonderland*. I'm going to buy that for Isolde if it's a good copy and not too expensive. I read to her from mine when she was small, but she'll soon be old enough to have her own.'

'So what will you buy Luke?' Olivia asked. 'Don't you always buy for both of them as they're twins?'

'Not always,' Olivia said. 'We used to when they were very little, but Mama and Pa said they were individual little people and we should treat them as such.' She smiled. 'But perhaps I might buy a whip 'n' top for Luke. He'd like that.'

She bought the book, which was a second-hand copy but very clean, and murmured to the bookseller that she would never sell hers as it was so precious. Her mother had bought it for her eleventh birthday.

He'd smiled and looked over the top of his spectacles and said 'Quite right, young lady. Books are very precious,' and put it in a brown paper bag.

'Will you give it to Isolde on her birthday,' Olivia asked as they stepped along the street, 'or will you give it to her now?'

'It's not their birthday until June; I might give it to her next time I go home, or wait and give it to her at Christmas.' She smiled. 'That would be a nice gift, wouldn't it? Here we are. It looks as though the café's quite busy.'

'Someone's just coming out,' Olivia said. 'Isn't that Laurie's friend?' A young man was just inside the door and appeared to be waiting for someone at the counter who was handing over money.

'It *is* Daniel,' Alicia said. 'What a coincidence. Pity he's just leaving,' she chuckled.

'Yes, but you know we couldn't—' Olivia broke off as Alicia stepped inside.

'Good afternoon, Mr Gough!'

'Alicia! Hello! How lovely to see you.' He looked towards Olivia behind her and gave her a polite greeting too, but she was trying to catch the eye of the young woman clearing the tables, who looked up, acknowledged her, and pointed to an empty table.

'It's really nice to see you both again,' Daniel went on, putting his hand to his chest. 'We're just off to the Assizes. I'm shadowing a lawyer as part of my studies, and my father's clerk is coming with me to show me the ropes, so to speak.'

The man coming towards them was putting away his pocket book and gave a polite nod to both the young ladies as they moved towards the free table, Alicia murmuring, 'We mustn't keep you then. We'll meet another time, perhaps? Goodbye, Daniel.' She nodded in the direction of the other man.

'Yes, we really must,' Daniel agreed and turned to usher his colleague out of the door, but he was staring back at Alicia and Olivia. The café was small and there wasn't much room. 'Come on, Rand, we're going to be late.'

The lawyer's clerk was still staring back at the café as Daniel took him by the elbow to marshal him along the street. 'That young woman – who is she? Do – do I know her?'

'Alicia? Shouldn't think so. Her parents are friends of my parents. Though you might have met them: Fawcett-Newby, they're clients.' He blew out a sigh. 'She's lovely, isn't she? She'll have a lot of suitors when she's old enough, I expect.'

They were hurrying, almost running now. If they were late they wouldn't be allowed into the court.

People were milling about on the steps of the stone-built Assizes as they rushed towards them; an usher was standing by one of the pillars looking anxiously about him. He spotted them and indicated with his hand that they should hurry. 'Mr Rand, sir. A message for you from your wife: can you go home immediately?' His face broke into a smile as Rand put his hand over his mouth. 'Good luck, sir.' He turned to Daniel, who was looking anxious. 'If you come now, sir, I can let you in, but we'll have to be quick.'

Rand turned quickly and ran across the courtyard, back the way they had come and out into the street, dodging horses, traps and wagons, lifting his arm in farewell to Daniel, who had already crossed the Ionic portico, through the door and was running up the stairs to the County Court, the usher opening the door and whispering where he should sit to watch, listen and learn from his father, who, in his robes, was already rising to his feet.

James Rand and his family lived only minutes away from the Assizes. The door to his house was unlocked, and he took the stairs two at a time, knocked and opened the bedroom door and saw his wife, flushed and smiling, sitting contentedly in bed with a small white bundle in her arms.

'Sweetheart!' His voice broke. 'Darling Ellen. Are you all right? The baby?'

She moved back the shawl so that he could see the infant's face. 'A girl!' she said. 'I thought you'd be pleased. Look at her hair! Black as coal. Isn't she beautiful? What shall we call her?'

'Clara!' Tears ran down his face as he gazed at his daughter, her rosebud mouth, her tiny shell-like ears, and her dark glistening hair; how perfect she was.

The sudden recall triggered by the dark-haired girl in the café faded away. He eased out a breath of release. Simply a coincidence, he thought; nothing more.

CHAPTER THIRTY-FIVE

Beatrix and Edward were in the sitting room drinking coffee; this was their morning ritual, an opportunity to discuss what was coming up in the day. Edward was still in his socks, having left his working boots at the kitchen door, and Beatrix smiled at him affectionately. 'When you drove into Hessle to visit the smithy a week or two ago, you said you'd met someone who kept you talking and would tell me about it later,' she said. 'But you never did. Who was it?'

Edward put his head back as he sought to remember. 'Mmm . . .'

'You'd been to get a new wheel on the trap?' she prompted.

'Ah, yes, that's right. I had to get two new wheels in the end. The wheelwright said it was hardly worth doing, but I said my wife was very fond of the old trap. Got old Harry shoed by the blacksmith as well whilst I was there.'

'Did you get receipts?'

Edward sighed. 'I expect I did, but I've no idea where they are now!'

She shook her head. 'Hopeless,' she said. 'You'll never make a businessman!'

'I know,' he groaned. 'But it's my good fortune that I have a wife who's very clever in that direction.'

She gave a tut-tut with her tongue. 'So it was the blacksmith *and* the wheelwright who kept you talking, was it, and that's why you wanted to change our usual luncheon?'

He considered and looked sheepish. 'No, not exactly, although I had to wait for the jobs to be done. Old Harry kicked up his heels on the way back after being shoed,' he added. 'No – I remember now. Do you recall the Highcliffe-Rand family from Hessle? They have that rather ugly brick house with a tower?'

'Erm . . . oh, yes, I know which you mean. I was invited to call, a lot of years ago. Rosie came to collect me. Rosie's a good friend of Amelia, the daughter of the house. I only went once; I was never asked again. Must have blotted my copy-book somehow or other. Perhaps I used the wrong cutlery.' She laughed. 'I seem to remember that Amelia's mother was a veritable dragon and kept barking questions at me.'

'It wouldn't have been anything to do with you,' Edward commented. 'Mrs Highcliffe-Rand was rude to everyone she met, apparently.' He took another sip from his cup and went on, 'It was James, the son, who I met, and he was in rather a state of – of confusion, I should say.'

Beatrix shook her head. 'I don't know him; I didn't know there was a son until just now. I only know Amelia; I've met her a few times at Rosie's. I think she goes there to escape from her mother.'

'Apparently there was another sister,' he went on. He leaned forward, cradling his cup with both hands between his knees. 'I was asking Aunt Hilda about the family, seeing as she's from Hessle, you know, and she confirmed some of what James Rand had told me.'

'Removed the Highcliffe, did they? Two surnames are a pain to manoeuvre, aren't they?' Beatrix gave a slight smile as she thought of their own.

'Only James did that,' he told her. 'I suspect he wanted to disassociate himself from the family name because of his younger sister's unexpected death.'

Beatrix frowned. 'Why were you discussing their family affairs in the middle of Hessle? I wasn't aware that you knew this . . . James Rand.'

'I hardly know him,' he said. 'I only ever met him occasionally. He's younger than me; we didn't attend the same school, but for some reason he remembered me, and – but I'm only guessing – he must have spotted me pushing the cart across to the wheelwright's and needed some company.'

He sighed. 'He'd been to the churchyard to visit his sister's grave and, as I said, he was, well, in a terrible state and he needed someone to talk to. Someone who had no dealings with his family, but knew of them – I knew Amelia, and his parents by hearsay, and the only thing he knew about me was that I had married a widow!'

'Good heavens! And all this came out as you were talking in the street or the blacksmith's or somewhere?'

Edward shook his head. 'No, he asked me if I'd the time to go across to the Admiral Hawke for a glass of stout.' He rubbed his beard. 'So I thought I might as well whilst I was waiting for the cart to be fixed.'

She gazed at him. 'I'm sorry to hear such a sad story, but I wonder why you're telling me?'

'Well, there was a lot more,' he admitted, and proceeded to tell her the rest of the sorry tale, of his sister dying in childbirth and his parents putting out the story about the influenza, and him leaving home and now living in York and being married with a child and only coming home after his father's death, until Beatrix was completely muddled.

'I'm only telling you because I mentioned to him that maybe we could have him and his wife and Amelia, and Rosie and Esmond, over to supper one evening. I thought it would be neighbourly.'

'Edward!' she said. 'Does that mean we'd have to invite his mother too?'

CHAPTER THIRTY-SIX

The following morning, Kitty handed Beatrix the silver salver. It held one letter and an envelope that felt as if it had a card inside.

'Shall I bring coffee, ma'am? Mr Newby has just come in.'

'Please, Kitty, if you will. Has Cook made shortbread biscuits? I shouldn't really eat so many but I can't resist.'

'Sally and Cook have both made a batch, ma'am. Cook says she'll take a taste of Sally's to see if she's up to the job!'

Beatrix put down the envelope. 'Has Cook not allowed her to make them before?'

Kitty put her hand to her mouth and giggled. 'No, she said this is a final test. If Mr Fawcett-Newby approves then she can stay on!'

'We'd better not tell him, then,' Beatrix suggested. 'He'd be nervous of saying that Sally's were better than his aunt's.'

The maid dipped her knee. That was what she liked about working here: everybody was equal. She would definitely put a few of each biscuit on the plate. Sally had made rounds, Cook had done fingers.

Beatrix pulled the card from the envelope. It was white, with a silver edge and silver lettering. An invitation! Oh! To a wedding. How lovely. *Mlle Lucille Leblanc to Mr Joseph Snowden.* She glanced again at the envelope; it was addressed to Mr and Mrs Fawett-Newby and family. She wondered if Alicia had received her own invitation at school. Alicia had told her that Olivia had talked non-stop about the forthcoming wedding, and that she hoped she would be invited.

There was a note inside the envelope with her name on it, and written in an elegant hand. Lucille again, Beatrix thought. Everything Lucille does is stylish and chic. She might not have had much of an education, but she has certainly taught herself the art of taste and beauty.

The note began with *Dear Beatrix*, which she was pleased about, for she thought of Lucille as a friend since they'd had the conversation in her café. Lucille went on to say that their daughter Olivia would be chief bridesmaid at their marriage and they had invited Alicia to be the second bridesmaid and stand by her side as a witness. She also asked if their youngest daughter Isolde would like to be a flower girl.

I have no relatives in England, as you know, Beatrix, she wrote, and I would be thrilled if you and your family would agree to take their place. Joseph's mother has asked if she might give me away, and of course I am delighted, as she has been like a mother to me ever since I came to live here.

'How lovely!' Beatrix murmured. 'Alicia will be thrilled, and Isolde ecstatic!'

Would the others like to be there, she wondered? Laurie? If he has the time. Ambrose? Maybe not. Luke? Perhaps. Sometimes he likes to do the same as Isolde but more often nowadays he will follow Ambrose. They must choose for themselves.

Edward came in and she waved the card at him. 'An invitation to a wedding,' she said jubilantly.

'Oh? Whose?'

She read from the card. 'You'll come, won't you? Lucille has invited Alicia to be a bridesmaid alongside Olivia, and Isolde to be a flower girl if she would like to be!'

'Oh, excellent!' Edward said. 'Yes, of course. Good of them to ask us, especially as we haven't known them long. I like Joseph,' he added. 'He's a good sort, I think.'

Beatrix agreed. He must be to take on a child who wasn't his own and make her his ward, as Alicia had told her he had, and she wondered if after their marriage Olivia might also become Lucille's ward. That would be such a lovely thing to do, she thought, or am I just being romantic and sentimental?

'I regard Lucille as a friend,' she told him. 'I like her tremendously. I'm sure she has gone through such a lot, coming to England when only a girl, and then making a successful business for herself; and on top of everything becoming a young mother to Olivia.'

'When is the wedding?' he asked. 'And where?'

'Six weeks.' Beatrix gazed into space. 'She'll be the most elegant of brides. St Mary's in Hull – I don't know it. I thought they might have chosen Holy Trinity, but perhaps it's too near her bakery shop and cafe!'

'I know St Mary's,' Edward commented. 'It's a very old church, but it was knocked about by Henry the Eighth when he was in his demolishing mood. He had a manor house in Hull, did you know?'

Beatrix shook her head.

'Apparently he built the house from some of the church stonework and the church wasn't rebuilt until a couple of centuries later.'

'You never cease to amaze me with your knowledge!'

Edward laughed. 'I liked history, and we had a good teacher at the village school. St Mary's will be in their parish, I suppose.'

'They'll want a quiet wedding, too, I expect; Holy Trinity is very grand – quite magnificent, I'm told, though I haven't been inside.'

'A winter wedding.' Edward whistled. 'We'll all need our winter drawers on,' he said irreverently, and caught the cushion she threw at him.

The other letter was from Alicia, who was writing to say she was thrilled to be asked to be a bridesmaid; when Isolde was told about the wedding she couldn't contain her excitement. Then letters went back and forth: Beatrix wrote to Alicia

215

asking her to find out about the colour scheme Lucille was planning before they started looking in some fashion books for style. She knew how she would like Isolde to be dressed, but not yet the colour.

Alicia wrote home to say that Lucille wouldn't tell. *Not even Olivia, so we have decided that we will both wear satin in a deep rose colour; it will suit both our colouring. What do you think, Mama? That would be lovely, wouldn't it? Olivia says that her grandmother will make her dress, as she makes most of her clothes. She will write and explain the style. We would both like a crinoline, just a medium-size hoop, before they go completely out of fashion. Will you have time? Perhaps Dora might help?*

'Oh, my goodness!' Beatrix exclaimed. 'So little time. I have a catalogue of materials somewhere.' She got on to her knees to rummage in the cupboard where she kept her sewing threads, scissors and measuring tape, and on the bottom shelf was the catalogue she was looking for, with samples of materials, including satin, attached to some of the pages.

'Mama!' Isolde bounced into the room. 'Luke says he *will* come to the wedding but he's not going to wear any clothes!'

'Oh!' Beatrix said solemnly. 'It'll be rather chilly. What if there's snow?'

Isolde gazed at her, her mouth half open, and then caught the raised brows and laughing eyes of her mother. 'Luke didn't mean he wouldn't wear *any* clothes. He wants to wear the same as Ambrose.'

'Smelly old breeches, then?' her mother suggested, and Isolde screeched and flung her arms round her mother's neck, almost knocking her over. Beatrix laughed and pulled herself up to sit on the sofa and patted the seat. 'Come and help choose,' she said, opening the fabric catalogue. 'Let's see what would suit a beautiful flower girl.'

She wrote to a fabric company in Hull and someone came out and brought a selection from which to choose; she ordered the rose satin for both her daughters and a soft lining material, bearing in mind that the weather would probably be cold.

'Anything for yourself, ma'am?' the young salesman asked.

She shook her head. 'No, thank you. I have something suitable to wear, and I won't have time to make anything else.' She asked him to send the material as soon as possible, with the matching thread and another packet of sewing needles.

After he had left, Dora, who had let him in and stayed whilst Beatrix made her choices, said, 'I can help you with the sewing, ma'am. I don't have so much to do just now; Kitty has been doing most of what I would normally do.'

Beatrix nodded. 'I know,' she said. 'I've asked her to take on some of your work.' She smiled at Dora's set face. 'I want you to take it easier, Dora, not always be running about after me and mine. You must enjoy this short period of leisure before you have the child, for you won't have much of it afterwards. But I really would appreciate your help with the sewing. We can sit and chat too, can't we?'

She saw the easing of tension in Dora's face, and went on, 'We can talk about old times, when it was just you and me in this great old house; two young London gels' – which made Dora smile – 'who knew nothing about the country.'

And so they did, and reminisced about finding their way round the old house and meeting the neighbours, who had all been so welcoming and friendly, and neither mentioned Charles or the unhappiness he caused. Nor did they mention his sudden death, which had set Beatrix free, but talked softly of Dora's baby to be, and how pleased her mother was and whether Dora would like a girl or boy, and her reply that she didn't mind as long as it was healthy, and together they laid ghosts to rest and dwelt on present happy times and children who were growing so fast.

CHAPTER THIRTY-SEVEN

Once the sewing was under way, Beatrix wrote to Lucille. Something had occurred to her. Alicia had told her in one of her letters home that Olivia had said that Lucille and Joseph would not be going away for a holiday after their wedding, as Lucille in particular was coming up to her busiest time: she was taking orders for Christmas cakes, French style, and preparing selections of pastries and bon-bons for people to buy in pretty boxes as Christmas presents.

And they're planning a reception at the Station Hotel for their guests, she'd added.

'Mm,' Beatrix said to Edward. 'That's such a shame. A short break for them would be rather nice, wouldn't it?'

'What are you thinking of? We could ask them if they'd like to stay here? At Little Stone House?'

'Yes.' She smiled. 'They would be completely private. Mrs Snowden could stay here with us, if she wished. And they could stay for just as long as they liked; Sally could cook for them, and Kitty could wait on them, and they could drive out whenever they wanted.'

'You know, you could quite easily be an entrepreneur,' Edward said quite seriously. 'You come up with such ideas.'

So she wrote, excusing her intrusion into their arrangements. *The offer is there,* she wrote. *You could also, if you wish, use Little Stone House for your reception. It's empty at the moment, but fires are still lit at least twice a week; every day if anyone is staying.'*

She sent the letter off post-haste, and then worried that she was being meddlesome.

A reply came back immediately. They would love to come and stay and how kind it was of her to ask them. They would keep the reception at the Station Hotel, as it was booked and local people had been invited, but to come afterwards to Little Stone House would be wonderful, as they would both be ready to relax.

Beatrix immediately set the housemaid to work on polishing the tables and chairs, washing the inside windows and making sure that the cushions and antimacassars on the backs of the chairs were washed or shaken, and that fires were constantly burning in the sitting room and the largest bedroom and bathroom.

She asked Sally if she would like to be in charge of the cooking for a few days in Little Stone House, adding that one of the guests ran her own French pâtisserie in the heart of Hull.

'I've heard of her!' Sally said. 'Ooh, yes please. I might pick up some advice.'

'She'll be on her honeymoon,' Beatrix smiled.

'Ah!' Sally noted. 'Well, mebbe not, then. But, yes, ma'am. I'd love to be Cook.'

When the day dawned, whilst Isolde was waiting to be dressed by her mother and Luke was being buttoned into his waistcoat by Ambrose, who had decided that if everyone else was going to the wedding then he would ask for time off too, Aaron was charged with driving Alicia into Hull to the Snowdens' house, where she and Lucille and Olivia, helped by Irma Snowden, would dress in their wedding clothes.

When Alicia arrived, Mrs Snowden was already dressed in a fine wool morning gown of silver grey with a fur-trimmed matching jacket; a grey hat with pink, grey and navy feathers was waiting on a sideboard.

'Such extravagance,' she muttered, when Alicia said how

very nice she looked, but she seemed pleased with the compliment.

Lucille went upstairs to her room, followed by Mrs Snowden, who was to help her into her gown, whilst Olivia took Alicia to her room to change into their finery.

'I'm so excited,' Olivia said, as they helped each other into their hoops, and then the underslips, before pulling their gowns carefully over their heads. They fastened each other's buttons and compared their white fur shoulder capes and elbow length gloves, which were almost identical.

'You look – *wonderful*, Olivia,' Alicia said softly. 'If there are any young men in church they'll immediately fall in love with you.'

'So do you, Alicia.' The girls smiled at each other, and then Mrs Snowden came into the bedroom to ask if she could help, and pinned flowers in their hair.

'You must come and look at Lu— *your mother*,' she murmured to Olivia. 'So beautiful.'

Lucille stood on the top landing waiting for them. Her face was pale, with just a slight blush on her cheekbones.

'*I can't believe this is happening to me, cherie*,' she murmured in her own language to Olivia, who stood transfixed at the sight of her.

Lucille wore a high-necked, long-sleeved dusky rose sheath gown of silk velvet fitted close to her slim figure, and a low-set *tournure* or French bustle pulled back to make a short train which fell in deep folds to her feet. Perched on her head she wore a creation of lace and silk flowers with a short veil that covered her forehead and eyes.

Alicia joined them and she too was silent for a moment before saying, 'How lovely you are, mademoiselle.'

Lucille swallowed, and then moistened her lips. 'Are we ready?' she whispered, the others nodded, and all four went carefully down the stairs to the hall, where all but Mrs Snowden picked up their bouquets.

Joseph had been staying nearby at an old school friend's

house. Maurice had agreed to be his best man, and defying convention Joseph was driving his bride, her attendants, his mother and his best man to St Mary's in the landau, pulled by Captain, his mane dressed in dark red ribbons.

Joseph stood holding the reins as the front door opened and his mother stepped out, looking as he had never seen her before. She moved to the side to make room for Alicia, who came slowly down the steps, looking lovely, to stand next to the landau. A smiling Olivia followed, and Joseph held his breath: was this beautiful girl his very own daughter?

His mother put out her hand as a vision appeared in the doorway, and somewhere he heard clapping and cheering from the neighbours who had come to share his special day and see his beautiful bride to be.

He strode halfway up the steps and stretched up his hand for Lucille to take, his eyes filling so much that he could hardly see. Why had he waited so long to claim this beautiful, talented woman? He wanted to kiss her cheek, but knew he must wait until they were married.

Maurice opened the door of the landau and Joseph handed in his bride; she sat facing him next to Olivia, who reached for her hand. Alicia and his mother sat behind him and Maurice next to him on the driving seat. Joseph took up the reins, and turned again to look at Lucille. She was smiling, and he blew her a kiss.

'Come on then, Captain.' He shook the reins and Captain whinnied and set off. 'Let's go and get wed!'

CHAPTER THIRTY-EIGHT

If anyone was shocked or perturbed that Joseph Snowden was driving the carriage carrying his bride to be, her attendants and his mother to church, no one breathed a word of censure; Joseph was well liked in the town, where many people had known his father, and knew that the son, like the father, was a hard-working honourable man who had achieved all he had by his own efforts.

His bride, too, was known to many as a creative professional woman who had lived in the town for many years with Joseph's mother, and if she could please Mrs Snowden then she was acceptable to them. As for being driven to her wedding by her future husband, well, that was all right too; she was French, after all, and maybe that was their custom and nothing wrong with that.

Joseph gave Lucille's hand to his mother and he and Maurice walked ahead into the church, nodding at friends and acquaintances who were already seated. He smiled at the Newby family. How kind and generous of them to offer them some quiet time in their lovely old house. He and Lucille were both ready for some relaxation in their busy lives, and perhaps his mother would appreciate having her home to herself for a short time.

He turned as the organ began to play and was surprised to see the church so full: townspeople who had followed him in, older men who had known his father, neighbours of his mother's – for he still thought of the house as belonging to his mother, even though it was his – and shopkeepers and others who had known him since he was a boy and used to work on their accounts.

But his eyes were drawn to the church door as a crescendo of music swelled and Lucille, a vision in her elegant gown and something lacy on her head, came in, holding a bouquet of roses and his mother's arm. His mother, dressed so stylishly, walked with her head held high, nodding here and there to people she knew.

And then the little daughter of the Fawcett-Newbys' – he couldn't recall her name – so pretty in her satin dress and flowers in her hair, clutching a basket of yet more flowers, the colours matching her gown, and looking from side to side at the congregation and smiling at them. And then Olivia, his beautiful girl, coming up behind, with the lovely Alicia at her side.

Lucille was standing beside him and giving Olivia her bouquet to hold, and he hadn't realized how he had been holding his breath; it didn't seem possible that someone so lovely, so talented, could possibly want to marry him, such an ordinary man. But she put out her hand to him and he saw the love in her eyes.

She's been waiting for me, he breathed. All this time and I didn't know. What a fool I've been. I've been so protective, concentrating so hard on keeping Olivia safe, that I hadn't realized that Lucille wanted the same.

Laurie was standing next to Ambrose at the end of the pew on the right-hand side of the aisle, both very smart in their dark jackets and pinstriped trousers, their parents flanking Luke in the pew in front of them. They had all stood up as a fanfare from the organ silenced the whispered conversations, and the bride with her hand on Mrs Snowden's arm came slowly past. And then his sister, looking very pretty, had glanced at him and discreetly lifted an eyebrow, and his gaze fell on Olivia next to her and he swallowed and felt his throat tighten as he felt the touch of her sleeve.

She caught his gaze and lowered her lashes and gave a small smile. Does she know how incredibly beautiful she is? She can't possibly. She isn't vain; when she helped at harvest with the horses she chatted quite normally and I felt like a fool. Oh, how long before I'm old enough, and brave enough, to tell her that I'm absolutely besotted by her.

She turned her head slightly to smile at his parents in the row in front of them, and glanced back at him again and he thought he would die of happiness.

After the reception at the Station Hotel, guests came over to congratulate Joseph and take Lucille's hand, and the Newbys began to gather their children together. 'Alicia, are you ready for home?' her mother asked. 'Do you have to collect anything from Mrs Snowden's house?'

'We'll bring her, Mrs Newby,' Joseph said. 'We all need to change before we take advantage of your kind offer.'

'Are you sure?' Beatrix asked. 'You can come any time at all. We'll have champagne waiting in the larder for you. Is your mother coming to stay with us?'

Mrs Snowden came up to her; she'd taken off her hat and her silver hair shone. 'Thank you, my dear,' she said, 'but I won't. I'll come back with you now, if someone will bring me home, but I won't stay; I intend to spend a day or two on my own, perhaps reading, or doing a bit of sewing and thinking of the lovely time we've had today, and maybe popping out to see a friend or two. But another time, perhaps?'

'Of course,' Beatrix said. 'You are very welcome any time. We always have plenty of room if you feel like a change of air. What about you, Olivia? Perhaps you'd like to stay overnight with us and we'll drop you back at school tomorrow evening with Alicia?'

Both Olivia and Alicia beamed. 'That would be lovely,

Mrs Fawcett-Newby,' Olivia said. 'Will that be all right, Papa? Mama?'

Lucille opened her arms and everyone felt a tightening of their throats as Olivia embraced her newly named mother.

Laurie raced upstairs as soon as he got home. He hung up his formal clothes and changed into casual home things, but putting on a waistcoat and looking anxiously at himself in the wardrobe mirror as he did so; then he brushed his hair and ran his fingers through it.

'She's coming,' he muttered to himself. 'I'll have the rest of today and most of tomorrow with her. What can I talk about? Shall I tell her about wanting to be a vet? But of course I have to get to university first and then veterinary college, so what if I fail?'

Old insecurities came hurtling back at him. 'But I'm *not* going to fail,' he said out loud.

Cook and Sally had prepared a buffet for when everyone came back and laid it out in the dining room: hot chicken soup and crispy bread rolls, onion tarts, egg and cheese flans, sausage rolls and pork pies, a baked ham with an accompaniment of mustard or red-hot horseradish and coleslaw, if people liked something spicy to add to it; and then apple pie or gooseberry flan with a jug of cream.

Some of them were hungry, having been too excited, nervous or busy to eat earlier, such as Lucille and Joseph, Olivia and Alicia; Ambrose and Luke tucked into pork pie and pickled onions, whilst Isolde ate gooseberry flan, drawing in her cheeks at the tartness. But in the presence of Olivia Laurie completely lost his appetite. He tried not to look at her, for she was sure to see how he felt, and he didn't want to embarrass her or himself.

Later Edward opened champagne and proposed a toast to the newly-weds, wishing them good health and happiness, and a happy life together; then he toasted all the beautiful ladies of the day, and raised his glass to Beatrix, and to the matchless elegant matriarch Mrs Snowden, who, after imbibing champagne and sherry, sidled unsteadily up to him and said in a loud whisper which reached everyone that he could address her as Irma.

Beatrix had earlier murmured to Lucille, still in her wedding gown, that the Little Stone House was ready for them and that Kitty was prepared to show them where everything was whenever they wished; and so as the sky began to darken and fill with stars the couple slipped away, blowing a kiss to Olivia and Joseph's mother as they went. Following Kitty, they went next door and found a low fire burning in the sitting-room hearth, a bottle of champagne standing in an ice bucket, a plate of bread with beef and slices of chicken beneath a cover, a box of chocolates on a small table next to a vase of roses; and at the top of the stairs a lamp was burning on the landing.

'What a lovely day,' Beatrix said, as the rest of the family settled into the sitting room. 'Olivia, Mrs Snowden, you must both be so happy!'

'I *am*,' Olivia said. 'It's what I've always wanted; and I think it's what they both wanted too, but somehow they didn't talk about it, and I think Papa maybe didn't think that Lucille – I mean Mama – would want him as a husband.'

Mrs Snowden, nodding sleepily in a chair, agreed. 'That's men all over. Joseph was once smitten by Lucille's friend . . .' She waved a hand vaguely. 'Bold minx she was, flirtatious, knew what she wanted and who; French, of course, and you know what *they're* like!'

Beatrix put a hand to her mouth to hold in a gasp and Olivia inhaled and said 'Grand-mère, Mama is French too!'

Mrs Snowden frowned. 'Oh, I know, but not 'same as *she* was. Margot her name was, I'd forgotten it for a minute, but,' she went on, 'Lucille took her off to London to stay with an aunt, and left her there. So we were well shut of her,' she said triumphantly. She looked round the room. 'I think I'd better get off home. I'm keeping all you good folk from your beds; it must be getting late.'

'Too late for you to be out, Mrs Snowden,' Beatrix told her. 'We've made up a bed for you.' She had asked earlier if Olivia would mind sharing with Alicia so that her grandmother could have her room. She was bothered about the elderly lady being at home alone. She had not held back when imbibing champagne and sherry.

'I don't mind at all,' Olivia had said. 'We share at school, after all.'

Followed by Olivia, Mrs Snowden clung to Edward's arm on the way upstairs. 'Whoops,' she said. 'I think I might have had a glass too many, but why not! It's not every day that my lovely boy marries such a beautiful lady. I've waited and waited for this moment.' She tried to turn her head to Olivia, and Edward held her in his grip. 'You know that, don't you, Olivia, and now we're a proper family.' She waved a finger at her. 'And now,' she slurred, 'you can become her ward too. They can apply to Courts of Chancery, I think it is.'

'I know, Grand-mère,' Olivia said. 'We'll look into it, but there's no hurry; I'm almost grown up now.'

Her grandmother nodded her head. 'Of course you are. Of course you are. It seems like just 'other day when . . .'

Edward opened the bedroom door. A fire was burning and the room was warm; a lamp glowed on a side table, shedding a golden light. The room was warm and welcoming; at the bottom of the bed was a small portmanteau that Olivia had brought.

'I packed a few things for Grand-mère,' she whispered, 'in case she stayed overnight. I'll see to her now, Mr Fawcett-Newby. Thank you so much.'

Edward smiled. 'You're very welcome, my dear.'

CHAPTER THIRTY-NINE

The next morning, being Sunday, Beatrix yawned sleepily and turned over. Edward's side of the bed was empty. Six thirty, and he must be already downstairs eating breakfast or having his first cup of coffee. For farmers, she thought, Sundays were much the same as any other day; animals still needed to be fed and watered, and they could rarely squeeze in a visit to a church service.

She wouldn't go back to sleep now, so she decided she would get up and join him. She sat up and gathered her thoughts together. Ah! They had guests next door and Mrs Snowden in a bedroom across the landing. Olivia and Alicia were on the next landing and neither they nor the others would be stirring yet, except perhaps Ambrose. Laurie, Alicia and Olivia had stayed up after she and Edward had gone upstairs and she had heard them chatting and laughing long after she and Edward had climbed into bed.

It's so nice that Alicia and Olivia have become such good friends, she mused. Laurie too has plenty of school friends, but none as close as Olivia is to Alicia.

That will change, I suppose, once he goes away to university. She had no doubt that he would, now that he was set on a veterinary career. I wonder which university he will choose – if he has a choice, that is. I suppose it will depend on the grades he achieves. She wasn't in the least concerned that he would fail, for his previous exam results had always been high.

She dressed and quietly went downstairs; she could smell coffee and fried bacon: Edward's breakfast. She peeped in the dining room. The table was set for nine, as the children were at home and they had two guests, though often on Sundays everyone came down for breakfast at different times, as did she and Edward.

Edward looked up from a newspaper when she opened the door and smiled at her. 'Good morning, my darling. How are you this morning? You were fast asleep when I came down. Coffee?'

'Tea,' she croaked. 'It's the only thing to wake me. Wasn't it a lovely day yesterday?'

'Splendid! It was a good idea to have them here, so that they could unwind. It's all quiet next door; the curtains are still closed. I don't suppose either of them often gets the chance for a sleep in on a Sunday morning.'

'No,' she agreed, 'and it's still early; not yet seven o'clock.'

The door quietly opened and Ambrose peeped round it. 'Good morning: I thought I could smell bacon and eggs.' He lifted the lid from one of the serving dishes on the dresser. 'Mmm!' He licked his lips. 'Are you having this, Mama? Can I serve you?'

'That's very kind of you, Ambrose, but I'm going to ring for a pot of tea first; you have the rashers. I'm sure that Cook or Sally will be cooking more for everyone else.'

'I'll just eat this in the meantime, then,' he said, and Beatrix hid a smile when Edward looked up and grinned. Ambrose had a huge appetite, but he remained lean and spry.

Kitty came in with a tray laden with more bacon and eggs that she put into the serving dishes to keep hot, and a pot of tea for Beatrix. Am I so predictable, she thought?

'Hallam has just called in, sir, ma'am,' Kitty said. 'He wondered if it was too early to bother one of you?'

Edward shook his head and Beatrix said, 'No, not at all. Has something happened? Is he still here?'

'Yes, ma'am.'

'Will you see him, Edward, or shall I?'

'I'll go.' Edward stood up. 'You have your breakfast. I've had mine.'

Beatrix poured her tea; she'd wait to find out what brought Hallam so early before she began breakfast. I hope Dora is all right, she worried.

Edward came back in within five minutes. 'Can you have a word?' he said. 'Your department.'

She raised her eyebrows. Did something need smoothing over? Hallam saw to the men and the assignment of work, but if there was any dispute then Beatrix was asked her opinion.

He was waiting in the hall. 'Morning, ma'am. Sorry to disturb you.'

'Part of the job, Hallam. Is everything all right? Dora?'

'Dora is fine, thank you. I left her in bed. But I need to report to you that Arnold Thompson, one of our tenants, passed away yesterday. He farms over at—'

'Oh yes, I know Mr Thompson,' she said. 'I'm so very sorry to hear that. Come into the study, won't you?' She heard the tread of feet upstairs. 'Yesterday, you say? I must drop by and see Mrs Thompson. Was it sudden?'

The Thompsons had farmed a small acreage at the far side of the estate. She recalled meeting Mr Thompson when she'd first arrived at Old Stone Hall fresh from her first marriage and had decided to visit and introduce herself to the farm tenants. His first words to her had been, 'What's a slip of a young lass like you doing running 'Dawley estate?' and she had charmed him by saying, 'This is why I've come to see you, Mr Thompson. I've heard that you have more knowledge than anyone else round here.'

His wife had stood by, her hands folded one over the other, and given her a wry smile, then turned to go back into her kitchen, returning with a freshly baked loaf wrapped in a clean tea towel and thrusting it into her hand. 'Tha'll do, miss,' she had said, nodding sagely. 'He'll be putty in thy hands now.'

It was only a small acreage, and on it he kept a milk cow for themselves, a few chickens, a very noisy cockerel, a vegetable plot and, in the largest field, pigs. They had very little money except when he sold a pig, but he always paid the annual rent on time. Beatrix liked them, so she made sure that the fences were repaired when necessary but never charged them for the labour.

Hallam used to frown at that, saying it was up to the tenant to keep the fences in good repair, but she'd replied that the land belonged to the Dawley estate, as it was then, and one day it might be back in their hands so they must still take care of it.

'What about Mrs Thompson, Hallam?' she asked now. 'They have a son, I think, but will he want it?'

Hallam shook his head. 'No. He went off to work in industry some years ago. Said he wasn't going to scratch out a living on the land like his father did.'

'But farming was in Mr Thompson's blood, wasn't it? He must have been very disappointed.'

'I think he was, though he never said. Mrs Thompson has asked if she could have a word with you. She knows she can't stay on, but there's something she wants to tell you. She's going to live with her sister, it seems. It's what they do round here.'

'Yes, indeed.' Beatrix was thinking of Mags and her sister Hilda, their cook. Cook was still dithering about leaving her cottage in Hessle, where she'd brought up her large family, and coming to live with Mags. She must have another word with both of them, too.

'What about you, Hallam? You and Dora? Would you like the Thompson farm? Though there might be another option coming up.'

He gave a slight frown. 'I'd like the house if it's available, ma'am, but not the land,' he said.

'I understand.' She smiled. 'You want to relax in the house when you arrive home at night, not work the land. But in any case, I was thinking that the land might be merged with the estate, perhaps just leaving a garden area round the house. I'll speak to Edward after I've seen Mrs Thompson.'

When she went back into the dining room when they had finished talking, Laurie had joined his father and brother and was tucking in to scrambled eggs. Edward said they should drive the children back to school before dark, taking Olivia and Alicia on to York after they'd dropped Laurie and Ambrose in Pocklington.

'In that case,' Beatrix said, 'I'll slip over to see Mrs Thompson just as soon as I've finished breakfast.' She told them about Mr Thompson's death and Ambrose looked up from his refilled plate and immediately asked, 'Who'll take his pigs?'

'I don't know,' she said. 'You can come with me to see Mrs Thompson if you'd like to? Maybe add to your stock if they're suitable?'

'That's what I was thinking!' Ambrose said eagerly.

'You'll have to offer the market price,' Edward told him. 'Mrs Thompson will be glad of the money.'

Ambrose nodded. 'I'd better check what it is,' he said. 'Have you got the farming page from the newspaper, Pa?' Then he added, 'Of course, their value depends on what breed they are. I'm trying to keep mine pure.'

'Of course,' Edward said, 'it goes without saying,' and felt unbelievably proud of Ambrose. Laurie gazed at them both and felt a slight surge of envy. He hoped that, one day, Pa would be as proud of him as he was of his brother.

Beatrix saw his expression and realized that although Laurie was exceedingly intelligent, he still thought that he had yet to prove himself. His chance will come, she considered, but he has to wait a while yet. He will succeed, I'm sure of that; he has the will and determination and that in part comes from me, not from Charles, whose attempts to influence him failed so completely.

CHAPTER FORTY

Ambrose drove the pony and trap up the hill and came to the Thompsons' farm – or Top Farm, as it was more generally known – from the back road.

It would be shorter and quicker coming up from the estate across the land, and Beatrix envisaged treading a footpath alongside the hawthorn hedge for ease of access if Hallam and Dora wanted the house, but she had sensed a slight reluctance in Hallam. She thought again of what had once been Home Farm, where the Newbys had lived for a time and where Mags still did. *If I can persuade Mags and Cook to live in Edward's bolt hole, then Hallam and Dora can have Home Farm, which should suit them very well once Dora gives birth to their child. And she thought that it would suit her too to have Dora living closer, for she missed her.*

Mrs Thompson was in the kitchen packing her best china and dinner plates when Beatrix and Ambrose knocked on her door.

'Mrs Thompson, I'm so very sorry to hear the sad news about Mr Thompson. It must have been very sudden?'

'He'd not been well for about a week,' Mrs Thompson explained stoically. 'Feverish, you know. But I didn't expect him to go as fast as he did. Still, it was typical of him: he nivver did like hanging about. Funeral's at 'end of 'week. Friday,' she added. 'It would be good to see you there, Mrs Newby, and

Mr Newby too. We've known Edward a long time, since he was a lad, but I expect he'll be busy. It's a big estate to run.'

Beatrix agreed that it was and thought that there would be many local people who would assume that it was Edward Newby's estate now and she was just the wife at home, never in the least imagining that it was Edward who had come into partnership with her and not the other way round. They were joint partners in the business and looking after the estate for their heirs. But she didn't mind that assumption. It was sometimes difficult for people to change, especially farming families who had followed tradition all their lives.

'There's no hurry for you to move, Mrs Thompson,' she said gently. 'You can take your time.'

'Ah, but there is.' Mrs Thompson shook her head. 'If I keep busy I won't be inclined to ponder on what has gone before and what might be coming next. I'll be going to my sister's,' she went on. 'We'll be all right together, though I expect we'll fall out now and then.' She stopped her packing. 'But what I wanted to show you and this lad o' yourn is Mr Thompson's pigs. You've seen 'em afore, haven't you, laddie?'

Ambrose said yes, he had. He'd been to see the last litter. Beatrix was surprised. Had Ambrose been visiting the Thompsons unbeknown to her? Not that he had to tell her; he was old enough and sensible enough at thirteen to go off on his own. But he hadn't mentioned it.

They followed Mrs Thompson out and she took them to the field where the pigs were kept. There were three pens, all filled with plenty of straw; a boar was snuffling in a muddy pool, and the sow was lying on her side feeding four or five piglets.

'Oh, they're new,' Ambrose said. 'What happened to the last litter?'

'Went off to market. Mr Thompson got a good price for 'em; and what he said to me just afore he got ill was for me to tell Master Ambrose that he could have 'pick of 'next lot.'

'They look like Tamworth,' he said. 'See, Ma, they've got that gingery look already? Same colouring as me,' he joked.

'Aye, that's what Mr Thompson said.' Mrs Thompson laughed. 'He said you'd allus recognize your own if you picked Tamworth.'

'That was very kind of him,' Ambrose said earnestly. 'Could I have one of the boar piglets? I'd like to breed from them. I've got Gloucester Old Spot already, but it would be good to have both breeds and see which comes out best.'

Beatrix was impressed. 'Would you like any of the others?' she asked him. 'I'm presuming you're selling all the livestock, Mrs Thompson?'

'All but my old hens,' she said, 'and I'll tek those with me. But I don't know what price to say for 'pigs. I was going to send 'em to market and see what they'd fetch.'

Ambrose looked at his mother. 'It would be better to ask Pa or Hallam,' he said. 'Then it would be all above board, wouldn't it? You'd get the best price then, Mrs Thompson.'

'Oh, but I trust you,' the old lady said.

'Even so,' Ambrose said solemnly. 'Shall we shake hands on it that I can have first refusal of all of them?'

Well, my goodness, Beatrix thought as they drove back. That's Ambrose on his way into farming; a pig specialist. With these and the pigs he already has, he's off to a very good start, and entirely by his own efforts.

Ambrose hardly spoke on the way down. He seemed to be concentrating, and when they saw Edward and Hallam out in one of the fields he drew in and asked his mother if she would mind driving on without him while he spoke to them.

'Is it all right if I buy them, Mama? I must strike whilst the iron's hot; other farmers might be calling round to see Mrs Thompson, knowing that she'll be selling up.'

'Yes, it is, but Mrs Thompson made an agreement with you and she won't go back on it. Tell Hallam and your father that I have given my approval, you just need the market price. We won't want any of the furniture but we'll purchase the livestock.'

Ambrose grinned and kissed her cheek. 'Thank you,' he said, as he handed her the reins. Jumping down, he ran across the fields calling to his father and Hallam to wait.

Beatrix sat watching him, and then she noticed exactly where she was. She could see a slight pull-in, slightly off the road, and in the days when she was unhappy in her first marriage, afraid of losing her children and even for her own safety, it was here where she came to find peace, looking over their land and down towards the estuary.

She smiled. And here I am now, married to Edward who has constantly loved me; and we have made a life for ourselves and our children, who are so blessed to have stable and loving lives with good fortune and opportunities to make something of themselves. And that's Ambrose taken care of, she considered; next for him is farming college.

She picked up the reins and shook them, and then pulled in again when she saw Edward racing towards her. 'Give us a lift, missus,' he said, jumping in beside her. 'We've got guests at home, haven't we?'

'I believe we have.' She smiled. 'They'll resurface soon, I expect, as they'll want to say goodbye to Olivia before she leaves for school.'

He nodded. 'What have you been doing up here, apart from buying pigs? Rekindling old memories?'

'Some,' she said, as they trotted on. 'But only good ones.'

He squeezed her hand. 'Do you know what I was thinking?'

'Yes; that we should amalgamate Top Farm into the estate and bring the pig pens further down so that Ambrose can separate his unit from the other animals. I thought that Hallam and Dora might like the house, but I don't think he wants it.'

He looked at her in astonishment. 'How did you—'

'I can read your mind,' she teased. 'But it makes sense, doesn't it? Though if Hallam doesn't want it it will remain empty—'

'Not for very long,' he interrupted. 'I rather think there might be another wedding in the offing.'

She frowned. 'Do you? Whose?'

'Well, I could be wrong, but I reckon that Aaron is sweet on Sally. Aunt Hilda has given out a hint or two, and whilst Sally has been cooking for our guests at Little Stone House, twice I've caught him coming out of the kitchen door.'

'Oh, I do hope so! They would be so well suited. She's so level-headed, and fun to be with, and Aaron – well, he deserves someone as nice as Sally.'

Edward nodded. 'And his ma would be thrilled. She really likes Sally and has longed for someone for Aaron.' He grinned. 'And if they were married, I'd be sure that he wouldn't try and run off with my wife!'

'I'm too old for him,' she claimed. 'And besides, I'm a happily married woman.'

As they drew towards the house they saw a carriage pulling up the hill: Joseph and Lucille in the landau.

'Here they come,' Edward said. 'The newly-weds. I hope they've enjoyed their time with us.'

'I'm sure they have,' Beatrix said. 'I wonder where they've been? So nice for Joseph to be able to have a leisurely drive without passengers in a hurry. They will have come back early to see Olivia off to school.' She sighed. 'I'm so pleased we still have Luke and Isolde at home. I feel that our older children are stretching their wings as if they're almost ready to fly their nest.'

CHAPTER FORTY-ONE

Lucille stepped down from the landau. 'We have had such a lovely morning,' she exclaimed, coming towards Beatrix, whilst Joseph drove the pony on down the drive. 'We've been to Beverley. We walked in Saturday Market and along Toll Gavel, I think it is called, and looked in shop windows. They weren't open, of course, as it is Sunday, but quite a lot of people were about, coming from the church and chapel services. Such a pretty town, with beautiful meadowland. Joseph showed me where he might bring Captain for a gallop. Perhaps I'll come again on a weekday and see how it is, and also visit the churches. They look very fine.'

'A bustling little town,' Beatrix said. 'With market days on Wednesdays and Saturdays. Perhaps we could meet one day and visit a tea shop? Oh, but you are busy with your own, of course!'

Lucille shook her head. 'I can take time off sometimes; otherwise it is all work. I wonder, is there a French patisserie in the town?'

'N-no, not as far as I know.' Beatrix's eyes widened. 'Are you thinking of opening one?'

'Perhaps. I had been thinking of opening another in Hull, but perhaps Beverley might be better.'

'Would you bake on the premises?' Beatrix asked.

'It depends,' Lucille mused. 'If I could find somewhere big

enough for a kitchen, I would, otherwise I would transport the cakes from Hull. Joseph would get me a leetle cart to drive, or I could hire a boy to drive one and unload the cakes. I will see. The premises have to be good, somewhere tranquil, should I say, like the café in Hull Market Place. I am very particular where it should be.'

Edward and Joseph were discussing the transportation of the children to Pocklington and York. 'I feel you should enjoy the rest of your short holiday,' Edward was saying, 'so I'll drive them to school. If you are leaving us tomorrow, perhaps you would give us the pleasure of having supper with us tonight?'

'That's kind of you, Edward,' Joseph said. 'We hardly ever take time off, so this has been a real treat.'

'I know what you mean,' Edward said feelingly. 'The men get time off, but we rarely do.'

It was decided. Edward and Beatrix would drive to Pocklington and York and Joseph and Lucille would relax on their last evening in the company of their hosts when they returned.

The front door opened and Olivia came hurrying down the steps to greet her parents. 'Have you had a lovely time?' she said to Joseph, giving him a hug.

'We have. Have you missed us?'

'Not a bit!' she declared, and then laughed. 'Of course I have missed you both. I wish we had a few more days, but I'll soon be home again. You'll give my love to Grand-mère, won't you? Aaron took her home earlier. I hope she hasn't been lonely without us.'

Joseph drew in a breath. He hadn't thought of his mother once when he had had the company of his beautiful bride. He caught Edward's eye and managed not to return his broad grin.

Alicia and Olivia were looking forward to describing the wedding day to their school friends. Ambrose said he would tell his friends about the pigs he was buying, and they'd all put their hands over their mouths and pretended to yawn but he didn't mind; he had put the question of price into his father's and Hallam's hands, and he said he knew he could trust them to get the best deal while making sure that Mrs Thompson didn't lose out.

They all had tea and collected their coats and luggage, and then Aaron came up from the kitchen into the hall. 'I can drive them back, Edward,' he murmured. 'No need for you to go, you've been busy all day.'

'Oh, but – well, if you're sure,' Edward said. He saw that Aaron had something more to say, and added, 'Was there something else?'

'Erm, do you think that Miz Beatrix would object if I took Sally for the drive? I don't think she's ever been to York,' he finished awkwardly. He narrowed his eyes when he saw a flicker of his cousin's mouth, but Edward said not a word, except to agree.

'Course she won't mind. Tell Sally to take a blanket, though; it'll be a bit chilly coming back,' and then he did grin.

It was a merry party that the grown-ups waved off, and Lucille blew a kiss to Olivia. She and Joseph were going back into Little Stone House to rest and change for supper, and Beatrix and Edward said they would do the same, with Beatrix apologizing that they would have a cold collation of meat and salad for supper as Edward had given Sally the night off and Cook had gone home.

'Oh, is there a romance?' Lucille asked. 'Sally will make the perfect wife for someone. She is an excellent cook and very sociable.'

They all turned and watched the carriage as it drove down the track to the bottom road, and they could hear the sound of laughter and see arms and hands waving from the windows.

A mere half-mile alongside the estuary waters Ambrose asked, 'Alicia, would you mind swapping places with me? I always feel sick if I travel with my back to where I'm going.'

'No,' she said. 'I mean yes, I do mind. You'll have to get used to it.'

'I'll swap, Ambrose,' Olivia said agreeably. 'I don't mind either way, I'm a good traveller. Perhaps because I ride so often and get used to the movement.' So Ambrose immediately jumped up and Olivia sat down next to Laurie, who instantly went hot and then cold with delight.

'Where do you ride?' he asked, although he knew she rode in Hull's Pearson Park, for her father had told him so.

'Pearson Park,' she said. 'It's lovely. Papa and Mama and Grand-mère took me to see the grand opening of it, though I don't remember much as I'd only have been about five, but I remember the brass bands playing and the soldiers marching. Most of the grass is set with flower beds now so I can't canter, but Papa and I have sometimes travelled up to the coast, to Hornsea or Withernsea, but only if the weather is good, as the cliffs are not stable and eroding rapidly. But it's exhilarating to canter on the sand.'

'You must come to Beverley sometime when you're home for the holidays and we could ride on Westwood meadowland, or even on the racecourse,' Laurie said. 'Or we could ride up to the Wolds. It's wonderful to climb up higher than our flatland and look down on the estuary. It's like looking down on a silver ribbon.'

'I'd love that,' she said softly. 'Perhaps when we're next home again?'

He gazed at her; what deep brown eyes she has. He touched his lips with the tip of his tongue and then realized she was waiting for an answer. 'Yes,' he croaked. 'I'll look forward to that. It would be wonderful,' and daringly he touched her hand in agreement.

Alicia dropped a kiss on the top of Ambrose's head as Aaron pulled up outside the boys' school door. He huffed. 'You're not my mother, you know. Suppose somebody's looking!'

'Sorry!' she said, hiding a smile, and leaned towards Laurie as he bent to kiss her cheek, and Laurie without thinking kissed Olivia as she reached to offer her cheek too. 'See you again soon,' he mumbled.

'Cheerio, lads,' Aaron called, and Sally gave them a wave.

Alicia and Olivia spread themselves out as they moved off. 'Laurie will be all of a quiver now, you do realize?' Alicia teased. 'I bet you're the only girl he's ever kissed.'

'Well, of course I will be,' Olivia said, 'When do we ever get the opportunity to kiss anyone? You are so lucky having brothers and meeting their friends.'

'Mm, I suppose, but I haven't met any of them that I'd like to kiss,' Alicia said.

'Not Andrew? He's likeable, isn't he?'

'Not my cup of tea; he seems quite young still, even though he's older than Laurie. No,' she said lazily, 'the only one I've met and think passable and possible,' she dropped her voice even though there was no one to hear, 'is Daniel Gough. Daniel Robinson Gough, our lawyer's eldest son. That's his full name; his father dropped their middle name, just as we changed ours too.'

'Mm.' Olivia seemed thoughtful. 'My name would have been Rushton had I been named after my birth father. I don't know what my birth mother's family name was – *is*,' she added. 'I suppose they're still alive. Not that I want to know them.' Her voice had an edge to it. 'Why would I want to meet people willing to give up a child of their blood?' She heaved a breath. 'Do you know, I think I'm going to try for university, to study science; the human kind. Biology, in particular.'

Alicia turned to her. So, happy and content as Olivia is, she still cares about the question mark over her beginnings; and even though she has met the father who begat her, to use an old term, she is curious about her mother's bloodline.

And though, like her, I know the man I call my father didn't sire me, I know he loves me, and I love him, and for me that is enough.

*

Aaron drove on to York to deliver his young ladies, as he thought of them. He'd regaled Sally with the things that Alicia had got up to when she was a little girl, when she'd considered him her very own older chum: someone who was there simply to do her bidding, or to answer any of her questions no matter what they might be.

'I'd love to be a father to someone like Alicia. A little girl – or boy – who'd completely trust me.'

'You'd need to find a wife first,' Sally had said. 'Have you considered that?'

'I know.' He'd glanced at her as they drove on. 'I'm hoping that's in hand.'

In the school courtyard Sally walked with them to the door whilst Aaron carried their belongings inside. When he came out again he glanced at her quickly before turning to the girls.

'Cheerio, Miss Alicia, Miss Olivia. See you again soon.'

'You will, Aaron.' Alicia put her arms round his waist and gave him a squeeze. 'Thank you.' She turned to Sally. 'Thank you for coming with us, Sally. I hope you've enjoyed the ride?'

'I have, miss, thank you.'

Aaron touched his coachman's hat to Olivia and Sally dipped her knee; they had seen them safely to their destination and Olivia added her thanks to Alicia's, marvelling at how they were all at their ease.

'Well, madam,' Aaron paused before pulling out into the road, 'it's not yet dark. Would you like a quick tootle around this fine city before heading for home?'

'Yes, young man,' Sally agreed, 'I would love to see the old city walls.'

'No sooner said than done,' he said. 'Two minutes and before your very eyes!' He drove up the road and through Bootham Bar into the city itself. 'And here we are. I brought you this way as it's the best sighting of the Minster.'

'It's wonderful,' she said, gazing at the inspiring towers

against the darkening sky and the glowing limestone walls surrounding the ancient city.

'We'll come again,' he said, gazing at her. 'Too late tonight, as the walls close at dusk, but on another day, and we can walk along them?'

She turned her head towards him. 'Yes. Please.'

'A honeymoon walk, perhaps?' he said softly.

She sighed. 'I thought you'd never ask.'

CHAPTER FORTY-TWO

The last months of the year came quickly, and were eventful. Alicia and Olivia spoke separately to their headmistress to tell her that they would like to continue with their studies in York and would not travel to France. Alicia asked if she could continue with maths, and also study law with a view to eventually attending university. Law wasn't taught at her present school, so it was suggested that she should apply to study for two days a week at one of the colleges in York that was open to female students, and this she agreed to do.

'Will I get in, ma'am?' she asked.

'Yes,' the head said promptly. 'With our recommendation! You might find some opposition to your attendance, as not all teachers, or students either, are open to the education of females.' She gave a small and rare smile. 'But I expect you will survive.'

'I have three brothers, headmistress,' Alicia replied. 'I won't have any difficulty.'

Olivia was able to continue with her study of science and biology at the present school, and they were both pleased with their decisions, as was the headmistress, who didn't want to lose either of her outstanding pupils.

Laurie had received such excellent results in his examinations on all counts that although he was still young he was allowed to take the University of London entrance examinations. He was given extra tuition and qualified; his aim, he advised the examiners when he was brought in to speak to them, was to study animal biology with the intention of becoming a veterinary surgeon.

And, as everyone in school knew, Ambrose was going to be a pig farmer, specializing in rare breeds. When some of his fellow scholars honked as they passed him, he didn't even notice.

Christmas was coming up fast, and soon they would be going home at the end of term. Alicia and Olivia asked permission to go into York to shop for gifts, and Alicia dropped a note to Laurie and Ambrose to ask if they'd like to join them.

'Will we be able to meet sometime over Christmas, do you think, Olivia?' Alicia asked. 'We're quite a large jolly party: our grandparents, our mother's parents that is, always come to stay, often in the Little Stone House. Grandpa Ambrose loves it there; he can be quiet when he wants to be. Then there's Granny Mags, Pa's mother – you've met her – she likes to help Cook in the kitchen and then comes in to eat with us on Christmas Day. Cook's family as well, and she could eat with us too if she wanted, but she won't – she prefers to eat in the kitchen with the other staff, those who haven't gone home for Christmas. Then there's Aaron, who's Mama's special pet – he's in and out all the time, mostly driving on errands, but Mama always insists that he should come in for a glass of sherry or wine with us. I'm not sure what will happen this year, though – we think that Aaron is sweet on Sally, and he might want to be with her, which would spoil the tradition.'

'Could she not come in too?' Olivia asked.

'Of course, if she would like to, but we don't insist, and wonder sometimes if we're a bit too loud and noisy because there are so many of us. Then on another day we have Mama's friend Rosie – you'd love her, Olivia, she's so eccentric – and she brings her quiet husband, Esmond, who just sits and watches us all, and makes sure that his boys behave.'

'How many boys do they have?' Olivia asked, getting more confused by the moment.

'I can't remember.' Alicia began mouthing their names and counting on her fingers. 'Five, I think, or maybe six.'

'Ha!' Olivia mocked. 'I thought you were a mathematician!'

'I thought I was too, but they've given all the boys names beginning with the letter E like their father, and I can't recall which one comes where, but they've got Eamon, Ebenezer, Edgar, Edwin, Elijah, Emanuel – how many is that? Not that it matters. They all answer to any name – or not,' and they both fell about laughing.

They did their shopping, and with time to spare before meeting Laurie and possibly Ambrose started exploring York's narrow streets and snickleways, the name given to the alleyways and passages which cut through from one street to another, until they found themselves, quite unintentionally, in a little square which seemingly had no exit.

'We'd better go back,' said Olivia.

'No, it's this way.' Alicia pointed to what looked like a mere slit in the wall, but it was wide enough to walk through in single file, and as Alicia emerged she walked slap into someone coming in.

'Daniel,' Alicia exclaimed, and the young man stepped back.

'Alicia, I do beg your pardon.' He glanced at Olivia behind her. 'Miss – I'm sorry, your name escapes me.'

She dipped her knee. 'Olivia Snowden.'

'Of course,' he said. 'Do forgive me. Where are you off to? I'm on my way to meet Laurie; I thought you were too.'

'We are,' Alicia said. 'Or at least we were, but it seems we are going in the wrong direction!'

'Indeed you are going in the wrong direction. So please allow me to be your escort,' he said. 'It can be very confusing. You need to find King's Staith and then it's easy from there. So let's about turn to go back the way you've come and I'll show you for next time.'

They followed him through another alley to find a wider

road leading to King's Staith and the river, where he invited them both to take an arm, saying, 'If you'll forgive me for offering unsolicited advice, preferably don't travel the snickleways alone, or in the dark. As in any city, you might find yourselves in trouble, or become lost.' Then he smiled. 'I must say, I hope I see some of my fellow students on our way, for it's rare for me to have one beautiful young lady on my arm, let alone two!'

He's very smooth, Alicia thought. Is it an act? Is he showing off, as boys – young men – tend to do? He's not at all like Laurie, who quivers in any young lady's company, even though he has a sister – two sisters in fact, although Isolde won't count yet. Then an unexpected thought struck her: or is it only in Olivia's company that Laurie gets into a pickle?

Well, we'll see, for there he is waiting for us. She waved with her free arm and Laurie saw her and waved back. And then she had another thought. Is Daniel as chivalrous with other females, or is he putting on a show for me, or maybe Olivia?

She felt a tiny stab of envy. Olivia is so beautiful that any man, young or old, would turn round to look at her. She thought of the man who had been with Daniel when they had last met and had stared so intently at the oblivious Olivia: he was an older man. Not old, but twice the age that Olivia is.

'Are we late?' she asked her brother when they reached him, and he shook his head and told her that Ambrose had decided not to come; then he touched his chest to Olivia and gave her a short bow.

'We got lost in the snickleways,' Olivia explained. 'Luckily Mr Gough came along and rescued us.'

'A knight in shining armour,' Daniel said, giving a sweeping bow. 'Come to the rescue of fair maidens.'

Olivia gave a laugh. 'So that's only you, Alicia, for I've been told that my hair is as black as coal.'

'Or Whitby jet,' Laurie offered, blushing slightly. 'And as fair as . . . oh, come on, Daniel,' he said, clearly embarrassed at joining in the jesting, 'you're the one for spouting metaphors!'

'That's because – oh dear, I'm going to look like a fool.'

Daniel hung his head. 'It's because I'm going into law, and will have to think of different ways to impress a jury. I'm sorry,' he said penitently, turning to Alicia and Olivia. 'Tea and cakes on me as I've been such an idiot.'

Alicia and Olivia exchanged glances. 'Does that mean, Mr Gough,' it was Olivia who spoke up, 'that you didn't mean any of what you said?' Laurie, his hand on the café door, turned to his friend with a quizzical look.

Daniel smiled at Olivia, then glanced at Alicia as he said, 'Every word, I assure you.'

They returned to normal conversation, and Daniel asked Olivia and Alicia what subjects they were taking at school and if they were intending to take their study further.

'Human biology for now,' Olivia said, rather shyly. 'I'm not sure of other subjects yet.'

'Mathematics,' Alicia said boldly, 'and then perhaps law. But Olivia is the one with brains. No one in the top form can hold a candle to her.'

'Oh, I'm very impressed. Perhaps medicine?' Laurie asked.

'Not as a doctor.' Olivia blushed. 'Perhaps in science.'

The two young men exchanged glances of admiration. 'In what field, do you think?' Laurie asked her, but she shook her head and murmured, 'Too early to say.'

'You're quite right to think seriously about it,' Daniel said. 'It seems to me that it's harder for women to achieve their goals than for men, and yet they are often more capable than we are.' He turned to Alicia. 'My mother studied law, though she was unable to sit for a degree. I get as much of my thinking from her as I do from my father. She gave it up after they had children, but she now acts as a councillor to women who need assistance with legal matters. The law is not always on a woman's side.' He tutted, showing self-rebuke. 'Tell me if I talk too much, won't you? I'm inclined to do so.'

He's a bit older than Laurie is, Alicia thought, and was about to ask him when he would be going to university when he tapped the side of his head.

'I've just remembered something. When we met here last time, I was with my father's chief clerk. I didn't introduce him as we were racing off to County Court – though as it so happened,' he added, 'he couldn't come into court with me as there was an urgent message waiting for him to go home immediately. His wife had given birth to their second child and I didn't see him until a few days later, when I'd called in the office to ask my father something. He told me that his wife was well and had been delivered of a baby daughter. He was almost jumping for joy, but then his mood changed and he started to ask me about the day we'd seen you in the café. I'd told him I knew you, Alicia, but he seemed to be more interested in "the dark-haired one" . . .'

There we are, Alicia thought, rather piqued. I knew he'd noticed her.

'. . . but I'm afraid I didn't recall your surname, Olivia, so I couldn't help him there.'

'Why did he want to know about us?' said Alicia, who was never fearful of asking questions.

'He thought he knew Olivia – or you reminded him of someone,' he said, turning to Olivia, 'and he asked me, if I saw you again, whether I would ask you where you were from. Naturally I said I couldn't possibly ask such a personal question; that it would be an infringement of a young lady's privacy. Which he should have known, and he apologized for his lack of judgement. I do know, however, that Rand is a thoroughly genuine and honest person.' He frowned. 'But it was very odd that he should ask, and there's no doubt that after he saw you that day he seemed to be in a strange state of mind.'

'Perhaps he was worried about his wife's condition,' Alicia suggested.

'Maybe so. Anyway, I thought I should tell you.'

Olivia seemed to relax. 'I don't know why he might think he knew me. I'm hardly ever in York, apart from when I'm at school.' She shrugged. 'I live in Hull,' she told him. 'Born and bred. There's no reason why he should know me. However,

I'm disappointed to hear,' she observed, taking a leaf from Alicia's bold and engaging manner, 'that there's someone else in York who looks like me!'

Laurie shook his head, and gazed at her; Daniel too denied it, and smiled. 'There can't possibly be!' He glanced at Alicia. 'Not either of you. You are both unique.'

'We are!' Alicia agreed; and added in a prim school-marmish manner, 'Perhaps he wanted to call his new daughter after you, Olivia, as you so obviously made a great impression on him!'

'Perhaps,' Daniel agreed. 'But as he didn't know your name, they've christened her Clara.'

CHAPTER FORTY-THREE

They didn't meet Daniel again before the Christmas break as he was preparing for examinations for London University in the middle of January. Alicia and Ambrose were busy revising; Laurie was too, hoping to achieve good enough results to win an early place at university. He wouldn't be eighteen until May, and it would be most unusual if he gained admittance.

Ambrose was the most nervous of them all. He hated exams and was still far too young for farming college, but Edward had found him some part-time work at a pig farm in Brough and he would be able to drive himself there and back in the old trap. He had ten days' work before the Christmas holiday and came home each evening exhilarated and exhausted and worried that he wasn't giving his own pigs enough attention. Edward warned him that if he wanted to be a farmer he must be prepared to work at all hours every day of the week and sometimes at night. Ambrose said he was.

Alicia celebrated her sixteenth birthday after she came home for the holiday and said she really didn't mind not receiving presents as it was too near to Christmas and that she'd have an extra one on Christmas Day . . . except perhaps some bon-bons or chocolate would be rather nice, so that was what everyone gave her.

They enjoyed Christmas Day as always. Beatrix's parents were staying with them until the following week, which had some bearing on choosing the date on which to invite other people to visit.

Beatrix had sent out invitations for friends and neighbours to call for light refreshments from two o'clock until four on Boxing Day, which meant that those who wanted to go to a church service would be able to. She wondered if the Snowdens would be able to come but Lucille wrote back accepting on behalf of them all, including Joseph's mother, who was looking forward to the visit. Joseph had arranged for one of his most dependable men to organize a rota for the drivers.

Beatrix had also invited Rosie and her husband and as many of their boys as wanted to come, which she fervently hoped would not be all of them. She had asked Rosie's mother Mrs Stokes too, but not her husband, as she knew from Rosie that he would refuse. She also invited Rosie's friend Amelia Highcliffe-Rand, but not her mother, as she had been advised that she was a recluse and never went anywhere and certainly never called on people.

'I wondered, Beatrix, if we should invite Amelia's brother James and his wife as well?' Edward said. 'Do you recall me telling you that I'd met him that day in Hessle?'

'Mm, I do,' she answered, 'but we don't really know him, do we? I've invited the Goughs, though, if they don't mind the drive over from York.' Alicia, who had joined them in time to hear part of the conversation, said, 'Mama, do be sure to ask if Daniel will come. Laurie would be so pleased.'

Her mother looked up and smiled. She seemed to be hearing Daniel's name rather often from Alicia's lips these days, but thought she was far too young to be too interested in young men yet. 'Will he, dear? Then I'll ask the whole family, and then Daniel's brother won't feel left out.'

'Yes, of course,' Alicia said. She didn't want to appear to be too keen, and it's not that I'm really interested, she pondered, but I would quite like to flirt, if it doesn't look too silly or pretentious. She gave a small sigh. I do hate this in-between time, being neither child nor grown-up.

They just had time to arrange the changeover of houses. Mags and her sister had at last made up their minds about moving house and went up the hill, meaning that Hilda could live comfortably just a short distance from Old Stone Hall, and that Mags was again in the old cottage which she and Luke had moved into when they first married, and Edward had commandeered when they moved down the hill to Home Farm, for when he wanted somewhere of his own. Both houses had since been renovated, and Home Farm could now be offered to Hallam and Dora.

'We'd better be quick,' Dora told Hallam. 'I'd like my first child to be born in my own home.'

'Strictly speaking, it's not ours,' Hallam said pragmatically.

'I think you'll find that it is,' Dora smiled, and continued stitching baby sheets and pillow slips and knitting small white blankets for the crib that Beatrix had asked Edward to bring down from the storeroom on the top floor of Old Stone Hall, saying that she was as excited as Dora was.

She'd also asked Dora if she'd like to borrow the christening gown that had been her children's. Dora thought for a moment, and then said, 'I think my ma might still have ours; I'm sure she'd like me to use it for another grandchild. She stitched it herself for her first daughter, my eldest sister.'

'Oh, then yes, of course you must,' Beatrix said, 'and we must arrange for her to come to be with you when the baby's born. How long – when should we fetch her?'

'After Christmas will be soon enough,' Dora said placidly. 'I think.'

The guests began to arrive on Monday and were taken upstairs to the drawing room, which was still dressed in its Christmas finery. Rosie and two of her sons, Edgar and Eamon, were the first to arrive. The boys looked very similar. Alicia thought that Eamon was very chatty, like his mother, whereas Edgar spoke little apart from an initial greeting. 'He's very like his father,' Rosie explained, and moved up on the sofa to accommodate Mags. 'But he did say he'd like to come.'

'I was curious,' he muttered. 'I thought there would be young ladies here.'

'There are,' Alicia said. 'Me!'

'Yes, but I *know* you, Alicia.'

He's gawky and spotty, Alicia thought, but I suppose he can't help that; some young men are. It's their age, I believe. 'Isolde will be down soon; she'll want to play games with you.' He pulled a face, so she went on, 'And there'll be my friend Olivia, who is lovely, but you can't have her as I want her for someone else.'

'Oh! Who do you want her for?' He seemed mildly interested. 'Is she fair or dark?'

'Never you mind. She's spoken for. But she's dark-haired and fair-skinned.'

'I only like fair-haired,' he said.

'No one then,' she sighed, tossing her own blonde hair, and excused herself to go and talk to her grandparents, who were sitting near the window. Glancing down at the driveway, Alicia saw a rather shabby governess trap that needed a lick of paint drawing up at the foot of the steps, a dark-haired woman of about her mother's age holding the pony's reins. As Alicia watched, she stepped down, to be greeted by Aaron, who climbed up in her place and drove the trap away.

Mrs Gordon was at the door to meet people and bring them up, and very soon she announced 'Miss Amelia Highcliffe-Rand.'

'Amelia!' Rosie waved to her. 'I'm so pleased to see you!'

Beatrix came over to greet her. 'I'm very pleased that you could join us, Amelia. Come over and meet my parents, and then you can talk to Rosie. She was hoping that you'd be here.'

'How's the old dragon?' Rosie asked brightly as Amelia kissed her cheek. 'My mother is a bit out of sorts today, so she didn't come either.'

If Amelia Highcliffe-Rand was shocked by Rosie's words, she didn't show it. Alicia, listening in to snippets of conversation, paused to hear a sharp reaction, but there wasn't one.

'You wouldn't believe the relief I felt when Mother said that she wouldn't come, but permitted that I could.' Amelia lowered her voice. 'I didn't tell her that her name wasn't on the card!'

'You should have said that, as she never goes out, everyone thinks she's dead!' Rosie boomed, laughing heartily.

Alicia saw her mother swallow and put her hand to her throat in embarrassment, but Amelia didn't turn a hair at Rosie's echoing proclamation, and instead lowered her own voice. 'She wouldn't have allowed me to come, except that, can you believe this, *James* came yesterday and brought his wife and two children, the youngest only an infant. Mother knew nothing of James's marriage, or his children; he had decided long ago that he wouldn't tell her, but after a fearful tantrum she finally agreed that they could stay the night.'

Alicia, hanging about to listen, was intrigued, until she saw Laurie's swift movement to the window and saw the pleased expression on his face.

Olivia and her family, she thought, and alerted her mother that more visitors were arriving. Her father was busy handing out glasses of champagne, wine and fruit juice to anyone who wanted one. However, it wasn't the Snowdens, but the Gough family arriving from York, Daniel and his brother Robin accompanying their parents.

Oh, lovely. Alicia beamed with delight, and she and Laurie eased themselves to the door. Alicia behaved beautifully, dropping a curtsey to Mrs Gough, whom she had met previously. 'Thank you for coming,' she said politely. 'Such a cold day for driving.'

She dipped her knee to Stephen too, and then Daniel and Robin. She saw Daniel's mouth twitch as he dropped his head in a short bow and put his hand to his chest, and then, taking her quite by surprise, he took her hand and pressed his lips lightly to it.

'Miss Newby,' he said. 'Charmed to meet you again.'

She gave a roll of her eyes and controlled a laugh, saying, 'And I you, Mr Gough. *Delighted.*'

She saw puzzlement on Mrs Gough's face, and astonishment written on his father's, but just in time to save either of them any embarrassment her mother arrived at her side to greet their guests and Edward followed her, twirling an empty tray, saying merrily, 'I know my place!'

Dora and Hallam came next. Beatrix took Dora over to speak to Rosie as she knew her well, and Dora dipped her knee to Amelia, whom she didn't know at all, and then she and Hallam moved over to Mags, where Dora lowered herself into an easy chair next to her old friend whilst Hallam went off to speak to the menfolk.

Then came the sound of another flurry of arrivals and Laurie shot out of the door and down the stairs to greet the Snowden family in the hall. Alicia heard him telling Joseph that Aaron was totally capable of handling Captain *and* the landau and had kept a place for them both at the back of the house.

Joseph came in with Lucille on one arm and Mrs Snowden on the other, and behind them came Laurie, escorting Olivia. Beatrix said how pleased they were that they were able to come, and murmured softly to Lucille, 'How lovely you look as always, Lucille. I hope you have had a lovely Christmas?'

Edward shook hands with Joseph, gave Mrs Snowden a bow, and kissed Lucille's and Olivia's offered hands. 'Come,' he said. 'Let me introduce you to everyone. Have you met Beatrix's parents? No, well, here we have Mr and Mrs Ambrose Fawcett.'

They shook hands, and Edward moved on. 'You know Hallam already and the treasured Mrs Hallam, and my mother Mags? But you won't know Mr and Mrs Stephen Gough, or their sons Daniel and Robin, who are from the fine city of York.'

Everyone shook hands again, then Edward took them to meet Rosie and her sons. 'And may I also introduce you to

Miss Amelia Highcliffe-Rand, who also lives in Hessle – Mr and Mrs Joseph Snowden, and their daughter Olivia.'

Only Edward and Lucille heard the sharp intake of breath that Joseph gave when he heard the name, or saw how his face blenched before he recovered enough to give a short bow to the dark-haired pretty woman who dipped her knee to him and his very attractive wife before turning to smile at their daughter.

But they all saw Amelia's face drain of colour and saw how she put out a hand to reach for a chair and whispered, 'How do you do?' before fainting clean away.

CHAPTER FORTY-FOUR

Everyone jumped, startled, but Joseph who was nearest stepped forward and caught her, lowering her on to the chair from which she had just risen.

'*Sal volatile!*' Lucille cried out. 'Quick, quick.'

Mrs Gough appeared by Amelia's side within seconds, crouching down beside her and opening her handbag. 'Lavender oil,' she said. 'It has the same effect.'

Olivia clutched her hands at her chest. 'Wh-what happened?' She whispered in French to Lucille, '*Maman! She fainted when she saw me!*'

Mrs Gough looked up; she obviously understood what Olivia had said. 'Perhaps the sudden movement as she stood up made her dizzy?' She looked about her and found Beatrix looking on anxiously. 'Perhaps she should sit down somewhere quiet for a moment or two.'

'Yes, of course.' Beatrix looked at Joseph. 'There is another room off the landing. Could you . . . would you mind?'

Joseph scooped up the limp Amelia into his strong arms and followed Beatrix out of the room to another, where there was a desk, several bookshelves and a small sofa. He carefully sat her there, then picked up a cushion and placed it at her back.

'I'm so sorry,' she said in a small voice. 'I don't know what . . .' Mrs Gough slid silently back out of the room, as if her role was done, and put the small bottle back inside her bag.

'It was Clara, wasn't it?' Amelia put her hand to her forehead. 'But Clara is dead,' she whispered. 'And she has – had – never been here, so how . . . why . . .' Tears welled from her eyes and ran down her cheeks. 'Why would she visit me here when she never came to me at home, even though I wished and wished that she would?'

Beatrix and Joseph exchanged glances; Beatrix thought that Amelia's mind was wandering. Perhaps she should ask Aaron to take her home. She'd ask Rosie what she thought.

But Joseph forestalled her. 'Mrs Fawcett-Newby,' he said formally, 'I think I should bring Olivia in here. This lady' – he didn't want to use her name – 'has mixed her up with someone else.'

'Would it not be better to take her home?' Beatrix murmured.

'No, please.' Amelia swung her feet to the floor. 'I'll be all right now. It was silly. Just for a moment, I had . . . an apparition. I thought I saw my sister, who died many years ago. I'll come back in; I'm spoiling your party. I'm so glad that I didn't bring my mother; she would have been so cross with me.'

Joseph led Amelia back into the drawing room, where the other guests were talking quietly together. They gazed anxiously at Amelia, who murmured she was so sorry.

Olivia was standing with Lucille, and Alicia was doing her best to entertain their guests while Laurie and Ambrose were filling up glasses or handing round plates or inviting people to eat, and Mags was doing the same.

Then Cook came in wearing a fresh crisp white apron and carrying a tureen of hot soup; Sally followed behind with a platter of warm bread, a dish of butter and a large ladle. Another maid brought in another tureen, placed it on the serving table and stood behind it.

'Sally!' Amelia declared in a croaky voice. 'I didn't know you'd come here! Well done. What a nice household to come to, especially after ours. Mother is a nightmare, isn't she?'

Sally bobbed her knee. 'If you say so, Miss Amelia, I wouldn't disagree with you.'

She placed herself behind the serving table next to the other maid and raised her voice. 'Soup, anyone? Chicken broth, mixed game soup, fresh bread.' She sounded like a market trader and everyone laughed, breaking the ice.

Luke and Isolde, who had been absent until now, appeared as soon as the food was brought in, Isolde giving a pretty curtsey to the room at large and Luke a polite bow with one hand behind his back.

At Beatrix's invitation, the guests began to sit at the two round tables that were laid with cutlery and napkins, and the young maid distributed bowls of soup whilst Isolde and Luke offered plates of precariously balanced bread rolls.

'Such a lovely idea, Beatrix,' Rosie said from across the table. 'Everyone enjoys a bowl of soup on a winter's day, and this is delicious.'

'Thank you, Rosie.' Beatrix smiled. 'We are lucky to have two excellent cooks. Dora, come and sit here by me. Hallam, why don't you sit by Edward, but you must promise not to talk only about farming!'

'Thank you, ma'am,' Hallam responded. 'That means I can only eat, and not say a word except perhaps about the weather.'

Olivia sat next to Lucille and her father sat across from her between Rosie and Beatrix's mother, but when Olivia looked up she saw that Amelia was sitting at the same table, and, pale-faced, was gazing right at her.

Olivia couldn't eat. She couldn't even lift a spoon to her mouth, and she found that she was trembling.

Amelia lowered her gaze, her thoughts in a jumble. It was uncanny. This young woman, a girl only, younger than Clara had been when she died, was the very double of her.

Mrs Gough leaned forward and spoke up. 'Miss Highcliffe-Rand, Mr Snowden.' Legally trained, she had no difficulty in remembering names. 'Are you related to one another? Your daughter' – her gaze rested on Lucille and Joseph and then on Olivia – 'could so easily be assumed to be a relative of yours, Miss Highcliffe-Rand, a daughter even. The likeness is quite incredible. Does anyone else see it?'

There were murmurings around the table, some saying they couldn't see it at all, others agreeing that it was remarkable. Laurie, sitting at the other table, saw how uncomfortable Olivia was; there is something amiss here, he mused. He glanced at Joseph and observed his taut expression, and then something clicked in his head and he glanced at Daniel, who was poker-faced. At the same time he saw Stephen Gough bending and murmuring something to his wife, and her lips parted as she listened intently.

Stephen raised his voice to the company. 'Isn't there a saying that we are all related to one another? That we are all cousins, in effect, but you'd have to be a mathematician to work it out.'

'There's one for you then, Alicia,' Laurie called, and everyone laughed. 'Go to the top of the class if you can solve it.'

'Well,' Alicia spoke up. 'I can certainly work out that you and Ambrose and Luke are my brothers, but there's a join in there,' she said and glanced at Edward, who smiled back at her, 'and no one would know where it was just by looking at us as we all have similarities, similar hair colour, even similar-shaped noses, except that Isolde's and mine are much prettier than the boys'.'

There was a groan of disapproval from Laurie and Ambrose, and Luke fingered his tenderly and everyone laughed and the subject was changed.

After the repast was over the guests spread themselves around into small groups. Isolde sat at the piano and began to play a soft refrain as her mother had requested that she should, and many of the guests turned in surprise and murmured how well she played for such a small girl.

Mrs Gough came across to Amelia and apologised to her if her question had made her uncomfortable. 'I didn't intend to

262

embarrass you in any way,' she said, lowering her voice, 'and I of all people should have known better. Your brother James is my husband's chief clerk, and I realize that you have both had a difficult time over the years.' She went on, 'I have a surgery to assist women in finding their way around various aspects of law. If ever I can help you, please don't hesitate to get in touch.' She surreptitiously handed Amelia a card.

'Thank you. I didn't know that you knew James, Mrs Gough.' Amelia sighed. 'He tells me little about his life, and yours sounds so interesting and worthwhile. I am impressed by what women can do if they have the stamina, which,' she sighed, 'I'm afraid I have not.'

Across the room, Olivia stood facing the window with her back towards the other guests as she thanked Alicia and Laurie for the distraction they had created to save her from the embarrassment that had occurred due to Mrs Gough's unfortunate comment.

'Do we look alike?' she asked. 'Miss Highcliffe-Rand and I – is there a similarity?'

'There perhaps is,' Alicia said, 'but merely because she is dark-haired and pretty.'

'But you are unique,' Laurie broke in, and then became embarrassed and added, 'as we all are.'

Olivia nodded. 'But I think that Papa is keeping something from me, and even from Mama.' Calling Lucille her mother came easily now, especially since Lucille had confided that she was hoping to conceive a child; a brother or sister for Olivia who would complete their family circle.

'And,' Olivia continued now, 'I can deal with missing pieces of my life. I'm old enough. I've met my birth father and his wife and my half-brother, and was pleased to do so, but my birth mother remains a mystery to me, except that her given name is also one of mine.'

Guests began to drift between groups. Daniel came across to Alicia, who introduced him to her grandparents, and Laurie took Olivia to meet Rosie and her boys, both of whom stared wordlessly at her until Edgar, mumbling, asked whether she was the pretty girl that Alicia had said was spoken for.

'Silly boy.' Rosie slapped his arm lightly. 'Of course she's not spoken for yet, but she isn't available to you! She's far too intelligent as well as lovely to want you by her side.'

'Poor boy,' Olivia murmured as Laurie led her away. 'His mother doesn't help his self-confidence.'

Laurie laughed. 'I don't think it will bother him too much. He probably knows his mother well enough, and my goodness, you should meet his grandmother. She's as crazy as a coot, and says the first thing that comes into her head!'

Olivia laughed too until she turned round and found herself face to face with Amelia Highcliffe-Rand.

The two women gazed at each other, and Laurie didn't know what to say except, 'How do you do?', for he didn't know Amelia and had never met her before, but Olivia was standing close to him and her skirts were brushing against him and it seemed so natural for him to reach for her hand.

Amelia moistened her lips with the tip of her tongue and breathed, 'May I ask your name?'

'Olivia,' she answered softly. 'Olivia Clara Snowden.'

'You're her daughter,' Amelia whispered. 'You have to be.'

CHAPTER FORTY-FIVE

Beatrix looked about her; the occasion had gone very well, she thought, apart from when Amelia fainted . . . and ah, there she was, speaking to Olivia and Laurie, and oh my goodness, Laurie is holding Olivia's hand! I'd better go over.

'Amelia,' she said. 'Are you feeling all right now?'

'Yes, thank you.' Amelia turned to her hostess. She patted her throat and spoke rapidly. 'It was just a silly turn; I've had a few days of tension,' she excused herself. 'My brother arrived for Christmas with his wife and children, and my mother . . . well, she's difficult at the best of times, but oh dear, such tantrums, and I was glad to come out today because now he'll know what I go through with her. His wife is very nice,' she added, 'and seemed to know how to deal with Mother. But you don't want to hear all this, and dear Rosie is here and is always such a tower of strength, and I must say how much I have enjoyed being here' – she knew she was running on but didn't seem able to stop – 'and you have such a beautiful home, Beatrix, whilst we, well, Mother won't let me touch a thing to change our old ruin . . .'

Her voice was at a high pitch and her eyes darted continually at Olivia, who kept her head low and only glanced up at her from beneath her lashes.

Beatrix saw that Olivia looked apprehensive and rather tense and kept checking to see where Lucille and Joseph were, so she made all the appropriate comments and allowed her and Laurie to escape, hands unclasped. After a few more minutes she made her excuses and left Amelia's side, moving on towards where Stephen Gough and his wife were talking to Edward and Alicia. I wonder what Lucille and Joseph will think of that misunderstanding with Amelia, she thought, and did Edward and Alicia see Laurie holding hands with Olivia?

Looking round for her parents, she saw Joseph and her father chatting amicably together and Lucille, Olivia and Irma Snowden talking to her mother. She glanced about for Laurie and saw him in deep conversation with Daniel; the twins were sitting together on one stool at the piano, with Mags standing behind them.

Dora was sitting quietly, looking content, and Hallam was bringing her a cup of tea. Beatrix smiled. Dora has got him house-trained.

A merry tune broke out on the piano, where Luke and Isolde were now accompanying Mags as she sang a jolly ballad about a farm boy. 'That's what I'm going to be,' Beatrix heard Luke say to his grandmother when they'd finished. 'I'm going to be a merry farm boy!'

'Good lad,' Mags said, patting him on the shoulder. 'Just like your Grandpa Luke!'

'No!' Luke said. 'Like Ambrose!'

Mm, Beatrix thought, and where is Ambrose?

Ambrose, it seemed, had slipped out to lock up his pigs.

Some of their guests were preparing to leave; Mrs Gordon and the maids were patiently waiting in the hall with coats and hats, and Aaron and the lad were bringing traps and barouches to the front door. Aaron told the boy not to touch the landau: that he would bring it round himself.

The Goughs were giving their thanks and shaking hands with everyone and saying how splendid it had been to meet them all. Daniel said to Laurie that they would meet when they could, and then said goodbye to Alicia and Olivia, wishing them good luck with their school work and saying he hoped to see them again soon.

Amelia and Rosie went off in their traps, Amelia waving a sad goodbye and Rosie letting Edgar drive and almost falling backwards with her legs in the air as he cracked the whip and the pony shot away. Those watching from the window put their hands over their mouths to hide their laughter.

'Don't ever let him near any of my horses,' Joseph said to no one in particular as he stood on the steps outside, waiting for Aaron to bring Captain and the landau round to the front.

Beatrix's father, not knowing what Joseph did for a living, asked, 'Why, how many have you got?'

'Ten at the last count,' Joseph said mildly. 'Eleven with Captain, but he's not a working horse.' And the elder Ambrose, the former banker, blew out his cheeks and thought there was a lot of money about in these parts. 'Some of mine, sir,' Joseph explained, 'are what you might call bankrupt horses.'

Ambrose Fawcett frowned. 'What does that mean?'

'Well, sir, people buy horses thinking it will be cheaper than hiring, but they don't take into account the cost of feed, a good stable to keep them warm and dry, or keeping them well shod and harnessed. And on top of it all there's veterinary fees. It costs a lot of money to look after them properly, and folks shouldn't buy them if they can't care for them and keep them well fed, especially if they're working horses as mine are. I buy those that they can't afford to keep, and I'm sure the animals consider themselves to be in clover!'

Ambrose senior went inside, as it was getting chilly, and Edward came out to talk to Joseph, who said, 'Miss Highcliffe-Rand. Have you known her long?'

'Erm,' Edward sighed, 'I've known *of* her for years; the whole family, really. They're one of the *elite* families in the district so everyone knew of them, but they never bothered with the likes of us unless they needed some job doing. My mother has known them for a long time, but that's only because she and my father worked for Neville Dawley, who used to own this estate before it went to Beatrix's first husband.'

'So you weren't one of 'elite?''

'No,' Edward grinned. 'But I might be now since I married Beatrix! Not that I give tuppence about people like that. Amelia's all right,' he added. 'She's had a rough time with her mother, by all accounts.'

'And – erm, her father? Is he . . . ?'

'Oh, long gone!' Edward said. 'He had a seizure, apparently; he was an ogre, worse than his wife so they say, not that I knew him. Their son left home at sixteen, dropped out of school, dropped the Highcliffe and only kept the Rand and went off to make his own living.

'Funnily enough,' Edward scratched at his beard, 'I met him a while back. I didn't recognize him but he remembered me, don't know how. He looked dreadful; he said he'd been to visit his younger sister's grave and that's the only reason he ever comes back, except for when he came to sort out his father's estate after he died.'

He gave an ironic laugh. 'According to Rosie, the old buzzard left the estate to his wife, a pittance to Amelia and nothing to James. Unless his mother leaves it to him, he has nothing. He works in York as a solicitor's chief clerk; they were here, the Goughs, the lawyers he works for. Good people. We've known them a long time. Did you get to meet them?'

Joseph nodded, listening and thoughtful.

Edward frowned. 'I don't think Amelia knew who they were even though they were introduced. James can't have told her who he worked for, unless she didn't make the connection. She's a bag of nerves. James hadn't even told his mother that he had a wife and child, maybe two children by now. They have their secrets, I suppose; don't know why.

'Here's your fine horse and carriage, milord. Would you like a warm drink before you leave? You must be feeling chilled out here.'

'No, not me,' Joseph said. 'All my years of waiting to pick up passengers have hardened me, but my ladies will want their blankets and they're under the seats.'

He went back inside with Edward. It was time they were leaving for the drive back into Hull. A rime of frost was making the grass glisten and soon it would be dark, but he always carried a lamp, to be seen rather than see, for his sight was keen.

He collected his womenfolk: wife, mother and daughter. He was content, apart from the niggling uncertainty that perhaps there was something waiting to be done. The right thing, after all these years.

'Goodbye, *darling* Olivia,' Alicia said in an exuberant manner. 'I suppose we'll have to work for the rest of the holidays, but if your papa should be travelling this way perhaps you'd come with him and call on us?'

'Perhaps I would,' Olivia said. 'I'd like that.' She looked tired, Alicia thought.

Laurie kept his eyes lowered; his mother had seen him holding Olivia's hand. It was nothing, he convinced himself; he was only giving comfort to Olivia, who was shaken by that silly woman's protestation that she had seen her dead sister. But it was odd, all the same, after Daniel had told them about the clerk who had seen Olivia and also thought she was someone else.

Olivia is quite sensitive, he thought as they crowded to the door to wave them off, even though she appears to be confident; I understand that feeling only too well. We understand each other. We are – *compatible*! And he suddenly smiled, and Olivia looked up from the carriage window and smiled back and waved.

CHAPTER FORTY-SIX

Lucille had realized that Joseph was troubled, but she knew also that he would want to resolve the problem himself; the decision had to be his. Nevertheless, she said to him that she would like the four of them, including his mother, to arrange an interview with Mrs Gough, who had been highly recommended to her by Beatrix.

'Why would we want to speak to Mrs Gough?' he asked.

'She is legally trained, her husband is a lawyer, you met them at the Newbys' home, and she deals with aspects of law appertaining to women and children.'

He realized how this conversation had come about: his mother and Olivia were listening for his compliance or defiance, so Lucille had already discussed it with them.

'And why do we need this discussion?'

'Because, chéri, I wish our daughter to be my ward as well as yours and your mother's.' She glanced at her mother-in-law, who nodded. Irma Snowden hadn't changed her mind; she had already agreed that it was the right thing to do, as had Olivia.

'And then,' Lucille went on, 'we will know that Olivia will always belong to both of us, unless she decides to marry.'

'She would still be our daughter,' Joseph interrupted, 'even if she married.'

'Of course, Papa,' Olivia murmured. 'For ever. But Mama

270

should be formally included too. She's the only mother I have known.'

Joseph swallowed. 'This is because of – because of meeting Miss Amelia Highcliffe-Rand?'

'Partly, yes,' Lucille explained, 'but that has merely brought it to the front of my mind. It is what I have always wanted, Joseph. I was too young to be included when Olivia was born, but time has gone swiftly and now I am old enough and a married woman and . . .' She gave him a brief smile and her eyes were bright as she continued, 'I was there at her birth. Olivia was already mine as I ran to fetch the midwife and the doctor to save her and the young woman who had given birth to her; and I held her when she was born and placed her in Oliver's arms.'

Joseph wiped his eyes, and Olivia came and stood by him and put her arms around his waist and laid her head on his chest. 'So you were,' he murmured. 'So you were.'

'And then,' Lucille hadn't quite finished, 'if you both wish it, chéri, we can take Olivia to visit her other family, her aunt and uncle, and maybe give them some peace of mind too, but mainly to confirm that the child born to their dearest sister is loved. Joseph – you are the only one who knows where they live.'

Joseph was silent for a moment, and then said softly, 'It hadn't occurred to me before I met Amelia and talked to Edward at the Newbys' party that anyone from that family would care. I hated that poor girl's parents.' His voice became hard. 'They cared for nothing but their damned name and reputation!'

He remembered how a distraught Oliver Rushton had told him where Clara's family lived and asked him if he would go to them and tell them what had happened; of their daughter's death and of how she was lying in the undertaker's parlour, and of the child that lived; and so he agreed, but her father had shouted at him to get out and her mother had screamed at him that he was a liar.

In a sudden burst of anger, he had shouted back at them, and then, as realization hit him that they too were shocked and horrified, begged their pardon and pleaded with them to bring their daughter home for burial.

Clara's father died never acknowledging that he had a grandchild. But Joseph had met Clara's young brother and seen how he had wept over his sister, and he had been haunted by the boy's grief. But that was then, he acknowledged, and it was now time to reflect.

Mrs Gough was swift in her endeavours to have Lucille and Joseph made joint guardians of Olivia.

'If there is no property or title involved and if Olivia has no objection – for you are of an age to say, Olivia – there is no legal issue and therefore the Court of Chancery is not required to be involved. The emphasis is placed on the child's welfare and best interests,' she told her, 'and that has obviously been considered throughout your life. Presumably you are content with that?'

'Oh, yes, thank you, I am,' a smiling Olivia declared, 'and I'm *very* happy that Tante Lucille has now become my mother.'

The formalities completed, they thanked Mrs Gough and left the office. Lucille's face was wet with happy tears. 'One more thing,' she said, 'and then we're done. We need to meet Miss Amelia Highcliffe-Rand and tell her what really happened to her sister.'

The door behind them opened again and a man in his early thirties came out.

'Mr Snowden,' he said. 'Mrs Snowden. Olivia! Won't you come back inside for a moment?' He gazed at them with an anxious crease above his nose. 'I am James Rand. Amelia and – and Clara's brother.'

Joseph heaved a breath; he had thought the clerk looked familiar. They went back inside and saw that Mrs Gough was no longer in the front office; she must have had business elsewhere.

Joseph put out his hand to shake James's. 'I remember you,' he said. 'You were just a boy when we last met.'

'I remember *you*,' James said, and already tears were

spilling down his cheeks as he looked at Olivia. 'You came to tell us what had happened, and then you took my father and me to the undertaker's. My father didn't want me to see Clara, but I said I wouldn't believe she had died if I didn't. I'm so pleased to meet you again; I've always wished I knew how to find you so that I could tell you how much I at least appreciated all you did that day. Thank you, Mr Snowden.'

Joseph looked at the man who had been that terrified youth seeing death for the first time, and a little of the bitterness he had harboured for so long fell away.

'Olivia,' James said, 'I thought I was seeing a ghost that day when I saw you in the café. I was already overwrought with worry over my wife; she was expecting our second child and I wanted to get home, but seeing you . . .' He held out his hand again and Olivia gave hers to him.

'I'm very glad to meet you at last, James,' she said softly. 'I have had a good life with my parents, Joseph and Lucille, and I have a wonderful grandmother, my father's mother.'

He was still holding her hand as he said, 'I'm pleased to hear it,' and gave a grim throaty sound. 'You wouldn't be able to say the same about my children's grandmother, not on my side, though my wife's parents love them very much.'

He released her hand. 'Will you see Amelia?' he asked. 'She told me that she had made a fool of herself at the Fawcett-Newbys' house and has been so upset ever since.' He sighed. 'There is little I can do to help her, and she thinks that I don't do enough. I do what I can, but our mother holds the puppet strings, I'm afraid.'

They promised they would visit Amelia, and as soon as they arrived home Lucille penned a letter to her asking if they might call the following weekend, choosing that time in the hope that her brother James would also be able to be there, and so it was duly arranged.

Joseph remembered exactly where the house was situated. It was imprinted indelibly in his mind, but he didn't recall the long grass in the meadow that fronted the house or the wild flowers that grew in it, nor the high straggly hedges. As they drew near they saw the weeds in the gravel drive, the cracked windows, and the great wooden door that needed a coat of paint.

He tied Captain to a metal post at the bottom of the steps, then helped Lucille and Olivia down from the landau before pulling the chain on the old iron bell. Someone had been watching, for the door was pulled open immediately and a very elderly housekeeper beckoned them in, even before Joseph gave her their name.

'Drawing room, sir, ma'am,' she was beginning, when Amelia hurried down the stairs, calling back to someone presumably in a bedroom, and a second later James Rand came into the hall, opened the drawing room door and invited them in. It was very cold, and only a small fire burned in the grate. Both Lucille and Olivia were glad they were wearing their long wool coats.

'Please, won't you sit down,' Amelia said, following them into the room. She seemed nervous, and cleared her throat. 'Mother says she will come downstairs today,' she murmured. 'She doesn't often, but is insisting on doing so today. It isn't because James is here, for she rarely speaks to him, but she knows me very well and can guess when I am agitated about something.'

'You don't need to be worried about our visit,' Lucille told her. 'We have only come because we felt that Olivia should meet you and your brother, her aunt and uncle, properly; we want nothing from you, and nor do we blame you for what happened in the past.'

A voice was calling from upstairs and they heard the old woman who had opened the door to them calling back 'Yes, yes, in a minute!' and then the sound of a door opening into the hall, presumably from the kitchen stairs.

'Our mother blames me for everything,' Amelia began abruptly, looking down into her lap. 'And rightly so, as I was the one who had booked the carriage to collect Clara and Oliver. I never told anyone *that*, not even you, James.'

Joseph took a sudden breath. He had often wondered who had arranged it. He had received an envelope containing money for the fare and a postcard telling him when and where he should wait, just outside the gate, and under no circumstances to come up the drive, but to be ready for the journey to Hull's railway station. He had done as instructed and turned the horse and carriage to face in the right direction, and within five minutes of the arranged time the young couple arrived in great haste.

'Unfortunately, my mother heard the front door open, looked out of her bedroom window and saw them hurrying down the drive,' Amelia continued. 'She screamed for our father and saw me standing at the top of the stairs, and I told her she was too late, they were gone: gone to find a place where they could be together and be happy because they'd never be happy in this house.' She was holding back tears and could hardly speak. 'She slapped me and pushed me into my bedroom and locked the door.'

'Amelia was locked in there all night.' James took up the tale. 'Father saddled up his horse and galloped off in pursuit. When he came back he said he couldn't find them but that if he had he would have whipped the varmint to within an inch of his life.'

Joseph remembered that mad drive. When Oliver had banged on the carriage roof he had pulled into a space under some overhanging branches and had got down from his seat to ask what the trouble was. He saw a horse gallop by and guessed the rider was looking for the young couple.

'I think he passed us, when Oliver and I were discussing what should be done,' he said. 'But I know all the lanes and short cuts and he would never have found or caught us; and my priority then was to get away from the district and take the young woman to a safe place where she could give birth to her child.' He smiled at Olivia, who had tears running down her cheeks.

'And you found one, Papa, didn't you? None better.'

They left as soon as was polite. There was the sound of shouting coming from the upper floor as they came into the hall, and each thought what a dreary house it was.

'I'm coming, Mother,' Amelia called up the stairs. 'Just a minute, please.'

James opened the front door and an icy wind blew in. Joseph and Lucille stepped outside as James held the door; Amelia followed them, shrugging into her shawl, but Olivia paused for a moment, looking back and thinking what an unhappy house it was. There was nothing friendly about it, no sound of laughter or singing, no smell of cooking. It was filled with dust and gloom.

She lifted her eyes upwards to the top of the dark stairs and saw a movement: something white. She stepped forward to give herself a better vision and saw an old woman at the top, not the one who had opened the door to them, but someone thinner, with wild silver hair, wearing a white nightgown and a long dressing robe with a loose belt that hung crookedly to the floor.

She saw the woman gasp and put her hands to her face and then lift her arms up as if to call out or signal to someone. Olivia moved back out of view and went outside, suddenly wanting to get out of this house and go home.

She dipped her knee to Amelia, who said, 'Thank you for coming, my dear Olivia. I'm so very grateful, and so pleased to see how happy you are.' She leaned towards her and gently kissed her cheek. 'How fortunate you are to have such lovely parents in your life. Cherish them.'

'Thank you, Aunt Amelia,' Olivia whispered, just as they heard a shout and a crash inside the house. She dipped her knee and thanked James and said how pleased she was to meet him properly, then turned to her father, who was holding the landau door open for her, and stepped inside with a huge feeling of liberation and emotion.

'Let's go home, Papa,' she murmured. 'There is nothing and no one here for us.'

James and Amelia watched the landau until it reached the open gate, and then they turned to go inside. 'Well,' James murmured. 'She now knows how lucky she is not to have been born into this household.'

Amelia gave a slight nod, and looked again down the empty drive. She sighed. 'Yes. What a blessed escape she has had.' She came inside and closed the door and for a brief moment leaned her head against it. She sighed, and turned. James was standing stock still in front of her, and their mother was lying in a crumpled heap at the bottom of the stairs.

Amelia rushed to her side, James following more slowly as if he couldn't bear to look. 'Is she dead?' he asked, but Amelia shook her head.

'Mother!' she said. 'Mother, speak to me. What have . . . ? I told you to wait.'

'Did you . . . see her?' Her mother's voice was cracked and hoarse. Her head was bleeding. 'Clara! She's come back, just as I always – I told you she would, and no one ever believed me. She's come back to say she's sorry for running away. Fetch your father, he'll have something to say . . . but bring her to me first. I'll tell her – tell her that she did right to come home.'

James turned his back and walked into the cold, dank sitting room and picked up a blanket that was draped over the threadbare sofa. He took it back into the hall and silently handed it to Amelia, who wrapped it over her mother.

'I'll just go down to the kitchen,' she muttered. 'Mrs Henderson can go home; there's no need for her to be here – especially on a Sunday. She'll want to be with her family. I'll lock the back door after her.'

CHAPTER FORTY-SEVEN

1873

'How long the days seemed to be when we were children,' Beatrix reminisced, 'and when our own children were small, and then suddenly,' she heaved a deep sigh, 'the years are gone and we're preparing for them to fly the nest.'

'They fled a few years ago, my lovely.' Edward turned a page of his newspaper. 'Or some of them did. Laurie flew before he was eighteen, when he gained a place at university; we didn't realize we had such a clever son.'

'Oh, I always knew!' Beatrix boasted. 'And now the wait is on for entry to veterinary college.'

Edward put down the newspaper. 'He will get in, won't he?'

'He'll be extremely disappointed if he doesn't,' Beatrix murmured. 'There's so much prestige attached to both London and Scotland, but he wants London, doesn't he? The first veterinary college in London to be granted a Royal Charter. It's wonderful.'

They heard the front door open; they could always tell when it was Ambrose coming in, for he never shut the door behind him and would be halfway across the hall before someone would shout 'Door!' and he would hurry back to close it.

Isolde was coming downstairs, and she it was who called out this time, 'Shut the door, Ambrose. Were you born in a field?'

'Might have been,' he answered without any malice; he never took offence, or gave any. At sixteen he had the calmest, most unflappable nature anyone could hope for: 'Exactly right for a farmer,' Edward said.

The only thing that made Ambrose cross was that he was still too young for farming college; university would pass him by, as he was not in the least interested in academic work, but he most certainly was a man of the soil – or, as Edward always said, of pig muck.

Isolde was still of the mind that she was going to be a concert pianist, and although she was still very young her music teacher said that it could be possible. It would be hard, though, and he wasn't sure if she had the stamina for study; it isn't only about being able to play well, he'd said. Her brother Luke had no such academic or artistic ideas; like Ambrose, he was set to be a farmer.

Alicia, as they'd always thought she would, had found her own path. When she was still eighteen, she had sailed through her exams and with the assistance of the headmistress had been interviewed at a ladies' college and moved from her school in York to the college where she began studying law and accountancy. When she was asked why, she'd replied that she would become the financial director of the family business when her mother retired, but she was also interested in legal studies. 'Because,' she said ambiguously, 'women do not always know their rights, even the few that we have.'

Her mother wondered if Alicia had subconsciously been aware of the difficulties she had been through with Charles, even though she had been so young at the time. Beatrix had always tried to shield her children from the knowledge of the worries she had had; but Alicia had simply said that law was a very interesting subject.

She had also developed a friendship with Mrs Gough, who answered any questions appertaining to law that Alicia asked, and then it crossed Beatrix's understanding that her daughter always seemed to call on Mrs Gough when Daniel was home from university.

They were waiting now for the telegram that Laurie had promised he would send as soon as he heard the decision from the prestigious veterinarian college. It came an hour later, when Beatrix and Edward had just agreed that it wouldn't be that day, but possibly the next.

The year before Laurie had sat his university examinations, Beatrix had received a letter from her father. He had, for many years, looked after the tenancy of the terraced house in London where Charles had clandestinely spent most of his time with his Spanish mistress, Maria, rather than in the home that Beatrix had made for their family on the Yorkshire estate.

When Charles had died, suddenly and accidentally, Beatrix, feeling desperately sorry for Maria, who had loved Charles dearly, allowed her to stay on in the terraced house where she too had created a home for herself and Charles. Beatrix's father had disapproved and advised that she should sell it and get rid of bad memories. Beatrix said no; it hadn't been Maria's fault, and if she were evicted from the house she'd shared with Charles she would become destitute.

Then came the letter from Beatrix's father advising her that Maria was moving back to Spain; her bullying husband had died, in the same week as had Maria's father, who had always sworn that he would kill her if ever she returned.

She told me that she would move back to live in Spain with her mother – and that she also longed for some warmth in her old bones! She intends to give her mother some luxury and freedom for the first time in her life,' Beatrix's father had written, and he admitted, *I suppose she is a decent woman at heart.*

Beatrix had smiled and nodded as she read it; she had nothing against Maria, who had known Charles since he was very young, much longer than Beatrix had, and it had given her some small comfort to know that Charles had had a warm and loving portion in his heart, even if it was given to someone who was not his wife.

'I'll keep the house,' she had told her father. 'We'll strip it out, knock down the wall that divides the bedroom and dressing room, and then put up another wall so that there are two equal-sized small bedrooms, and perhaps a minute bathroom. We might need it for Laurie, and he can share the accommodation with a friend if he gets to university or college in London.'

Her father was astonished, but couldn't come up with any argument against it. He had seen what Beatrix had done with Old Stone Hall and couldn't fault it.

'Very well,' he'd agreed. 'You know best.'

And that was what happened. Laurie had gained his place at university, and Daniel Gough was already there. They were studying different subjects, Daniel reading law with the intention of joining his father when he gained his degree; Laurie would probably take longer, but he lived in hope that the veterinary college would accept him once they had seen his exam results, which they did. So the two young men shared the house, and Dora's mother, who was the soul of discretion and lived at the poorer end of the street, agreed to be their housekeeper, cook, washerwoman and holder of the spare key.

'It's come, it's come!' Edward called up the stairs, telegram in hand, to Ambrose and anyone else who might be within hearing. Within minutes, Isolde, Luke (who asked 'What's come?'), Aaron, who happened to be in the kitchen with his newly wed wife Sally, Cook, Mrs Gordon and Kitty all knew that Master Laurie had achieved the next step toward his aim of becoming a veterinary surgeon.

'Will he have telegraphed Alicia?' Beatrix asked, wiping the tears of joy away with her handkerchief.

'Everyone he knows,' Edward grinned, 'including your parents, so they'll get the news twice.'

Alicia and Olivia had both gained places at the University of London, knowing that neither of them would gain degrees as it was not yet permitted for females to do so. Alicia was reading law and mathematics and staying in her mother's old room at her grandparents' house overlooking the gardens in Russell Square, and Olivia, reading science and biology, was in Beatrix's brother Thomas's room, which had been decorated in pale and pretty colours. A plain, large wooden desk, which Thomas had rarely used, being a soldier, was removed and a dressing table and mirror put in its place, with a smaller desk and bookshelves against the wall.

Ambrose and Emily Fawcett had been delighted when Beatrix had asked if they would be willing for Alicia and her friend to stay. 'They'll be safe with you, I know,' Beatrix said, knowing that they would be chaperoned whenever necessary but also given freedom; and also aware that her father was a fund of knowledge that would be useful to both of them.

Laurie felt as if he were walking on air as he took the road back to the house just off Judd Street. He'd sent telegrams to his parents, his grandparents and Alicia, who he knew would share the news with Olivia; he hoped she would be interested. They'd receive them by dinner time and he debated whether or not to catch the afternoon train and go home. He might even go over to Russell Square first and visit his grandparents.

He wasn't really looking where he was going as he strode along, full of bright thoughts and plans. The course at the veterinary college would be long and difficult and he hoped he would be up to it – but I will be, he determined, I will; I've managed so far – and so busy in his head was he that he bumped slap bang into a man coming in the opposite direction, who expostulated and said in no uncertain manner, 'Look where you're going, young man!'

'I'm sorry, sir.' Laurie bent down to gather up some papers and magazines that the man had dropped on to the pavement. 'My fault entirely.' He looked the man in the face and held out the papers for him. 'I do beg your pardon,' he began, and then realized that the elderly man he had crashed into was staring straight at him.

'Are you all right, sir?' Laurie gazed about him; there was no seat or bench for the man to sit on. 'Are you shaken up?' He didn't see how he could be; Laurie hadn't knocked him over, but only caused him to drop his papers.

'Charles! No, not Charles, of course not, but by heavens you have a look of him.'

Laurie frowned. 'No, sir, my name isn't Charles.' He wasn't going to give the man his name. He was rather shabby, although his coat was of good cloth, and he hadn't visited a barber recently, or had a haircut.

'But you're Charles's son, aren't you?' The man pointed over his shoulder to where Laurie would shortly be turning a corner. 'He lived just along here.'

Laurie hesitated for a moment, and then said, 'My late father was indeed named Charles.'

'I knew it was,' the man said exultantly. 'I know who you are now! You're Laurence – Laurence Dawley – and you're heading to the house where your father once lived with—' he broke off, as if reading something in Laurie's expression, and finished, 'lived before he married your mother Beatrix.'

'Yes!' Laurie said in astonishment. 'And – forgive me, sir, but who are you?'

Alfred Dawley's face paled, and it was as if all light had disappeared from within him and left an empty hollow shell.

'I, Laurence, am your grandfather. Alfred Dawley.'

Laurie had been well brought up and had been taught always to be polite, especially towards elderly people. He was still holding the papers, but he transferred them to his left hand and put out his right to shake his grandfather's.

'How do you do, sir? I'm very pleased to meet you.'

CHAPTER FORTY-EIGHT

Alfred Dawley shook Laurie's hand vigorously. It was as if he hadn't felt human touch in a long time, like someone being rescued from a desert island.

'Look,' he said. 'I don't want to keep you, but . . . have you time for a cup of coffee?' He pointed up Judd Street. 'There's an Italian café where I sometimes go to pass the time, you know. I don't eat the food, oh dear no, I only eat English food . . . although I must say it smells good.'

'Erm, well, I'm a bit pushed for time . . .' Laurie didn't want to be rude, but he did have things to do; however, he knew the café was only a few steps away. 'But yes, all right,' he agreed, and saw the relief and eagerness on the old man's face.

It took more than a few minutes, of course, as Alfred Dawley showered him with questions; the first was how old was he now and what was he going to do with his life.

'I'm twenty, sir,' he said. 'And I've just heard that I've gained entrance to the Royal Veterinary College.' He couldn't help but have a great smile on his face; this was one of the reasons why he wanted to get back to his lodgings: to tell Daniel, if he was in, that he had passed the prized exam.

'Oh, and what does that mean?' Alfred Dawley looked puzzled. 'Will you not be running the estate? It becomes yours, you know, when you're twenty-one. It's always been in Dawley hands. Then you'll need to find a wife and produce a son for him to take over when you die.'

'Oh, no! It isn't like that any more,' Laurie began to explain, but saw a sudden burst of anger in his grandfather's eyes which made him wary, and he stopped.

Dawley leaned forward, slopping coffee into his saucer. 'Are you under pressure?' he said in a low voice. 'Is someone trying to take over?'

Laurie smiled. 'No, not at all, sir. We took legal advice some years ago, after I said I didn't want to run the whole estate, which is considerable, on my own; we are now a limited company and all the family have shares in it, with my mother as head!'

Dawley remembered his mother. A beautiful woman with a brain, who had taken charge of the accounts from the very beginning; but when Charles died she moved everything from Alfred Dawley's London-based bank to one in Yorkshire. He frowned; he didn't get as much as a sniff at it.

'It's a pity you're not in banking, you know.' Dawley changed tactic. 'There's good money in it; private banking, I'm talking about. I'm still chairman of Dawley's and I don't know who I'll put in charge when I've had enough of it.' He raised his bushy eyebrows enquiringly, suggesting that Laurie might take the hint.

'I'm going to be a vet,' Laurie told him. 'I'll be specializing in horses, and probably other large animals.'

'Hm,' Dawley said wryly. 'Missed opportunity there, my boy; but you have a brother, don't you? What's he going to do? How is he with figures, eh?'

Laurence was on the point of saying that he had two brothers, but just in time he thought that perhaps his grandfather might not know of the twins, or of their parentage.

'Ambrose? No, he's going to be a pig farmer, specializing in rare breeds. He's already started and is waiting to get into agricultural college.'

'What? But—'

He appeared to be lost for words, and then Laurie had a brilliant idea. 'What I could suggest, sir, if you want to keep the bank in the family, is to ask my other sibling, who is incredibly gifted and is studying mathematics as well as law.'

'That's more like it.' Dawley sat back and rubbed his hands together. 'I'll take a good pension, of course, and probably keep hold of the purse strings for a while.' He frowned. 'I thought there were just the two of you? Your mother didn't marry that other fellow, did she? Newby? I'd not have that.'

'Not a brother, sir.' Laurie almost held his breath, fearing an outburst, and said carefully, 'My sister. Alicia. She's the one with the analytical brain in our family.'

Dawley's mouth opened, and then he laughed loudly. 'Takes after her mother, does she? Well, that would set the cat amongst the pigeons! Not sure how those old duffers on the board would react to having a woman at the head of the table in the boardroom.'

'Stir them up a bit, would it?' Laurie laughed too. 'She couldn't do it yet, of course, she has to study and then finish her exams. She's set on completing both studies before she decides which path to take.'

'Not set on catching a rich husband, then? Of course, she doesn't need to; she'll be very eligible.' Dawley touched the side of his nose. 'We'll keep in touch, shall we? It would be nice to. My wife died, you know; there's no one else.'

Laurie didn't know. He didn't know about either of them; as far as he knew they had never kept in touch, except . . . 'My mother used to exchange correspondence with your daughter Anne, I think, but I don't know if she still does.'

'Really?' He seemed very surprised. 'I suppose she's still in France?'

'I'm afraid I don't know, sir.' He stood up. 'I'm really sorry, I have to go. I have letters to write and a hundred other things to do.'

Alfred Dawley got to his feet. He seemed reluctant to part

company, but held out his hand. 'It's been . . .' he cleared his throat, 'really nice to talk, Laurence. I hope we can meet again. I rattle around in that great house of mine up on the Heath with nobody to talk to for days on end, except for my housekeeper, and she doesn't have much to say.'

'I was at school in Hampstead,' Laurie said. 'We were on the Heath.'

Dawley nodded. 'I remember,' he said. 'My old school too. You ran away!'

Laurie laughed. 'I did.' And then his smile faded. 'My father died not long afterwards, so I never went back.'

'That's right; that's right,' Dawley murmured. 'And everything changed after that. And I lost control. Lost my son, lost my daughter.' He paused. 'Lost my wife.'

Laurie waited for him to say he'd lost his family, but he didn't.

He hurried back to the house. It was true that he had lots to do, including writing letters to former tutors who had helped him to achieve his goal. He could hardly believe it. It had been really hard work, but so much had been interesting and stimulating.

He thought it very strange that he should meet his paternal grandfather like that, and wondered why he was so far from his home in Hampstead so early in the day. Bored, perhaps, with nothing to do and the day spreading before him. Laurie didn't imagine that he would have many friends; he didn't seem the type to cultivate friendship, being too brusque in his manner, perhaps even bullying.

He knows where the house is; did he influence my father's plans? Laurie rarely thought of Charles, but when he did his senses shrivelled and a cold shiver ran through him as he thought of how he had tried to manipulate his mother when they were children. Had Charles inherited this trait from his own father, Alfred Dawley? It seemed likely.

'Well, what happened? Any news?' Daniel called from the

parlour as soon as he heard Laurie's key in the door. He'd still been in bed when the telegram had arrived, and Laurie had gone out immediately to spread the news.

He was sitting at the long table at which they both worked and dined. There was a good smell; their help, Mrs Murray, had obviously brought some freshly baked food in with her when she came in that morning. She dusted, washed, polished and tidied, but never ever moved a single scrap of paper or a book from that table, knowing this was their work station.

Laurie took off his coat, trying to conceal the huge grin that was threatening to break out. 'Oh, you know!' he said, nonchalantly, then 'Yes!' he shouted. 'I'm in!'

Daniel rose from his chair and put out his hand. 'Oh, well done! That's incredible news and well deserved! Now starts the hard work.'

'I know. I'm thunderstruck. I can't believe it!'

'Have you sent your telegrams? All the important ones? Your parents, grandparents?' Daniel reeled off the names. 'Alicia, Olivia?'

Laurie nodded. 'Yes, yes, that's where I've been. Erm, not Olivia. I expect that Alicia will tell her.'

Daniel gave him a questioning look. 'She's not important enough to have her own telegram?'

'Oh, no, no! Not that at all. It's just . . . well, wouldn't it seem odd for her to have her own message when – when Alicia and our grandparents can tell her?' It was a feeble excuse, and he knew it.

Daniel went into the small but immaculate kitchen. 'Coffee?' he called, and Laurie muttered, 'Yes, please.'

Daniel came back with two steaming cups of black coffee. 'You know,' he said, placing the cups on table mats, 'everybody knows that you're sweet on Olivia, including, I should think, Olivia herself.'

'She's never given any indication of it,' Laurie said gloomily. 'She's too young, anyway. She's younger than Alicia.'

'That I know,' Daniel replied laconically. 'And you're young too, but if you're serious then you should tell her, because if you don't have some kind of understanding there might be some other fellow in the wings just waiting to sweep her off her feet!'

'Huh,' Laurie said. 'Have you met her father? You'd have to be somebody really special to gain his permission to even look at her.' He laughed. 'I really like him. He's what everybody might call a typical straight-talking Yorkshire man, and a Hull one at that!'

'Well, we all know that you're not that special.' Daniel sipped his coffee thoughtfully. 'I mean, anybody can gain entrance to the Royal Veterinary College. Even a dunderhead like you.'

Laurie grinned, embarrassed. 'Yes, but it's not about being brainy, is it, when you choose someone? I mean, what actually are young women looking for?'

Daniel shook his head and sighed. 'It's no use asking me, old fellow; what do I know? Tell you what: why don't you ask her? By the way, are you catching that train home today or not?'

'Oh, heavens, yes.' Laurie glanced at the clock on the cloth-covered mantelshelf. A plain new fireplace that his mother had put in when she was renovating the house, a painting of a sailing ship at sea over the mantel, rather than a mirror, two small and comfortable sofas, plain curtains without swags at the window and no frippery made it a suitable room for two young men to live and study in.

'I'm going to call and see the grandparents first and ask if Alicia or Olivia is going home for the weekend too. What about you?'

Daniel shrugged. 'I think not, much as I'd like to; I'm snowed under, if I'm honest, and not getting on particularly well. I'll make it for your party, though, in a couple of weeks' time.'

Laurie threw a few things in an attaché case, plus pencils, textbooks and notebooks, enough for him to put down his thoughts as he was travelling; now that he was guaranteed a place, he could ease off a little. He knew that his parents would be glad to see him and hear exactly what had been said at the interview before he received the good news via a telegram.

And he might also see Olivia.

CHAPTER FORTY-NINE

Laurie rang the bell at his grandparents' house, looked up and saw someone waving from the upstairs window. When the door opened it was Olivia standing there.

'Laurie!' she said. 'How lovely. The telegram came; what wonderful news! Congratulations. How clever you are!'

She pulled open the door and he stepped inside, and without thinking he bent forward and kissed her cheek. 'Thank you,' he said, and then gasped. 'S-sorry. I—' He gulped and flushed. 'I beg your pardon. I was, erm, I was thinking of Alicia!'

'Really? Were you?' Her eyes were bright and merry. 'Come in. Alicia has gone out with your grandmother. They won't be long.' She gazed at him, and taking advantage of his embarrassment said softly, 'Would you like to kiss Olivia now?'

'Oh!' he breathed out. 'Y-yes, I would actually. I'd like that very much. Is, erm, is anyone else here?'

'Only your grandfather.' She pointed to the side door in the hall and dropped her voice. 'He's in his study, so probably reading his morning newspaper.'

They both heard voices outside on the steps and stepped apart. 'Damn,' Laurie muttered, and Olivia put her hand over her mouth to suppress a giggle. He grinned and pulled the door open to let his grandmother and Alicia in.

'Hello!' Alicia said. 'And who's a clever fellow?' She reached up on tiptoe and kissed his cheek. 'Well done. Why are you here so early? You could have saved money on the telegram!'

'Because my grandparents live here and I can! And I'm not such a skinflint as you are.'

'Give me a kiss then,' his grandmother said. 'We are so proud of you, Laurie. We ought to have a celebration!'

'He'll be having one soon,' Alicia said, 'for his twenty-first birthday. We don't want to spoil him!'

'I came to ask if both or either of you would like to come home for the weekend with me.' He glanced at Olivia. 'I'm catching the one o'clock train. I hope,' he added, as the grandfather clock in the hall began sounding out twelve chimes.

'Not me,' Alicia said. 'I've masses to do.'

'Oh, yes please.' Olivia was eager, but flushed. 'Mama is – did you know that my mother is, erm, expecting a baby very soon? I'd like to see how she is.'

'Laurie has studied biology and anatomy, Olivia,' Alicia teased. 'You don't need to be embarrassed. He knows about babies, even human ones!'

Laurie frowned at her, but Olivia joked back, 'Yes, but he's *your* brother, not mine!'

Alicia wrinkled her nose. 'Oh, so he is,' she said with a sly smile.

'You are such a tease, Alicia,' Laurie murmured, as Olivia ran upstairs to pack a bag.

'She understands me,' Alicia assured him. 'Probably better than you do. Have you spoken to Grandpa yet?'

'I'd only just come through the door. I don't know how we missed each other.'

'Different end of the garden?' she suggested.

'Maybe.' Laurie lowered his voice. 'Must tell you this first. When I'd sent the telegrams earlier this morning, I was on my way back to the house when I bumped, actually *bumped*, into an old man. He dropped some papers he was carrying, and when I stood up after picking them up he was staring right at me.' He dropped his voice further. 'It was our other grandfather!'

Alicia frowned. 'Who do you mean?'

'Dawley! Charles's father. Alfred – or Albert? Alfred, I think.'

'But he doesn't know us.' She too dropped her voice, sensing it was the right thing to do. 'I wouldn't know what he looks like; I don't think I ever met him.'

'Nor I. I don't think we were of great interest to him when we were infants, except that I was the son and heir; but he does know about us. He knew I had a brother, though he didn't mention the twins. He was desperate to talk – lonely, I thought – and so we went to that little Italian coffee house, the one on Judd Street, and he wanted to know what I was doing after university. He wants someone to follow him into the family banking business.' He grinned. 'Chairman of the board, when he retires. I told him that I was already committed to being a vet, and that Ambrose was going into pigs, so I suggested you! I said you were the brains of the family, the one with the analytical mind. He seemed impressed.'

She began to smile. 'Really? I'll sound out Grandpa Ambrose; he was in banking, and he'll be bound to know him. Chairman, eh? Or chairlady, chairwoman?' She raised her eyebrows. 'Chairperson?'

They started to laugh. 'That would be rather impressive, wouldn't it?' Laurie said. He tapped on the study door, and at a grunted 'Come in' he opened the door and put his head round it to see his grandfather with the newspaper on his knee, just as Olivia had predicted.

'Just popped in, Grandpa,' he said. 'I'm on my way to catch a train home. I'll see you when I get back and we'll have a proper chat.'

'Wait a minute, wait a minute.' Ambrose got up from his chair and put out his hand to Laurie. 'Well done, my boy, very well done. We read the telegram this morning and we're very proud of you; goes without saying, but we are!'

Laurie was touched, and gave his grandpa a hug. He couldn't

imagine doing that with his grandfather Dawley. He remembered when he was little that he received a hug from Gampa Luke, Edward's father, and suddenly he missed him.

'Alicia going with you?' Ambrose asked, extricating himself.

'No, but Olivia is.'

'Well, take care of her. Lovely young woman. I suppose she's a woman? Little girls grow up so quickly.' For a moment his eyes drifted away from Laurie, as if he were reminiscing. 'All right,' he said. 'We'll see you on your return. Mind yourself, now.'

Laurie carried Olivia's bag as time was getting on and they needed to walk quickly to give them long enough to buy tickets. 'Two first-class returns to Hull, please,' he said at the ticket office, and Olivia looked at him.

'I can continue on to Hull on my own,' she murmured. 'You can get out at North Ferriby.'

He nodded. 'The fare is the same,' he said, although he didn't know that, but it was irrelevant in any case. He was travelling to Hull with her.

They had a carriage to themselves for some of the journey and both took out notebooks, although Laurie didn't really need to, but then they began chatting and Olivia began to ask him questions about his upcoming course work, but he couldn't tell her much except for what he had read in the syllabus. He stretched his arms and breathed out. 'It's such a relief! Do you know, I think it was when you came to help with the harvest that summer, do you remember, and we looked after the Shires, and I think – wasn't one of them in foal? And I fell in love with your father's Morgan?'

She shook her head vaguely. 'I remember looking after the Shires with you and talking about how the mares went on working when they were carrying a foal.'

'Mm,' he said. 'Well, it was about that time that I began to think that was what I'd like to do. To look after them if they had a health problem, and to diagnose it and know what to do to make them well again. I used to watch the vet when he came to look at the animals – not just the horses, but the cows too. I helped him one time when one of them was having difficulty calving. I was fascinated.'

The train steamed into a station. 'I won't be able to discuss such matters if anyone else gets in our carriage,' he murmured, and sure enough, someone did. They both put their heads down to look at their textbooks as a man and a woman came in.

'Is anyone else sitting in here?' the woman asked tersely, addressing Olivia.

'Not at present,' Olivia said, so solemnly that Laurie sucked in his cheeks to stop himself laughing. 'Laurie,' Olivia went on in a little girl voice, 'can you help me with this problem, please?'

He gave a protracted sigh. 'Let's have a look. Ah, yes.' He bent towards her and she to him so that their heads were almost but not quite touching, and Laurie could feel her hair on his cheek.

'This is what you have to do,' he said, and closed his hand over hers, which was holding a pencil. 'Like this.' He turned a page and drew a heart with an arrow through it.

'Oh,' she said softly. 'I had no idea. Thank you.'

'Very good,' the elderly man opposite said. 'I like to see young men helping their sisters with their lessons. Stimulates their brains, you know, even if they don't achieve a great deal.'

His wife turned to look at him, and then caught Olivia's eye. 'Silly old duffer,' she mouthed. 'Doesn't know what he's talking about.'

CHAPTER FIFTY

'Next stop, Doncaster,' Laurie said softly, gathering his notes together and putting them in the side of his case, and thinking that he'd been an absolute idiot.

He helped Olivia down the step on to the platform as if she were incapable of doing it herself, and she turned and glanced at the couple still in the carriage. She found they were looking back at them, the man benignly and the woman with a slight frown. She gave them a little wave and then turned to follow Laurie.

'Sorry,' he said.

'What for?'

'For making a blithering fool of myself.'

'It is ridiculous, isn't it, that women can't travel with a man unless he's a brother or a cousin or her father without someone thinking she's unworthy – or a wanton.'

He smiled at her. 'There is no possible reason why anyone would regard you as unworthy. You look like a—' He stopped and shrugged.

'Like what?'

'Oh, a perfect young English woman,' he muttered. 'I think this is our train . . . yes, it is. Let's try to get on at the front.'

He began to move down the platform, taking her arm.

'Just be careful,' she said jokingly. 'Someone might be watching!'

'It's not funny,' he said. 'I would hate it if I were a woman.'

'Good thing you're not, then,' she answered, as she put her foot on the step up into the carriage. 'And we do; hate it. But we have to joke about it so that it doesn't get to us. Don't forget to ask the guard if the train stops at North Ferriby,' she added, looking over her shoulder.

But when the guard came he just slammed the door shut, waved his flag and blew his whistle and they were off.

'Doesn't matter anyway,' he said. 'I'm going through to Hull in any case.'

She didn't answer, just looked at him and smiled, and he felt happy. It doesn't matter, he thought; we understand each other. We're like . . . well, no, not like the couple on the last train: she understood her husband, but he didn't understand her, but I'd bet that she makes all the decisions anyway. But Olivia understands that I want to travel with her to keep her safe; but I don't know yet if she knows that I love her, and that I'm not too young to know that I do.

He felt her hand creep into his and his fingers covered hers. 'Thank you,' she said softly.

The train arrived in Hull and he checked with the guard the time it would be leaving again. He had eight minutes to get back from seeing Olivia off in a cab; he hoped one of her father's. It wasn't so much dark as gloomy, with heavy clouds threatening rain.

They stopped at the exit where the hired carriages were waiting and he saw one bearing the Snowden insignia pull up to be second in the queue.

'I'll be all right now, Laurie,' she said. 'I'll see you on Sunday for the return journey, shall I? Enjoy the weekend. Your mother will be delighted to see you.'

'She will,' he said. 'That's why I wanted to come. Yes, until Sunday, the midday train. Save a seat for me.' He wanted to kiss her, but she would be known in the town, not least by her father's drivers.

'Bye.' She turned and headed for the waiting cabs, where

her father's vehicle was now first in the queue. She walked towards it, and was surprised to see a driver she didn't know: most of them had been driving Snowden's carriages for many years.

'Hello,' she said, as she approached. 'Are you new?'

He got down from the driving seat, holding on to his whip. He seemed a little unsteady, she thought, but he couldn't be. Joseph had a strict no-drinking rule for his business.

'Hello!' he said in an over-friendly manner. 'So what's a pretty girl like you doing out on your own?' He opened the carriage door for her to get in, but she hesitated. 'Need a hand, darling?' He put his palm under her elbow and eased her towards the door, his hand slipping from her elbow to her waist and then to her hip. She froze, and turned towards him. 'Going far?' he whispered. 'I can take you anywhere you want,' and he winked.

'No!' she said. 'I've changed my mind,' and in one swift movement she dropped her bag and seized the whip from his grip, lashing it in the air so that it cracked once, twice, and bringing it down so that it hung enticingly close to but not quite touching the driver's nose. People turned round at the sharp thundercrack of the whip, including another Snowden driver, Bowden, who jumped down from his driving seat and ran towards her.

'Miss Olivia,' he said. 'Are you all right?'

'Yes,' she said, lowering the whip. 'Perfectly, thank you, Bowden. But this driver isn't. He's drunk, for one thing, and isn't fit to drive any passengers or any of my father's horses.' She picked up her bag and threw it inside the cab, banged the door closed, and turned to the now snivelling driver. 'You're suspended immediately and without pay; if you want to take up this decision, then speak to Joseph Snowden first thing in the morning.' She turned to the other driver. 'Thank you, Bowden,' she said. 'I'll drive home. I'll tell my father what's happened and I dare say he'll find another driver to bring Swift back.' She knew the names of all the horses, and how to ride and drive them.

'Yes, miss.' He touched his hat and grinned admiringly. 'Well done.'

Laurie, alerted by some kind of commotion outside, came back in time to see Olivia hitch up her skirt and climb on to the driver's seat. Holding her whip high, she cracked it, and drove out on to the road towards home.

'Papa,' Olivia said, wondering why he wasn't at the stables and why he was opening the front door.

Joseph was looking at the horse and cabriolet standing outside his house. He kissed her cheek, and said, 'It isn't that I'm not pleased to see you, but why have you come home, and why are you driving one of my cabs?'

'Well, I'm sorry to say, Pa, that I've given one of your drivers notice to quit. I'm afraid I didn't get his name, but Bowden will know: he was there and witnessed everything. The man was definitely drunk, so I had to drive home, but I'm only pleased that I was the one he tried to take advantage of and not some other woman travelling alone.'

Joseph drew in a breath. 'That is the first and last driver I'll take on without a reference. You're all right, are you? A bit shaken?'

She shook her head. 'No, quite exhilarated as a matter of fact. I'd been having a conversation with Laurie, who was concerned about women travelling alone and insisted on travelling into Hull with me, rather than getting out at his station.'

'Ah,' Joseph said with some relief. 'So he was with you?'

'Actually, no,' she said cautiously. 'We'd seen your carriages there so he went back into the station to catch his train home. Where's Mama?'

'She, erm, I'm glad that you're home. Really good timing.' His face glowed with a huge grin. 'Your gran is with her. She's started with the baby.'

Olivia squealed. 'Oh, I just knew it! I wanted to come home, and when Laurie called to ask if Alicia or I wanted to come with him today – he's passed his entrance for veterinary college so he decided to come even though he's sent telegrams – I jumped at the chance. I must go in and see Mama straight away,' she added. 'I just must, so will you see to Swift, poor fellow? He'll be wondering why he's here and not at the railway station.'

Lucille was in the parlour and in her dressing robe. She opened her arms wide to embrace Olivia. 'I was hoping and hoping you would come, chérie! But I had given up hope as we hadn't heard.'

'It was a last-minute decision,' Olivia told her, and went on to explain why. 'Where is Grand-mère?'

'Preparing,' Lucille explained, smiling. 'Making up a bed, looking for old sheets. You know, chérie,' she lowered her voice, 'this child being born here will dispel the fear and sadness that came with your poor mother. Your papa is nervous, though he says he is not; I know him well and he is afraid. But I am strong and I'm not going to die.'

'I understand,' Olivia said softly. 'But *you* are my mother,' she emphasized. 'Clara was my carrier, bringing me to you and Papa and bringing you together.'

'That's a lovely thing to say, chérie.' She kissed her. 'Thank you.'

Joseph was back within ten minutes. There was another driver at the stables taking a break and he took Swift and the cabriolet back to the railway station. Olivia was making tea and had set a tray with cups and saucers. She had been upstairs to see her grandmother and helped her make up a single bed with old sheets and pillows.

'Have you put a cup out for the midwife?' her grandmother asked. 'She'll be here any time.'

'Will she? Already? I thought it took hours!'

'Now I wonder why you thought that?' Irma Snowden creased her brow. 'Sometimes it's quick to deliver a bairn, sometimes it's not. Lucille is so relaxed about it that I think she'll tek no time at all.'

They heard a rap on the front door, which was quickly opened, and the sound of feet on the stairs.

A plump, elderly woman came in and took off her coat. From her large black bag she brought out a clean white apron, put it on and fastened it with strings at the back. She looked at Olivia. 'Are you stopping?'

Olivia looked at Lucille. 'Only if my mother wants me to.' In French, she told Lucille, '*I'd like to, but only if—*' She was suddenly overcome. '*Only if I can help. I don't want to get in the way.*'

'*You won't get in the way,*' Lucille answered in her mother tongue. '*I'd like you to. You can hold my hand.*'

Olivia looked at the midwife. 'I'd like to stay, please,' she said.

'Right then, if you're stopping, mek sure 'kettle's on 'boil,' the woman told her. 'We'll need hot water in a bowl and some clean towels. You'll remember, Mrs Snowden,' she said, 'from 'last time. How did that poor bairn get on?' she added. 'Did you ever hear?'

Irma Snowden kept a poker face. 'Oh yes,' she said. 'We hear regularly. Lovely young woman. One of 'family.'

'Oh, that's nice.' The woman busied herself and indicated that Lucille should get on to the bed. 'I love to hear good news about babbies I've brought into 'world. Beautiful bairn, she was. She'll go far, I'd bet. Come on then, m'darling,' she said to Lucille. 'Let's see how long you'll be afore bringing this one into 'world.' She turned to Olivia. 'Do you want to ask 'fellow downstairs who's walking up 'walls to come and sit on 'top step? Then he'll be ready to hold his bairn in his arms.'

Olivia wiped tears from her eyes with the back of her hand and mutely nodded. She went out of the door and found Joseph already sitting on the step. She sat beside him.

'I don't know how I can bear this,' he whispered. 'I keep thinking about Clara.'

Olivia nodded. 'Mama will be all right,' she murmured. 'She's in good hands and she's fit and well.' She heard urgent voices inside and stood up. 'I'll go in and find out if anything is happening.'

'Rinse your hands, miss, if you want to help.' Irma Snowden was by Lucille's side, holding her hand, and the midwife was looking at Olivia. 'Don't mind a drop o' blood?'

Olivia shook her head and stood in position; Lucille smiled and pushed, and Olivia bent and gathered up the squalling miraculous infant into her hands.

'It's a boy!' she exclaimed. 'Papa! Mama! You have a son. I have a brother!'

CHAPTER FIFTY-ONE

It had been a time for babies and a time for funerals. Dora had given birth to a boy, much to Hallam's delight. They had moved into Home Farm cottage just in time. Sally married Aaron and had a baby girl and warned him that they wouldn't name her Beatrix; it just wouldn't do. They named her Sarah, which was actually Sally's name.

Hilda Parkin, Aaron's mother, otherwise known as Cook, was overjoyed not only with the baby but that Aaron had married such a lovely girl as Sally, who gradually, over time, took on more cooking duties whilst Hilda looked after Sarah. That only continued until Sally became pregnant again and gave birth to a boy, by which time they had moved into Mr Thompson's cottage, and the land, apart from a small patch in which to grow vegetables, and a yard and stable that Aaron used for a horse and trap, had been drawn into the estate to give more room for Ambrose's pigs.

The funeral had been for Mrs Highcliffe-Rand, who according to Rosie had fallen down the stairs and wasn't found until the following morning.

'There was nothing to be done,' Rosie had related; by the time they, meaning Amelia and her brother, who happened to be staying there, had found her it was too late for recovery. She was buried in the same churchyard as her husband, a few yards from her youngest daughter. Only Rosie, her mother and Amelia were at her funeral; her son had been unable to come for some reason and the few people who knew her stayed away.

'I'm going to sell the house and land,' Amelia told Rosie. Her mother had left it to her in its entirety, but she said she would share the proceeds with her brother James, who had been left out of his father's will.

'I shall buy a small house by the sea,' she went on, 'and plant a little garden. I shall have a dog and a cat and keep my pony and trap for getting about and I will start my life anew. I will be a rich woman and tell nobody.'

But she had told Rosie, so perhaps she would be found out.

'Laurie,' Beatrix called to her son on the eve of his twenty-first birthday. 'We wanted to talk about your birthday present.'

'Oh, Ma', he said. 'I told you that I needed nothing. I have everything that anyone would want. Well, almost everything.'

Beatrix wrinkled her forehead. 'And what is it that you haven't got that you would like?'

He looked up; he was reading some of his notes. In front of him were at least three years of study and then he had to find a veterinary practice to take him on before he would qualify. He had already made some enquiries and there was a practice in Beverley that seemed promising.

'I can't tell you that,' he replied, smiling a little.

'Goodness,' his mother said provocatively. 'And I couldn't possibly guess?'

'I'll wait until Pa comes in,' he murmured. 'And then I'll think about it.'

'You've been in a strange kind of mood since you came home,' she said.

'Since the weekend he came with Olivia.' Alicia had come into the sitting room and caught the end of their conversation, and with her usual perspicacity had winkled out the subject. 'She's been the same, although she says it's because she was there to see her brother born. She's so excited.

Practically glowing. Samuel, they've called him, after Joseph's father apparently.

'Everybody's having babies,' she went on. 'Dora, Sally, Lucille. Isn't Lucille a little old to be having babies, Mama?'

'Certainly not!' her mother said. 'She's younger than me.'

'Oh, good,' Alicia said. 'Because I don't want any until I'm at least thirty. If I'm to be chairwoman of Dawley's Bank,' she said airily, 'I don't want to be hampered by babies.'

'*Don't*, whatever you do, mention that idea to your father!' Beatrix warned, whilst Laurie just laughed. 'You haven't met Alfred Dawley yet. He's a tyrant.'

'He won't be, not in my hands.' Alicia arched her eyebrows. 'I asked Grandpa Ambrose about it after you told me what you'd said, Laurie, and he said he'd introduce me at some point; he says it's about time women were put in charge.'

Beatrix stared at her. 'My father said that?'

'Yes. He said it was *paying-back time*, but I didn't know what he meant. He's a very forward-thinking man is Grandpa Ambrose.'

Neither she nor Laurie understood why their mother fell into fits of laughter.

When Edward came in, he looked at Beatrix. 'Have you mentioned anything?'

'No,' she said. 'I thought we'd leave it until tomorrow.'

Laurie and Alicia both looked up. 'Leave what?' they both said.

'Nothing,' their mother said. 'It can wait.'

'But it's my birthday tomorrow,' Laurie complained. 'You're not going to be working, are you?'

'Of course not, but the Goughs are coming over for lunch, as it's officially your coming of age, and Stephen will need to know if you've changed your mind about the inheritance.'

'Can I change my mind?' Laurie asked, astonished. 'I thought we'd signed and sealed it all.'

'You'd better not have changed your mind!' Alicia jested.

'I thought it was all amalgamated into one pot.' Laurie

305

rubbed his chin. He'd decided to grow a beard for his twenty-first birthday, but it was very itchy, and although he had been hoping it might be dark it was the same colour as Edward's, a sort of pale gingery colour, so he was going to put the blade to it in the morning.

'Well, perhaps I will keep it after all.' He shrugged off Alicia's onslaught. 'You'll have to be especially nice to me.' He put his hands over his head to stop her. 'Is Daniel coming?'

'Yes, I invited them all, so Daniel and Robin too.'

Alicia stopped beating her brother. 'What time are they coming?'

'Lunch time.' Their mother sighed. 'They're coming for lunch.'

'Anybody else?' Laurie asked nonchalantly.

'No, the rest are coming for supper, but the Goughs can stay if they'd like to.'

'You've invited the Snowdens?'

'Yes,' Beatrix replied patiently. 'Of course. I want to see young Samuel!'

'All the grown-ups will be cooing over him, Laurie,' Alicia said, 'he's just at that age when he's adorable. You'll have your nose pushed right out of joint! I'm going to my room to see what I might choose to wear.' She jumped up from the sofa. 'Although we'll all be cast in the shade when the beautiful Snowden ladies arrive.'

'They're not coming until the evening. I said they could stay overnight if they wished.'

'What about Granny and Grandpa Fawcett?'

'All arranged,' Beatrix said long-sufferingly. 'I have arranged birthdays and house parties before!'

'When are they coming?' Alicia paused by the door. 'I want to speak to Grandpa. I'm serious about this banking venture.' She gazed at her mother significantly. 'Very serious!'

'What does that mean?' Edward frowned. 'I don't always know what our children are talking about.'

'Don't worry too much,' Beatrix told him as she followed Alicia out of the room. 'They're going through a stage!'

Edward sighed, sat back and picked up a newspaper.

'Pa! Can I talk to you?'

Edward put down his paper. He'd been outside all day, come in, bathed and changed; all he wanted to do was relax.

'Is there anything wrong?' He thought that Laurie seemed a little anxious. 'It's just a formality, you know, seeing the Goughs. They're really only coming for lunch.'

'I wasn't going to ask you about business. It's something personal.'

'Oh?'

'Yes.' Laurie took his courage into both hands. 'Do you think – erm, do you think that I'm old enough to become engaged – to be married?'

'What! But you've just passed—'

'I know, I know! Nothing has changed there. It's still what I want to do – to be.'

'It's Olivia, isn't it?'

Laurie nodded. 'Yes. I love her. Absolutely love her. Adore her.'

'Well, that doesn't surprise me. She's very beautiful.'

'It's not only because of how she looks, Pa. She's just so lovely in every way; and,' he swallowed, embarrassed about sharing something so very special, 'I just want her in my life.'

Edward sat for a moment before speaking. Then he sighed and said softly, 'Well, you might not know this, Laurie, but I know exactly how that feels.'

'When you met Mama?'

Edward nodded. 'It was her first visit to the house and she was standing on the front meadow looking up at it and gazing around her; she didn't hear me coming and I caught her un-awares.' He sighed. 'I thought her the loveliest woman I'd ever seen; yet she was only a girl really, nineteen, totally inno-cent. Then when I saw her next, after her marriage to Charles and . . . well, you know the rest, and I shall *never* mention his name again – and I'd fetched Aaron to come and stay with her, I came back later after dark to check if they were both all right and I found her dancing barefoot on the grass.'

Laurie had heard the story before, but never tired of hearing it. Edward's voice dropped. 'And if I could have carried her off there and then, I would have done, but no, I had to wait ten long years.'

He seemed to come out of a reverie. 'And I love her even more than I did before, though I would never have thought it possible. So if you feel the same about Olivia, then yes, you're old enough to love her. And in case you've forgotten, it's your twenty-first birthday tomorrow and you don't need *anyone's* permission but her father's.

'But I'd advise you to wait a little while before marriage. Enjoy your youth together, if possible, without compromising her. Carry on with your exams and your career, and for heaven's sake, tell her father how you feel before you tell Olivia.'

Laurie felt a great weight slipping away. 'I was going to speak to Mr Snowden tomorrow. As for Olivia, I rather think she knows already.'

CHAPTER FIFTY-TWO

Alicia woke Laurie. She was still in her nightgown and robe, bounced on his bed and climbed in between his sheets. 'Happy birthday, big bruvver,' she said in a babyish voice and gave him a smacking kiss. 'Today is the first day of your grown-up life!'

'Alicia!' he complained. 'You're too big to come into my bed,' and then the door opened and Isolde, followed by her twin, came in and climbed into the bed too.

He sat up. 'We're one missing,' he said sleepily, accepting kisses from Isolde and even Luke. 'Where's Ambrose?'

'He said he'd come in after he'd been down to see to the pigs,' Luke said. 'But he won't give you a kiss!'

'Phew!' Laurie pretended to grimace. 'That was close. So come on then, where are my presents?'

'Downstairs on the dining room table,' Isolde told him, 'and my best present is that I've composed some music for you and I'm going to play it whilst you're eating breakfast!'

'Oh,' he said, putting his hand to his chest. 'I don't know what to say!'

'Say thank you,' Alicia mouthed. 'No matter how it sounds!'

Beatrix came in and smiled when she saw them all in Laurie's bed. 'Happy birthday, darling boy.' She leaned to kiss him too. Her voice was husky as she murmured, 'Wherever have the years gone?'

He put his arms round her and squeezed her. 'Can't imagine,' he said softly. 'They must have been good to fly by so fast.'

Mrs Gordon was crossing the hall, and congratulated Laurie as he came down the stairs followed by Alicia and the twins. He thanked her and gave her a hug; she had known him since the day he was born, after all.

As they all trooped into the dining room, Edward and Ambrose came downstairs, both in clean shirts and trousers and with well-scrubbed hands. Edward put his arms out and hugged him. 'Congratulations, Laurie. You've made a good man and a fine son. We're proud of you.'

Ambrose put out his hand too to shake, then grinned and hugged him. 'Happy birthday, brother.'

Laurie was so touched by their gestures that he could feel his eyes welling up. He knew that if he let them spill he'd never hear the end of it from Alicia or Ambrose, so he pretended to sneeze and took his handkerchief out of his trouser pocket to wipe his nose and his tears.

'Let's start breakfast,' his mother said to distract them all, and Isolde gasped. 'I have to play Laurie's piece,' she said. 'Leave the door open and I'll play very, very loudly so that you'll hear me,' and she dashed away upstairs to the drawing room.

The maid brought in a dish of kippers and they began to serve themselves, and then Cook came in with more dishes of bacon and eggs. 'Happy birthday, Laurie,' she said, and she too gave him a kiss on the cheek.

'At last!' Beatrix whispered to Edward when she had left the room. 'Your aunt Hilda has discovered her place in the family.'

Edward laughed, and then his mother came in to see the birthday boy. 'You're here early, Granny Mags,' Laurie commented as he received her kiss too.

'I could have walked down later, but Aaron collected his mother so I thought I'd come along too as it's a special day.'

'We're not listening to Isolde's music!' Ambrose, perceptive for once, shushed them.

She was just coming to the end of the piece so everyone

cheered and clapped and shouted bravo, and Isolde appeared flushed and proud, and Laurie said that it was perfect and that he'd love to hear it again, upstairs; and the others all nodded and said they would too.

'About your birthday present,' Beatrix said. 'It's coming later. It's being brought by special delivery by friends, as it's too big to be carried.'

'What we'd also like to say is that we know you might not be able to use it very often to begin with,' Edward picked up after Beatrix had finished. 'You'll be busy with your studies and won't always be here, but we've taken that into consideration and made, erm . . . arrangements.'

Laurie glanced round the table but met only blank expressions. Alicia definitely didn't know, as he could tell that she was trying to work out what it might be, and Ambrose would have joked that he knew, whilst Luke and Isolde just shrugged.

'I'm intrigued,' he said. 'I haven't the slightest idea.'

'Good,' his mother said. 'That's a huge relief – and incredible!'

It was true that there was no ulterior motive behind the Goughs' coming for lunch, although they also accepted the invitation to stay for the later party. 'You can all stay if you wish,' Beatrix told them as they sat down at the dining table. 'My parents are coming and will be here very soon, but we have plenty of room. Mrs Gordon is going to have the beds made up next door.'

Laurie saw Daniel glance at Alicia, and saw her lift her eyebrows and nod, and wondered; you could never tell when Alicia was fooling, and he hoped that she wasn't misleading Daniel. But then he reconsidered; Daniel was a joker too sometimes and he hoped he wasn't simply teasing and then going to break her heart.

Growing up isn't always easy, he thought as conversation drifted around him; sometimes it's more difficult than getting through childhood. But we've had the good fortune to be born to a lion-hearted, protective mother, who with Pa by her side has taught us how to get through life. Now it's time for us – me, at least – to make our own decisions as to what to do next.

Well, I know what is my greatest desire, and that's to have someone loving and special in my life. It's what I know, and am used to, and I'm fairly sure that Olivia wants the same. She could have arrived anywhere in her life if her mother hadn't been brought by chance to Joseph's house where she was born. A miracle, he thought. Life is a game of chance or good fortune.

Wine had been brought to the table and poured, with lemonade for Luke and Isolde, and Ambrose too. Laurie got to his feet, and picked up his glass.

'I'd like to make a speech,' he said, 'whilst it's quiet and we are with good friends.'

'Hey,' Edward butted in. 'That's my role!'

'I know, Pa. But later, perhaps? I have a quiet voice and maybe later I might not be heard above the sound of joyous laughter!' He turned towards his mother, who was gazing expectantly at him with a tender smile on her lips.

'I would like to raise a toast to our much loved mother, who, compliant in her promise, gave birth to me, her eldest son, as requested. Born to order, we might perhaps say; but with her strength and might and love she turned the tables and resolved that I wasn't to be given away; that I was her child. I know the story by heart, Mama, and I think I can imagine how difficult it must have been for you in those first few years, but then the stars aligned' – he smiled at Edward – 'and there was Edward, quietly and patiently waiting, and at last here was the perfect loving man with whom she was willing to share her precious children.'

He raised his glass. 'To our mother, Beatrix, and to our father, Edward. Mama and Pa.'

'My goodness, Laurie,' Alicia said later as they went upstairs to change for the evening festivities. 'You can be the speechmaker for my wedding, if ever I have one.'

312

He queried the *if ever I have one* remark. 'Not Daniel, then?'

'Probably,' she said. 'I'm very fond of him, but not yet. He feels the same, I'm sure, but he's too polite to say so; and besides, he has to prove himself before he can work for his father, so we have a kind of understanding. I'm going to work with his mother after I've finished the coursework on law. She's going to extend her work with women and I can help her with that, and I know everyone thinks I'm joking about Dawley's Bank, but I'm not.

'If Charles hadn't made such an ass of himself he would have become chairman of the bank; you wouldn't ever have wanted to. I know that you have your sights set on something worthier than money, but I think I'll be able to juggle law and banking at the same time. By rights it's ours once old Grandpa Dawley has shuffled off, and I'm not going to let a bunch of old men deprive us of what should come to us lawfully. You and I and Ambrose were Dawleys originally.'

He was astonished, incredulous and dumbfounded at her astuteness. Never in a million years could he have taken on such a challenge. Or wanted to.

They stood on the landing and he put his arm around her. 'You are so shrewd and clever and smart,' he said. 'Alicia, my fearless sister!'

The house was filled to bursting with friends and family, including the staff, many of whom had worked at Old Stone Hall from the beginning of Beatrix's time there, and some, like Mags and Edward, who had known it in old Neville Dawley's time, as had Rosie's mother. Rosie said when she was a child she used to sneak into the orchard and feed the pigs with apples.

But the Snowdens were not here yet, and Laurie was getting anxious although his mother was not. 'They have a young baby to get ready, don't forget,' she said, adding, 'in fact we have a few babies coming, Dora's, Aaron and Sally's, as well as the Snowdens'.'

Being mid-May, it wouldn't begin to get to dusk until at least eight o'clock. It had been a lovely day, and people had arrived early to make the most of the warmth of the evening. Edward and Ambrose had decorated the door with bunting and put braziers on the terrace, and here and there on the front meadow had lit small fires of wood and coal in old metal buckets with holes punched in the sides so that they glowed red. Tables and chairs were set on the grass near to the house with glasses and covered jugs of fruit juice.

Beatrix's parents, Ambrose and Emily Fawcett, had arrived just as lunch with the Goughs had finished. Aaron had picked them up in North Ferriby station and they'd unpacked and had a quiet lunch and a short rest in Little Stone House before getting changed. Emily was thrilled to see Dora's son, having known Dora since she'd come to work as a housemaid at the house in Russell Square straight from leaving school.

Alicia captured Grandpa Ambrose and took him off to tell him more about her plans, and Beatrix gazed after them thinking that she would never have believed it if she had been able to see that meeting of her father and her daughter when she was Alicia's age. And it made her catch her breath when she realized that she had been about that age when she'd married Charles. Sitting on the window seat, she followed their progress down the meadow, heads together.

Edward came across to Beatrix, and bending close murmured, 'Visitors arriving as planned!'

'Where's Laurie?' she asked.

'Outside, mooning about. Waiting.'

She laughed. Indicating to her mother to take her seat by the window, she strolled with Edward towards the open front door.

'Come on, Fawcett-Newby children,' Edward called through the house. 'Alicia, Ambrose, Isolde, Luke.'

'Alicia is already out,' Beatrix said. 'She's there with my father. Planning a *coup d'état*!'

The Snowdens' horse and landau pulled round on to the

front drive, Joseph driving Captain, with Lucille and baby Samuel sitting in the carriage wrapped in shawls and blankets and Joseph's mother next to her.

Laurie appeared beside his parents, but his face fell with disappointment. 'Where's Olivia?'

Joseph got down and shook Laurie's hand and then Edward's, and bowed to Beatrix. Opening the door of the landau he helped his mother down, then took Samuel from Lucille's arms. He handed her down tenderly and then gave him back to her.

'Where is Olivia?' Laurie raised his voice and asked again. If she hadn't come then the day would be ruined.

'Mm?' Joseph turned and put out his hand to shake Laurie's again. 'Congratulations on reaching your majority! Olivia's about five minutes behind. She's driving a young horse; can't rush him.'

Edward and Beatrix caught his eye, but Laurie ran back the way Joseph had come in.

'There's a young man in a hurry, I'd say,' Joseph said laconically. 'She's right behind, coming up 'track.'

Beatrix turned to Lucille. 'Let me look at Samuel. Oh, how handsome he is; and how are you?' She took Lucille by the elbow and led her up the steps to meet the other guests.

Laurie halted in his dash to the top of the track and stood by the gate. Someone, slim and wearing a dark green jacket with a top hat, was driving an alert and spry light chestnut horse steadily towards him, pulling a dark red landau. It wasn't a man, unless it was a very young one. The driver held up the whip in a sort of salute.

The horse, by his gait, was young too, with a light springy step, a high-set tail and a long full mane. He clip-clopped steadily up the track and gave a soft neigh as he saw Laurie. Laurie heard a sound, a hum of voices behind him and turned his head. Alicia, Ambrose, the twins, his parents, his Fawcett grandparents. Granny Mags. Daniel and his family; Joseph and Lucille. Aaron but not Sally. Dora and Hallam, their son left inside.

He walked towards the conveyance and Olivia slowed almost to a stop and invited him to climb up beside her. 'You look very handsome,' he said softly. She wore a dark green driving skirt, a fitted buttoned jacket and a neat light green scarf at her neck. Her dark hair was pinned back in a tight chignon beneath the top hat.

'So do you,' she replied.

'This is a very smart conveyance,' he murmured. 'But the horse? He's not a Morgan, is he? Is he? Yes, he is! Oh, let me down!'

They drew in to a halt, and Laurie leapt down and ran his hands over the horse's neck. 'He's magnificent,' he murmured, and the horse gave a little snicker as if agreeing and turned his large eyes to face him, his shapely ears pricked with interest. 'Whose is he? Is he yours? What's his name?'

'I don't know his name,' he heard her say. 'He isn't mine. I'm just the delivery maid.'

He turned, questioningly. 'What do you mean, you don't know? He must have a name.'

'He probably has, but I don't know it. The new owner will have to name him.'

He kept his hand on the horse's neck and looked up at her, and then back to the crowd watching from the gate: at his mother and father, his brothers and sisters, all of whom had their thumbs upright and were wagging them.

'The new owner? Who – who? He's not mine, is he? Is he?'

Olivia nodded and smiled. 'Would you like to lead him in?' she said softly. 'Introduce him to everyone. So that both of you can say thank you to your mother and father for acquiring him? To my father for searching him out?'

Laurie pressed his lips hard together. This he hadn't expected; he had stipulated no presents. But this wasn't just a birthday present. This was a lifetime gift. This noble steed would be with him for a long time, just as everyone gathered here would be. The name for him came immediately. Noble Knight.

He turned to look up at Olivia. 'Just so that you know, I love you.'

She beamed, her face lighting up. 'I know; I love you too, and I've prepared my father and mother too – just so that they know.'

He gathered up the reins and led Noble Knight through the gate and on to the drive and everyone waiting gave a rousing cheer, echoed by those inside, and clapped their hands, and Noble Knight lowered his head, up and down several times, in recognition of his designation and his admirers.

CHAPTER FIFTY-THREE

ENDING

It had been a lovely day; everyone agreed on that. Laurie had felt as if he was in seventh heaven and the day utterly magical. He had thanked his parents for their wonderful gift of Noble Knight and the landau, and also Joseph Snowden who had, when asked to do so by Beatrix and Edward, scoured the three Ridings, East, West and North Yorkshire, to find a young Morgan of good breeding. When he saw Noble Knight, as he was to be named, he took Olivia with him several times during her weekends off from college to try him out, riding and driving; he had his health checked by a veterinary surgeon; and finally consulted Edward, who went to see him for himself, and approved.

During one of those weekends at home, Olivia had offered her father a suggestion that she had been thinking through for some time. In view of her encounter with the drunken driver, he might consider hiring a female driver in his team to drive women travelling alone to their destinations.

Joseph thought it an excellent idea, and his present drivers were also pleased. It could be a risk for them too, they said, to drive a single woman. He found a sturdy country girl, used to horses, who had come to live in town and needed an occupation. He took her on, kitted her out in the dark green livery that Lucille had designed and Olivia had worn for Noble

Knight's debut, and although she didn't look quite as admirable as his daughter, she looked very professional, and didn't have any trouble with male would-be customers.

He advertised in the local newspaper and on his billboards that he also employed a Lady Driver and Carriage, and soon he hired another woman, such was the demand as more ladies began to travel alone.

Lucille, once their son was old enough to be left with his adoring grandmother, decided that she would, after all, open another café in Beverley. Joseph bought a small travelling van and kitted it out with shelves, and every morning the trained cooks in her Market Place kitchen would fill the van with French pastries which would be driven to the new café.

On the night of his birthday, Laurie had plucked up courage to ask Joseph for permission to ask Olivia to marry him; he loved her, he told him, and hoped that she would wait for him until he was in a position to make her his wife.

As Olivia had informed her father in advance that that was what she was hoping for, he was prepared with his answer. He was quite sure that he couldn't have hoped for anyone finer to take care of and love his precious daughter as Laurie would; he was a man of few words, but he knew what he wanted and had already been prompted not only by Lucille but his mother too to say the right thing, which was yes.

As for Alicia, she soared through her exams, exceeding all expectations and leaving her male counterparts reeling in awe and admiration, or dismay and consternation, depending on their nature. Their only consolation was that she was unable to obtain a degree as they were able to; but that didn't deter her, as she had employment to go to in the Goughs' law office, and eventually a role in Dawley's Bank as finance adviser to the chairman of the board, whose meetings she attended every fortnight, travelling to London from York where she had lodgings, or from her home in Old Stone Hall.

Her grandfather Dawley seemed to have taken on a new lease of life since she had approached him, and he recognized that she was as sharp with figures as her mother had been, but was unaware of her sweetly disguised but uncompromising objective of becoming owner of the bank, and was pleased to have her by his side and introduce her to the old duffers as a possible chairwoman of the future.

Alicia's grandfather Ambrose Fawcett, who had been in her confidence from the beginning, declared to his wife that he hadn't had such a good laugh in a long time, and on the strength of that he bought shares in Dawley's Bank and gambled that they would go up in a very short time.

Daniel Gough, too, was ambitious, and became a high-flying lawyer with a fine reputation. He and Alicia were known as an intrepid pair but they wouldn't marry until Alicia was twenty-five, thus ensuring that she was on her way to early success and Daniel at nearly thirty firmly up the ladder of law.

Isolde and Luke, too, were steadfast in their hopes of success. Isolde wouldn't become a pianist playing for money, but eventually she would meet and marry a handsome penniless concert-hall pianist and write music for him to play so much better than she could. As for Luke, he followed in his brother Ambrose's footsteps and after agricultural college joined him in the breeding of rare-breed pigs, and their company, being joined to Fawcett-Newby Farms, became eventually known in the vicinity as the Newby Brothers.

Laurie, finishing his training as a veterinary surgeon in Beverley, eventually took over the practice as the present vet was ready for retirement. His wife Olivia, who became known as the Lady Vet, looked after dogs, cats and other small animals. Laurie's expertise and renown grew over the years and he travelled many miles to attend sick horses, often driving Noble Knight, who sired many prize-winning offspring of his own, which made Laurie think that perhaps the idea he had nurtured in the past might yet be the future for him and Olivia and their two sons.

'What now for us?' Edward said, one sunny warm evening when the two of them sat outside enjoying a glass of wine. 'Lonely without our children?'

'Hardly,' she protested. 'They always come in pairs or three-somes, don't they? And they haven't really left home.'

Edward nodded; their family didn't always arrive together, but there were always two or three and sometimes more, and Luke and Ambrose were usually here. They were beginning to think that Ambrose would be an eternal bachelor, for he never mentioned any young woman by name. He was always busy, completely absorbed in his animals and regularly visiting other pig farms and country shows to look out for good stock.

Above them on that soft summer evening were the ever-present squawking gulls; and the honk of geese as they flew in V formation made them smile. As dusk fell they heard the rush of owl wings, birds out hunting and flying low towards the wood. Beatrix with her sharp ears could hear the rush of the estuary waters; the tide was high tonight. She heard too the musical notes of a song thrush from deep in the wood and she closed her eyes and listened as its harmony swept over her, delighting her.

And something else. She listened keenly. A rattle of carriage wheels, the clip-clop of hooves turning on to the track; more than one carriage, not just Aaron's wonky-wheeled trap. Then the joy of laughter came nearer and Beatrix's face lit up; Edward glanced at her and they both smiled as they heard the chatter of children's voices and running feet and blond and golden-haired children turned the corner and tumbled to-wards them. Then came Laurie and Olivia, Alicia and Daniel, Isolde, not yet with a beau, brought home from music college in Aaron's trap, with Aaron and Sally's children come out for the ride. Luke, cleanly bathed, came out of the open front door to ask,' 'What's happening?' and then Ambrose with his usual ambling gait, one of Laurie's boys on his shoulders and another holding his hand as he tottered beside him.

Holding his other hand was a brown-haired young woman with blue eyes and sun-browned cheeks.

'Ma,' he grinned. 'Pa, this is Juliet. She's come to stay.'

SOURCES

Books consulted for research purposes:

The Victorian House by Judith Flanders, HarperPerennial, 2004
Horse Breeds and Horse Care by Judith Draper, Anness Publishing Limited, 2002
A Time to Reap by Stephen Harrison. A celebration of East Yorkshire's agricultural history. Published by the Driffield Agricultural Society, 2000
Costume in Detail by Nancy Bradfield, Harrap Books Limited, 1968

ACKNOWLEDGEMENTS

I would like to thank the Transworld team once again for their constancy and dependability over the last twenty-eight years. Different faces from time to time, but some constant ones too, who have all been equally supportive.

To my editor Francesca Best, editor Sally Williamson, copy and production editors Vivien Thompson and Nancy Webber and the whole of the Transworld team who have worked under Covid difficulties in these most unusual times, thank you all.

And not forgetting my local team, Divine Clark PR, who steer me through the mysteries of social media and publicity with patience, good humour and encouragement. Thank you.

AUTHOR'S NOTE

After I had drawn to a close on the story of *The Lonely Wife*, as I always do when finishing a book I began to dwell on the characters and ponder on what might happen next. They had, after all, lived with me for some considerable time, and, in particular, I was left with a question mark over the lives and futures of Beatrix's children.

They were secure in monetary terms, but I wondered what effect the influence of their birth father and the trauma of his sudden death would have upon their young lives. Had they absorbed their mother's anxiety, born of her hidden fear of her late husband Charles, and, if so, would that stay with them as they grew into adulthood? Had they felt any doubt over their mother's remarriage to Edward?

Fortunately, Edward, being steadfast in his love for Beatrix, had gathered up her children in his caring embrace and loved them equally, and he was determined to erase Charles's influence and the effects of his avaricious power-seeking behaviour. These children, having known Edward all of their lives as a friend, as someone they could trust and talk to, must have felt secure in his show and strength of love.

Ambrose, for instance, being the youngest, didn't remember Charles at all, and as Edward had always been in his life, he didn't see why he shouldn't bear his name; Alicia, having a strong belief in herself, also knew that she could trust him. It was Laurence, the eldest child, who had doubts about himself. Charles had tried to influence Laurence with his own warped ideas of how his son should behave as heir to the estate. Children often feel an innate sense of what is right or wrong, and it was Edward's guidance that convinced Laurence to *be his own self.*

In real life, I have come across children with separated parents, with step-parents and adoptive parents; in most instances, although not all, the transitions have worked well, and safeguarding laws are in place now that were not there in the nineteenth century. In the time of *The Lonely Wife* – had it not been for his death – the risk of the divorce that Charles had threatened Beatrix with would have been very real, and she would have lost her children completely.

But as Laurence said so meaningfully on his twenty-first birthday: 'the stars aligned'.

Authors generally are observers of real people; we have to be, otherwise our fictional characters would be flat and as lifeless as cardboard. This is not to say that we use real people in our novels, but that we listen and learn and catch the nuance of what they are saying, and because of our observations we are then able to create fictional people with the attributes of real, living and breathing individuals.

Fictional lives and real ones do sometimes cross. I often hear from readers who describe to me the real-life traumas they have experienced that correspond with what they have read in my nineteenth-century novels – perhaps surprisingly realizing, or maybe proving, that some aspects of life don't change at all. The fictional novel therefore is a reflection of life.

Here is one of my favourite quotes, on which you might like to contemplate:

A novel is a mirror walking along a main road.
Henri Boyle (1783–1842)

Val Wood

Four Sisters

by Val Wood

Hull, 1852.

Matty has had to care for her three younger sisters
ever since their mother's death ten years ago.
She and the girls' beloved father have worked
hard to keep the family together and now it's
time to celebrate as Matty turns eighteen.

But their joy is short-lived when tragedy
suddenly strikes and their father disappears
on his way to London.

The sisters have no way of knowing what has
happened to him – only that he hasn't returned
home. With little money left, they're now forced
to battle life's misfortunes alone . . .

Four Sisters is available in paperback and ebook now